UPRISING

CHILDREN OF THE GODS
BOOK 2

JESSICA THERRIEN

FROM THE TINY ACORN...
GROWS THE MIGHTY OAK

Uprising
Children of the Gods, Book 2
Second Edition
Copyright © 2017 Jessica Therrien
All rights reserved. No part of this book may be used or reproduced in any manner whatsoever, including Internet usage, without written permission from the publisher.

Acorn Publishing
WWW.ACORNPUBLISHINGLLC.COM

This story is a work of fiction. References to real people, events, establishments, organizations, or locales are intended only to provide a sense of authenticity and are used fictitiously. All other characters, and all incidents and dialogue are drawn from the author's imagination and are not to be construed as real.

Cover design by Damonza

ISBN-13: 978-0-9963788-1-9

To Holly,
writing wouldn't be as fun without you.

and

To Ron & Mary Jane Therrien,
thank you for everything.

PROLOGUE

MAC LED US TO A CABIN IN THE THICKEST PART OF the woods. It wasn't old, but it had been lived in, and I wondered how many other visitors had taken refuge there. The kitchen stovetop was stained from overuse, and the futon that sat against the wall sagged in the center where people had slept. As I looked around I breathed in the earthy scent of the forest that had seeped in from outdoors. Aside from the common area, which was both the kitchen and living room in one, there was only a bathroom and a single bedroom.

"Sorry if I gave you two a scare back there," Mac said, collapsing heavily into a seat at the multi-purpose table in the center of the room. "Can never be too sure these days." He leaned back in the wooden chair, his brawny body testing its strength.

I raised my eyebrows at his casual brush-off. *Oh, sorry for shoving my loaded shotgun in your face.* Maybe it was smart though. Having me heal proved I was who I was—the last healer. Still, poisoning a deer was a little dramatic.

"Well, someone could have at least warned us you'd be armed and dangerous," William said, his voice cutting through the quiet cabin. He took my hand and led me to the futon.

"It's best you just assume that from here on out," Mac laughed back at him. I didn't find it as funny. It wasn't that he frightened me, or that I felt too uncomfortable in this strange place, I just had too many thoughts in my head to process those insignificant feelings. I still hadn't gotten my bearings. So much had happened in the last twenty-four hours or more. I wasn't sure how long it had been.

"You guys must be hungry," Mac said, breaking the silence.

Starving, I thought. When had I last eaten? My body had moved past hunger pains and was simply ignoring my need for food, at least until it was mentioned.

"I think my stomach is eating itself." William cracked a smile for the first time since the gun incident.

Mac stood up, his heavy weight dragging the chair loudly across the old wood floor. He was built like he was made for the military, like he could pick a guy up by his throat or bust a door down with a swift kick. It was strange seeing such a burly man in a dainty kitchen, but he seemed to feel well enough at home. He pulled two plates from the fridge, which he had already prepared for us.

"I'm not the best cook, but it should do the job."

I didn't care if it was mashed celery. I would have eaten anything.

"The zucchinis grow out back, and the meat is quail," he said tentatively, his guttural voice not matching his kind words. "Sorry it's cold. I could heat the beans up on the stove if you want."

I moved a little too quickly to the table. "It's fine, thanks," I said with gratitude. I could see he wasn't a cruel man, just protective. After all, he did have the power of safety in his blood. Could you blame the guy for being a little overly cautious?

He picked up his shotgun and examined it, making sure it was loaded. As if someone could have stolen the shells without him knowing. William and I watched with curiosity as we inhaled our meal, every cold, delicious bite.

"Anything else you need?" he asked as we finished, plates nearly licked clean. "We have to talk about what's going to happen here."

"I could use a shower," I answered honestly. I wanted time to think. I wasn't ready for more.

"Sure," he said, placing his gun to the right of the door. "You guys will have the room, so I put your clothes in the dresser in there. Towels are under the sink."

"Okay thanks," I answered, wondering how my clothes had ended up here in the first place.

The solitude was nice, so I didn't bother to be quick. I caught a glimpse of myself in the bathroom mirror and smiled at how unkempt I looked. Tired, chestnut eyes stared back at me. My dark brown hair was greasy and tangled, and my clothes were dirty from trekking through the woods. I looked like a doll that had been dragged around the playground by a five-year-old.

I gazed back into my reflection, trying to convince myself that everything was all right, that I had no reason to worry. But was it true? I stripped down and stepped in the shower, letting the steaming water wash away layers of salt and sweat as I ran through the facts, every stepping stone in the path that had led me here.

It wasn't that long ago that I'd considered myself alone. The only one cursed with long life while those around me died. Then, only two others shared my secret, my burden—Anna and her daughter. They were more than friends; they were family, despite the fact that they weren't Descendants. Things were so different now, like that reality was a lifetime ago. I'd dreamt that there were others, hoped it in the deepest parts of me, but I never imagined it would be so complicated. The world of Descendants, my people, with their supernatural abilities and secret lives, The Council, the laws, the prophecy, none of it had turned out how I'd hoped. Things were backwards, uncivil, and unfair in this new world. I shouldn't have had to risk my life to heal my best friend, but it had come to that. If it weren't for Kara, who'd once considered me an enemy, maybe I would be dead. I shook that thought from my head. It didn't matter.

All that mattered was that Anna and Chloe would be

okay. Their safety was at the forefront of my mind. Kara had taken care of them, and they'd be here soon. Thanks to William, Ryder was gone. I could let go of that worry, but there were still things unsettled. There was Iosif. The memory of his scream made my stomach turn, and I hoped he would be all right. Obviously The Council believed we were dead, so what more could they use him for? And what had come of William's family? Were they questioned? Tortured? Did the Council members get involved? I would have to ask Mac if he knew anything.

As for the prophecy, apparently everything had gone as predicted, despite the fact that I was kept in the dark about the true way it would play out. What was it Iosif had said? *You survived because you were meant to—to fulfill the prophecy. Your sacrifice set things in motion. Now it's only a matter of time.* But what did that mean, that I was supposed to start a war against The Council? Free the Descendants from their oppressive reign? Even as I thought the words, I didn't believe them. How was I supposed to do that? Especially stuck here with most everyone thinking I was dead.

Only one thing comforted me as I mulled over everything: There was nothing I could do about any of it. Not right now at least. If I thought of it any other way, it all might come toppling in on me like an imploding building. Today, all I could do was talk to Mac. He was the only resource I had. I just hoped he knew what was supposed to happen next, and that I would be up for it.

I changed into my favorite old Levis and a long sleeve black shirt. When I opened the bedroom door, I caught them sitting at the table, talking with their heads close together like I wasn't supposed to hear their conversation. It seemed odd, but Mac addressed me like it was nothing.

"Better?" he asked, his strong brown eyes too cheery for his rough face.

"Much," I responded casually, but I knew better than to believe they weren't keeping something from me.

"Did you see this?" William asked, trying to steer the subject.

He held out a hand-carved blow dart gun, the one Mac had used to poison the deer.

"Yeah, I've seen it."

"Up close?" he continued. "Mac made it himself." He thrust it toward me, and I took it.

It was handcrafted, with intricate designs and beveled edges despite its long, narrow shape. The finger grip was made of dried reeds woven into a tightly knit pattern, and it had a sight for aiming that was so thin and precise it must have taken ages to carve. Although it was an amazing work of art, I cringed as I held it. It was lethal. A weapon, meant to kill.

"It's beautiful," I said, trying to be polite.

"Glad you like it," Mac answered with a wide grin. "I made it for you."

I was confused.

"Why?" I reacted without thinking. Nearly ninety

years of avoiding interaction with strangers didn't exactly make me the best in social situations. I should have just said thank you, but he didn't seem to take my question personally. Instead he considered it carefully, glancing at William in between thoughts.

"It will protect you," William spoke for him. He had that desperate look he always got when he wanted me to see things his way, a mix between pleading and insistence.

"We're in a safe haven," I reminded him, handing back the weapon. "I don't think I'll need it."

"You will," Mac added, staring hard at me. "I'll start training you tomorrow."

My eyes moved back and forth between them, trying to pick up on what it was they were getting at. I didn't like where things were going, and I wasn't sure why they were pushing it on me. Without responding, I headed back for the bedroom.

"Wait." William sighed. "There's someone outside for you."

If it had been anybody else, I may not have picked up on it, but I could read him so easily now, the crease in his brow, the pulse of his cheek muscle as he clenched his teeth—something had happened.

"Who is it?" I asked, trying to get more out of them before I faced what was out there, but they both remained tight lipped, unable to answer.

I listened for a hint of sound, but everything was so quiet here, eerily quiet. I eyed the dart gun and tucked my wet hair behind my ears. Without much of a choice, I walked almost unwillingly toward the front door, looking back at William for strength.

It was still light outside, brighter than I'd expected. Judging by how exhausted I felt, I thought it should be night. I had lost all sense of time. The thick trees blew lightly in the breeze, rattling their dry leaves like nature's wind chime as I stepped out into the forest.

"Elyse," a voice called from behind me, and I spun around with a gasp.

"Oracle," I mumbled with surprise.

She laughed, the corners of her soft eyes wrinkling as she smiled. It made me uneasy the way she looked at me, like she had known me my whole life.

"It's Florence, actually."

Her loose linen clothing matched the color of the surrounding trees, like she was a part of the forest, and her hair tied up into an elegant bun had slipped slightly, letting pieces fall against her face. She looked too normal to have such brilliant power.

"Hello," I managed, my timid voice wary as I waited to hear the reason for her visit.

"Will you walk with me?"

I nodded and began picking my cuticles as I took up beside her, mimicking her slow, graceful steps.

"You've had to give up a lot," she began, her voice low and calm. "I understand how hard it's been for you."

She looked over at me as we walked, but I couldn't

look back. I was afraid to meet her eyes. Though they were kind, they'd seen things I knew I wasn't ready to face.

"It's not going to get easier, Elyse," she said, her tone dipping with remorse. "The road ahead will be difficult. Not everyone will survive."

My eyes reacted on their own, searching for any uncertainty in her expression. There was none.

"I'm here to tell you that you have a choice. You can always decide to take a different path." She clasped her hands behind her back. "But you won't. You are good. Selfless. That's why you are who you are. You will lead them. Not because you have no other choice, but because it is right."

I wondered how she could be so sure. If she asked me right now if I knew what to do, if I knew what was right, I wouldn't have an answer. She had such confidence in me, everyone did, but they were wrong.

"Elyse," she said, stopping abruptly. "The war has started, and they have made the first move."

Her face was so intense it scared me, her motherly eyes afraid to give me bad news.

"They found Anna and Chloe—" she began.

I stepped away from her. "No," I said, not wanting to hear the rest.

"Elyse," she continued. "Kara tried her best, but Christoph took them."

The words felt heavy, like gravity pulling me down.

"Are they dead?" As I asked the question, my voice

shook, and everything started to break into pieces. I couldn't look at her. I couldn't breathe.

"No," she answered, her hand settling on my shoulder, "not yet, but they will be if you don't go after them."

"How?" I asked, my heart desperate. "How am I supposed to do that?" The fear shook me from the inside, making me frantic and reckless. "If you just tell me how, tell me what to do, I'll do it. I'll go now if I need to, if you tell me where they are—"

"Listen," she said louder than I expected. It grabbed my attention. "This is what they want. They don't believe you're dead, and they're trying to lure you out of hiding. They're waiting for you, and they want you to come panicked and unprepared. Elyse?" She waited for me to look up. "You must not go until the last night of February."

"Three months? That's so long." I shook my head. "It's *too* long. I can't."

"If you go before then, you will fail, and they will die. Do you understand?"

I nodded and bit my bottom lip. "But where do I go? How am I supposed to save them? I can't do it on my own."

"You can."

My shaking hands clenched into tight, steady fists. "I need more than that. Give me something to go on," I pleaded on the verge of anger.

"I can only say so much without altering the future, Elyse." She leaned forward to kiss my cheek, but I hardly noticed. "I must go before I say more. I won't see you again after this. Good luck," she said, before turning to leave. I watched her walk away, too stunned to move.

"Wait," I called after her. "Where are they?"

"Where you'll expect them to be," she yelled without looking back.

"Where is that?" I shouted.

When she didn't respond I took off after her, running as fast as I could, but I was too late. She disappeared beyond the boundaries of the safe haven, through an invisible wall I knew I wouldn't be allowed to cross.

I leaned back against a nearby tree, too devastated and angry to move on. It all seemed clear to me as I stood alone in the forest. There was only one path ahead of me. I could choose to walk away, but I wouldn't. She was right. They were all right. Maybe this *would* be my war.

CHAPTER ONE

—

I DIDN'T KNOW WHERE I WAS. THE PARKING LOT WAS empty, and it was getting dark so I knew I should probably leave. I had a nervous feeling in my stomach. An old white Toyota was parked in the farthest spot, the only car in sight. I figured it must be mine, so I dug in my pockets and found the key.

Inside, a package rested on the seat, a sleek plastic box in a paper sack, and I remembered what I was supposed to do. I had to deliver it. 243 Park Lane. Somehow, I knew how to get there. It wasn't far, a few blocks from here.

The little house was quiet, no lights on, no cars parked in the driveway. Nobody home. The whole street looked that way, like it had been abandoned. I decided to go in anyway. I didn't want to wait out here alone.

The white fence creaked as I entered. I took slow, soft steps, not wanting anyone to hear me, and though no one was home, I was afraid. The front door was open, and the crunch of the grassy doormat beneath my feet seemed too loud. Again, the nervousness pulsed quickly under my skin. The house looked empty, but as soon as I entered, I knew it was because they were hiding. They were in the back room, waiting for me to return from where I had been.

I tiptoed quietly as I walked down the hall, not wanting them to know I was home. When I reached the door, I was startled by someone on my right, but it was just my reflection. Something wasn't right, though. I recognized the face in the gold-framed mirror hanging on the wall, but it wasn't mine. It was someone I knew, someone I was angry with. Then it hit me—Kara.

I looked down, confused, and realized I had opened the package I had carried with me inside. The contents of the sleek plastic box was in my hand, and my heart jumped when I saw what it was—a gun, heavy and threatening. I wanted to drop it and run, but I had no control over this body. It was Kara's. It moved forward without my consent, readied the gun without my wanting it to.

As I opened the door to the back room, I saw their faces. Anna and Chloe, scared and shocked. My hand was pointing the gun at them.

"Kara?" Anna pleaded, but I felt my finger tighten around the trigger.

"NO!" I screamed as the shots fired.

———

"HEY, YOU'RE OKAY," SAID A LOW COMFORTING voice, still tired with sleep. "Come on, wake up. It's a dream."

My mind struggled to comprehend. Trying to fight the anguish, my eyes pinched closed clinging to the darkness. What if I opened them and it was real?

"Wake up, Ellie," William said again. He pulled me closer, his hands warming against the skin of my waist. The heat that grew under his palms was familiar. It told us we were meant for each other, and the sensation lifted me out of the dream. He buried his face into the back of my neck, kissing the skin on my shoulder with gentle lips, and my eyes opened, taking in the room still dark with night.

"Thanks," I said, recovering. I was drenched in sweat, my lashes wet with tears.

He propped himself up on his elbow, leaning over to kiss my cheek, and his golden hair fell forward tickling my jaw. "Which one was it?" he asked.

My chest still ached with worry. "The one with the gun, and in the end I'm Kara."

He collapsed back onto the bed and pulled me into his chest. "That's the worst one."

I stared at the pitch-black window, as if it alone was keeping out the dreams. At any moment I was sure it would shatter, letting all my worry in to suffocate me.

It had been a few weeks since I had heard the news about Anna and Chloe being captured, but the nightmares kept on. I still hadn't forgiven myself, and I didn't know if I ever would. There was no guarantee I could save them, and if they died it would destroy me. If I hadn't tried to cure Anna, if I had just let them be, at least Chloe would still have had a chance. In the end, it was really their sacrifice that fulfilled the prophecy and began the war, not mine. They were the ones suffering, Christoph's prisoners to torture at his leisure and discard at his will. My heart hurt when I thought of it.

"Since we're all awake now," I heard Mac grumble from the living room couch where he slept. "Might as well get in some target practice."

"Mac, it's four o'clock in the morning," William protested.

"I don't care if it's a quarter to a kick in your ass. Get up, you two."

I rolled my eyes and grabbed my dart gun off the dresser. "All right. All right." I nudged William, whose face was still buried in the pillow.

"Maybe if I play dead he'll let me sleep in," he said with a muffled voice.

I laughed. "Either that or he'll pull you out by your toes."

It was still dark when William and I stepped outside.

"Four o'clock in the morning is as good a time as any to train. Battle can occur anytime, anywhere, and with anyone. I want you prepared for every scenario," Mac said as we walked between the trees.

I didn't mind. I liked the cool early morning, when

the sun was still asleep. It always felt like I had stumbled upon the world's secret, when the earth came alive thinking nobody was watching.

I had only just started to get used to the dart gun, the feel of the grass reed finger-grip as I steadied the weapon, the amount of force needed to propel the dart a long distance, the way the holster strap fit around my thigh.

I had been reluctant at first, unsure it would be worth the effort, but Mac was a good teacher, and he explained much more than how to use the gun.

"The thing is, Elyse," he'd said, "it's a war. That means if you don't come for them, they'll come for you. And when they do, if you don't have a way to protect yourself, then we're all outta luck."

I didn't see myself as a violent person, but what he said made sense. I had an ability at my disposal, one that could save my life and save others, but only if I learned how to use it. On one side, my blood was a deadly toxin, and on the other, its cure. But it was useless as a defense unless I had a way to transport it to my enemies. The darts would serve that purpose.

"Now that you've got the basics down—" he started, but I cut him off.

"I wouldn't say that." I felt like I hardly knew what I was doing, like I was lucky I didn't suck the dart down my throat every time.

There was a lot more involved than I had expected, so much to think about before I made a move. How much force did I need behind my breath, did I consider the balance of my feet and steady the grip of my hands, what was the weight of the dart I was using, had I taken notice of the direction of the wind, was I close enough to my target to shoot? So many factors played a part. The heavier the dart, the shorter it would go, but only the heavier ones stayed on course. The lighter darts went farther, but they tended to curve in the direction of the wind.

"Well, I think we need to take it to the next level. You need to feel comfortable with how your blood works with the darts, on more than just animals, and eventually we'll need to practice using enough to ensure the kill."

The kill. My hands felt shaky at the thought of it. Would it ever come to that? I had to consider the idea that it was very possible. The force we were up against, The Council, was capable of unspeakable things. Anna and Chloe were seeing that first hand.

I tried to feel empowered by my anger, to remember that I was fighting for my friends and that we were all fighting for a cause much greater, but I couldn't deny the fear. If I were ever forced to kill, I'd have to find the will somewhere down in the darkest part of my soul. Maybe I could do it, for them.

"I don't know, Mac," I said, shying away from the thought. "I need a lot more training before I'm ready for that."

"No you don't," he said as though it were a simple fact. "What do you have in your bag?"

I pulled out the largest dart in the satchel on my hip. "Aside from the standard? A few hollows."

"Nasty little buggers, aren't they?" He took it from me and looked it over, then handed it back with a nod. "Harder to carve than the standard, too. They'll snap like a dried spaghetti noodle if you aren't careful hollowing out the center."

It wasn't enough that I had to learn how to use the gun. Mac made me carve out every dart I used. I'd gotten much better at it, simply because a bad dart wouldn't fly, and I couldn't really train when a part of the weapon didn't function. That first week of training, I sat at the kitchen table for eight hours a day taking out my aggression on the tiny sticks until I had piles of them, until they were perfect.

"The good thing about the hollow is you can fill it with a hefty amount of toxin that will release into the skin on impact," he continued.

"So that's her kill shot?" William asked. He looked at me, studying my confidence, making sure I knew what I had to do if I ever needed to defend myself.

"Yep," Mac answered.

I stared at the slender wooden needle with a sick feeling. I imagined what it would be like to slide that dart into the gun, knowing it would be the end for whoever happened to be my target. I silently hoped to myself that I would never see the spotted black feather fly through the air, as sure to kill as a bullet to the heart.

Mac adjusted the shotgun on his shoulder. "What else?"

"I made some of these last night," I said, holding up a shorter solid version with light brown feathers.

"Tell me what it does," he added, testing me.

"This one is absorbent," I answered, examining the etchings my knife had made. "The wood will suck up moisture and slow release into the target."

"Right." Mac nodded. "That's the one I used on the doe."

I remembered the animal he had used to test me vividly. Her black eyes were full of fear as I bent down to heal her. It was the only way Mac could be sure it was me taking refuge in his safe haven, and not an intruder. Things had changed so much since then.

"And you," Mac said to William. "I'm glad you brought your arrows kid, but you won't be shooting this morning." He chuckled to himself like he knew something we didn't. Then mid-laugh his faced turned serious, and he stopped abruptly. His arms shot out in front of William and I, pushing us behind him. I'd never seen him get so quiet.

William stepped closer to me, becoming more alert. He removed the bow from his back and loaded an arrow.

"What is it?" I whispered.

Mac looked at me like I was the crazy one. "Don't talk to someone in situations like that, Ellie."

"Situations like what?"

"You don't talk, you look," Mac grumbled, pointing

from his eyes to the space in front of him. Without more explanation he continued walking ahead, waving us forward. "And what do you say when you meet someone you ain't sure of?"

"Once harm has been done, even a fool understands it," I repeated. It was something they'd used in the last war, a simple phrase that separated the good from the bad.

Mac looked at William. "And what should they answer?"

"The outcome of the war is in our hands; the outcome of words is in The Council."

"Good."

William scanned the trees ahead. "So, what was out there?"

Mac shrugged and smiled his crazy-man smile as he looked back at us. "Nothing to worry about."

I rolled my eyes and jogged a little to keep up.

"So, tell me again why I'm not training to use a semi-automatic or a sniper rifle?" William asked with a smirk. His eyes found me, and we shared a knowing smile. "A bow and arrow seems pretty weak in comparison." He adjusted the strap on his quiver and returned the weapon to his back.

William knew very well why Mac had him training to use a bow. He'd been having him hunt and bring home dinner every night for a reason, but it was still fun to rile him up over the subject.

"If you don't know that by now, I'm gonna to slap you

upside your head," Mac muttered.

William and I waited, knowing he would continue unprovoked.

"Sure you could use a shotgun, but that won't teach you accuracy. You could use a long-range weapon but that won't teach you stealth. The bow will train you in ways a gun never will. You get over confident with a gun, forget to stay low because you think you can take on whatever you encounter. We'll work with guns later. Right now we need to focus on how to make the most of your abilities."

He had been leading us into the woods as he ranted, but stopped to look William in the eyes, as he made his final point.

"Your ability is powerful, but it does nobody any good unless you can get in close, unseen. You can't affect people from a long way off, and what good will you be if you get yourself killed walking into an enemy camp like a bull in a china shop? Sure, a gun is a better weapon, but for us, better weapons don't mean you'll win the fight. During the first war I lost some good friends to a Descendant of Chronos. Doesn't really matter what kind of weapon you have if you get caught by somebody who can stop time."

"All right. All right," William answered with a laugh. "I'll listen. What are we doing first?"

"Like I said, Elyse needs to learn to use her blood with the darts." Mac turned to me with a menacing grin that had me worried he was about to get even.

"But I already have. I've practiced on hundreds of

deer." I didn't understand why he was anxious for me to paralyze more animals. It was kind of cruel.

His overly excited eyes moved back and forth between William and I, holding the suspense. "Well, today William will be the target."

"What? No way," William and I protested together.

He had to be joking. If he really thought I was going to try and gun down the one I loved with sharp needle-point darts, he had another thing coming.

"Are you going to take this seriously or not?" he roared.

"I'm not doing it," I said, firmly standing my ground.

He bent down to my level, unaffected by my strong voice, and stared into me.

"If you don't do it, I will," he threatened, "and I won't use the little splinter of a dart you'll use."

"What the hell, Mac," William said with outrage.

Mac changed his focus to William. "You have a thirty second head start. If Elyse finds you in the next thirty minutes, she gets a hammer dart to the thigh, so if you don't want her to get nailed with this, you better stay out of sight."

I could see how this would motivate William to hide. He wouldn't want to see me impaled with the massive spike Mac held in his hand. It was the length of a pencil and at least twice as thick.

"I might as well sit down right here and wait for the thirty minutes to be over. Why would I want to find him if I'm just going to get a dart in the leg if I do?"

"Well, if you don't find William in that same time, *he's* getting the hammer dart to the thigh."

There it was, the condition that would have me hunting down my lover like a wild boar. In order to save him from the pain, I'd have to find him and take it myself. After what happened with Anna, it wasn't a hard decision, and he knew I wouldn't let him win.

"Who's it going to be?"

A sick grin curled into Mac's cheeks with such a disturbing sense of pleasure, it was hard not to believe he'd follow through with his threat. William and I looked at each other, both knowing neither of us was going to forfeit, to let the other take the dart willingly.

"You're crazy, Mac," William said as he ran off into the forest away from me.

I tensed to run, but Mac stopped me with his thick hand.

"He gets thirty seconds."

CHAPTER TWO

—

"ALL RIGHT," MAC SAID WITH BOOMING ENTHUSIASM. "He's all yours."

I threw back a nasty look before charging into the thick mass of trees. I ran until Mac was completely out of view, scanning the area with each step. William had gone in this direction, but I had no idea if he had changed course. He could be anywhere.

I tried to pull myself together. I only had thirty minutes to find him. I stood perfectly still, listening for any sign of movement, a rustle of leaves, a snapping twig, the crunch of heavy feet as they tip-toed over dried foliage—there was nothing.

I walked with quick, quiet steps in one direction, then the other. My eyes flickered from tree to tree, up in the branches and far into the distance, hoping to spot some sign of him.

After what felt like twenty minutes, I leaned my back

against a nearby trunk and sat completely hopeless on the ground. The sun was starting to rise, and faint light was brightening the forest. Maybe if I just waited quietly he would expose himself.

That's when I saw it, a small freshly broken branch dangling and swaying in the breeze. I pressed myself up, looking around for another sign of him, but tree trunks and shadows in the distance only played tricks on my eyes. I smiled as I approached, realizing there were tracks. A vague impression I could only assume were his footprints led me hopping through the woods like a fox following a trail.

As I pursued the tracks, I started to notice something was off. They were small, too small to be either Mac's or William's, and I had never been to this part of the woods before.

I froze when I sensed the presence of someone other than myself up ahead. There, behind that tree. My heart hammered, and everything I had learned over the past weeks kicked in as I reached for the dart gun. I pulled out a thin but sturdy dart from the satchel strapped to my hip, thin because I was being cautious. I didn't know who was out there. I pressed the two gold buttons on my bracelet, which was wrapped snuggly around my left wrist, and felt the blades slice into my skin. I was used to it now, and didn't flinch. As the blood began to flow, I dipped the dart in the small hole at the bottom of the gold ring. It would be just enough to debilitate the person, to slow their reaction time down and hinder their muscle movements.

I crouched, hiding behind a cluster of brush as I loaded the blood-dipped dart slowly, careful not to make noise. I readied my grip, took a few silent deep breaths to prepare my lungs, and stood up to shoot. I was hoping it was William, even though deep down I knew I'd meet someone else's gaze. The eyes that found me were more familiar than I'd expected.

Kara's expression was nervous, but prepared. She could see every thought I was having and knew I had a dart ready and meant for her. I didn't know if she was armed, but if she was, it was only a matter of who would act first. My face hardened as I looked at her, but neither of us spoke. She didn't try to communicate with her mind as she tended to do. Instead we stared, predator and prey, into each other.

Even with my gun still aimed and ready, tears began to well up against my lower lids like unsteady dams ready to burst. I held them in, and her face dropped as she read my thoughts. She knew I blamed her for the loss of Anna and Chloe. How could she have betrayed me like that? Without thinking I took a breath, deep and full, aimed the gun, and shot the dart into the fleshy part of her shoulder. Maybe I had it in me after all. Maybe I could be a killer.

She cried out a quick, painful moan and crumpled to the ground. I'd never shot anyone before. Her wild black curls covered her face, so I couldn't see if she was conscious. I watched her, waiting for her to move.

Another cry echoed through the forest with such unrelenting agony that I shivered at the sound. It was William. It must have already been thirty minutes, and I had failed to find him. I sighed with frustration as I glanced back at Kara's limp body on the ground. If it wasn't for her, I might have. My heart gave a lurch as I took off in his direction, leaving Kara behind to fend for herself.

I didn't have room in my mind to think about her, to bother with how she had gotten into our safe haven. What if she had brought The Council? What if William's screams were not from the hammer dart but from something far worse? I sprinted with all my might to him, switching the bracelet to my right wrist, the healing side. If he needed it, I would be ready.

I found him moaning on the forest floor, holding his thigh where the dart protruded from his leg.

"Is everything okay?" I asked Mac, using my hands to brace myself against my thighs.

"Well, not exactly," William answered with a wince. "I have a hammer dart in my leg."

My dry throat ached as I caught my breath. "So The Council's not here?"

"Did you poison *yourself* somehow?" Mac laughed. "No. The Council's not here."

I looked around, still worried, but lowered myself to the ground beside William. "I can't believe you did it," I said, glaring at Mac.

He shrugged like it was nothing. "Said I would."

"Will someone please do something?" William pleaded.

"I'm sorry," I apologized as Mac pulled out the thick wooden dart. William's cry of pain made me clench my teeth with regret. "It's my fault. I'm so sorry."

I pressed the two gold buttons on my bracelet willingly. The blood dripped steady and quick into the wound as William sighed with relief. I caught myself glancing into the woods as the skin on his leg healed up. Kara was still out there.

"I can't believe you, Mac," he muttered as he rubbed his thigh, the new flesh pink and tender.

I was distracted and didn't realize William had a hold of my left hand until he spoke.

"Why didn't you use my blood to heal yourself?" he asked, suddenly worried about my blood loss. His blood was my cure as much as mine was his.

"I forgot," I answered, looking down at the two cuts resembling a snakebite on my wrist. "It's nothing, though. I'll be okay."

Without asking he took a knife from his pocket and slid it across his thumb. "William, it's fine. One cut from the bracelet won't affect me—"

"Wait," he interrupted. "Why did you need blood from the left side? You weren't anywhere near me."

"I was about to ask the same thing." I raised my eyebrows at Mac, remembering that nobody was supposed to be able to get in here. It was his safe haven. If Kara was here, he had *let* her in. "Mac let somebody in. I shot her in the forest."

"Who?" William asked, sealing up my wounds.

I ran my fingers across my newly flushed skin. "Kara," I answered with resentment.

Mac's face twisted in shock. "You shot her?"

"Well, yeah."

"Did you kill her?" His voice raised with worry.

"Why do you care?" I shot back. First he let her in, and now suddenly she meant something to him? "I thought you wanted me to start shooting people anyway."

"You *killed* her?" William gasped.

"No," I answered. "Of course not."

You only thought about it. Kara's voice was in my head.

I whirled around, expecting her right behind me, but she was concealed in the trees a short distance out.

"What?" William asked.

"She's there," I said, pointing to her through the trees.

Mac followed the direction of my finger, looking eagerly for the girl I'd taken down.

"Kara, come on out here," Mac called. "If she tries to shoot you, I'll give her the hammer dart she deserves."

I gave Mac a look that said go ahead and try, but he only smiled at the threat. I didn't know why he was being so nice to her.

We all walked in silence back to the cabin. Kara stayed up front, under the protection of Mac, who shot warning glances back at me every few minutes. Although her gaze stayed forward, I was sure she was sorting through my thoughts. I tried to keep a clear head, but she still had access to my memories. It was infuriating that there was no privacy around her, not even in my own mind. I thought perhaps she would respond to my anger by forcing her own opinions into my head, but she stayed quiet.

"What are we going to do with her?" I asked when we were inside.

"*Her?*" Mac answered. "What are we going to do with *you?* I invited her in, Elyse. She's not an intruder. She's our guest. You're acting like a lunatic."

Coming from Mac that was saying something, given the man would be considered insane by most people's standards.

"Fine," I said under my breath as I retreated to the couch.

William followed, at a complete loss for words. It was smart for him to stay quiet. My emotions were razor sharp and unstable.

As the morning began to light up the room, I could see Kara more clearly. She looked worn and ragged, like she hadn't slept or eaten in a while. The sight of her made me wonder what she'd been through, and for the first time since I'd shot her I could feel the slightest bit of sympathy and regret form in my chest.

"Elyse," she spoke aloud, probably taking advantage of my moment of weakness. "Will you let me show you?"

"Show me what?"

"Show you what happened," she said, her face pleading. "I know it won't change anything, but at least you'll know."

I wanted so badly to blame her. It was easier for my enemy to be one person, a simpler opponent to defeat than the massive powers of The Council, but I knew better. Even if she had betrayed me, it wasn't her that I had to face. She was just their pawn.

"All right," I said, straightening up as she approached. Her offer was too tempting. I couldn't resist knowing the details of the nightmare that had been haunting me.

She pressed her palms against the sides of my head. Much like Kara could access the thoughts and memories of others, anyone could access her mind as well, as long as she let them in. I found my way through her memories much easier than the last time. Unfamiliar images streamed past me, faces I'd never seen, places I'd never been, but Anna and Chloe were somewhere. I just had to find them. That simple thought drew them out.

The memory I was looking for was clear and began with her coming home from a job. It was an easy one, just a lookout gig, but the guy never showed. She was carrying groceries I knew could only be for Anna and Chloe, two new toothbrushes and an assortment of non-perishables.

There was a spring in her step, or mine as it seemed. It was a strange perspective living out her memory, seeing what she saw, feeling what she felt. She was happy to be doing what she could to make up for the atrocities The Council forced her to partake in. But as her eyes found the front door of her apartment, I felt her skin prickle with fear. It was open. I picked up on the sick feeling in her stomach as she pushed it in, expecting what I still refused to believe—that Christoph had found them.

The place seemed empty at first, but even if Anna and Chloe were there, she knew they wouldn't be up and about. They were hidden below the floor in a secret room she had discovered a few months after moving in. It was a good place to keep them safe until Dr. Nickel contacted her about joining Elyse and William.

Suddenly there were voices, and Kara stopped. They were coming from the back patio. *Be calm*, she thought. It was probably a Hunter sent to validate her story, their casual way of checking up on things. She knew how to deal with Hunters. They were ruthless and intimidating, but they were also stupid and easy to manipulate. How else could The Council use them for clean up jobs? As she peeked around the corner to get a glimpse of the intruders, her heart sank with such a hopeless sense of dread and panic that I couldn't help but react.

What? I yelled. *What is it?* But her memory answered for her—Christoph.

She should have known he'd come to question her. Just as she caught sight of him, he turned his watchful eyes, catching her in the doorway.

He reminded me of a sleazy businessman, corrupted by power and greed, as he stood up to straighten his suit jacket and tie. I wondered how many people he had fooled with his sophisticated style and expensive taste. His hair, a gray that was once blond in his prime, was short and nicely styled, but he couldn't disguise the evil in his face. His features were sharp. The point of his nose, his protruding cheek bones, the tips of his eyebrows, all unnaturally symetrical. He had thin, tight lips and perfectly white porcelain veneers that made his smile deceitfully charming.

The way he carried himself was intimidating. Kara stood her ground, but with every step he took forward, I felt the urge to step back. His eyes were a cold, pale blue. They were empty, like he didn't have a soul, and they narrowed in on Kara as if his stare alone could strip her of her life. I could only imagine how much death those eyes had seen, how many times they had widened with excitement at the sight of human suffering.

As he opened the sliding glass door, the two individuals that accompanied him came into view, and with a rush of fear, Kara knew it was over. The man with him was Dimitri, and he was only used for one thing—punishment, or at least the threat of punishment. He could make any living thing age until its death, taking years away from a person's life, or killing them entirely. He didn't have the look of a killer; his eyes were gray and indifferent, almost bored. He was short and athletic, younger than Christoph, but still had shades of silver laced through his head of brown hair. The woman was Amber. Kara only knew of her by description—tall, thin, blonde, and beautiful. Since The Council used both Kara and her for essentially the same purpose, they had never worked together. She was used to extract information by deciphering the truth of a person's words. In an interrogation, there was no use in lying.

"Hello, Kara," Christoph greeted her with a smile. His voice was surprisingly smooth, almost too kind.

"Christoph." She nodded briefly, returning his greeting.

"No doubt you know of Dimitri and Amber," he added. He had eyes like a snake, ready to strike.

"Of course," she answered with a polite smile, but despite their etiquette, I could feel the tension in the atmosphere and in the quick pulse of Kara's heart. "Please, make yourselves at home."

The four of them took their seats in silence, Amber choosing to sit beside Kara on the love seat, while Christoph and Dimitri chose the couch directly across from them.

"Let's not play coy, Kara," Christoph said pointedly. The tone in his voice sent a chill down Kara's spine, and I shivered from the feeling. "You know why we're here."

"Do I?" she answered calmly, though her fear was so immense it was almost painful. The question was the best response she could think of. It wasn't a lie, and it wouldn't give away the fact that she knew exactly why they were there.

Christoph glanced at Amber, clearly noticing how Kara had evaded his question.

"You are quite clever," he laughed, but the sound was menacing, not joyful. He leaned forward before he continued.

"Where is Elyse?"

My heart stopped dead in my chest as he spoke my name, but Kara's slowed with relief.

"I don't know," she answered honestly. Only Dr. Nickel knew of our location, and he hadn't entrusted it to Kara.

Amber gave a subtle nod, letting him know her words were true, and he continued.

"So she is alive?" he pursued the topic with a disturbing grin.

"I have no way of knowing that for sure." Amber nodded again, but Christoph didn't need her to tell him that Kara was avoiding straight answers.

"Do-not-mess-with-me," he hissed each word slowly and clearly with black anger in his eyes. "Are you hiding something from us, Kara? Yes or no?"

"What could I be hiding?"

He shook his head in disapproval. "Dimitri, take away 100 years the next time she does not give me a yes or no." He tilted his head and came back to Kara. "Would you like to try again?"

This time it was Kara's heart that throbbed frantically. "Please don't," she begged. "It won't help you find her."

Christoph smiled with indifference as he gave Dimitri a slight nod. "Do it."

"Please," she cried, but Dimitri obeyed, locking his gaze on her.

I felt it, as she began to weaken, and her skin began to

itch as it aged.

"Wait," she screamed frantically, her body nearly paralyzed with shock.

Christoph held up a hand, and Dimitri looked away, ending the torture.

The panic began to grow in me as her thoughts became clear in my head. She was afraid, and she had no other choice. It was her life or theirs. I felt the tickle of her tears as they slid down her cheeks, the pain in her chest when she knew she couldn't win, and the guilt that spread through her like an unwelcome disease as she answered with a heart-sinking: "I'll tell you."

"The human she healed and her daughter. They're in the basement," she confessed, overwrought with distress. "Under the bedroom floor."

No, I cried out into the empty space of the memory, but nobody heard, and Christoph's pleased expression made me sick with anger.

Kara refused to look, but I heard the latch lift and the hinges of the hatch door open. There was no hope. As they were pulled out of their hiding place and into Kara's line of sight, I broke down. Anna's worried eyes looked deep into Kara's, past her and into me, like that silent plea for help was meant for nobody else. Chloe's face, flushed and swollen from crying, never looked away from her mother. Dimitri escorted them quickly by, and although I wanted to call out, grab them, hold them, save them, *something,* Kara's body paid no attention to my mental commands.

She stood helplessly by and watched as they were taken.

"Thank you," Christoph said with absolution as he turned to leave, "for doing what is right for our people."

"Yes, sir," she said through silent tears, but I felt the hatred she had for him.

His last words were a futile plea for understanding. "I only need their child," he confided. "Once she bears it for me, Elyse will be free to go. Without the next generation oracle, we have no chance."

CHAPTER THREE

—

HIS RESOUNDING LAST STATEMENT BLINDSIDED ME, and I pulled out of the memory with force as he closed the door behind him. I'd known I was flagged untouchable for being the new mother. I just never realized it was because he wanted the child. I should have been expecting it. Of course he didn't want me dead. He needed me. My insides clenched up with worry for a child William and I had yet to conceive.

I almost forgot the three of them were sitting wide-eyed, waiting for my reaction.

"So?" Mac asked, but I had no words for him. My mind wouldn't move away from what I had just learned.

"Elyse?" William urged, setting a gentle hand on my arm. The warmth in his touch brought me back momentarily, but I couldn't look him in the eye. This time the heat from our skin didn't give me comfort. Not when it promised William and I would bear a child Christoph wanted. Instead I addressed Mac directly.

"Christoph and Dimitri were there. They were going to age her until she gave them up." Though I would have given my life for Anna and Chloe, I couldn't expect someone else to do the same. "She had no choice."

"I want to help you get them back," Kara said. "Whatever you have planned, I want in."

"Are you okay with that, Elyse?" William asked, still wary of Kara's presence.

"Yeah," I answered, unable to ignore the feelings I had experienced through her memory. As much as I'd denied it, the oracle was right. Kara had done her best. It wasn't her fault.

"All right!" Mac declared, slapping his heavy hands together. "I'm going to start breakfast now that I know you aren't going to go for her jugular."

How long have you known that, Kara? I asked. *That he wanted our baby?*

Not long, she returned the thought. *I didn't know until he told me.*

"You okay, Ellie?" William asked, interrupting my busy mind.

"Yeah," I lied, keeping my eyes on Kara.

He must be keeping the idea to himself. I haven't heard anyone thinking about it.

Why would he tell you?

I don't know. I guess he assumed I already knew.

"What's going on?" William asked, picking up on the

unspoken communication between us. Our eyes finally met, but I couldn't bring myself to tell him. He had reacted so harshly about the prophecy, I didn't want to worry him more than he already was.

It doesn't really matter anyway, I thought to her. *There is no oracle baby.*

Not yet, Kara added.

"Sure," William said with high eyebrows, "don't mind me. Just continue on with your silent conversation like I'm not here."

"I'm sorry—" I started, but Mac jumped in.

"Girls, I need a wood run. Pile's getting low."

I thought William would protest, eager to get more information from us, but Mac gave him a look that kept him quiet. I felt bad about leaving him out, but I needed more details, and I needed to come to terms with the facts. I would pull myself together, then confide in him what I knew.

"No problem, Mac," I said, jumping to my feet. I picked up the canvas wood hauling sack by the door and stepped out into the cold. The cool morning air was refreshing as we walked in silence away from the house.

"So, he wants the baby," I let out, once we were some distance away. I still couldn't believe it. My brow wrinkled in thought. "It doesn't matter. It's not going to happen, Kara. There won't be a baby. I mean, we haven't...you know..."

"So."

"So," I said, ripping a loose branch from a dead tree trunk a little too aggressively, "babies don't just happen, and I'm going to make sure it doesn't."

She laughed unconvinced. "Yeah, because I'm sure that will stop fate, no problem."

"Why does he want her anyway? It'll be years before she'll be able to tell the future."

"Her?" Kara answered with a smirk.

"Oh, you know what I mean. *It,* okay? Maybe he just wants the baby so he can kill it?"

We found a nearby fallen tree and began scavenging small logs and twigs.

"I don't think so," she answered skeptically.

"You're supposed to know these things," I spat, still feeling the need to blame her for Anna and Chloe. I sighed when I heard myself. "I'm sorry."

"It's okay. It *is* my fault you're in this situation. I should have hidden them better. I just thought—"

"It's fine," I interrupted. "We have a plan. We'll get them back."

"About that," Kara said, loading an armful of logs into the bag. "We have to be careful. Things are more complicated than they seem."

Our eyes connected and I got quiet, waiting for her.

"I think that's why they were flagged. Think about it. There must have been a reason. Maybe it was so he could use them as bait when the time was right. He's smart, Elyse. Don't underestimate him. He knows you're alive.

I'm sure he's expecting you."

I took a seat next to her on top of the fallen trunk. "Even if he is expecting me," I said, finally sure of at least one thing, "the oracle gave me instructions. If we follow them, it'll work."

"I hope that's true."

We sat in silence for a while taking it all in.

"What happened after they took Anna and Chloe?"

She didn't say anything at first, but slid off the log with her back turned, distancing herself from me. "You mean how did they punish me?" Her shoulders shrugged before she answered. "They threatened my family, like always, and gave me extraction assignments." She turned, trying to keep her expression unaffected like these were the simple facts. Nothing to take personally. "The ones no one wants."

My eyebrows lowered. "Like what?"

Her gaze dropped, and I saw through her hard and distant demeanor. "Children." The word was soft and colored with shame. Our eyes connected briefly, mine horrified, hers desperate for forgiveness. "But I couldn't do it, Elyse, not anymore," she said quickly, needing to be absolved. "I ran out. I knew they'd find me, but I didn't care. I was tired of being their slave, and I knew I deserved to die anyway after giving the two of them up to Christoph, after everything I've done in my life."

"No, Kara..."

"They didn't find me though," she kept on. "The

oracle did. She said I had been on the wrong side, but she would help me find the right one, where I was supposed to be."

"Did you look into her mind?" I asked with quiet hopefulness.

"There was too much. Fear. War. Death. I just didn't know what was real and what was prophecy. I didn't see anything that could help us."

"It's okay." I looked away. "So, it's pretty bad out there?"

Her lips tightened. "It's tense."

"But William's family is okay, right? And our friends?"

"They're fine," she answered, tucking her short thick curls behind her ear, "but you should know…"

"What?" I demanded.

"Iosif." She shook her head. "He didn't…they killed him, Elyse."

"Oh," I whispered, swallowing down the ache in my throat.

"Sorry." She was trying to be sensitive, but Iosif's death didn't hurt her as it did me. It was my fault that he was killed.

I felt sick. "We should probably go back."

"You go," she said with a subtle smile. "I have a feeling I should stay here for a while."

"Stay here?" I didn't want to explain things to William on my own. I couldn't be the one to tell him about Iosif. "No, come on. Let's go."

She rolled her eyes. "Don't be pushy, Elyse. Just trust me. We'll both be happy you did."

I gave up easily, realizing there was a reason she was being resistant. I just had no idea why. When I got back to the cabin, something seemed off. There was no sound of Mac's booming voice, or anyone's voice for that matter. Things were too quiet.

It was hard to believe we weren't safe in the haven, and with Mac around, I couldn't think of a more secure place we could be, but my hand still clutched my dart gun.

I twisted the handle slowly, trying not to make a sound, but the place was so small, it was almost impossible for it not to be obvious I was entering. I flung the door open, in case I needed to act fast, but William's hearty laughter settled my adrenalin rush.

He sat wide-eyed and amused at the table, which was set with two plates, wildflowers in a vase, and steaming hot breakfast.

"Somebody's a little paranoid."

I smiled, embarrassed. "Well, in my defense, the most powerful Descendants in the world are hunting me as we speak." I closed the door behind me.

"Touché," he conceded. "Anyway...Surprise!"

"What for?" I asked, stepping toward the empty seat.

"We missed your birthday. It was a month ago."

I had forgotten, completely. There were just too many things on my mind these days.

"Yeah," I answered with surprise. "I guess we did.

How old am I again?"

"In human terms or ours?" he played along.

I shrugged. "Easy. A girl always goes for the lesser number. Eighteen sounds so much better than ninety."

"Eighteen it is," he said, coming around to push in my chair. "So, for the birthday girl we have pan-fried potatoes, quail eggs, and oranges."

"You did all of this?"

"Mac helped," he said, giving him credit. "We both thought you could use a little normal in your life." He sat down across from me. "We all could."

He was homesick, and I didn't blame him. If I had a home and a family like he did, I would miss it too. But he was my home, and seclusion was what I was used to. I felt perfectly content living this way.

"Not that quail eggs are normal." He laughed. "But close enough."

"It looks amazing. Thank you," I said, digging in.

I watched him from across the table, feeling lucky to have him. Whatever the circumstances, as long as he was with me, I knew everything would be all right.

"Just for the record, you're my normal," I added.

No matter how crazy or bad things were going to get, we could always come back to our secret world of each other, even if the universe of others was crumbling around us.

He combed his fingers through his blond hair, the muscles in his square jaw flexing as he chewed. "Are you going to tell me what else you saw in that memory?"

I picked up the small vase of purple and yellow flowers, taking in their earthy sent.

"Not right now."

"That bad huh?" he asked, cutting into an orange. "I just wish I knew what was going on out there."

"Kara said it was tense."

He looked up. "What does that mean? Is everyone safe?"

"Not everyone," I said with regret.

William's eyes became grave as he braced himself for the worst. "Who?"

"Iosif," I answered. "They killed him. Because of me."

The guilt felt like rocks in the pit of my stomach. All of this was because of me.

"It's not your fault," William said as he came around the table. "You can't blame yourself for everything that happens." My eyes were down in shame, stubborn tears beginning to fall despite my attempt to hold them back. He wiped them with his thumbs as he held my face in his hands. "None of this is your fault. You didn't choose this, Ellie."

He moved his face closer to mine so I would look up. When I did, his lips lured me in. His kiss was home, my relief from everything. It was soft and gentle at first, but soon the rush lifted me to my feet. It was easy to get lost in the moment, with the romantic breakfast and the privacy. My fingers found the buttons of his shirt, forgetting everything else.

"Bedroom," he said against my mouth.

His lips moved to my neck sending a chill over my shoulders as he picked me up, wrapping my legs around his body. I wanted the distraction, needed his firm arms to hold me, and he gave in too. He closed the door behind us, leaving our breakfast half-eaten on the other side, and sat me down on the bed. His fingers tickled my sides as he lifted my shirt over my head. Our lips met again, the only sound our heavy breath as he slid in next to me, pulling me closer. When his hand grazed my stomach and settled on the button of my jeans I pulled away, heart beating.

"Wait," I breathed, sitting up and turning away from him.

"What's wrong?" he asked, surprised by my resistance. "Am I going too fast?"

"No." I looked back at him. "It's not that."

He pressed himself up to sit next to me, and slid his warm fingers in between mine. "What is it?" "I have to tell you something."

"Okay." He tightened his hold on my hand.

"In the memory, Christoph said something." I swallowed hard, wishing I didn't have to tell him. It wasn't that I didn't love him. I knew more than anything that I wanted to be with only him, forever, and this might have been the moment we would have completely opened up to one another. Now that I knew what Christoph was planning, we couldn't risk it. "This isn't just about me starting a war, William. They want something from us. Christoph wants our baby."

"What baby?" he laughed. "There is no baby."

"Exactly," I said. "And we have to keep it that way. There's no way I'm going to let him have my child. I'm not going to ever let that happen, even if it means...taking every precaution." The roomed hummed with silence. "We just shouldn't tempt ourselves."

"And you heard *him* say that?" he asked.

I nodded. "Yeah."

A sense of hopelessness clouded the moment. Even after all we had overcome to be together, Christoph still managed to weasel his way into our world. I didn't want to live by his terms. I wanted freedom. I could feel it in what I had found with William, a chance to love and be loved, to live a full life like everyone else, but even that had been tainted by The Council.

William looked off into the distance, his stony expression a mixture of surprise and disgust. "Well, you're right. We'll just make sure it doesn't happen." Even through the grim atmosphere, his subtle smiled shined through. "I'm assuming protection isn't really effective if the baby is...pre-destined."

I laughed. "Probably not."

He picked my shirt off of the floor and slid it over my head.

"Thanks," I said as I pulled it on the rest of the way.

We stared into each other, the forbidden making

things all the more tempting. "To be honest," he said brushing my hair back, "there are other reasons we should wait. I mean, other than making an oracle baby, which probably isn't the best idea."

"Definitely not the best idea," I agreed, leaning into his shoulder.

"I don't see why we can't keep things innocent, though," he said, moving in for a kiss. It was too easy to agree. His lips were persuasive as they moved softly over mine.

"Okay," I whispered with our mouths touching.

My hands found the buttons of his shirt once again, but this time I clasped them shut, one by one, as he kissed the parts of my neck that were still bare. "You know I love you, right?" he asked.

I smiled. "Even though I'm plagued with prophecy?"

He laughed as we headed back into the living room to finish our breakfast.

"You know what? On second thought, the whole prophecy thing's kind of a hassle. I'm not sure this is going to work out."

When we reached the table I threw my arms around his neck. "Yeah. We're no good together anyway," I played along.

His warm fingers grazed the skin on my hips as he pulled me closer, but before our lips met, the front door flew open with such force I heard wood splinter. Suddenly I was pinned between the wall and William. His protective stance blocked the door from view, making him a human shield against me. Even so, my hand grasped the loaded dart gun ready to defend him at all costs. But none of it was necessary.

"Dad?"

Hearing the shock in William's voice, I ducked under his arm. Dr. Nickel's face was strained with worry.

"They're coming," he said.

CHAPTER FOUR

I DIDN'T NEED TO ASK WHO. I KNEW THE COUNCIL would be looking for me as long as I was alive, but that fact had never scared us off before, not with the safe haven to protect us.

"They can't get in. They won't be able to find us," I said. "Right?"

"Christoph is with them," Mac added as he appeared in the open doorway with Kara. "My ability means nothing to him, kid. He can turn it off like a light switch."

"How close are they?" William asked, clasping his hand around mine.

"Close enough," his dad answered. "We need to leave."

We left everything but the weapons. Clothes, food, toothpaste. There wasn't time for things that weren't essential to escape. The five of us went on foot in a direction that was meaningless to me. I had never seen what was outside the edges of the safe haven, not since I'd been here.

When Mac stopped abruptly after our fifteen-minute trek into the woods, we all froze at once, bodies poised and ready to attack, eyes searching for threats.

"We're here," Mac announced. "What should we expect, Marcus?"

I had never heard Dr. Nickel called by his first name, and it made me realize he wasn't as untouchable as I had imagined. Just because he was here, didn't mean we were safe.

"I don't know," he answered. "Maybe an army, maybe nothing. Depends on where they are."

"Everyone best get down on the ground just in case," Mac decided with a nod. "Weapons ready."

As I lay belly down in the dirt, I noticed Dr. Nickel pull a gun from his belt, and my stomach gave a heave.

"When I remove the haven walls, there will be a van. Everyone get in back. If anything goes wrong..." Mac paused, uncomfortable at the thought. "It's been nice knowin' ya."

After Mac's last words, our surroundings began to change. Everything outside the protective walls of the haven came into view like a heavy fog was lifted by the wind. As the haze cleared, I could make out a few small-town houses and a single dirt road that ran along the edge of the forest. There were no streetlights or any sign of a highway nearby, but the van was there.

"Should be clear," Kara announced after searching the area for subconscious thoughts. "I can't hear anyone but us."

"Move," Mac commanded, and we all scrambled to our feet.

Within seconds somebody was there, but only briefly, disappearing so fast I couldn't get a good look. For a moment, I thought I was seeing things, but I wasn't the only one stopped dead in my tracks.

I looked at William, confused. "What was—"

"Go," Kara yelled, her voice shattering the silence. "Run!"

We were too late. A circle of fire entrapped us. The flames leapt high above our heads encapsulating us in heat. Beyond its borders three figures came closer, but I couldn't keep my eyes open long enough to see who. Dr. Nickel, capable of mimicking abilities, fought fire with fire. But even as he pushed the flames away from us, the heat stung my face and the smoke burnt my lungs. I reached for my dart gun, ready to fight my way out of the raging flames. As I lifted it to my mouth, an unnatural feeling of heavy sadness weighed me down, and I lowered the weapon. I tried to ignore the oncoming waves of grief, but they had me.

"Don't let it get to you," William said, reaching for my face. "The sadness. It's just an ability. It's not real." But in my mind we'd already lost. I'd already lost William. Anna. Chloe. Everyone.

I buried my face into William's chest, but he failed to hold me the way he should. I could see in his eyes that he was giving up, too, sinking deeper into the hopelessness with me as the fire hissed and cracked around us. I wanted it to take me, to end the crippling ache of sorrow that had pulled me to my knees.

We were already dead. Why fight it?

My eyes lifted at the sight of someone new amongst the flickering flames. He wrapped Kara's limp arm around his neck and shuffled toward us. I didn't care who he was, why he was here to die with us. I was hypnotized by the flames and didn't bother to watch him, but when I felt a hand on my shoulder the world disappeared.

I was blinded by white, everything around me erased. Whatever had a hold of me knocked the air from my chest, and the pressure of the white space pushed in from all directions. Maybe this was finally it. Maybe this was death.

———

I WASN'T THE ONLY ONE WHO WOKE CONFUSED. William gasped, and my eyes opened to darkness.

"William?"

"Are you all right?" His warm fingers grazed my arms and shoulders, searching me for injuries. "What happened?"

"You got me," Mac answered, sitting up. His heavy boots clanked against a metal floor.

There was hardly any light, so I had trouble making out our surroundings. Once my eyes adjusted, leaving behind the blinding white, I realized we must be in the back of the van. In the blackness of the cab, with no windows and a cave-like feel, I assumed we were prisoners.

"Where do you think they'll take us?" I asked.

"There's nobody out there," I heard Kara say, though I could barely see her sitting in the corner.

"Dad?" William asked, realizing his father hadn't spoken.

"He's not here," Kara answered. "He chose to stay back and fight."

I heard William take a deep breath next to me.

"He'll be all right. He knows what he's doing," I comforted.

He stayed silent at first. "If it wasn't my dad, how'd we get here? What was that, the white?"

"It was one of Christoph's messengers. Apparently he helped us escape. I guess I'm not the only one rebelling against The Council," Kara answered. She opened the rear hatch, letting sunlight spill into the cab.

"All right, well, we need to keep moving," Mac said, sliding out the door and closing it behind him.

"Did you guys feel it too? The sadness?" I asked, remembering the ache in my chest. It still lingered.

Neither one of them answered, so I took that as a yes. I heard the engine start as the three of us sat in silence, and when the van started forward my body bounced and shook with each bump on the uneven road.

"I'm sorry, okay?" Kara said aloud. "There. Does that make you happy?"

William sighed. "Come on, Kara."

"What are you sorry for?" I asked.

"William thinks they followed me to the haven. That it was my fault they found us."

"Well, they showed up right after you," he added.

He was probably right. It was an unlikely coincidence. I closed my eyes, immediately regretting the thought. I wished she couldn't hear what I was thinking.

"Don't worry. I'm used to it," she said under her breath.

If it was her fault they found us, I knew it wasn't intentional. I'd been inside her head, felt her guilt at the loss of Anna and Chloe. She was with us now. I was sure of it.

"Even if they did follow you, Kara, they were supposed to. Everything happens for a reason. I've learned that by now."

I couldn't see her through the dark, but I could feel her looking at me. *I really am sorry*, she said with genuine regret. *I never should have come.*

I'm glad you did, I answered, surprised by the thought.

Whenever I expected the van to roll to a stop, it kept on. There wasn't much else to do but sleep. I rested my head on William's shoulder and tried to forget the flames as we huddled together in the deepest corner of the cab. Kara kept her distance, staying close to the back hatch. In time, we all drifted off, glad to be alive.

When I woke up, William was still asleep next to me, but we were alone. The back door of the van was left open letting the early morning light in. We'd driven through the night.

I nudged William, eager to get out. "Hey, we're here."

He sat up, his grown out hair sticking up in places, and I laughed as he squinted away from the light.

"What?" he asked.

"Rough night?"

He smiled. "Get me out of this van."

We shuffled out of the back, and my heart stopped when I realized where we were. William walked on unaffected, but I couldn't move.

"What's wrong?" he asked, turning back to me.

I couldn't believe it. Of all the places, how could they choose this one? I didn't like the feelings it stirred up in me, and I didn't want everyone rifling around here either. This place was a part of me that I didn't want to share.

"Why here?"

"Why not here?" William answered without understanding.

A buried ache I'd learned to keep hidden over the years suddenly throbbed in my chest. "This is my parents' house."

———

I LET WILLIAM GO IN ON HIS OWN. I WASN'T READY to face the inside of the house just yet. Instead I kicked past the sagebrush down to the creek where I used to play as a kid, giving myself a moment to think. There was so much to process. Rescuing Anna and Chloe was always at the forefront of my mind, but now there was the news about Iosif, Christoph's new plans, the attack, and knowing that The Council was actively hunting us down. They were close. Too close. Not to mention after all of that, being here forced me to relive moments with my parents before their death, each memory adding to the burden that already weighed so much.

They let me be for a while, but William was sent to drag me home before I was ready. Moments of peace were a luxury in war, one I'd have to live without.

"Are you okay?" he asked as he approached.

"No," I answered truthfully, chucking a handful of pebbles into the water.

He took my arms without asking and wrapped them around his waist. "Me either."

"Throwing rocks helps." I laughed, trying to lighten the mood. At least we had each other. I pressed my cheek into his chest, letting the soft sound of his heart settle my own. "They got to us so easily."

"I know." He ran his fingers through my hair. "But my dad's here. He says they've lost us. We should be safe."

"That's good," I said, feeling relieved for William. "Did he say how he knew they were coming?"

"He had Descendants in place, watching the area."

"Maybe one of them was followed. It might not have been Kara."

He pulled away just enough to look me in the eyes.

"You're sure she's on our side?"

I nodded. "Did you ask your dad about everyone? How are your mom and sister?"

"He said they're all being watched. There have been some disappearances, but nobody you know."

Being watched. I worried for them. If there were already disappearances, if The Council was tightening their grip, his family would be in more danger than anyone else. Why weren't they being hidden?

"Can I ask you something?" I pulled my arms from around his waist and folded them across my chest. I felt guilty for even thinking it. "Why was your dad never punished after he started the last war? He never went into hiding, never had to run. How is it he was even allowed to teach at the Institute? And now...he shows up, and suddenly we're attacked—"

"Wait," William interrupted. His eyebrows pulled together. "You're right. My dad's probably here to kill us."

I rolled my eyes. He wasn't taking me seriously. "Okay, so what? I'm just crazy."

"No," he laughed. "Come on. I'm just teasing you. You're being smart. It's good to be cautious, but I know my dad's one of the good guys."

"Then explain why he wasn't killed for starting a war, and why his family isn't being protected or hidden when The Council is out hunting us."

He reached forward and took both of my hands. "My family is different," he answered, folding and unfolding his fingers in the grooves of mine. "My dad's part of The Council and my…" He let his words trail off. "My *sister* is his heir." Something about that fact made him sad, but he continued. "He's protected in a way that most aren't. If a Council member is killed, the rest of them lose their powers and the next generation inherits them."

He let go of my hands and walked to the edge of the creek without looking back. His palm settled on the back of his neck the way it always did when something was bothering him.

"What's wrong?" I asked.

"My sister…she shouldn't be the one to carry that burden." He was quiet for a moment, watching the water, but when I put a hand to his arm he looked up, and I could tell he didn't want to talk about it. "Christoph didn't want to lose his power," he continued, "so they ended it with a truce. I think he's always been afraid my dad would take his own life just to spite him, so he's left him alone. My dad would never kill himself, though. He wouldn't want to leave Edith with Council responsibilities so young, but Christoph doesn't know that. Besides, my dad has a lot of Descendants on his side. Descendants who listen to him. If he disappeared or was killed, it wouldn't go over well. And I'm sure my mother and sister are protected. My dad wouldn't leave them alone if they weren't safe."

"So, your sister doesn't have your dad's ability yet?"

"Well, she does, it's in her bloodline, but it hasn't manifested. She won't be able to mimic powers until he or one of the other Council members dies."

I picked a flat rock off the ground and skipped it across the pooling part of the creek.

"Do you think Christoph has children?"

"I'm sure they all do," he answered, finding his own rock. "It's sort of an unspoken law. If there are no heirs, then there is no Council. Nobody's seen them, though." He smiled as the water splashed four times. "Beat ya."

"I'm sorry," I said, looking back at him. "I didn't mean to accuse..."

"It's okay. I forget sometimes that you don't know everything most Descendants know." He put his arm around me and kissed my cheek. "It's not your fault you were forced to live as a hermit."

I laughed, grateful for his light-heartedness and shoved him with my shoulder. "Well, who's the hermit now?"

"Yeah, I guess it's contagious." I could feel him smile without seeing it as he leaned his head into mine. "They want to go over the plan," he said, trying to coax me into going home. He knew it would work. Even with everything going on around us, there was one thing that kept me stable, focused. I was determined to get Anna and Chloe back.

Dr. Nickel, Mac, and Kara all looked up as William and I entered through the back door. I avoided Dr. Nickel's eyes, hoping he wasn't mimicking Kara's ability to look inside my mind. The three of them were seated at my family's kitchen table, and it was obvious they had been waiting.

I looked around, catching sight of the old iron stove that relied on a wood burning fire to heat its surface, the cutting board counter top that had large bin-sized drawers once filled to the brim with fluffy white flour and heaps of sugar. On my left, the hand carved sofa that my dad crafted in his shop still sat against the wall, the cushions rotted and disintegrating. Cobwebs clung to corners and layers of dirt and dust caked the old wood floor. My chest went hollow at the sight of it.

"Is someone going to tell me why we are here?" I asked, gripping the back of an empty table chair.

I expected Mac to answer, since my question was directed at him, but Kara spoke up instead.

"I told him to come here," she admitted. "I know you don't like it, but your parents knew Chilcoot was a good place to hide. The Council was never able to find you when you lived here."

As hard as it was to be in my old house, she did have a point. Maybe we would be safe here. I *felt* safe.

"I guess you're right," I accepted, pulling the chair out to sit with them. I pushed the ache away again, trying not to let the sight of my father's hand carved furniture affect me. "Did you find anything else of use while you were digging around in my memories?"

Kara and I smiled at each other. Me forgiving, her apologetic.

"So, what's the plan?" she asked.

"Don't look at me," I said. "Mac's in charge."

They all stared at each other like they knew something I didn't.

"I hate to break it to you, kiddo, but this is your call."

"*My* call?" I asked. Since when did I know anything about how to rescue people, especially from The Council? Sure, this whole mission was to help *my* friends, but Mac had been orchestrating this from the beginning. Now suddenly *I* was in charge?

"I don't remember my name being in no prophecy," Mac added.

My eyes shifted from face to face, getting a sense that they were all in agreement. "But I don't know anything about The Council," I said, pushing my chair away and rising to my feet. "I don't even know where they live." My voice was too high. Panicked. Frustrated.

"They live in Beverly Hills," Dr. Nickel answered.

His response surprised me. Beverly Hills? The name alone was intimidating, and it didn't help that they were all looking at me, expecting me to come up with the whole thing. I wasn't qualified. I had no idea where to start.

"I need a minute," I said, heading for my parents' bedroom.

I shut the door behind me, and wiped my clammy hands on my jeans. My parents' room was exactly how I'd left it, only now it was a ghost's room. All the color deadened by dust and decay. I went to the wooden chair in front of my mother's vanity and stared at the gray image of myself in the dust-covered mirror. We had been so focused on training I hadn't even thought about a plan, simply because it never occurred to me that I'd have to come up with one. But this was *my* problem, not anybody else's. In fact, none of them were required to take any part in Anna and Chloe's rescue. This was my responsibility, and I needed to get it together. I combed my fingers through my hair, brushing it out of my face, and took a deep breath.

"Okay," I said, coming out of my parents' room with newfound confidence. I'd avoided their room for so many years, and now I wondered why. My parents had been gone for decades, but maybe it was them who gave me the strength. "I don't think we should use numbers or force."

Mac laughed. "Good, because we don't have numbers."

"Stealth is the way to go. I want to get in and out of the house quickly and quietly if possible."

"So, the house in Beverly Hills, are we sure that is our target?" Mac asked.

I had only assumed. It seemed the most logical. If Anna and Chloe really were bait, why not lead me right to them? We only had one shot, one night that the oracle had said would work. My only reassurance was that if we did go on that night, we would succeed in rescuing them, which meant wherever we ended up would have to be the right place.

"It has to be," I decided, moving to sit back in my seat across from William. "It was the first thing I thought of, and the oracle said, 'they'll be where you'll expect them to be.' I remember that."

"They've kept others there in the past. It's as good a theory as any," Kara added.

"If that's the case, the place will be heavily guarded. I think I should go in first, ahead of you," William said decidedly.

"No," I reacted on impulse. I didn't like the idea of him being the front line. What if he got hurt or worse? "I don't think that's a good idea."

We stared at each other.

"Elyse, that's what Mac has been training me for, to get in unseen so I can clear the way for you. You know it should be me."

I didn't want to admit it, but he was right. He could use his ability to persuade those he encountered in our favor. Everything in me was fighting it, but I knew he was the key to slipping past security.

"Mac has to go with you," I added.

William glanced briefly at his uncle. "Yeah. I'm sure I'll have no problem sneaking a six foot three man-beast past everyone."

"Hey. Who taught you all the tricks?" Mac defended himself.

I ignored them, determined to keep focused. "Dr. Nickel, if it's okay, I think I'd like you to stay behind. I'm sure everything will go smoothly, but if it doesn't, I'll need someone to take my place." Mac had taught me to be prepared for every scenario, even if I was sure of the outcome.

"I'm sure that isn't—"

"Dad," William interrupted, his eyes drifting toward me. "She calls the shots."

Dr. Nickel stayed quiet.

"I want to keep this small," I continued. "Besides, we need you home, keeping an eye on everyone."

"All right," he nodded.

"Kara, you and I will follow behind William and Mac," I continued. "How well do you know the place?"

"Better than most," she answered. "I'll follow their thoughts once we get in close. I'm sure I can get us to where we need to be. I've seen most of the hidden passageways in the minds of others who work there. I know more than Christoph realizes."

"If I'm not going to be involved, the less I know the better," Dr. Nickel interrupted as he pushed his chair back and stood to leave. He looked at William for a long moment. "Be safe, son." Then he addressed the rest of us. "Good luck."

CHAPTER FIVE

—

THE NEXT MORNING I WOKE BEFORE EVERYONE ELSE. I hadn't slept well in my parents' room. The house made me tense, but thankfully the creek settled my nerves. I sat on the cold dirt as the sky grew brighter. The water at my feet trickled past stone making music with the mockingbirds as they sang proudly for the dawn. Four weeks until the end of February. I breathed in the cold sweet smell of nature and closed my eyes. It seemed like an eternity and nothing at the same time. At least here I could escape, pretend like war wasn't somewhere in my future.

"But it is," Kara said, sitting down beside me.

"I know," I answered, staring into the creek. "Can't I just pretend like it's not?"

"No." She looked at me, and I looked back. "You run, Elyse. You always want to run. How do you expect to beat Christoph or win a war when you're always trying to look the other way?"

"I don't expect to beat him," I answered honestly.

She ignored me and kept on. "You have to be ready for anything, anytime. Your mind should always be thinking of your next move, not acting like there isn't one."

"My mind doesn't work like that. I'm not...I don't know what to do first, let alone what I'm supposed to do next."

"First, you should know your enemy," she said, throwing a pebble into the rippling water at our feet, "what makes him tick. Christoph is very closed off. Not many people know much about him. I can't get inside his head, but I've been inside others, Council aides who've seen things." She offered her hand to me. "You could start there."

I stared down at her palm. It wouldn't hurt to know more about the man I was supposed to destroy. I nodded my head and turned to face her as she pressed her fingers to my temple. This might be the most valuable weapon she had against him—a secret.

The memory was distant, and I could tell as I looked through a young girl's eyes that it didn't belong to her. The details were washed and muted, the sensations dull and forgotten with age, but I watched secretly from another room as a young Christoph spoke to his father.

"You'll come to understand in time, Christoph." The man's stare was intimidating. He looked almost ghostly with his thick white sideburns and cheeks that sunk into shadows on his long face. "I used to be naïve as you are, but

I've seen things. They're not a race worth saving."

The boy's blond hair was combed to the side and fell forward slightly as he bowed his head. "Yes, sir. I only thought..."

"They're all the same, son." His voice was cold and unyielding as he busied himself with papers behind an oak desk. "I had to watch my mother burn at the stake for being taken as a witch. They'll never accept us. Look at them now. My mother was killed in 1692. It's nearly 170 years later, and they're still persecuting others because they're different. Their own kind, no less. Enslaving them because of the color of their skin."

"Nettie is one of us," the boy whispered. He stood some distance away, seemingly afraid to come closer.

"You know I've tried to help her. The railroad has aided many of our kind. She knows I'm a shepherd. I can't make her leave if she is not willing."

"But it's your job to find them, Father." His voice spiked as he stepped forward, the bravery shining through his still innocent blue eyes. His face was sad but hopeful, with a sweet naivety that I knew he'd lose with age. "Why can't you make her go?"

"It's her choice. She chooses to stay. For you."

The memory shifted in time, but not by much. I peered through different eyes, an older man as he watched Christoph run from afar.

"Nettie!" he screamed. His feet beat the dirt as he ran into town. His frantic face glistened with tears. The man hurt for him. I hurt for him.

In the town square, people were gathered around making a commotion over something. Men and women towered over him as he forced himself through the mob of angry protests and jeering voices. The man only stood and watched in horror. He was a Descendant. It could easily have been him in place of this poor girl.

"She's a monster!"

"Kill her!"

The gunshots fired before Christoph had made it through the crowd, and as he finally reached the front, he saw her chained and wounded.

"I love you, Nettie," he spoke through the riotous mob. His words were lost to yells and cheers, but the man heard.

"I love you too," she mouthed as her eyes closed.

Images blurred and yet again the boy sat facing his father, the same desk sitting between them. For a while they said nothing. Christoph's hair was tousled, his cheeks red from tears, but his eyes had changed. They were heavier, full of shame and anger as he stared across the room.

"She exposed her ability, and they shot her." He yelled the words, like he'd found power in his rage.

"I'm sorry, son," his father said without feeling.

"What are you planning?" Christoph demanded, wiping his wet cheeks with his coat sleeve. His voice was hoarse as more angry tears came. "I want to help you. I want to kill them. All of them."

Maybe it was me, but I thought I saw a glimmer of a smile in his father's face.

"Keep your wits about you, Christoph. Don't involve our kind. Soon there will be a civil war." He leaned back in his high back chair. "Let them kill themselves."

"Wow," I said, pulling out of the memories. I didn't want to admit it, but I sympathized with the boy I'd seen running with tears in his eyes. Was that wrong, when he was such a villain now? To see his perspective, to understand how his hate had been born? When love is plucked from your heart, little is left to keep you sane. But understanding his hate didn't change who he was to me—the enemy.

"It's okay that you understand him that way. It might help you," Kara continued. "That's all I can give you in terms of memories, mental preparation." She stood and paced with her hands in her pockets. "You seem to be pretty good with your dart gun, but has Mac taught you hand-to-hand?"

"Yeah. We've gone over the basics. Technique and things."

She smiled. "All right. Let's see it."

I rose to my feet, a little shy in front of Kara, and took a boxing stance. I threw a few punches at the air, the way Mac had instructed. Nimble feet, guard the face, turn with the jab.

"That's not what I meant," she laughed. "Nice form though. I meant, try and hit me."

"Fight you?" I asked. "Yeah right. You'd kill me."

She nodded. "I know, but you're not going to get any better swinging at nothing."

I stood there staring at her until I realized she was serious.

"Fine," I said. "Just…be easy on me."

"Yeah, sure," she said with a grin.

I dug my fingernails into my palms making tight fists and bounced on my toes. Kara watched me, more with amusement than with concern. I swung, but she dodged the hit, and I pulled back. She shook her head slightly, waiting for the next one. I sighed and swung again. This time she grabbed my wrist, twisting my arm around my back and locking my neck in a chokehold with the other.

"If you can avoid throwing a punch, you should. Unless you feel confident you'll make the right point of contact."

"Okay," I breathed as she released me.

"It makes you vulnerable," she said. "If you want to hit someone, and you're not sure how they fight…" She grabbed my hand and bent my wrist back, patting the lower part of my palm. "Use the heel of your hand, make a fist and use it like a hammer, or use your elbow. Try not to use your knuckles. You break those, it's over. Most people drop their head instinctively when they see a punch. You won't be able to do much more damage if you break your knuckles on someone's skull."

I nodded, taking her words seriously.

"Again."

I tried using my fist like a hammer, but she still caught it, swinging my arm around my back and locking me in the chokehold.

"To get out of this, turn your body and throw your leg behind me. This will give you leverage and throw me off balance."

I smiled when I was free. "It worked."

"When you throw the first blow, you have to lean into me. Don't be a timid fighter. You'll lose. You have to move your body forward, throw me off balance as you're swinging, so I can't grab you or hit back."

"Show me," I said, taking up a defensive stance.

"You want me to hit you?"

"Yes," I said, more determined.

With not much of a warning, she stepped forward, shoving both heels of her hands under my chin and knocking me off my feet. She moved so quickly I didn't have time to react.

"Hey," William's voice called from a distance. "What the hell's going on?"

"It's okay," I said, dusting the dirt off of my pants and rubbing my jaw. "We're training."

He looked at Kara and then back at me. "What's she teaching you? How to get knocked out?"

"I'm fine, really," I said, laughing it off.

He raised his eyebrows at me. "Maybe you should teach her how to block a punch."

"Why don't you teach her?" Kara said, challenging him to do better.

I tried to hold back a smile.

"What?" William asked me. "You think I don't know how to hold my own in a fight?"

I shrugged, unsure. "Well, you never showed me anything before."

"What can I say? Mac sort of steals the show, but I am ninety-four," he said with confidence. "I've learned enough."

Suddenly I was curious. The idea of William fighting to defend me was...sexy. "How?"

"I learned from my Dad. Don't let him fool you with his suave I'm-in-a-suit look. He can mimic abilities, so he learned from the best."

"Are you two going to fight or what?" Kara interrupted. "I really want to see this."

"Okay," he said. His warm fingers pressed against my upper arms as he pulled me closer. "When your opponent is close enough to throw a punch, nine out of ten times, they will. You just have to know to expect it. It's best to be in the offensive, throw the first punch, move toward your opponent—"

"Yeah, I told her all that," Kara added.

"But if you find yourself on the defensive," he continued without acknowledging her, "you try to push the punch to one side with your hand, like this." His touch was warm as he reached for my arm, extending it toward him slowly, moving his body to the left, my arm to the right. "After you've dodged the hit, you use the closest elbow to come in and drive it to their chest." He stepped forward, pressing his elbow against my sternum softly, then smiled at me. It was hard not to enjoy being close. In a fight, I imagined he would use his ability next. With his eyes inches from mine, he could make me do whatever he wanted. But there was no need to use his power on me. I would already die for him.

"Okay, forget this," Kara said, pushing William away from me. "She's never going to learn with you being all sexy-eyes at her."

"Hey, I was born this way. It's not my fault I've got sexy eyes."

"Throw a real punch at me," Kara continued, still focused on training.

William took a seat on the water's edge to watch.

When I came at her with a heavy lunging swing, she followed William's instructions pushing my fist aside with grace and stopping just before her elbow slammed into my chest. "Got it?" she asked.

I nodded. "Again."

———

I TRAINED WITH KARA EVERY MORNING FOR FOUR weeks. William watched, joining in only when he disagreed or had something more to add, but he remained serious. Mac took over in the afternoons, running drills, teaching technique, until it was finally time to make our move. Four weeks of training, the oracle's guarantee, and I still wasn't confident.

"We should probably leave soon," I said after we'd finished dinner. I began stacking my parents' old china plates and handed them to William.

"How d'ya feel about us leaving tomorrow?" Mac asked from the table.

"We can't," I answered simply. "We won't make it in time. Beverly Hills is a long drive—"

"Apparently we won't be driving," Kara said, turning to Mac with surprise.

He gave her an irritated look. "Mind stayin' out of my thoughts?"

"Well?" William asked, running water over the dishes.

"A young man's offered to help us. Name's Alex."

"The messenger," Kara added. "From the fire."

I stopped clearing the table and stood behind an empty chair. "Can we trust him?" I asked.

"Given that he helped us once, I think we're good," Mac answered. "Besides, Kara here can make sure he's not bluffing, right?"

"Count me in," she answered.

"He offered to help us get past the first gate with the guard tomorrow night, but after that we're on our own," Mac continued. "He doesn't want any part in the rescue."

"So why include him, Mac?" William argued, turning off the water.

I thought about the white pressure that saved us from

the fire. How we'd been carried away from the fight in a matter of seconds, ending up in the van far away from any threat. "He's a getaway plan," I answered, seeing the uncertainty in Mac's face. "He doesn't think we're going to make it out of there on our own."

"We might not," Kara added.

CHAPTER SIX

—

THERE WAS NO WAY I COULD HAVE FULLY PREPARED for this night. Too much was at risk for me to feel sure all would go as planned. If the slightest thing went wrong, someone could be killed.

I heaved a deep stress-filled sigh as I thought about it. My hands kept busy, sorting through darts at the kitchen table, picking out my favorite and most accurate pieces. I was sure I wasn't fooling anyone though. Kara, Mac, and William all knew I was nervous, but they also knew nothing would get in my way.

"Here," Kara said, tossing me a black piece of fabric. The look of amusement on her face made me curious.

"What is it?" I asked, examining it more carefully.

"It's your outfit." She smiled wide as I unfolded it.

"This is a dress," I said in disbelief.

She laughed. "I know. I can't wait to see this."

"I'm not wearing it."

"Yes, you are," Mac yelled from my old bedroom where he and William were getting ready.

Somehow when Mac said all black, I'd imagined sweat pants and ski masks. Not this.

"Isn't there something else?"

"Nope," Mac answered, emerging in a stunning tuxedo, fully shaved. "It's Beverly Hills, kid. You've gotta look the part. Anyone asks, we're attending a cocktail party, and we're lost."

I'd never seen Mac dressed so nice. It took me by surprise. If he was willing to go to such lengths, I guess it wasn't so unreasonable for me to do the same.

"Well, what are *you* wearing?" I asked Kara, feeling a bit singled out.

She rolled her eyes. "Same thing, different version."

The two of us locked ourselves in the bathroom and shimmied into the dresses. Mine was loose around the legs, stopping at the knee and tightening up around the hips and waist. I pulled up on the shoulder straps trying to heighten the v-neck, which was a little low for my taste. Over the years, fashion had gotten so revealing. I glanced at Kara who was staring at herself in the mirror.

"I don't know about this," she said, pulling the fabric down over her legs.

At least mine was long enough to cover the weapon I now had to keep strapped to my bare thigh. Hers was skintight and didn't leave much for the imagination.

I held back a smile. "Yeah, I'm thinking I got the

better deal."

We slid our feet into black flat dress shoes and stared at the makeup on the counter.

"Do we really need to wear makeup?" I asked. "This is a rescue mission, not a dance party."

She shrugged. "We have to look the part."

I used the toilet as a seat while Kara painted my eyelids with color. The brush tickled like feathers, and made my face relax. I wished I could enjoy getting ready with a friend, but it reminded me of playing dress up with Chloe when she was younger. Behind my closed eyes I saw her sweet baby face with blue eyelids and cheeks too pink. I saw Anna smiling as her daughter danced around in that worn out princess costume. It made my heart ache.

When we were done we pulled our hair up and faced the mirror.

I raised my eyebrows at Kara. "We're pretty," I said with surprise. I didn't recognize either of us.

"Are you ready?" I yelled, once we emerged from the bathroom.

"How do I look?" William asked. He slid across the wood floor in his socks, flashing his tuxedo, and nearly stumbled at the sight of us. "Wow." The subconscious reaction was mumbled under his breath, not meant for others to hear. "You're so...you look amazing."

I laughed to hide my embarrassment. "You too."

"All right, all right, can we go now?" Mac grumbled, pulling at the collar of his shirt.

Outside the boundaries of Mac's safe haven there was a limo, its black color camouflaged against the night. Here in Chilcoot, it was too cold for dresses, and I shivered as we walked across the dirt road toward the car. A young guy with milky white skin and pitch-black hair waited beside it. His eyes were a cool minty blue and they stared into me with intensity as I approached.

"Name's Alaximandrios," he said, thrusting his hand out in front of me. I took it and looked hard back at him. Something about his tone rubbed me the wrong way. "Do me a favor though, and only use it when you need to. Any time it's uttered, I hear it as a call for my services. People call me Alex."

"Nice to meet you," William said offering his hand. Alex still had mine tightly in his grasp, and I could tell it was bothering him.

Alex shook it and turned toward the limo without a word. "Don't go blabbing my call name to anyone either," he said over his shoulder as we followed him.

As soon as we entered the limo, I began to sweat. All my muscles went tense, and no matter how hard I tried to relax, my shoulders stayed tight. William smiled at me, and our eyes locked. That was when the ache started in my chest. By coming with me, he was giving me everything he had. They all were, risking their lives for me, for Anna and Chloe. The gripping fear that this might be the last time I saw William made it hard to breathe, but there was nothing I could say to make him change his mind. My love was his burden, and guilt took a swing, hitting me in the gut. There was only one way to keep everyone safe, if it got to that point. I had one last saving grace—a trade. Me for them.

The familiar white erased my surroundings before I had time to ready myself. I squirmed in the emptiness, unable to breathe, see, hear. Then within seconds it was over, and we were all staring at each other. I had expected to pass out, like before, but I'd been conscious the whole time.

"Is that unpleasant for anyone else, or just me?" William asked as we all tried to pull ourselves back to reality.

"No. Definitely not pleasant," I agreed.

It was hard to make out what was beyond the tinted windows as we drove through the neighborhood streets of Beverly Hills. The houses hid behind gated driveways, subtle light twinkling through tall hedges. The night made for the perfect camouflage. When the car came to a stop, Mac's rough voice cut through the silence. "Here goes nothin'."

Kara and Mac shuffled out the door leaving William and I inside.

"Would you stay back if I wanted you to?" I asked quietly.

He looked at me like he'd been expecting the question.

"Would *you*?" My eyes moved away from his. He knew I wouldn't.

"It's different for me. I have to go."

He shrugged. "So do I."

As far as I was concerned, he didn't *have* to do anything, but I knew he would never let me go in alone. In his mind, he had to protect me, and nothing would keep him from that.

He scooted toward the open door, and held his hand out for me. "Come on. It'll be okay."

I took it and climbed out behind him. As soon as I was out, Alex drove away, leaving us alone in the street. There was no going back.

"This way," Kara said, taking the lead.

I listened to William's footsteps behind me as we walked, but my eyes were alert, looking for movement. If they were expecting us, there was no telling when they'd make their move.

Kara stopped a block away from a tall wrought iron gate.

"Riley should be guarding the entrance. You'll have to approach from the far right to avoid the camera. Once you're there, William, have her freeze frames to the front gate and left side yard surveillance."

"Got it," he answered.

I bit my lips as I watched him.

"Don't go," I whispered into his ear as he came in to kiss my cheek, but he ignored me, and tipped my chin up with his finger.

I watched him walk away, feeling completely helpless.

As they turned the corner, he looked back with one last comforting smile and was gone. Immediately my chest caved in, and my mouth went so dry I couldn't swallow. I watched Kara's concentrated eyes as she followed William's thoughts, tracking their progress.

"What's going on?" I asked after waiting several minutes. "Are you telling them where to go?"

"Ssh!" she snapped.

I sighed and picked at my nail beds, staring at the gate, like if it moved I'd get my answers.

"They're in," she said, staying focused.

"Okay, should we go?"

"Just wait." Her voice spiked with irritation.

The girl next to me wasn't the Kara I'd been growing close to over the weeks. She was the harder version, the trained operative who'd worked for The Council on jobs for years.

I couldn't help but stare at her face, waiting for the muscles in her forehead to tell me if things were good or bad, but I didn't speak again.

Her glossy lips curled into a smile. "The guard is opening the gate for us. Let's go."

The hard soles of our flats clicked and scuffed over the surface of the sidewalk as we tried to be quick but discrete. Kara led the way, scanning the area for any threatening presence. The large black wrought iron gate swung open electronically, and a pretty face met us with a love-struck smile. She straightened her beige dress suit and ran her fingers through her auburn hair, trying to make herself look presentable.

"Hi, Riley," Kara said, apparently amused to see her under the influence of William's ability.

"Hello," she answered in a daze. "Please, come in."

Kara laughed quietly to herself.

What's so funny? I thought to her. I couldn't be anything but completely serious.

She can take a wall down with her fist. If it weren't for William, she probably would have ripped my heart right out of my chest. I don't imagine I'm welcome here anymore.

I looked around, feeling threatened by whatever ability lurked around the next corner. *Where are they?*

Close, but hidden. Where we should be.

I knew what came next, my role in this. William's ability would wear off as we moved on, and I needed to sedate those we encountered. I triggered the bracelet on my left wrist and loaded the dart with just enough toxin to put Riley under for a few hours.

Do it, Kara urged, sensing my hesitation. It was harder than I imagined it would be to shoot someone with this amount of blood. If I used too much, it could kill her. Every person's body was different, but no matter the outcome, I had no choice.

Riley pulled back her hair, exposing her neck to me, something William must have instructed her to do. I blew the dart at close range and heard her moan as it punctured the skin. Kara caught her as she fell limp, and we dragged her unconscious body, hiding it amongst the foliage of some blooming bushes.

The front yard was pristine, with clean squared-off hedges and trellises laced with climbing vines. The house was more of a manor or estate than a home. It was large enough to be a hotel. The entire façade was polished stone veneer supported by tall pillars that reached the floor of the second story.

Come on, Kara instructed as she ducked behind a porcelain fountain. Just as I took cover next to her, a flashlight beam cut through the darkness, searching like a roaming eye. Kara offered no silent words of advice to my thoughts. Neither of us dared to move. The heavy breath that could only belong to a Hunter took in air so fully, I thought he might be trying to sniff us out. The grass rustled under his shoes as he came closer, and I moved my hand silently to my weapon.

I don't think it will work, Elyse, Kara warned, *not on Hunters. They're built different, more durable.*

I guess we'll find out.

I slid the gun out of its holster, but before I had time to load a dart, a loud voice called out.

"Hey, Carl. You seen Riley?"

"No, she don't report to me," the Hunter answered from inches away.

"Yeah, but you're out here." The man paused. "You looking for something?"

"No, just a perimeter check." He seemed aggravated. "Why you on my case so much, huh?"

The Hunter's voice began to fade as he walked away, closing the gap between him and his antagonizer.

It wasn't a particularly warm night, but Kara's forehead still beaded with sweat that glistened in the moonlight. I wasn't the only one who was nervous.

Is it clear? I asked

Yes. William and Mac are waiting.

Kara and I kept to the shadows as we made our way alongside the house.

It's here, Kara said when we'd reached them. *Behind the vines.*

The hanging plants were nearly a foot thick and heavier than I thought, but Kara and I managed to squeeze our bodies through. Beneath the curtain of vines was a passageway, its swinging door propped open by Mac's foot.

William pulled me by the hand and scooped me up into his arms.

"What took you so long?"

There was a Hunter, Kara said inside my head as the vines closed the gap behind her. *Keep quiet.*

William nodded, and I realized he could hear her too.

The tunnels that ran secretly within the walls of the house were easy to navigate, with fake vents that peered into abandoned rooms, and dim light pooling from lanterns on the marble walls. I wasn't concerned about getting lost as we took stairs that led us deep underground. We had plotted and reviewed the route hundreds of times according to Kara's memory. The four of us knew exactly where we were going, the only problem was there was nowhere to hide. Each step was tense, and even though Kara would have fair warning, the suspense from turning the next corner was enough to make my stomach tighten.

It wasn't until Kara slowed her steps that my heart really began to thud. Her face told me what I needed to know— someone was coming.

Take a deep breath and hold it now, she advised sternly, *and get ready to shoot.*

Her warning must have been heard by all of us, because Mac reached down for the knife strapped to his ankle, and all of us sucked in as much air as we could. Gentle footsteps grew louder from up ahead, but something was wrong. The shadow of a man stretched long against the curved walls of the passageway, but he didn't come closer.

Too much time had passed. I needed air. A part of me dreaded whoever was around the corner, but I was so desperate to exhale that I willed him to come forward. I wanted this over with, to expel all my breath behind a dart and finish him, but he didn't show himself, and I couldn't wait.

The air came spilling out of me, and I was desperate to fill up my lungs again, but there was nothing to fill them with. I choked and sputtered, suffocating. I felt compelled to run, move out of the radius of this mystery man's ability, but William and Kara began to choke as well. Mac was the only one who maintained composure. I drowned in the absence of air, clambering to get to William, in what could very well be our last moments. I was hardly aware of Mac moving in the direction of the shadow, the near silent scuffle that happened somewhere up ahead, but suddenly there was air again. William, Kara, and I coughed and wheezed, inhaling faster than we should, greedy for more.

Mac sauntered around the corner waiting for us to recover, the knife in his hand dripping with blood.

"Who was that?" I asked, still recuperating.

"Victor," Kara answered. "He gets his power from Lelantos. The bloodline controls the air."

"He won't be controlling much of anything," Mac added. "Not anymore."

"Are you all right?" William asked, still holding on to me. I wasn't all right. How could I be? We'd almost died. Things had almost ended for all of us before we could even save Anna and Chloe. That wasn't the answer he was looking for, though. I could breathe. I would survive.

"I'm fine if you are."

"We've got to keep moving," Mac pressed, the reality of what he'd just done visible on his face. He had killed a man. Even for someone of his size and strength, I could see murder still weighed heavy on his conscience.

I didn't look down as I stepped past the body on the floor. William squeezed my hand, pulling me onward. It had to be done.

The four of us continued on in silence until we reached what seemed to be a dead end.

"There's supposed to be a door," Kara said, staring at the wall in front of us. "We just have to find a way to open it."

William ran his hands along the rough stone, looking for a loose brick or latch.

"I don't know," he said, frustrated. "I can't find any-thing."

My hands began to clam up, and I couldn't keep from looking behind me. With two members of Christoph's team dead or missing, it wouldn't be long before he realized we were here.

"Maybe there is no lock or trick," I said, desperate to move on. I pushed with everything I had against the wall, but it didn't budge. "Come. On. Open." I kicked the solid rock out of anger.

"Elyse, it moved," Kara said in amazement. "The rock moved."

I was on my knees in less than a second, prying the loose rock from the wall, but the brief moment of hope was crushed by what I saw behind it.

"It's a lock," I sighed, discouraged yet again.

"Well, let me see," Mac said pushing me aside. I knew what he was thinking, that maybe he could use brute force to break it, but this wasn't some flimsy padlock. It was a deadbolt that needed two keys to open it. We might as well be trying to crack a bank vault.

"Maybe we can pick it," William suggested. I looked over my shoulder, down the narrow passage, wondering how long it would be before they would come for Victor, for us.

Kara realized it at the same time I did, maybe because she had seen the thought come into formation—Victor.

"I'll be right back," I said, without asking for permission.

"Victor might have the keys," Kara answered William's confused look.

The body came into view within minutes of me sprinting, and even though the sight of him made me recoil inside, I moved forward without slowing. I tried not to look at him while I fumbled through his pockets, afraid if I did glance into his lifeless eyes, the image would haunt me forever.

I'd found nothing and was starting to lose hope when I heard something not too far off. I froze, straining my ears, and willing the blood pulsing loudly in my head to cease flowing. When I realized what it was, my hands began to shake. Whispers.

Think, I told myself. *He has to have it.* If it were me, where would I put the keys? I had to put myself in his shoes. Even through the fear, I smiled at the phrase. Shoes. It was my last and only option.

I pulled them off of his feet and thanked Victor silently as I removed the double-pronged key he had kept hidden under his heel. The low raspy voices grew louder, but I had what I wanted, so I took off at full speed away from them. I just wasn't fast enough.

"Hey!" a man yelled after me, and as I looked back I recognized the Hunter from earlier.

The air burned my throat as I pushed my body faster than it had ever gone. Something kicked in when I was running for my life. Instinct, adrenaline—whatever it was saved me.

"I have the key," I screamed while the three of them stared in shock as the Hunter chased me down.

"Don't let her get away!" the Hunter's antagonizer yelled at him.

"Kara," I called out, knowing she could see my next move. I chucked the thick gold key with every ounce of strength I had, and she caught it in the air.

As I bolted down the narrow hallway, the three of them worked to unlock the door. The wall swung open, heavy and slow, just in time for us to escape inside the dark room behind it. The door closed with a bang, separating all of us from the men at my heels.

"They know we're here," I panted, still coming to terms with what that meant. Would they find us soon? Would they kill us when they did? Would they let everyone else go if I gave in willingly?

"Elyse?" A meek voice sounded through the dim light, and my heart gave a leap.

"Anna," I answered back. "Where are you?"

"Here."

I reached through the empty room with my hands

trying to find her as my eyes adjusted.

The two of them were huddled in a corner against the wall, too frail and disheartened to move. Anna still had some strength about her. Maybe it was the remaining nourishment my blood had provided when she was healed, or maybe she simply needed to endure for her child.

I wanted to hold them, evaluate if they'd been hurt or severely mistreated, but with the men on the other side of the wall, I knew we needed to move.

"Can you walk?" I asked Anna. "Mac can carry Chloe. We need to go."

Anna's face didn't show an ounce of urgency. "We're locked in, Elyse."

"No," I uttered aloud, refusing to believe it. As I looked around, hoping to prove her wrong, my eyes fully adjusted to the dark and the room came into view. There was no furniture, no décor, no windows, nothing but hard walls and a bare floor. We were in a holding cell. The only light that kept the room from complete darkness came from a small glass peephole embedded in another door across the room, one that wasn't a secret part of the wall.

"Is there someone out there?" William asked. I hadn't been paying attention to the others, but they were just as busy trying to figure out an escape as I was.

"Usually a guard," Anna answered calmly, her voice sounding as though she'd already given up. She ran her fingers through Chloe's hair as she stayed unconscious, looking at her with a mother's love.

"He's out there," Kara confirmed, finding his thoughts with her mind.

"Do you think you could get him to open the door?" I asked William.

"He better. Put your training to use kid," Mac snarled, stepping over to Anna and Chloe. "We're going to get you girls out of here, okay?" He bent down and slipped his strong arms under Chloe's limp body and picked her up. She opened her eyes only slightly, too weak to care what happened to her. Mac and Anna looked at each other, sharing in the pain of the moment. "She'll be all right."

Anna managed a slight smile at the gesture, and accepted my hand as I pulled her onto her feet.

"He's coming," William said, concentrating his gaze through the small glass window.

"He's not going to let us out," Anna said with little faith.

William grinned wide and proud. "Yes he is."

The door handle turned and clicked, and a stout balding man looked at William with glazed eyes.

"He's just letting us go?" Anna asked in shock. "I don't understand. Why?"

"He's in love," Kara snickered.

"All right, have your fun once we get out of here," Mac scolded. "It's not over yet."

I stayed behind, making sure everyone was out before shooting a dart into the portly man's neck. He collapsed with a subtle bounce, and William locked him in the holding room.

I loaded my dart gun with a blood soaked hollow, just in case, and grabbed William's hand, giddy with satisfaction. "I love you."

He sauntered casually, acting cool, and flipped his hair back playfully. "I know."

The long hallway we'd found ourselves in ended at a flight of stairs that led up to the ground floor and out of what must have been a basement level. Kara confirmed that we were clear to move. The absence of people felt suspicious to me, but we didn't have much of a choice. The five of us, Mac still carrying a slightly more alert Chloe, crept up the velvety red staircase.

When Kara reached the top, she looked back at us with her eyes alight. *I know where we are. The front door is on the other side of this room.*

It seemed too easy, too quiet. The room we had to pass through was decorated in an elaborate Victorian style. The chandelier above cast dim gold light that reflected off of large framed mirrors and rich elegant furnishings that reminded me of a different time.

Just as we were about to make our move, Kara threw up a hand. *Wait.*

William stepped forward until he was in front of me.

There was nobody in sight, but Kara must have known a wandering mind was close. After a few minutes of heavy silence that had me tensed to draw my weapon, I saw him come into view—the Hunter from the passageway. His eyes hadn't found us, but they were focused. Looking. Waiting.

If Kara was right about the Hunters, it would take a lot of my blood to affect him. Maybe too much to deliver through a dart.

Through the haze of worry clouding my awareness, I didn't react right away when William started forward. I grabbed his wrist just in time. "What are you doing?" I mouthed silently, my face severe with disapproval.

He raised his eyebrows communicating his intentions without words. I tightened my fingers, refusing to let him go. What if it didn't work? What if the Hunters could resist more than just superficial powers?

Kara, tell him it might not work, I told her silently.

He knows, Elyse.

I shook my head wildly at him, but he only kissed my hand and released his own.

Every muscle in my body ached as I watched him approach the large, threatening man, but there was nothing I could do. When the Hunter finally laid eyes on William, he immediately drew his gun.

My insides lurched, and I felt my body propel forward. I had to do *something*, but Kara stopped me.

It's working, she told me.

Sure enough, the Hunter began to lower his weapon and stepped aside allowing William to open the door. There it was, our way out.

"Go," I whispered the command.

Kara led the way as everyone crossed the grandiose room in front of us, and I followed close behind, keeping watch from the rear, aware and protective.

Escape was so close I could taste it.

"Move fast," I said quietly as the group filed out into the night, leaving William and I to deal with the Hunter.

"I'll keep him influenced until you're out," William insisted.

"No, just walk out with me," I argued, as the rest of them made their way across the labyrinth of a front yard.

"I want you to have a head start, just in case I can't hold him for long."

I didn't like it, but time was persuasive. "Okay, but I'm waiting at the front gate."

Before he could protest, my lips were on his, stealing his ability to speak. I could have stayed in that moment forever, but he needed to concentrate, and I needed to go.

I tore down the steps, looking ahead for any sign of a threat that might get in my way, but the chilling voice that stopped me came from behind.

"Feel free to go." His sinister tone sounded slightly amused. "Though I'm sure William would miss you if you didn't stay."

I wheeled around, facing the man I'd only seen in Kara's memory, and looked him in the eyes. They were cold and calculating, a sick grin cutting into the side of his cheek. The Hunter, no longer influenced by William's ability, held him in a chokehold that threatened to break his neck. Though I hardly gave her notice, a woman with thick brown curls stood slightly behind Christoph, watching.

"Christoph!" Mac yelled from the gate as he started to charge forward.

"Mac, don't!" I shouted, holding up my hand for him to keep back. I needed him to stay with Anna and Chloe, to ensure they would be safe.

He obeyed, staying put, but his eyes raged with anger as he watched the situation play out.

"Take me instead," I offered.

"Please," Christoph scoffed. "I have him, I get you. Don't try and act as though you won't stay willingly."

He had me. It was true. Unless.

"Alaximandrios." I whispered the word like it would save me. Like it would save all of us. But he didn't show.

I squirmed uneasily in the silence.

"What's to stop me from killing you?" I spat with disgust as I imagined my thick dart stabbing him in the throat. "Let him go, or I'll do it." I never felt so sure of anything in my life. I wouldn't hesitate.

I knew he saw the truth in my words, but he only let out a slow, breathy laugh. "That's quite a threat, but you do realize abilities don't work on Council members, don't you?"

Descendants loyal to Christoph began to appear from both sides of the yard. First ten or so, then twenty. My heart began to race as the Hunter's thick elbow squeezed tighter around William's neck. I had no choice but to give in, and although William's eyes were telling me to run, I stepped forward with one last request.

"If I don't put up a fight, will you let the rest of them leave without being followed?"

William struggled in protest, but what else could I do?

Christoph's tight lips tugged at the edges, and he cocked his head to the side like a cat who had a mouse by its tail. He stood with his shoulders back, overly confident, clasping his pale hands together. "You have no chips to bargain with young lady, but simply because I have no use for them, yes. I will let them go."

I turned back to Mac who was still watching by the distant gate, looking for a promise that he would keep them safe. "We'll be fine," I yelled. "Just go."

Mac's hands balled into fists, and I watched as he nearly exploded into a fit of anger. He only had one option. As he walked away, his enraged bellow echoed through the streets.

CHAPTER SEVEN

I DIDN'T KNOW WHAT THEY WOULD DO WITH US, and I didn't want to think about it. Until Christoph decided, William and I were locked in what seemed to be a fairly elegant guestroom. Aside from the fact that it locked from the outside, it was rather comfortable, and didn't depart from the Victorian theme that continued throughout the house. In the silence that had started with my surrender, William sat speechless on a velvet stool near the door while I took a place on the elaborately decorated queen bed.

I wanted to console him, but I recognized the way he stared off at nothing in the distance. He was angry, and I could only assume it was at me. I had given myself up voluntarily in his eyes, I was sure. He wouldn't accept that I didn't have a choice, but I wasn't going to be without him ever again. I didn't care if he was upset.

At least Anna and Chloe were safe, and Mac and Kara

got out just fine. No matter what I told myself, it didn't change the fact that we both felt defeated, and the ominous future loomed over us with uncertainty.

"At least we have each other," I said, finally breaking the silence.

He sighed without looking up. "No, Elyse. That's exactly what he wants. Now he has us both and..."

He didn't need to finish. We both knew what was at stake. Christoph wanted our baby. The thought was terrifying, and I clutched the bedding beneath my damp palms. Although I felt comforted that William was with me, that comfort was only a distraction. Christoph had won, and our fate was in his hands.

"Dammit!" William stood and slammed his fist against the wall. I had never seen him so full of anger, and it held me in my place. He had his back to me, resting his forehead against the closed door that kept us in.

"I'm sorry," I let out, slightly defensive. "I couldn't just leave you with him."

He turned to look at me, full of regret. "It's *my* fault Elyse, not yours."

"This isn't your fault," I said, my brows wrinkling with confusion. How could he blame himself?

"If I would have just listened to you, walked away with you when I had the chance..."

He combed his fingers through his hair and closed his eyes.

"It wouldn't have mattered," I said, shaking my head.

The timing was too precise to be coincidence. "They knew we were there. The whole thing was a setup." I took a breath and forced myself to stop picking at my thumbs. "The woman with the curls, was that Adrianna?"

"Yes," he answered.

"See? She had to have been affecting Kara's ability. We had no way of knowing they were close." Suddenly I felt anxious. They'd probably been watching us the whole time, waiting for us to fall into their trap, and the idea of us being so easily manipulated scared me. "There was nothing any of us could have done, and there's probably nothing we can do now."

Maybe he saw the thoughts stir behind my worried eyes, because at some point, he decided to let me back in again and came to comfort me. He knelt down on the floor at the base of the bed and took my face in his hands.

"I won't let them hurt you." His words were sincere, but his square jaw tensed with worry, regardless.

I wanted to tell myself the worst wouldn't happen, but it might. I knew what Christoph wanted, and maybe he'd use any means necessary to get it. "At least we have right now."

My face lifted, and I looked into his leafy green eyes, grateful for the love in them. He pressed himself up and pushed his soft mouth into mine, his warmth spreading through me. I wanted the kiss to last forever, to carry me out of this place. My heart's frantic beat could easily be blamed on the feel of William's strong body pressed against me. Nothing could get to me in moments like this. Fear didn't exist.

Just as our lips parted, the doorknob clicked and turned. The portly balding man who had been guarding Anna and Chloe emerged with a disgruntled look.

"Christoph wants you," he said to me, his fat throat distorting his voice.

I looked at William, waiting for him to use his ability as he'd done before, but he shook his head. Christoph had stripped him of it, and I could feel the blood draining from my face. I couldn't move.

"Why doesn't he come himself?" William sneered.

The fat man pulled out a silver handgun from the back of his pants, and pointed it in William's direction. "I really don't like you."

"I'll go," I said, standing immediately, eyes wide with alarm.

A smile pressed into the man's full cheeks as he took pleasure in my reaction. "Good," he said, and he waved me forward with the gun.

William stood to follow, but the man turned the gun on him. "Not you."

"She's not going alone," he argued. A loud crack punched the air, and I jumped. I didn't understand what had happened at first. William collapsed to the ground with a look of shock on his face before I saw the pain register, before I realized he'd been shot.

"William!" I screamed, as the man lowered the gun.

William grabbed his shoulder in disbelief, and I tried to run to him, but was caught by a thick forearm. The fat man was quicker and stronger than he looked, and he dragged me out into the hall ignoring my kicking and yelling.

"Stay here," he said with distain, training his weapon on me, the only thing he knew would make me obey. I watched him lock the door trapping William inside the room, his gun staying pointed at me while I begged for mercy.

"Please. I can heal him," I sobbed, shaking frantically. He pulled me onto my feet and pushed me forward down the hall. "Please, let me go back." It was all I could do. They'd taken my weapon, my bracelet, even my shoes from me when they locked us up. I had nothing but my words, and they didn't work.

He walked behind me, digging the gun into my back. I didn't doubt that he would shoot me if I tried to run. The pain I could handle, but if I wanted to heal William, I needed my blood.

"If it isn't little miss save the world," Christoph sneered with amusement as we entered what I assumed was his office.

I didn't respond at first. I didn't want to give him the satisfaction. He wasn't worth the breath. He wasn't, but William was.

"William was shot," I told him, hoping somehow he would at least allow me to heal him. "I need to go back."

"Yes, I know," Christoph answered, his eyes fixed on me. "I needed to make sure you knew I was serious."

I wanted to look away, to fold under the pressure of his intimidation, but I forced myself to stare daggers back at him. I couldn't let him beat me, couldn't let him know how weak I felt as the love of my life slowly bled out in some room with no one to come for him. My stomach gave a heave, and I had to try something. "Well then, I guess he'll die. So much for your precious oracle." I felt like a serpent, spitting flames of hate.

"He's not going to die," Christoph scoffed, rolling his icy eyes. "It's a shoulder wound. Besides, we have you, the benevolent healer, to save him. He'll be fine."

"So can I go?" I seethed through gritted teeth.

He looked at me with intolerance. "Sit."

The fat man shoved me forward, and I sat in the leather chair that faced Christoph's desk.

"I want to get straight to the point," he said from his presidential chair. "You have something I want. The oracle, your child."

Who did this man think he was? I would never give up my child, not to anyone, and especially not to him. "Never," I answered simply, working hard to contain my rage. "I will never give up my child for you."

He leaned forward, resting his elbows on the desktop, smiling his crooked smile. "Elyse. I always get what I want." His black suit and impressive looks didn't fool me. This man was as close to the devil as any human or Descendant could be.

"Not this time." My words were strong, as if believing them would make them true.

He sighed, frustrated by my resistance. "The child would be safe with me. We could provide protection. That's all I want."

"I'll protect my own child." It felt strange discussing a child that had yet to be conceived. She, if I were to have a she, was little more than a thought in my head, and truth be told, if I had it my way, she would never be anything more. That was how I would protect her, by never bringing her into this world.

"Please. You can't even protect your friends."

"They are free aren't they?"

"Elyse. Don't tell me you actually believe that was your doing. I had no use for them, the oracle came through with her promise, and for her, I let them go." He laughed. "Don't be such a fool."

My lips parted in disbelief, too taken aback to respond. He had to be lying. "That's not true," I stated flatly, trying to control the tone in my voice.

"Think about it. What exactly did she tell you? That you would save your friends if you came tonight? She just left out the part about our little trade. You and William for them. She knows I get what I want. She knows that the only way you'll conceive this child is if I..." he thought about the right word, "*encourage* you to do so. Don't blame her, Elyse. She is simply ensuring the continuation of her bloodline. It's common sense, really."

I didn't want to believe him, but it did make sense. Why would she tell me to come on this night when she must have known William and I would be captured? Maybe she had her own plan all along. Maybe I was never meant to bring an end to Christoph. Was it possible that part of the prophecy was never true? It would be the perfect way to build protection around her one and only heir, a lie that would keep me safe until the time came for me to birth her bloodline. *No*, I told myself, *I'm letting him manipulate me. That's what he does.* Even if it was the truth, and she had given me up to him, there had to be an explanation. The oracle had to make hard choices. I tried to remember the sincerity in her eyes when we had met, the gentle love I saw in them when she looked at me.

He had given me time to process everything, but my silence might have gone on forever.

"Elyse, I know you've been plotting against me, made to believe I am your enemy, so you can't see that my intentions are good."

He waited to see if I had taken the bait. I hadn't.

"The oracle is a precious and powerful ability, and I can't simply let her be born into a world of conflict, tainted against me as you've been. The consequences of my father's decisions are undeniable. Letting the oracle do as she pleases has divided our people with talk of prophecies and war. We are a people of superior being, and we should not be in conflict. I've done my best to keep us protected from human prejudice, but I hope for peace amongst ourselves. Peace comes with a price you will never understand."

I hated him for his ability to persuade. He had such a slick tongue, like the serpent in the grass tempting Eve to eat the apple.

"Don't ever say I didn't try things the easy way," he concluded.

"Go to hell."

"Oh come on now. I'm not all that bad. I'll even have Adrianna restore your power temporarily so you can heal William."

I glanced back at the door, desperate to leave. "What's the catch?"

"Well, like I said, things always have their price." He pulled a syringe from his desk drawer, removing the sterile cap. "I need a vial of your blood."

"Why, so you can kill someone else?"

"The healing side, actually."

He waited impatiently for me to speak, but I couldn't. All I could think about were the reasons I hated him, the proof that he was evil. The murders of innocent people, Kara's forced involvement, Anna and Chloe, William shot and bleeding, his need for my unborn child.

"I hate you," I said through gritted teeth.

He smiled. "That may be, but I'm the only one who can help him."

I didn't really have a choice, and it was the healing side. William needed me. I looked away and thrust my bare arm toward him. "Take it."

He knocked the wall behind him with his knuckle, and a part of it swung open—a hidden door. I recognized the woman who emerged as Adrianna. At first her dark brown eyes stared into mine, but when I didn't look away she let them drop.

"It's done," she said, standing at his side.

His cold hands grasped my arm firmly. I couldn't watch, so I didn't see his face. Only when he was done did I look up, catching sight of something below his nose. Blood. I wouldn't have thought it strange, but it dripped from both nostrils, a deep scarlet. Something was wrong with him.

"Your nose is bleeding," I said, waiting for his reaction.

He looked alarmed for the briefest moment, but I saw it—vulnerability. He grabbed a handkerchief from his jacket pocket and held it to his nose, no longer concerned with me. With a nod of his head, the fat man had me by the arm, yanking me onto my feet. "Make sure she gets what she needs," Christoph said as I was pushed out of his office, back into the hallway.

"Hope nothing's wrong," I yelled from outside his door, a smile starting to sneak past my lips.

I held on to Christoph's words as I was followed by the man once again, gun pointing at my back. *Make sure she gets what she needs.* I needed to get back to William, I needed a shower and food, but when I heard the sound of a knife sliding out of its holster, I realized there was one thing I needed more—blood.

Before I had time to ready myself, he stuck the knife through the fleshy part of my right side. The shock alone stole the air out of my lungs, and I doubled over, too overcome by the searing pain to react. I was paralyzed. I couldn't move or breathe or scream. No air, no sound, nothing would come, until finally he yanked it free, and I inhaled sharply, like coming to after the wind is knocked out of you. Every muscle tensed in resistance to the throbbing wound, and although I wanted to fight back in retaliation, I felt grateful for the blood slowly seeping into my dress.

I stayed still and hunched as he unlocked the door and ushered me into the room. I tried not to moan as I hobbled in. William sat slumped against the foot of the bed, pale from blood loss and pressing a balled-up pillowcase against his bare shoulder.

"What did they do to you?" he demanded, mustering energy from somewhere, and suddenly hopping to his feet.

"Nothing. It's fine," I said through staggered breaths as he helped me to the bed.

"Nothing? This looks like something."

The door locked behind us. "The fat man stabbed me."

"He what?" William raged.

"It's so I can heal you." I sat still for a moment, bracing myself against the edge of the mattress. "We needed the blood."

That didn't seem to satisfy him.

"Don't defend him. There are other ways...this is... How deep is it?"

He laid me down and peered through the sliced fabric of my dress, wincing at what he saw. "Oh my God, Ellie." His eyes closed with a sigh. "I'm going to kill him."

"Not if I beat you to it," I joked, struggling to laugh with my muscles constricted from pain.

William smiled, though I could see he was worried. "What should I do?"

"Come here." I pulled at his hand, and he leaned forward so I could see his shoulder. "We need to get the bullet out right?"

"It hit the soft part," he said, turning to show me the exit wound. "I think it went all the way through."

"Good." I touched his taut skin gently, examining the wound with care. I pressed lightly against his firm muscle, and rich red blood oozed out easily. He gritted his teeth, but let me test the flow. "It's still bleeding well enough."

As the shock started to wear off, I was confronted with the pain head on. It made me cringe and shake, as I put my head back on the pillow.

"You'll be all right," William promised, bringing his face close. He brushed my sweaty hair out of my eyes and touched his lips to mine with the slightest kiss.

It was a relief to give up control, to know that he would take care of me, and it would be over soon. He rolled me gently to one side, unzipping my dress, and I moaned when I returned to my back. Tears slid into my ears as he pulled the straps off of my shoulders.

"Did I mention I'm going to kill him?" he said, trying to distract me.

I smiled, not wanting to tense my muscles by laughing, and nodded, still shaking. He peeled the blood soaked dress down to my hips, leaving me in my bra and exposing the wound, then climbed onto the bed positioning himself over me.

"The pressure will probably hurt at first," he said, without acknowledging his own pain. "Are you ready?"

"Yeah," I answered, and clenched my jaw to brace for it. He laid his body on top of mine, matching his shoulder with my side to seal our injuries together. He was gentle, but the weight of his torso was excruciating, and I cried out in agony.

"I'm sorry," he whispered, but stayed held in his position, head resting on my chest. "It will feel better soon."

As we waited for our wounds to heal, giving in to emotional and physical exhaustion, we drifted off. Without food or water, our bodies demanded only one thing of us—sleep. At some point we folded into each other like flower petals pulling close together to endure a cold night.

CHAPTER EIGHT

—

I WOKE UP ALONE. MY SKIN WAS HEALED, AND A tray of breakfast sat untouched, but William was gone.

I did my best to resist the food, telling myself I would accept nothing from Christoph, not even if my belly was twisting with hunger. I cringed at the sight of his fancy silver platter. Did he really think nice things would make me forget I was a prisoner? It was probably laced with something anyway.

"Alaximandrios," I whispered over and over under my breath, but no matter how many times I tried to call him, he never came.

I couldn't keep from growing anxious as each minute passed that William didn't walk through the bedroom door. What if I never saw him again? I had no way of knowing where or why they had taken him, what they were doing. What if William was dead? My chest tightened. If so, I hoped they would kill me next.

I tried to put myself in Christoph's shoes, to imagine what I would do if I had finally captured the two most valuable people in a war set against me. We had something he wanted, we wouldn't cooperate, what other use was there for us besides death? The death of the last healer and the new mother and father would be the ultimate blow to a people already wary of revolution. What better way to reestablish his stronghold than killing us both?

When the door finally swung open, I had already come to terms with what it would mean. I didn't know if it would be Christoph or one of his many pawns who would do the job, but I was ready. Without William, I couldn't muster the will to fight for any cause. As far as I was concerned, without him, there was no prophecy, no war, no oracle, no future.

"It's you," I uttered in disbelief as William was shoved into the room. I jumped to my feet and threw my arms around him. Our eyes met, but his were no comfort. "I thought they killed you." His face was pained as he looked into me, like maybe they were still going to.

"What's wrong?" I asked.

He looked away. "You didn't eat your food."

"I don't want it," I said, falling for his distraction. "I don't want anything from *him*."

He lifted my arms from off of his shoulders and headed for the platter. "You should eat, Elyse," William insisted. "He isn't planning on letting us go any time soon."

His somber expression was daunting. "What happened

when you were gone? Did you talk to him?"

He hung his head, recoiling from his own thoughts. "Come here," he said when he finally worked up the courage to look at me. "Eat, and I'll tell you."

I sat on the edge of the bed and wheeled the room service cart close enough to use as a table. My mouth watered at the smell of bacon and eggs as I lifted the lid covering my food, and I couldn't resist. I grabbed a piece of bacon and took a bite. "Did you eat anything?"

"I had breakfast with him."

My eyes fell into a scowl.

"His idea, not mine," he clarified. "I didn't have much of a choice." He sat close to me on the bed, watching me eat. "Elyse, I need you to know that I love you."

"I know," I said, my heart clutching at the suspicious way his words were colored with sorrow. "I love you too."

"I'm so sorry, for everything. I was supposed to protect you, and it was me who...this is my fault. I know you don't see it that way, but I do. I just hope you can forgive me. You don't blame me now, but you might later, after..."

"After what?"

"Even if you can forgive me, I'll never forgive myself," he continued.

"William?"

"I have to ask you something, before I tell you. I need you to know that it comes from the heart, and even if it were a different situation, and we were free, I'd still feel this way. I've always wanted you and nobody else, like I've known you forever." He fell to one knee and my heart shot up into my throat.

"What are you…Why are you doing this now?" This couldn't be right. It wasn't like William to be so careless with sentiment. If this was his proposal, something was wrong. "Is he going to kill us?"

"If we don't do what he wants. Yes. He'll kill us."

I shook my head, trying to deny what I knew was inevitable from the moment we were captured. Christoph wanted one thing, the next oracle, and unless we gave him what he wanted, we were as good as dead.

"I won't do it," I said without thinking.

"Then he'll kill you, Elyse," William said in distress. "He'll kill both of us."

"This isn't your fault, it's *hers*," I sneered in anger.

"Who?" he asked with surprise.

"The oracle. She's been working with him. She told him we would be here. She meant for us to get caught."

He rose to his feet and sat next to me on the bed. "How do you know?" he asked, ready to defend her.

"He told me," I answered. "Think about it. She wants her bloodline to continue. This makes sure it happens. How else would he have known we were here?"

"But why would she put her trust in Christoph? It doesn't make sense. She's on our side."

"Is she? What if she kept me alive this whole time for this moment? She gets what she wants."

He shook his head. "Ellie, Christoph killed Iosif. Why

would the oracle side with someone who killed her husband? Christoph manipulates. Whatever he told you isn't true."

"Maybe," I answered, not sure what to believe.

"What should we do?" he whispered into the silence, his eyes pleading for a miracle answer, one I didn't have.

When I thought William was gone, death was an easy thing to accept, but with him sitting inches away from me, I couldn't give in that easily. If I refused to cooperate, it would be my decision that took William's life.

I turned to face him. "I don't think we have a choice."

"I don't want to force you," William said, releasing his guilt. "He tried to convince me it was the right thing to do, that I'd be saving your life, but I just can't do it." We looked at each other, both pained by the decision. "I can't take that from you, not if you don't want it."

"It's not that," I pleaded. "I do want it. I just…" Tears began to form, but I refused to blink. I would not let them fall.

He nodded. "Just not like this."

A thousand things were telling me to stand up for myself, for my virtue and my future child. I couldn't let Christoph manipulate us like this, and I wouldn't play into his game, but it was William. Was it worth dying over? How could I give up everything, deny myself the genuine love that he had for me, just out of principle? It seemed foolish. If it were anyone else it might be a worthy battle, but to give in wasn't necessarily defeat. It was per-severance in the name of love.

"We'll find another way," William insisted with little hope.

I chuckled to myself at his noble suggestion, and turned to him with dry and confident eyes. I found his lips, kissing them gently.

"What are you doing?" he whispered.

"It's not worth losing you."

"It shouldn't be like this," he said, shying away from my affection.

"Just forget Christoph, forget this place, what it means. I won't let him take this from us. It's not like the oracle would be born tomorrow. This doesn't mean he wins, it means we win, because we aren't doing this for him, we'll be doing it for us."

"I don't see it that way."

"Why? We've both wanted this for a long time, and I'm tired of holding out because I'm scared. I won't let Christoph control us."

He brushed his hair back out of his face. "If we give in, he *will* be controlling us."

"How do you know? Maybe he wants us to resist. Maybe he's just looking for any reason to kill us. We have to stop thinking about Christoph, and what he wants. We need to decide for ourselves." I laced my fingers between his. "If this was our last day together," I said, "if we were never meant to survive this, what would you choose?"

His eyes softened at the thought. "You."

"Then kiss me because you want to, not because you

have to."

He looked at me for a moment before he gave in. His warm palm slid against my cheek, his fingers settling on the back of my neck as he inched closer. Goosebumps crawled across my shoulders, and the feel of his lips made me breathe deeply, like I'd thirsted for his kiss for too long. "Are you sure?" he asked when our mouths parted.

"Yes, I'm sure," I answered.

"Okay, just wait one second," he said with a renewed sense of acceptance. He reached around to the back of my head and gently loosened my ponytail, letting my hair down. With the hairband in his hand he came to one knee yet again. "I've always known I'd marry you, Elyse, but I have to ask. Will you marry me?"

"Yes," I answered through a smile. Despite the circumstances, I was determined to let myself feel joy, as if the feeling alone was a victory. "Absolutely, yes."

He wrapped the black elastic band around my ring finger, twisting it until it fit. "I was planning on giving you my grandmother's ring. This doesn't quite do it justice."

"It doesn't matter."

He took my face in his hands again and kissed me softly, but this kiss was different. It was our end and our beginning in one. My chest heaved with breath as his pillowy lips slipped against mine. His fingers grazed the skin of my shoulders, taking in every inch, every feeling like it was the last moment we'd ever know.

With a hand against my waist he moved me to the

center of the bed using the pressure of his kiss to guide me. My body trembled knowing this was it. We'd lost, but giving in was a freedom I'd never felt before. My fingers shook and fumbled with the buttons of his tuxedo shirt, peeling it over his shoulders. His face, freshly shaven, slid like silk into the crook of my neck, and I closed my eyes. I breathed deeply as he reached for the zipper of my dress, but before he pulled it down he stopped, holding us in that last moment before everything changed.

"I love you," he whispered, his face inches from mine.

Our eyes connected. "I love you, too," I said, pressing my mouth into his. Defeat never felt so good.

———

I WOKE UP TO SILENCE. THE ROOM WAS DARK, BUT my eyes were used to it, and I could see the white sheets glowing against William's back. At first I smiled to myself. He was there, next to me, safe. I slid my hands over the sheets across my flat belly. Blood pulsed under my palms and the feeling made my chest flutter. I swallowed down the nervousness. Maybe it didn't work. My eyelids slammed shut. I didn't feel any different. Please tell me it didn't work.

Without warning, the door flung open. It crashed against the wall, startling William out of sleep. His body jumped, and he rolled off the bed, taking the top cover with him and leaving me with the sheet.

Adrianna sighed, and her eyebrows climbed up her

forehead. "I'm guessing I'm too late," she said. William and I stared at her, afraid to move, and she looked back at us with wide expectant eyes. "Well? Get up. Get dressed." Her voice was sharp and demanding and had us on our feet in seconds.

I held the sheet to my body as I scrambled to find my clothes. William buttoned up his shirt with quick fingers and was by my side to help me pull on my dress. My eyes drifted to the black cloth bag Adrianna held as she knelt down and began feeling under the bed. She lifted a key from around her neck and slid it into a lock hidden discretely under a wooden panel on the leg of the bedframe. The floor began to groan and the entire bed turned on an axis creating an opening in the floor.

"Move," she urged, beckoning for us to take the stairs that led down into the opening. "Quickly."

She followed us, sliding her key once again into a lock somewhere in the dark wall of the tunnel. The floor creaked and strained again, sealing us up in darkness below.

I couldn't see, but I felt her body brush against me as she pushed past us. "Follow me."

CHAPTER NINE

—

THE AIR WAS DAMP IN THE NARROW CORRIDOR, AND
the walls were sharp with jagged rock. I thought about
resisting. She had no weapon, but something told me not
to test her. A distant glow coaxed us onward, toward the
end of the tunnel.

When we got there, she opened the wooden door,
flooding the passage with a dull light. I felt William's hand
on the small of my back, urging me forward.

Cast iron cells lined the length of each wall of the
flame-lit room, but only one woman was being held here.
I figured we were next and wondered which would be
ours. The woman stayed quiet, and watched us through
loose strands of shiny blonde hair as we passed. Though
she looked healthy and well kept, both her feet and hands
were chained to the floor.

I heard William's footsteps stop somewhere behind
me. "Lilia?" he whispered.

"Keep walking," Adrianna warned from ahead. "Don't push your luck, William."

He glared at her with distain, but kept moving.

"Here." She thrust the black bag into my hands. "I'll restore your power within the hour."

I stood taller, facing her in the dim light. "Why?"

She opened a cell door, the hinges creaking with rust.

"Because I'm letting you go," she answered. "Help me lift this." Her eyes fell on a stone-carved bench that sat against the wall. "Behind it there's a hole that leads to the storm drain system."

I didn't move at first. I didn't believe her, but William must have because he stepped forward and gripped the edge of the bench with his fingers. The muscles in his forearms and back flexed as he braced his body to counter the weight of the stone. It crackled against the rough granite floor as he slid the seat far enough out for us to squeeze our bodies through. I stepped forward and saw the opening, an ominous black hole that led into the wall.

"Thank you," William said to Adrianna as he tugged at my hand. I didn't budge.

My eyes focused on her. "Why are you doing this?" I couldn't trust anyone blindly. Mac had drilled that into our heads.

She smiled, and shadows elongated her features. "It's just my little way of paying back Christoph."

"For what?"

Her eyes tightened, but her lips smirked as she answered.

"A lovers' quarrel. What is it they say? Hell hath no fury like a woman scorned."

I stared past her into the opening. It could lead us anywhere. This could be a trap. "How do we know we can trust you?"

"You don't." Adrianna sighed impatiently. "Look in the bag."

I opened the black satchel and stuck my hand inside. The familiar feeling of my dart gun graced my fingers, and I found my bracelet near the bottom.

I didn't know what to say, whether to hate her for who she was or thank her for her help.

"What about William's ability?" William stayed quiet, but I felt him standing strong against me. I was pushing it by asking.

"That is up to Christoph." She shrugged. "But he is weak. He has many enemies, and the more power we take, the sicker we get. Every Council member has their limitations. He'll give it up soon enough."

I glanced at William. I hadn't known that fact.

"Good luck."

William insisted on going through first. Adrianna had put a flashlight in the bag, but its single ray was lost easily in the blackness. His feet tested the rungs of the flimsy metal rebar that protruded from the cement as he lowered himself deeper.

My eyes floated toward Lilia while William climbed. She was the key, the only Council member who tied them all together. Without her, none of the Council's abilities worked. Adrianna cleared her throat to get my attention. She was watching from a distance and had to know what I was thinking. If I could get Lilia out and away from them it would strip their power. Christoph wouldn't lose his authority, but he would lose his ability. He'd be vulnerable. How fast could I load my thickest dart and shoot her?

"Okay," William spoke from below. "The ladder ends short. We'll have to jump."

I heard the echoing splash as his feet hit wet ground. If I decided to take the risk, I was on my own. There was no way back up. He pointed the light at me and I squinted back. I had to try.

"Elyse," Adrianna said before I made a move. "She's been conceived. I already feel her."

I opened my mouth to respond, but my breath caught in my throat. If those words had come from anyone else, I might not have believed them, but Adrianna was of Hera. Her bloodline was linked to the abilities of others. I couldn't dismiss that.

"How do you...you feel her?" I managed, my heart squeezing and pumping in my chest.

"Like I feel every female Descendant."

I stood there, unmoving.

"Come on," William beckoned from below. "What are you waiting for?"

Something in me switched on, and I couldn't bring myself to draw my dart gun. I glanced at Lilia, and she stared back at me with kind eyes like she was telling me something—*go*. She nodded her head at me, and I turned away, hoping I wouldn't regret the decision as I ducked into the hole. My bare feet found the rungs guided by the flashlight, and when I came to the end, I hoped I wouldn't break something or cut my toes off.

"Be careful," he said. "Do you want me to try and catch you?"

"No. I can make it," I answered. "Just point the flashlight at where I should land."

I made the jump, and the sting of the impact shot up my legs as I toppled into William.

"You okay?" he asked.

I got to my feet and stared at the hole above us. "Fine."

"What did she say to you?"

"Nothing. Come on."

There was no way back up. The ladder had dropped us into a cement tunnel just high enough that William didn't have to duck. In one direction, the space narrowed too tightly for us to continue. There was only one way to go.

Water ran sluggishly around our ankles as we made our way through the maze of tunnels. The smell was stale and offensive, like old toilet water, and it burned my nose. At first, the stream looked black as oil in the dim light, but when William pointed the flashlight at my toes it seemed clear enough to be safe.

"Walk on the sides," William instructed. "And go slow.

Watch where you step."

The tunnel walls changed shape from circular to square-edged, and every so often red and orange stalactites stuck out from the cement pipe walls like fingernails reaching out to grab us.

After the fifth turn had led us nowhere, I wondered if Adrianna's plan was to leave us scurrying around like rodents in an inescapable maze of tubes. William bounced the flashlight from one wall to the other hopelessly as we walked. I was starting to imagine us stuck down here, dying of starvation in the stink.

"There," William's voice rang out through the still air. His feet splashed the shallow water as he ran forward, and I hurried after. Two peepholes of light gleamed down on us as we stared at the bottom of a steel manhole cover.

"What's the plan?" I asked.

"I have no idea."

"Should we just go for it?"

"No. Let me at least see where we are," he said, handing me the flashlight.

I pointed the beam at the bottoms of his shoes as he climbed up through a chimney-like opening toward the street.

"What do you see?" I asked.

He closed the lid. "Fancy heels and valet workers," he answered as he made his way down. "We're right in front of a nice restaurant. We need to keep moving."

"No. We're here. Let's just jump out and run."

"Run where, Ellie?"

"I don't know."

He sighed, unsatisfied with my plan, but began to climb anyway. "Just let me make sure the coast is clear, okay? Wait sixty seconds before you come up."

My head stayed tilted back as I counted. Twenty-two, twenty-three, twenty-four. The lid lifted before I got to sixty.

"Elyse! Come on. Hurry," William ordered through the hole.

I didn't think. I moved. As fast as I could from bar to bar.

"What's wrong?" I breathed once I'd popped out into the open air. Eyes were starting to find me. People were staring.

"Get in the car," William said through clenched teeth.

I didn't argue.

The car was silver and smooth. One of those types men usually compare to a woman. I made my way to the passenger side and ducked in, eager to escape the looks.

"What are you doing?" I asked, once William began to pull slowly and casually away.

"Escaping," he said, enjoying himself a little too much. "What does it look like?"

"By stealing a car?"

"Well, technically it's not stealing." He hiked his shoulders up. "The guy gave me the keys."

I glanced out the rear window. "What? Why? Is your

ability back?"

"No." He smiled to himself. "When I stood up, he was getting out of the car and thought I was the valet."

"Seriously?" I laughed, despite my worry. "But you're a mess. Your tux is all wrinkled and wet. There's blood on it."

"I know. He hardly looked at me. Just threw me the keys and ran in. He must have been in a hurry or something."

I looked around in disbelief at the smooth black leather seats knitted together with white stitching. The dashboard was a glossy gray wood, equipped with navigation, XM radio, and an array of lit up features. Here we were clean as sewer rats fleeing our capture in a luxury sports car.

"What kind of car is this?" I asked, brushing the door handle with my fingertips.

William's eyebrows lifted, and he tightened his hands around the wheel with a grin. "A Maserati."

He revved the engine pressing the pedal to the floor. I let out a scream, and my head flew back into the seat as we launched onto the freeway.

My fingers gripped the door, the dash, anything to steady myself. "Slow down!" I yelled.

"It's a Mas-er-at-i," he tried to clarify.

"I don't care. Don't drive like a maniac. What if we get caught?" I felt my brow tighten. "This is too risky. We need to get rid of this car."

"Come on," he coaxed. "We have at least an hour before he reports anything."

"Where are we even going?"

"I was thinking my parents' house. My dad probably has security around the place."

I sighed. "It's too far away. How are we going to get there?"

"What's the matter, Ellie?"

I didn't realize I'd had an attitude until he mentioned it. I'd been snapping. Everything I said came out with a sharp edge, like he was to blame for something, but for what? We were safe, free, alive. I had no reason to be upset. No reason except the idea of a baby.

"So? Are you going to tell me?"

I didn't answer. Instead, I stared out the window, feeling guilty about acting mean. It wasn't his fault.

I could feel him looking at me. "We're going to have to talk about it eventually."

"About what?" I said, denying what we both knew he meant. I tried to make my words sound gentle, but they were still coming out rude. "I'm sorry. I'm just stressed."

He took my hand, kissing the top as our palms warmed. "Well, you shouldn't be. We're free."

I cracked a smile at the thought.

"Which means," he continued, "the baby is free. I'm actually excited—"

I pulled my hand away. I didn't want there to be a baby, not now anyway. Not when I was being hunted, not when there was supposed to be a war, not when I was supposed to lead. I could barely protect myself, how could I expect to protect and care for a baby? I wasn't ready.

"I don't think it worked," I lied. I hoped. Maybe if he thought it, it would be true. At least he wouldn't talk about it.

"Oh." His eyed drifted back to the road. "You don't know for sure though, right? You said yourself it was the oracle's plan. Maybe you were right. Maybe she knew we would escape."

As far as the oracle was concerned, I didn't know what to believe. All I knew was that you should never trust someone blindly, and I would never make that mistake with her again.

"I'm sure," I answered. "But it doesn't mean—"

Blue and red lights interrupted me. They flashed on the dashboard like a disco ball, and a siren wailed behind us.

I whipped my head around.

"Are we getting pulled over?"

William eyed the rearview mirror. "Yeah."

"Were you speeding or something?"

"No. 65 exactly."

"They know. Should we try and outrun them?"

"Yeah, and get a whole fleet on our tail and a TV spotlight? No. Just let me try and talk him out of it. Open the glove box."

CHAPTER TEN

—

I COULDN'T SEE THE OFFICER'S FACE AS HE SPOKE TO William.

"License and registration," he said through the open window, not bothering to bend over and look at us.

William already had the document in his hand. The car belonged to a Jeremy Wright. I couldn't imagine him as a Jeremy.

"Sorry officer. I left my wallet at a restaurant. We were just driving back to get it."

The man reached his hand in, and I stared at the blue cuff of his uniform, then the gun on his hip as he took the paper. My feet tapped against the floor of the car. This wasn't going to work.

"Do you know why I pulled you over?" he asked. I could hear the amusement in his voice.

"No, sir," William answered quietly. Then silence. I recognized the look on his face, the sharp concentration in his eyes. Was his ability back? "I don't believe we did anything wrong."

The prompt was subtle, but it seemed to be working. Maybe this would turn out all right after all.

A burst of laughter exploded from the cop, and his rounded belly shook. "Nice try, son. Get out of the car."

"If he arrests me, just drive," William whispered before opening the door.

"No," I said sharply under my breath.

I stared out the back window as William was patted down. I couldn't hear what was being said over the rush of the freeway, but after a moment the man removed a set of cuffs and pulled William's hands behind his back. My throat when dry, and for a second I began to panic but stopped myself. *No. Figure it out, Elyse.* I forced myself to think. I wasn't going to let us be held prisoner again. I'd do whatever I had to. Then I remembered my dart gun in the sack at my feet. My ability might be working by now. It was worth a try.

I punched the two gold buttons on my bracelet, grabbed a dart from the pouch, and dipped it in. The rest of the blood slid into the palm of my hand and I cupped it, just in case I needed more. As I turned to open the door, the cop was there opening it for me. I froze.

We looked at each other for a moment, and I expected him to draw his gun or order me to put my hands up, but he just stared. The blood had dripped through my closed fingers onto the tops of my legs. The dart dyed scarlet was ready to be loaded.

"It's you," he said, an unexpected and cheerful smile warming his face. He had friendlier eyes than I had imagined. They matched his dark brown hair and tan skin. "Come on." He spoke quickly, ushering me out of the car with sudden urgency. "We need to get you out of here. Careful not to get your blood anywhere."

I grabbed the black sack with my blood free hand, still wary of what was happening, and stepped out into the wind. Cars zipped by feet away from me, blowing my hair away from my face.

William's eyes widened in confusion as the officer came jaunting back toward him with a sudden change in mood. He looked at me for answers, but my brows were still pinched together with uncertainty, and I shook my head at him.

"Come on. Get in. Get in," the officer urged as he nearly forced William into the back seat.

William looked at me through the window, mouthing the words *run*, but I stepped forward. The cop beckoned me eagerly with his hand and pushed open the passenger side door from the inside. I took a breath, avoiding William's gaze, and got in.

As he drove away neither of us spoke. William didn't have to say anything for me to know what he was thinking, but I wasn't about to leave him now after all we'd been through. Instead I sat up front in silence. I glanced at the man's nametag: OFFICER GOMEZ. When I looked up,

I realized he was eyeing me as well, my bloody hand in particular.

He nodded his head uncomfortably as he looked back at the road. "I'm David, by the way," he said, breaking the ice.

"Where are you taking us?" I tried to make my voice sound strong.

"Oh." He looked in the review at William with bright eyes. "To my house." He'd completely dropped his I'm-a-cop-bad-guy role. "I'm descendant of Pasithea." As he spoke his posture changed. He straightened up and concentrated on more than just driving. When his ability took hold, I felt my shoulders relax, my eyelids soften, the muscles in my face let go of tension, as if he was taking all of it upon himself.

"Relaxation?" I asked in surprise, and I couldn't keep myself from enjoying the feeling.

He nodded and smiled. "Apparently you need it."

I closed my eyes for a moment, before the weight of my nerves was returned.

"I'm glad I found you," he said. "The community has been panicked since word spread of your capture. We need to keep you safe."

I turned to look back at William with a smile of relief, but his face hadn't changed. "Once harm has been done, even a fool understands it," William said, leaning forward to talk through the grate. His hands were still locked be-hind his back as he waited for the man to react.

I watched him through the corner of my eye, suddenly more suspicious. It had been a long time since I had heard those words. I'd almost forgotten them. Mac had made us memorize the phrase for this very reason, and I'd neglected to use it. I bit my lip, angry at myself.

David lifted his eyebrows as he shifted forward and stared back at William through the rearview. "The outcome of the war is in our hands; the outcome of words is in The Council," he replied with a nod.

The response settled my mind. At least luck was on our side. "How do you know who we are?" I asked.

"Well, I didn't at first, but after I saw your face, of course I knew you." He held the wheel with one hand and removed a photo from his shirt pocket. It was of me. "You're the last healer."

I took the photo from his hand. "Where did you get this?"

"A messenger brought it to the station just before I left for my shift. He said they'd lost you. I guess they were expecting you to show up."

"What kind of messenger?" William asked.

"I'm not sure what bloodline, but he can be called when you're ready. He's a young guy. It his nineties like you. His name is Alex."

When we pulled into the driveway of David's suburban cookie-cutter home, he opened William's door for him and removed the handcuffs.

"Sorry about that, William," he said. "It's not every

day I almost arrest the last healer. I got a little excited back there."

He nodded. "Yeah, she'll do that to you."

I shook my head, trying to hold back a smile, and followed David through the front door. As we entered, a woman stepped into the living room to greet us. When she saw our faces her almond eyes widened with surprise. She pulled a picture out of the pocket of her apron, and her mouth opened.

"David, how did you..."

"Offer them something to drink, Mags," he pressed. "Don't just stand there."

"Sorry. I'm Maggie," she said, brushing thick waves of amber hair from her face. She reached forward to shake our hands. "Please come in. Make yourselves comfortable. Can I get you anything?"

Her hurried speech had William and I looking at each other.

"Some new clothes and a shower would be nice," William answered.

"And something to eat maybe," I added. My stomach had a voice as well, and it continued to growl at me as we moved to their brown suede sofa.

"Sure." She nodded. "Of course. I'll start on some sandwiches while you two shower up."

David offered William some khaki shorts and a T-shirt, and escorted him to the downstairs bathroom.

"These are probably not the best fit," Maggie said as

she handed me some jeans that were a little too big, a tank top, and a sweatshirt.

"They're fine," I answered as I followed her up the stairs. Anything was better than this dress. "Thank you."

It felt good to let hot water run over my cold, bare skin. I tried to be quick, drying and dressing as soon as I was out. I brushed my wet hair out of my face and stared into the mirror over the bathroom sink. As I looked into my own eyes, I was surprised at what I saw. They weren't the eyes I was used to seeing. They were older, wiser, like they'd changed with experience. I didn't recognize myself. My muscles were strong and toned, and there was something different about the way I stood. I looked capable, tough. The last few months I'd allowed myself to focus on training, helping Anna and Chloe, and getting away from Christoph. I hadn't realized how much it had changed me. I only wished I felt as confident as I looked.

"Word is out," David explained after escorting us to the kitchen table. I sat across from him and took eager bites of my sandwich while I listened intently. "Communities have started to talk, take sides even." His eyes shifted to mine, hopeful. "They're waiting."

"Things have changed," Maggie added. "Headquarters in all communities have closed. They're worried about people congregating. We have to watch what we say. We've heard of Descendants disappearing."

"Do you..." David's voice lacked confidence as he stared at me. "Have a plan?" he finished.

"We have a plan," William said with reassurance. He glanced at me briefly, knowing I wouldn't have an answer. "We just need to get back home. We need to call Alex."

I leaned forward, resting my arms on the table. "How do we know he's not still working for Christoph?" I asked. "I called him before. He never came."

"I'll use the code," David answered. "Just like you did with me."

I nodded. "Good."

"But you two should hide," Maggie suggested. "In case he doesn't give us the right response."

We hid behind long dresses in Maggie's closet and waited. The sweet smell of clean laundry and rose scented perfume wafted around us as I pressed my back against the front of William's warm body.

"Thanks," I whispered to him.

"For what?"

"For saying we have a plan when we don't."

He wrapped his arms around my shoulders and kissed the spot behind my ear.

"We'll think of something."

I didn't know if "something" meant a way out or a way to fight. I tried not to think about it. The doorknob to the master bedroom clicked and footsteps were muffled against the carpet.

"All right," David said. "You can come out. He's one of the good guys."

William smiled at me, released his arms from around

my shoulders, and we ducked through the drapes of cloth.

"Let me go first," William said. "Just in case."

He closed the closet door behind him, but I could still hear their voices.

"What happened? We tried calling you."

"Relax. I tried, okay? Besides, the oracle told your dad you'd escape on your own."

"Can you take us back now?" I asked as I stepped through the closet doors and into the room. I needed to be home again.

"Just waiting for you," he said grabbing hold of William's shoulder. "Come on already."

"Thank you, David," William said as he held his hand out to me.

As soon as my fingertips touched William's and the three of us were linked, Alex made the world go white. I couldn't see my body, my surroundings. I couldn't breathe, and my lungs wanted air. Then, as if I had simply opened my eyes, the world was there again. My parents' house visible in the distance. I was home.

"I hate that," I said, catching my breath. "What is it?"

"What do you think it is, genius?" Alex said through a sideways smirk. "I'm of Aether. It's the upper air."

I couldn't keep my face from tightening with irritation as I glared at him, but with each step toward the house I felt my heart relax. Something was different, though. There was a distant droning that threw me off.

"What's that noise?" I asked.

"William!" a voice shouted from the front yard.

Edith ran toward us, a bright smile stretching across her face, and Kara followed close behind. I'd only seen William's little sister in pictures, but she didn't look much different. She was still growing into her forties, a child of eight or nine in human terms. Her shiny copper hair bounced as she ran, and her freckles stood out in the sun. When she got to us, she threw herself at her brother running full speed and wrapped her arms around his torso. "You're alive."

He smiled back at her and tousled her hair. "You know it."

"I was worried," she sighed, looking up at him.

"You know I'd never leave you alone with Mom and Dad. They'd drive you crazy."

She laughed and held his hand. "Hi, Elyse," she said with timid eyes.

"Hi, Edith," I answered. It was cute to see William with her. He would be a good dad.

You're pregnant? Kara asked me silently from a distance. I could see the reaction of the thought on her face.

Get out! I demanded. *Don't say ANYTHING.*

She looked away as she approached. "What the hell," she said, pushing William hard in the chest. "You weren't supposed to get caught." Her hard and resentful expression was only for play these days, and her scowl turned almost instantly to a smile. She wrapped her arms around him, the bond they'd formed as children still holding strong. I watched them as they hugged, and noticed she held on a little too long.

Her eyes found mine as she heard my thought, and she pulled away awkwardly.

"Yeah," he teased. "Thanks for coming back for us, by the way."

"Well," Alex said looking from face to face as we stood a distance from the front porch. "This is...boring. Can we go in now?"

"Are you ready for that?" Kara asked out loud.

I shrugged. "For what?"

"There's about a hundred people out back. They're all waiting for you."

The noise was so obvious now as I listened. Voices. People.

"No," I admitted. "I'm not ready." I grabbed William's hand for support.

"Great," Alex said with distain. His black hair contrasted his white skin in a way that made him look unworldly and threatening, like a snake's color reveals that it's poisonous. "This is what we've been waiting for?"

"Hey," William said with a low voice. "Back off."

"I'm just saying they're expecting someone who can lead them." He looked at me with his piercing blue eyes that matched the sky. "Can you do that?"

I stared back at him defiantly. "Yes," I answered.

"Good."

"How'd you find them?" Kara asked, catching up to

Alex as he continued toward the house. She seemed unaffected by his brazen nature.

He reached for the door. "They found me."

"I don't like him," I said to William once Kara and
Alex were out of earshot.

"Me either," he agreed.

"Yeah, me either," Edith added.

CHAPTER ELEVEN

—

"YOU FINALLY MADE IT," MAC GRUNTED AS WE walked through the front door of my parents' house. Dr. Nickel was there, eagerly waiting for us, and Mrs. Nickel was fixing big pots of soup in the kitchen. Anna stood next to her with Chloe at her side. She smiled as she saw me, letting go of all the worry.

"Elyse," Chloe's voice shouted from across the room. She ran toward me and hugged me as tightly as she could. Her skinny body was still weak from malnourishment, but I could tell she was in good spirits. "You're here." Her smile was contagious, and I couldn't keep my cheeks from lifting as I looked back at Anna.

"You all right?" Mac clapped his large hands around our backs and pulled us in for a hug.

Before I could answer, Mrs. Nickel was throwing her arms around my neck, then Anna, all of them bombarding us with smiles and questions and kisses.

"William," Sofia chimed with relief, quieting the rest of them. "I was so worried." She held her son's face between her hands, examining him. "You look all right. They didn't hurt you did they?"

"Well, they shot me."

"Shot you?" Dr. Nickel said from behind his wife.

The chaos started back up again. I hadn't been around this many people in so long.

"Relax. Relax. Elyse took care of it."

Sofia grabbed the sides of my face and kissed my cheeks. "You sweet girl."

I bit the inside of my cheek, trying to keep calm. All the excitement was getting to be a bit much. I squeezed Mrs. Nickel's shoulders and put on a fake smile. "No problem. I'll be right back, okay?" I said through five voices talking at once. "I just need a minute."

I slipped away and headed for my parents' room, leaving everyone to fawn over William. My head was in too many places to handle that sort of attention. I closed the door behind me and sighed. Someone had cleaned in here. My lips tightened. This was my parents' home. What gave anybody the right to even be in here? I clenched my jaw in anger and ran my fingers over the fresh towels that hung in their bathroom, the new bedspread that covered their bed. The dust was gone.

Remembering the voices, I made my way to the window and pulled the thick cloth drapes to one side. At least they remained. My mouth opened in surprise as I looked out over the backyard. Kara had been right. Nearly a hundred people, maybe more, had set up camp on the sloping land that led to the creek. They milled about large white canvas tents as if this was their home. A pop-up canopy covered a cooking area with grills and tables. A massive fire pit with logs for seats sat at the heart of the setup. Tables near the deck were strewn with maps and books. Had these people all come to fight? Had they come for me?

I turned away from the window, but left the drapes open. I couldn't hide from it forever. Maybe this was what my parents wanted, for me to lead. I tried to draw strength from them in their room. I needed strength to do this.

I opened my mother's bedside table, looking for a note, a keepsake, something, but all I saw was an old dusty book. I'd seen it there before, but never cared to touch it. As though if I left it frozen in time she might come back and pick up where she left off. Whoever had cleaned had missed this spot.

I picked it up and turned it over. *The Art of War*, by Sun Tzu. I sat on the bed and opened its cover.

Use this as a guide, my love. You are stronger than you know. – Mother

My chest tightened and tears rolled down my cheeks. I stared at the words, imagining her holding the pen and writing the advice she knew I would need.

Somewhere within me, a fire began to lick at my heart.

I was born to do this, meant to lead. Determination settled in the pit of my stomach and I started to read.

"Military action is important to the nation—it is the ground of death and life, the path of survival and destruction, so it is imperative to examine it."

I don't know how long I had been reading, but when I was halfway through, the door cracked open. "You all right?" Anna asked. I stared at the window, peering out at the scene. Eventually I'd have to show my face.

"Look at all of these people," I said as she closed the door behind her.

"I know. It's amazing. They're all here for you." She made her way over to the bed and sat down beside me. "Do you know what you're going to do next?"

"Whatever feels right, I guess."

"Well, that's worked so far."

"I'm so glad you're here," I said leaning into her and pressing my head to her shoulder.

"Me too." She let out a deep breath. "You saved my life, Ellie."

"Barely," I said, and for some reason I laughed. We laughed. It felt good to laugh about something so frightening. It meant that it was over.

"Is Chloe okay?"

"She's fine. Loving it here, actually. Sofia's just trying to fatten us up now." She slapped her skinny thigh. "We're more worried about you."

"Me?"

"You know they're all waiting for you to come out of this room."

"I know."

"You may doubt yourself, Elyse, but I know better. You're strong. You're determined. You will be a great leader."

—

WHEN I STEPPED OUT OF MY PARENTS' ROOM, VOICES hushed and heads turned my way. I didn't know how long I'd been in there, but I did know one thing.

"I'm ready," I said.

William stepped forward from his place between his father and Mac at the map-strewn kitchen table. "To go out there? Are you sure?"

Kara and Alex looked up with anticipation from the couch.

"I'm sure."

"Well you're not going out in that," Alex scoffed. "You look like a homeless person."

I stepped toward him with newfound confidence. "You know, this is my house, and I can kick you out."

Alex's face stayed blank and unfazed. "Just saying..."

If he hadn't been right, I might have.

I changed into tight fitting jeans and a solid black T-shirt. I tied my hair back into a smooth ponytail, strapped my dart gun to my leg, and tucked a spare knife into my back pocket. I had to be armed at all times.

The sun had set by the time I was ready, but tall torches kept the camp alight. As I stepped out onto the porch, silence overcame the crowd. I waited for people to gather, trying to stand tall and sure. Trying to breathe.

"Welcome," I spoke with force, keeping my voice strong and steady. "We all know why you're here. You think I have a way to take down The Council." My gaze floated over the faces of the people, meeting eyes that were full of hope and anticipation. "The truth is I need you just as much as you need me. This won't be easy. We'll have to fight. We'll have to win a war." I walked from one side of the porch to the other and smiled as I remembered what gave me hope. "But I've seen him. I've looked into Christoph's eyes, and he's weak. I've seen him bleed. He's not invincible. He's not all-powerful. He doesn't control us." My voice got louder and stronger as I continued. " *We* control our future. Not him. Not The Council. Not anymore." I nodded, satisfied with my message. "I have a plan, and we start tomorrow. So get some rest."

I turned away, heading for refuge in the house and forgetting the crowd, but a man's voice whooped somewhere amongst them, and I looked back. The cheering began to spread, and before I knew it they were all clapping. I smiled, humbled by their support, and walked through the back door before the excitement had time to fade.

"Where did that come from?" Alex asked as my inner circle followed me into the kitchen.

I just looked at him. I didn't know.

"Seriously, what was that?" he asked again.

I laughed. I couldn't help it. "It was what they needed. For me to be... confident."

"Whatever it was, it worked," added Kara.

Ten pairs of eyes were on me. Suddenly I felt uncomfortable again. Unsure. "We need to talk about what's going to happen," I said, walking toward the kitchen table. "We need to decide what we want from this. What's our goal?" It was the first thing mentioned in the book I kept hidden in my mother's bedside table. Know the way. Have the same plan, be on the same page. I just had to figure out what page *I* was on. "Are we talking human integration or—"

"Kill the Council members," Alex interrupted. His eyes were cold. He wanted vengeance. I could see it in his tight muscles. "Take out the enemy. Isn't that always the plan?"

"I agree," Kara said.

When no one countered, I looked at Dr. Nickel. I couldn't be the only one who didn't have that goal. "I don't," I admitted.

"Why not at least Christoph?" William asked, his brow low and heavy.

"Because it's what they're doing." My voice spiked. "It makes us no better than them."

Before I had time to continue, Alex was in front of me, his hands gripping my arms. We were gone before anyone had time to reach us. The familiar white abyss. The absence of air. The pressure.

When I opened my eyes, I immediately pinched them into a glare.

"Where are we? Take me back," I demanded.

He just laughed and stared past me at an abandoned shore, watching the waves float over the sand. Wherever we were, the sun was still out, which meant he'd carried me off to a different time zone. I couldn't do much but stand with my arms crossed.

"Well? What do you want, Alex?"

He looked at me, like my presence annoyed him. "The only reason I'm with you is to make sure Christoph dies. I'll kill him myself if I get the chance…I just—"

"I hope it doesn't come to that."

"I do," he said. "You can't be so weak. It's pathetic." He threw his arms up into the air. "He doesn't deserve sympathy."

"If we can find another way—"

He stepped toward me. "There is no other way. They die, or I'm gone. Then how will you communicate with anyone outside your circle, huh?"

"We'll manage," I said with a shrug. "It's not like you're really on our side anyway. I called you. You never came." I was in his face. Something in me felt strong enough to take him on.

"He took my ability! I couldn't come." He was glaring at me with his pool-blue eyes, but behind them, somewhere deeper, there was guilt. "I should leave you here," he said, his voice low and quiet.

"Fine."

It was a bluff. He stepped away, shaking his head. "You don't know what you're doing. You don't even know what you want."

I didn't speak. I was too angry at him for being right.

He looked back at me and touched my shoulder. "Figure it out," he said, and the blinding white took us back to my parents' house, amongst everyone else.

As soon as we appeared William's fist slammed into Alex's cheek. He looked at William, staring him down. "Ouch," he sneered, as he rubbed his jaw.

"Do that again, and you're gone," William said, slapping his hand a little too hard on Alex's shoulder.

"As I was saying," Dr. Nickel said, continuing the conversation I hadn't been a part of.

"Dad," William interrupted. "Don't take this the wrong way, but I think it's best you stay out of this."

Dr. Nickel cleared his throat. "Why's that, son?"

"People aren't going to be on board if a Council member is leading. Just lay low. Whatever Elyse decides is how it will go. We're here to follow her."

Dr. Nickel nodded at me to continue.

"Aside from whether or not they live or die," I said, "we need to agree on one thing." I looked at Anna sitting quietly with Chloe on the couch like they were trying to go unnoticed, and realized what I wanted. "Human integration. It's the only way to truly be free, and that's what we're fighting for. Freedom."

"I think we can all agree with that," Mac said. I was surprised to hear his voice. I didn't think he'd be on board with the idea, but then I followed his eyes. They were on Anna in a way that made me have to hold back a secret smile.

"So what's this plan you say you have?" Alex jumped in aggressively. "Because I don't believe you."

"What is your problem?" William said, stepping forward. I grabbed his arm and pulled him back. "No, he's right, William," I admitted. "I don't have a plan. I was hoping we could come up with one, all of us."

"Can I say something?" Kara asked. "No matter what our plan is, we need to train those people out there to defend themselves. Anyone on our side is at risk. They need to know how to fight."

"Okay," I agreed.

"What about dividing them into groups," Anna said from the couch. Everyone turned and stared at her, like she wasn't one of us. It made my skin crawl. Even they saw her as an outsider.

"What kind of groups?" I asked, trying to ignore everyone else.

"You know, like in the army they have recon, front line soldiers, cooks even." She shrugged and fidgeted with her hands. "I just mean, some people can't really fight, so—"

"That's a great idea." I folded my arms over my chest and raised my eyebrows at everyone around the table.

"Sounds smart to me," Kara agreed.

"We have to consider the threats," Dr. Nickel added. "Our last attempt at war failed because he threatened human life. He'll do it again, and we have to be prepared for that."

"You were aggressive before. We won't be," I said. "We'll lay low. Act quietly. They'll have no reason to kill humans or attack us if we aren't posing a threat."

"So, it's a coup d'état," William said, smiling widely. "I can live with that."

I nodded. "We'll just get more and more people on our side until they no longer have the control. Then we'll deal with human integration after that."

CHAPTER TWELVE

—

I WOKE UP TO THE SMELL OF BACON AND THE SOUND of jovial voices over the clanking of serving spoons on plates. William's chest was pressed against my back, and his heavy arm was draped over my side. The idea of a baby must have still been on his mind, because his hand was on my stomach. I didn't want to talk about it so I rolled over, forcing his hand to move to my back and nuzzled into his chest. It felt good to wake up here, where we were safe.

"Bacon," he moaned, his voice deep and crackling with sleep.

I laughed. "After all we've been through, and all the people waiting out there, your first thought is of cooked pork?"

"I know. I'm an animal."

His eyes finally opened, and we stared at each other across our pillows. "I'm nervous."

"You, nervous? I don't believe it."

I rolled my eyes. "Shut up."

"Come on," he said more seriously. "You were great yesterday. I've never seen you like that before. You were... amazing."

"What if they see through me?"

He reached forward and tucked a loose strand of hair behind my ear. "Then they'll see a person, like them, doing all she can to do what's right. Nobody's perfect. You can't expect yourself to be."

"Sometimes I feel like I should be wiser," I said. "I mean, I've lived ninety years. Why do I still feel so naïve?"

"I think everyone's different. There are old souls and young souls. For a lot of us, we act as old as we feel. Who wants to walk around acting like a grandpa, right?"

"Yeah, but you'd think after ninety years of life, I'd have a little more experience or knowledge...something. Sometimes I feel like I'm still a child."

He pushed his pillow down and moved his face closer to mine. "You've been sheltered. So have most of us, really. You know how my parents are. Kept me living at home for almost a century. Ninety years really isn't all that long if you think about it. My dad, now he has some stories."

"Like what?"

"He used to tell me about the Civil War. It was a different time. Boys had to be men. Now, life's too easy."

"It won't be. Not for much longer."

He leaned over to kiss my cheek, and as his fingers grazed my skin, I wanted more. I pressed a hand to his chest, holding him down so he couldn't escape my kiss. It was the perfect way to avoid what was waiting for me outside. At first he fell for it. He pushed against my lower back, scooting me closer to him. Every time our lips parted I breathed. There was no reason to stop.

I peeled his shirt up over his head and reached for my own.

"Ellie," he said, stopping me.

I paused with the hem of my shirt in my hands. "What?"

"I just don't think this is a good idea."

"What do you mean?" I protested.

"You know," he said, hiking his shoulders. "Do you think you're really...pregnant?"

I didn't answer. I knew I was, but he didn't.

"Because if you're not," he continued. "This could mean..." He shook his head. "Do you really want to take that chance?"

I slouched back into the soft mattress. So maybe I didn't know for sure. I was taking Adrianna's word for it. "No," I answered.

———

WHEN I STEPPED OUTSIDE AMONGST THE PEOPLE LINING up for breakfast and gathering at tables, everyone got quiet. They stared at me like my presence meant something. It startled me. I wasn't expecting such sudden attention. I looked around, meeting curious eyes and smiled, like I was trying to pass myself off as one of them. I couldn't think of what else to do.

"All right. Let the girl get some food," Mac yelled from behind me. It seemed to lighten the mood and voices began again. I turned to him with gratitude, but he was too busy tucking a knife into the side of his belt. "Well, get in line. You're not expecting special treatment are you?"

I laughed. "No."

"I was," William said as he stepped up beside me. He grabbed my hand, and we walked toward the back of the line. Eyes followed us, but I was met with kindness when I looked back, and each person stepped aside to let us go ahead of them.

"No, it's fine," I resisted uncomfortably, but hands pushed me ahead until William and I were beneath the white canvas canopy.

I tried to stand taller and keep my shoulders straight, hoping to seem more worthy of this treatment, as we inched forward toward the table of potatoes, eggs, and bacon.

"Good morning," Cearno said cheerfully from behind the grill. "Help yourselves."

It was a relief to see someone I knew. "Hi, Cearno."

"Take some extra bacon," he said through his gray beard, and I gladly accepted. Anything he made was bound to be delicious.

"Thanks." We shared a look, and I followed William to a nearby table.

The camp was set up in a circle with clusters of tents

bordering its edges. To the left was a large white canvas hut. I couldn't see what was in it, but I assumed it was a meeting place. In the center of camp was the largest fire pit, but I could see others in the distance. Small pillars of smoke billowed up from places amongst the tents, providing warmth in the chilly morning air. The familiar pine and birch trees from my past surrounded us. Some had no leaves this time of year, but all had grown since I was a child. It was strange to see my family home transformed like this. It used to be my own secret place. Now it was just...a place to be.

Beyond the canvas hut were a few rows of brown multi-purpose tables with metal fold-out chairs. Just before William and I took our spots at one of them, Sam and Nics caught sight of us and ran over with wide smiles.

"So, what? Only the *special* people are allowed inside the house? Best friends don't get access?" Sam punched William in the shoulder playfully and then slapped his big hands on his back as they hugged.

Nics nearly tackled me, squeezing her arms around my torso until I couldn't breathe. "We were worried," she said, shoving me.

"I wasn't," Sam said with a shrug.

"Everything I say, he has to say the opposite," Nics complained. The tops of her ebony cheeks gleamed in the sunlight.

I missed their bickering. It was nice to be back amongst friends. As they continued, I caught myself eyeing the streaks of gray in Sam's sand-colored hair. Kara's memory had taught me what he must have gone through for trying to save that human girl on the beach so long ago. It wasn't right to have years stripped from your life for trying to do something good. Those were the reasons we were here. That type of punishment had to stop.

"So what has everyone been doing?" I asked, trying to get a feel of what would be expected of me.

"We've just been waiting," Nics answered as she sat opposite us.

"For what?" I asked.

Sam looked at me like it was obvious. "For you."

Without warning, Rachel and Paul ambushed us. The two of them flew in spiral formation through the air, Rachel nothing but a tiny rainbow ball of light. After nearly crashing into our table, Rachel returned to her bodily form and wrapped her arms around my neck. Locks of her wavy blonde hair fell into my eyes as she smashed her face close to mine. "You're here!"

Paul sat next to William and put a strong tan arm over his shoulders in a half-hug. "Why didn't you guys come say hi last night?"

William shrugged. "Escaping from Christoph is a little exhausting."

"So it's true? That was the rumor, but we weren't sure."

"That's crazy," Rachel beamed as she slid in beside me. "How'd you escape?"

"Naturally cunning instincts," William answered.

I laughed. "Yeah. Right." I took a bite of my pan-fried potatoes, savoring the flavor of garlic and pepper. "It was pure luck."

I let William tell the full story, only interrupting when necessary or to reel in his exaggerations. For a while, I hardly noticed the crowd developing in the large white tent to my right.

"So, now that you're here," Nics asked, "what's the plan? What's this morning's meeting about?"

"Meeting?"

"Yeah," Nics answered. "You said we'd start in the morning. Everyone's expecting you to tell them what to do." She looked back and forth between William and me. "You do have a plan, right?"

People were flocking toward the tent, watching me as they passed. I knew they were waiting for me. They had the same question Nics had.

"Yeah," I said, staring at the groups of people coming together. "We get ready to fight. We organize our troops, prepare for attacks, and communicate exactly what it is we're fighting for."

My words took them all off guard. I didn't know what they were expecting me to say, but I could tell they were surprised.

"All right!" Paul said, slamming the table with his fist.

When we finished eating I stepped into the tent, but this time, people didn't stop talking to stare. The air was charged. I could feel their energy as a hundred conversations jumbled together. Their anticipation made my stomach flutter with stage fright, but I knew what I needed to say.

Against the canvas wall of the tent, I saw Anna and Chloe. Anna smiled at me, even though I knew she didn't feel comfortable here. Most didn't know they weren't Descendants. I beckoned for them to come to the front where I stood with William, our friends, Kara, Alex, Mac, and Dr. Nickel. Every single person here was in this tent, and they were all waiting for me to step forward and speak.

Logs had been placed in lines like rows of benches, and people sat on and against them while others stood. The younger ones sat in groups cross-legged on the dry grassy dirt in front, giggling and whispering secrets.

"Can you get me a chair?" I asked Rachel. She snapped into her messenger form, the small multi-colored ball of light, and zipped outside to get a metal folding chair.

I hugged Anna and Chloe as they stepped next to me. "Somebody's popular," Anna said with a sarcastic smile.

"Want to trade places?" I joked. She knew this wasn't me. I was shy and nervous. I wasn't a leader, but I needed to be, and I'd surprised myself these days.

"Are you going to tell them about us?" she whispered into my ear.

I nodded. "I have to."

She raised her eyebrows and gave me a look that said, "All right, here we go."

They couldn't be kept a secret anymore. Their presence

here was a symbol of what we were fighting for.

I squeezed her hand and stepped onto the chair.

"Good morning," I spoke, loud and confident like before. The crowd quieted, and my heart pounded. "If you're going to stay here, you should know what we're fighting for." My eyes drifted from face to face, and I straightened my shoulders. "We're fighting for a life free of The Council's oppression. One where we don't have to fear for our lives if we show compassion to someone who needs a helping hand. We shouldn't have to live in hiding, afraid to be ourselves, afraid to help others. Those who are here are fighting for the right to undo some of the wrongs in this world. We're fighting for a future where years of our lives aren't stolen from us for doing good deeds." Sam stared back at me with a hard jaw and passion in his eyes. I shifted my gaze to Kara. "A future where we don't kill for someone else's cause out of fear for our families, where we aren't forced to take human life to save our own." I swallowed down the heat and anger brewing in my chest. "I want to live in a world where humans and Descendants can live in peace together. A world where the consequences of loving another race isn't death. People who stay are those who want a new way of life. Who want to fight for freedom." I put my hand on Anna's shoulder. "This is Anna. I've known her since I was in my fifties. I was there when her daughter Chloe was born. They're my family. And they're human."

Not a sound was uttered amongst the crowd. My

throat felt dry as I waited for them to erupt into a protest, but no one said a word. I searched the sea of nervous eyes for someone who didn't approve, but only found surprise and acceptance in the faces that stared back at me. "If you don't believe that human integration is the key to freedom, that is your right, but you don't belong here." I stood confidently with William closely beside me. He smiled with pride, and that alone gave me strength. If everyone left but him, I'd be okay.

I expected at least a few people to straggle out with their heads down, but not a single person moved from their spot. "It's not going to happen tomorrow," I continued. "It will be a long and slow transition, and we'll need your support, your loyalty. You are the beginning." I took a deep breath. "To freedom."

"To freedom," a few responded with zest. Fists rose into the air, and soon the tent erupted, not with protest but with approval. I laughed. I couldn't help it.

The whole morning was chaos. The older moms put together lunch for everyone. Sofia and Anna had gotten close, and they organized the effort as a team. William took charge of separating people into groups by their abilities or skills and set up a table alongside the house to start interviews. Dr. Nickel and Mac sat at one end, Kara and Alex in the middle, and William and I to their left. Three lines formed and people joined them anxiously.

"Bloodline?" William asked the first person, who happened to be his best friend.

"Seriously?" Sam said with raised eyebrows.

William just smiled and wrote *Dionysus* on his list next to Sam's name.

"So what group do you want to be in?" I asked, resting my forearms on the table.

"What are my choices?" Sam asked.

I looked over at William's list. "Reconnaissance, Personnel, Food Service and Supply, Medical Care, Infantry, Recruiting, Weaponry, or Communications." The groups reminded me that this wasn't a game. Under the heading *Command and Control* were six names: Elyse, William, Mac, Marcus, Kara, and Alex.

"Reconnaissance," he said with a nod.

"Me too," Nics added, cutting in line beside him.

Rachel and Paul landed behind us and peeked over William's shoulder.

"Reconnaissance?" Rachel whined.

"Why?" Paul said, pulling her close to him and kissing her cheek. "What would you choose?"

"Personnel maybe."

"B-o-r-i-n-g," Sam said in monotone.

"So pick personnel," Nics told her. "You don't have to be in our group."

"I'm not going to be alone," she scoffed. "Put me in recon."

It took most of the day to assign everyone to a group, and the atmosphere was thick with anticipation. Training would begin in the morning.

It was easier to see the campfires at night. There were seven throughout the tents, and the cold air carried the smell of burning pine. I sat with the largest group gathered around the central fire. They were telling stories and playing games, but I only sat and watched. My mind was on other things. The prophecy. Thoughts of my people fighting for their lives. These carefree nights wouldn't last. Who would they blame when things went wrong, when things got worse?

"Come on," William whispered in my ear. He took my hand and pulled me off into the darkness.

It was easy to keep from being seen when we were outside the dim glow of the fire. We headed for the creek leaving the laughter behind us.

"Everything okay? Too many people?" His hand was warm against mine, despite the cold. "You know, we could forget this whole prophecy thing and elope," he said with a laugh.

"We could," I answered, letting myself give in to the idea, even if just for a moment. "Where would we go?"

He looked at me through the moonlight, judging my sincerity. "Come on, I know you're not serious."

"Just for fun then." I pulled my black jacket tighter around me with my free hand. "Where would we go?"

"I don't know," he said, thinking about it. "Europe, maybe."

"Are there Descendants there?"

"Some. Not a lot." I could see his breath as he spoke.

His answer didn't seem right. "Why is that? Why America? Why not Greece?"

"America used to be undiscovered."

I nodded, making the connection. "The perfect place to hide."

"If you ever want to get out, I'm sure we could find our own perfect place." He pulled me in close, holding me to his chest. "I'm not above running and hiding."

I laughed, knowing he was smiling as he rested his cheek against my forehead.

We both knew that wasn't an option. I couldn't run. I couldn't hide. Everyone had been waiting for me.

CHAPTER THIRTEEN

—

FOR THE NEXT WEEK MAC WOKE EVERYONE AT 6 A.M., his voice bellowing through the trees.

"Get up, you lazy dogs. All right, get up."

Every morning eyes were wide as people began to stir. No one seemed tired. Instead it was how I imagined the first week of summer camp to be. I didn't understand it. I ate breakfast quietly, letting the rolling pitch of Rachel's voice fade to the background. Only she could find a reason to be excited about training for war.

"First rule," William yelled to our training group after breakfast. "No abilities." He paced in front of everyone with his hands on his hips, and I noticed how much older he looked having gone without shaving the past few days. "We all know Christoph and Adrianna can strip us of our powers, and everyone needs to be ready to defend themselves physically, even if it's a last resort." He looked at me briefly, and I was reminded of Helen's class at The Institute when we thought she was crazy for having us duel. This seemed crazier. "Second rule. We're not trying to kill each other here, but don't hold back either. Christoph won't be taking it easy on us if it comes to that. We have a healer and a medic team if needed."

The name Christoph stuck in my head, and for a moment I thought I saw him standing across from me. I closed my eyes to clear my head, but when I opened them, he *was* standing there. He glared back at me clear as day, right next to William. My heart picked up as I looked around. Didn't anybody see him? I opened my mouth to warn everyone to run, to shoot, to kill, but William walked right through him like he was a ghost. Before I'd uttered a word, the image disappeared like smoke.

You okay? Kara asked from beside me. She stared forward as she spoke.

I turned to her, knowing she must have seen him too, at least through my mind.

What was that? I asked.

What?

You didn't see him?

I heard you get all worked up about it, but there was nothing there.

Even through my mind?

She shook her head. *No.*

"Kara and Alex will demonstrate," William announced to the group. I tried to pay attention, but my eyes wandered in search for Christoph. The sight of him had left an uneasy feeling in my stomach.

Kara stepped forward, facing Alex with a smirk on her face. "This really isn't a fair fight," she said.

Alex raised his eyebrows. "We'll see."

No Christoph. I had imagined him. I relaxed my shoulders, and my heart began to settle as I focused on Kara and Alex. It was stress. Just stress.

"Remember. No abilities," Mac reminded them, but I could see from the way they looked at each other, his rule wouldn't last.

Kara was already swinging before Mac had a chance to say go. Her fist found the air to the right of Alex's face. He was fast, even without his ability.

Kara tilted her head, impressed.

"What?" he said with a cocky grin. "You're not the only one who's gone through Council combat training."

Despite their words, there was enjoyment behind their eyes as they stared each other down. They were so much alike. I wondered if they realized it.

She swung again and missed, but her punch was strong. If she made contact, she could easily knock him out. Next Alex threw a fist, but Kara grabbed his wrist and knocked him in the jaw with her elbow.

"Oops," she said, and I noticed a hint of flirtation in her voice.

Alex opened his mouth wide, stretching his cheek muscles and shook his head. "Here I was taking it easy on you."

Kara bounced on her toes. "Oh, sure."

With each snarky comment the small crowd around them reacted. I caught William's eye, and he gave me a look after watching Kara revel in her hit. He'd picked up on it too, and I pressed my lips together, trying not to smile at their strange way of flirting.

After a few seconds of circling, they lunged at each other. One slipped in and out of the other's grasp, both dodging blows until Alex finally had Kara's neck in the crook of his elbow. "Good thing you're a girl. It wouldn't be right to hit a girl," he said loudly into her ear.

She stopped struggling, which made him loosen his grip. This time a cocky grin settled into *her* cheeks before she smacked him in the mouth with the back of her head. "Good thing you're a boy," she said. "I have no problem hitting boys."

The people around me laughed, including William. Even I couldn't help but smile.

Alex licked the blood off of his upper lip and disappeared.

"No abilities," Mac grumbled from the sidelines, but Kara didn't let it distract her.

When Alex appeared at her side she was ready. With her eyes closed she blocked every blow as Alex snapped in and out of place trying every angle. First her palm knocked him in the chin. He disappeared. Then an elbow to the throat. He disappeared. A knee to the gut.

I'd never seen Kara fight like this, and I couldn't look

away. Everything was so fast, impossible to predict. The next time Alex reappeared it was from a distance.

"All right," he said, feigning indifference. "So you win. Who's next?"

Sam pushed Paul into the center of the crowd. "We are," he said, throwing a few fake punches into the air.

Nics rolled her eyes. "Oh, give me a break."

"All right," Kara said. "I'll take you, Sam. Alex gets Paul."

Sam's smile dropped. "Wait, what?"

"This is going to be good," William laughed next to me.

Neither one of them knew what they were doing. Sam's long lanky arms threw awkward punches, and Paul was slow without his ability to fly. By the time it was over, tiny Kara had Sam on his belly in a chokehold crying for mercy. Nobody could keep from laughing.

I tried to relax and have fun that night, but I couldn't get away from the image of Christoph standing in the middle of our camp. I hadn't told anyone and wasn't planning on it, but it was haunting me.

"Whoa don't mess with Kara," Sam said as we huddled around our little fire. I hadn't been listening to the conversation, but his loud voice caught my attention. "You saw what she did to Alex today. She's a beast."

I watched Kara through the flames of our campfire. She looked away from us, but she was holding back a smile.

"What she did to Alex? What about what she did to

you?" Nics jabbed Sam in the ribs.

He shrugged. "Whatever. I don't feel too bad if badass disappear guy can't even touch her."

"Yeah, yeah. Laugh it up," Alex shook his head. His eyes stayed on Kara too long. She pretended not to notice, though I knew she did. She raised her eyebrows at me.

Really, Elyse?

I smiled at her through flickering ribbons of orange flame.

"Say it's the perfect world," Rachel said to the group. "You're free to be who you are. No consequences. No prejudice. What's the first thing you would do?"

"Start my own wine label," Sam said without hesitating. "I'd make a killing." All of us laughed, because he would. His wine was amazing.

Our laughter was contagious. The group next to us cheered and hollered at something. They sang too loudly, lyrics to a song I didn't know. Anna and Chloe were over there somewhere with Mac. The stars were out. The air was fresh. People were happy tonight.

"I'd travel the world," Alex answered. "My way." He scooted forward, warming his hands by the fire.

"You can do that now, can't you?" Rachel asked.

He shook his head. "Too risky. You can't just appear on top of the Eiffel Tower without someone noticing."

"I think we'd do the same," Paul said looking at Rachel, and she nodded.

"How about you, William?" Sam asked.

He leaned forward, resting his forearms on his knees. "Not much. Get a house." He looked at me with mischievous eyes. "Make babies."

His last two words threw the rest of the group into a riot of taunting jeers. I threw my hands over my face to seem like it was out of embarrassment, and maybe it was a little, but really I was hiding. Hiding from the truth. He bear-hugged me from the side and kissed my cheeks until I lifted my hands and kissed him back. Just a quick touch of our lips to bring closure to the moment.

"But seriously," Sam protested. "You could be a crime-fighting superhero. Hypnotize bad-guys with your love stare."

I let myself lean into William now that the focus was off of me, but I was still red.

"That's what I'd do," Nics continued. "I'd be a good superhero, right?"

"I don't know," Sam answered. "You're not so good at taking orders."

"What?"

As the bickering started, I stopped listening. Kara was the only one who noticed. I couldn't get my mind off of the idea of a baby, my baby. She didn't say anything. She didn't need to. Her eyes said enough. *It'll be okay.*

But would it?

I tried to stay positive. Everyone else was. Things were looking up. We had a system. We were preparing for battle, talking about plans of action. Sure, nothing was decided about when to act against Christoph, when to expose our race and how, but we had a long way to go before we got there. At least we were headed in the right direction. We were closer to being where we should be, closer than we were when I was alone with Mac and William, or when I was locked in the mansion.

"Well tomorrow, I'm challenging Elyse," Rachel said with sass. "I want to see what kind of a wild woman she's turned into, training with Kara and Mac all day." She smiled at me. "You and me, baby."

I laughed at her feisty attitude. "You're on."

As I lay in bed next to William that night, I realized they never asked me what I'd do. Maybe to them it was obvious: try to heal the sick as best I could. That would have been my answer, but would it have been the truth? The thought scared me. The pressure. The expectation. The consequences. I knew what was right. What we should be fighting for. We all wanted freedom, but freedom wouldn't come easily. Would all of this backfire? Would I find myself in a lab, held captive, being tested if things didn't go as planned?

As I slept, I dreamt I was alone in the camp, walking in between patches of scattered sagebrush and picking off the tops of tall weeds that reached for my fingertips. The sun warmed my shoulders and the wind carried the spicy smell of pine trees with it.

Out of the corner of my eye, I saw someone, but every time I turned to look, no one was there. Sweat collected on my palms with each glimpse of a man just out of sight. I didn't need to see him. I knew who it was. *Don't be scared,* I told myself. *This is just a dream.* My heart ignored the thought. It was too real. It kicked at my chest, and I heard it in my ears as I waited for him to come from a direction I did not expect.

My eyes were alert, snapping back and forth from tree to tree. They caught sight of something in front of me, just beyond a distant trunk—Christoph.

I knew I should run, but he just stood there, staring.

"Whether it's the humans or me. One of us is going to get to you. There's no way out," he said, his voice ringing with sick amusement as his lips curled.

He looked at me, snapped his fingers, and flames shot up the trees. Everything was burning.

I woke to the feeling of fire all around me.

CHAPTER FOURTEEN

—

THE MOMENT MY EYES OPENED, I FELT THE HEAT. MY lungs, eager for air, sucked in nothing but black smoke. I couldn't breathe. I cupped my hands over my mouth and nose, but it didn't help. Orange flames whipped around me, reaching for my bare skin and searing my clothes.

"William," I choked. His face was beaded with sweat. "William!" I shook him, and he woke up gasping and coughing.

Without saying a word he jumped off the bed and wrapped a blanket around us. I grabbed my dart gun and bag of darts from the bedside table, clutching them to my chest. Flames were shooting through the window, so we headed for the bedroom door.

"Let's get out of here," Alex yelled from across the burning living room. He and Kara were next to us in seconds.

"Anna!" I screamed. I pulled away from William, leaving

the blanket and heading for my old room. I coughed and hacked as I inhaled the smoke, but I ignored my body.

Kara caught my arm. "Elyse, they're not here," she said over the crackling and popping of the fire. "Come on."

"Wait!" I cried. I panicked as the remnants of my family home went up in flames around me. I needed one thing. *The Art of War.* I couldn't leave without it.

No, Kara told me. *It's gone. Let it go. We're going to die in here.*

My eyes were watering, or maybe I was crying. I was angry, irrational, crazy. William threw the blanket around me again and dragged me toward Alex. Then, all I saw was white, and we were gone.

When we landed I didn't recognize where we were. Everything around me was burning. People were running, screaming, fighting for their lives. We were being attacked. I strapped my dart gun holster to my leg and hit the buttons on my bracelet without thinking. William looked at me with worry, and I stared back, both of us pleading for the other to be safe. Without a word we took off toward the fight.

I recognized most of the faces around me, but no Anna or Chloe. Gunshots punched loud holes in the air. A woman fell, and I shot my first blood soaked dart into the back of a tall man with a gun. The dart was a hollow. He fell. He was as good as dead.

Out of the corner of my eye I saw Kara wrestle a thick girl to the ground. She slit her throat with one fluid motion, and for a second I couldn't look away. The screaming was carried through the wind—incessant.

To my left, a young boy began to sink into the ground like it was quicksand. I sent another dart into the chest of the older woman who was trying to bury him alive. I shot a second one into her neck just because the idea of burying someone alive made me sick.

My throat stung as I searched for Anna and Chloe. What sort of horror would they face? How would they defend themselves? I felt nauseated, but I couldn't lose it now. I didn't know if they were dead. They could be safe. Please let everyone be safe.

People ran, fought, shot weapons, scattered. Fire curled around the house and the trees. Smoke billowed into the sky turning it black. From the left a man charged at me with a knife, and I couldn't get my dart ready fast enough. My heart beat wildly. I turned to run. Then I heard him fall and saw the arrow in his back. I didn't know where he'd gotten the bow, but William stood behind him. He stared at me, warning me to be quicker.

"Be careful," he yelled. We both turned and shot a pair of gunmen in the distance. "You need to get out of here."

I shook my head and charged after the man causing the fire. It shot from his hands as he burned the world around him, the flames consuming trees, the house, people.

Heat waves blurred my vision and sweat rolled down the sides of my face as I closed in on him. I punched the buttons on my wrist again. Blood soaked the dart and dripped from my fingers. I aimed at the man with fire, but he spotted me and dodged the shot. I loaded again, but he was closer, aiming the flames at me. The heat, the smoke, everything began to swarm in. I grabbed a knife sticking up from the chest of an unfamiliar body and threw it in his direction. It spun fast, but he was quick, trained. The knife grazed his cheek, and that only made him angry.

I loaded another dart, but it was too late. I turned as he threw fire at me. The flames caught my back, and no matter how fast I tried to run, the heat kept up. I inhaled from the shock of pain, unable to breathe or scream. Then William was there. His arrow flew past me, and I prayed it hit the man, that it would extinguish the fire. I heard him cry out behind me and knew the flames must have stopped, but the burning continued.

I fell forward in agony, and rolled along the ground, but the fire ate away at my flesh. I saw William's tortured face as he ran toward me. Then the familiar euphoria spread. His ability held me even when I was in pain. I no longer cared about pain. All I cared about was him. I couldn't look away. I didn't care that I was burning. When his knees slid in next to me, I heard him whisper into my ear.

"Sleep," he said, and I obeyed.

———

I AWOKE SUBMERGED IN WATER. MY FIRST INSTINCT was to breathe, and it was wrong. Water filled my lungs, and my body convulsed, desperate to escape. Someone pulled me to the surface. I coughed out water and choked on air.

"You're okay," William said, and I wrapped my arms around his neck. He picked me up, and my legs looped around the front of his body as he carried me to the shore. I was shaking. It felt like my back was still on fire, but I tried to stay calm and still.

"Take us back," I insisted when I saw Alex. I didn't know how I'd move, but I knew I had to try. "We have to go back. What about Anna, Chloe, Mac, everyone—"

"*We* aren't going anywhere." Alex looked at me like I was crazy and disappeared.

William set me on my feet, and I cried out. Even the smallest movements set me on fire again. The air against my skin felt like flames.

"Try and lie on your belly," he said to me. My breath was shallow and quick, but I made my way to the ground wincing as each muscle in my back flexed. I let out a full breath when the front of my body relaxed against the dirt. William knelt down next to me, his ability flooding me with euphoria once again, until I no longer cared about the pain.

He took the knife from my boot, and I felt his fingers examining the burns on my back. His touch was thrilling, even though it stung. The knife cut my shirt in places that hadn't been burned through so my whole back was exposed.

It felt good to get the fabric off, but the wind still

licked my wounds with its fiery tongue. I was thankful the euphoria at least muted the pain.

"You're okay," he said softly. "It'll be gone soon."

I turned my head toward him and watched as he slid the knife across his palm. He didn't flinch anymore, and I loved him so much for being here, for helping me.

As the drops trickled across my skin, I sighed with relief. "Thank you," I said, feeling his blood heal my burns. He kissed my head, and I closed my eyes as he used his unwounded hand to spread it.

When he was done, he released his hold on me. I waited for the pain to return as I stood, trying not to move my back, but I didn't need to. It didn't hurt anymore. I held the remnants of my shirt to my chest, realizing it was the only shirt I had left. Everything was gone. I silently hoped my friends and family were still alive.

"Better?" William asked.

I nodded. "Yeah. Thank you." I moved my bracelet to my right wrist, hit the buttons to draw blood, and unclasped it. "Here."

His familiar grip wrapped around my new wounds, and we healed each other. It still amazed me. I looked at my newly healed flesh and re-clasped the bracelet.

With the pain gone, I was finally coming back to myself. William's face was splotched with soot, his clothes singed and black. Despite the fact that we were safe, I couldn't relax. The fight was still taking place.

"Alaximandrios," I said, waiting for Alex to reappear

and take us back. "Alaximandrios." I tapped my toes against the ground impatiently. "Why isn't he coming?"

"It was intense back there. You can't expect him to drop everything and come back for you." The muscles in William's jaw pulsed, and I could tell it was hard for him to be away, too.

I brushed my wet hair back and started pacing. "I don't understand how this happened."

"Christoph found us," he said like it was obvious.

"But how?" I moved to sit against a nearby tree and William sat next to me. "The safe haven...I just."

"Someone must be playing both sides. Either that or he has someone with the ability to find people, but I really doubt it. I don't think it exists."

"So you think there's a mole?"

He picked at the dry grass between us. "Something like that."

I started to remember flashes of what we left behind. People screaming, running, dying. How could anyone want that?

"This is my fault, William," I said. "I'm supposed to lead. I'm supposed to protect everyone. They trusted me—"

"Hey," he said, interrupting my rising voice. He looked at me, his eyes steady and serious. "This is how it's going to be now. You can't keep blaming yourself for things, and you can't cave every time there's bloodshed. It's a war, Elyse."

It wasn't what I expected from him. I expected sympathy,

comfort. I wanted him to tell me everything was all right even though I knew it wasn't. "I know. It's just...I didn't think it would actually happen."

"Well, it has, and they're counting on you to be strong." His words weren't mean. They were honest.

"But I'm not strong. I'm not a leader," I said, still floundering.

"You are. When you want something, when you have something to fight for, you don't let anything or anyone stop you. Just like you didn't let anything get in the way of saving Anna's life. You just have to remember what you're fighting for."

"I don't know," I confessed.

"You do know," he said, moving to face me. He took my hands in his, and the warmth of his palms gave me confidence. "You're fighting for those you love. For Anna and Chloe. For Kara. For us. So we can live in a world free of oppression."

"But what if I'm wrong? What if human integration isn't the right choice?"

"You can't dwell on what ifs. You do what you believe is right."

I nodded, trying to convince myself that what I believed in was worth the lives of those who had already died. William pulled me closer, and I lay against his chest looking out at the lake in front of us. Ripples broke the smooth plane of the calm water, and pine trees crowded the edges of the clay beach. I realized where we were and felt safe.

"If anything ever happens and we get separated. Meet me here, okay?"

His warm fingertips stroked the bare skin of my back. "I don't even know where we are."

"It's called Frenchman's Lake," I said, remembering my feet sinking into the muddy bottom when I was a kid. "I used to come here with my mother and father in the summer. This was our favorite spot. Crystal Point."

"Sure," he said, "but I won't ever let that happen."

When Alex reappeared, I stood immediately. "Where have you been?" I demanded.

His face was too serious, and he only looked at me before reappearing in the branches of a nearby tree. "Mac told me to keep you away." He reached for the blue shirt hanging in his back pocket and threw it at me. "You're welcome."

"Is it over?" William asked.

"Yeah," he answered. "But it's bad. Your dad's taking care of things."

"What about Anna and Chloe?" I added after I had the shirt over my head. "What about everyone else?"

"They're fine. Most people got out."

"Most?" William repeated.

I stared hard at Alex, trying to muster as much authority in my voice as I could. "I need to be there."

"I agree," he said, "you shouldn't be kept in the dark. Even if he is trying to protect you." In less than a second

Alex was next to me, and William's hand was in mine.

The sky was shadowed with smoke when my eyes opened, and the land was scorched black. The three of us stayed alert as we headed toward the house, still smoldering and collapsing in the center. Voices came from the front, orders being shouted. My feet quickened, crunching the burned grass with each step.

Something stopped me in my tracks when I reached the back of the house—bodies. The dead were lined up in a neat row along the ground. A wave of nausea hit me, and I broke into a cold sweat. I turned back, catching sight of William and Alex behind me. "So many." The thought triggered panic. Who had he murdered? My heart picked up speed.

"Elyse!" The sound of Anna's voice made me whip my head around, and there she was, her face smeared with soot and dirt like everyone else.

"Chloe?" I ask, my voice hurried.

"She's fine. We're okay." I hugged her tightly, grateful she was alive. "Luckily I know the place. We hid in the abandoned truck by the road."

We stared at each other, speaking mostly with our eyes. I didn't know what I would have done if something had happened to them.

I took her hand. "I'm glad you're okay." William's words echoed in my head. *Remember what you're fighting for.*

"Come on," she said, leading the three of us toward a

large white canopy set up in front of the house.

"I told you not to bring her here," Mac yelled as he saw us approaching.

"Yeah. I don't always do what people tell me," Alex said, "just so you know."

Mac tightened his lips and his eyes hardened.

"She should be here, Mac," Anna said, stepping beside him.

"If they come back—"

"Where's Mom and Dad?" William interrupted. "Is Edith okay?"

"They're fine," Mac answered. "Your mom and sister are looking after the injured. Your dad is seeing to the dead."

I turned my head to the right, forcing myself to look at the bodies lying in a line a few yards off. I didn't want to see their faces, but my feet carried me in that direction regardless, and William followed.

"Son," Dr. Nickel said with relief as we approached. His disheveled gray hair fell into his face, and he clutched the sides of William's shoulders as they hugged. "I didn't know if..." His father's eyes fell as he released him. I could see tears glistening in the corners. "I thought I'd lost you, too."

I kept my distance, trying to stay out of their moment. I'd never seen Dr. Nickel so fragile.

"I'm fine," William said, his words little more than a whisper.

They stared at each other, speaking more than I knew. "I couldn't lose another son."

I went still at his words, trying not to let the shock show on my face. William had a brother? Apparently I wasn't the only one keeping secrets.

"War has its price," William answered, his brow tight with tension. "This is what you wanted."

Dr. Nickel shook his head. I felt like I shouldn't be listening, but it might distract them if I walked away. I picked my cuticles and tried to keep my eyes down.

"I never wanted your brother to die, and it's not what I want for you either, but...I won't let Luke's death be in vain." He rested a heavy hand on his son's shoulder, and I looked up for a moment, just in time to see the anger in William's face.

"How many did we lose?" William asked, changing the subject.

Dr. Nickel looked at his notebook. He must have been taking names. "Twenty-seven," he answered with a sigh. His eyes found me for the first time, like I'd appeared out of nowhere. "Most of them were ours. Some were his."

I looked down at the man at my feet. Gray hair. Small and stout. I covered my mouth with my hand when I recognized his face.

"Cearno," the word slipped from my lips without me realizing. I swallowed and tried to settle my heart.

"He was a good man," Dr. Nickel said, before he continued walking down the line.

William took my hand as we said our silent goodbye to him. I couldn't imagine how it felt for William to see Cearno lying lifeless at his feet after so many years of friendship, but he only stood there, holding it all in just as he had with his brother. I wondered how many other friends of ours had died. The thought made me sick to my stomach. Sam, Nics, Paul, and Rachel were supposed to have left that morning on a recon mission. I assumed they were safe, but I hadn't seen Kara.

I couldn't look at Cearno anymore. "I'm sorry," I said.

I turned and stared at the place my parents' house once stood. There was nothing left but a black heap of charred wood and ash. Nothing could be salvaged.

"Are you going to be okay?" William asked. He put his hot hand in mine as he led me away from the dead.

I didn't answer.

"When were you going to tell me about Luke?" I asked when we reached the remnants of the house. Part of me knew it was the wrong time to ask that question, but I couldn't help it. The lives of everyone who'd died in their fight against Christoph weighed on me, including his brother.

He rubbed the back of his neck. "I wasn't."

His answer surprised me. "Why?"

"It's in the past," he said with a shrug. "I've moved on." The muscles clenched in his cheek telling me he hadn't really.

I looked at him. "That doesn't mean you should

forget about him."

"I haven't." His lips tightened. "It's just not something I like to talk about."

I nodded, accepting the fact that he didn't want to tell me what happened. A part of me was a little hurt, but I understood secrets. I had my own.

I squeezed our palms together and turned back to the rubble, taking in the feeling of defeat. The smoldering wood smelled smoky and sharp. It stung my nose, but I didn't care. It was all that was left of this place. I didn't want to let it go.

"He died in the last war," William said, pressing the tips of his shoes into the ash. "My dad tried to keep him out of it, but Luke had his bloodline. It was in him to fight. He felt like he had to."

"So he was next in line to join The Council, before Edith."

"Yes." The way his voice dropped I could tell he was worried for his sister.

"What happened?"

"He heard word of an attack and snuck out. He was only seventy-three. My dad didn't even know he was there. He found his body the next morning."

"I'm sorry," I said, looking at him, but his eyes stayed forward.

"I guess I always thought of it as my dad's war before, so I blamed him." His face twisted into a scowl. "He's so eager to fight, even though it puts everyone he loves at risk." He turned to face me. "I'm not like that. I don't want this. I don't want there to be a war, and I don't want you to fight or lead." It all came spilling out, and a part of me knew he felt that way, but he'd been keeping it inside.

I didn't know what to say. I didn't really have a choice. Instead, I leaned into him, wrapping my arms around his body as he held me.

"I realize that's selfish," he continued, "and I'm trying not to focus on what I want. I'm trying to be like you and do what's right, it's just...we can't let this happen again." He turned to face the line of dead and clustering wounded behind us. "We can't stay here."

I bent down, picking up a twisted piece of metal that used to be a framed picture of my mother, still taking in everything he'd said. Deep down I felt the same. I worried for the ones I loved, but I couldn't turn back now. Not after this. "You're right," I said. "They'll be back, and they'll keep coming until they find me."

I looked out toward the groups of limping and groaning people under a distant canopy, and began to walk in their direction. I knew I'd have to see to the wounded. I was the only healer. Still, I didn't want to face the broken hearts, the gruesome wounds, the pain I knew I'd find there.

The moment eyes caught sight of me people began to trickle out. They moved faster than I'd expected, until they were swarming. I wouldn't be able to heal them all.

"Can you heal her burns?" A mother asked me, pushing her young daughter forward.

"And my leg," a boy said. He limped alongside me as I walked toward the canopy where more wounded had gathered.

"I've lost my sight," another man said. "Can you heal that?"

Voices began to grow into a cacophony of sound as people begged for help. They pushed closer until William and I were encircled.

"Wait," I shouted as people started to push and shove to get to me, but none of them listened. They were desperate. I felt a hand grab my wrist, fingers on my neck, but William's grip stayed strong as he tried to pull me through the crowd.

When he stopped, I panicked. "Go," I yelled.

The groping hands didn't hurt me, but they suffocated. I needed out. I shut my eyes to try and escape any way I could. The noise, their heavy breath, their cries for my help, it was too much.

I tried to focus on the one hand I needed, William's. His grip was warm, solid, and as the seconds passed it grew warmer. I felt the heat travel up my arm, and my eyes opened in surprise. William stood still and focused next to me. "Back up," he said to the people around us.

Their shouts silenced, their hands pulled back, and the crowd widened around us, like Moses parting the sea. Their eyes were locked on him now, not me. He had a hold of them. All of them. "Thank you," I whispered. My heart still pulsed in my throat, but I stood there, stunned. How could he be influencing so many? At once?

"Go sit in your places under the canopy," he commanded. They obeyed, like drones, still following him with love-struck eyes as they walked away.

He turned to me, amazed. "That was insane."

I laughed. It didn't seem like the right emotion, but I was in shock. "Yeah." I looked down at our hands still clasped. My knuckles were white from squeezing, and I could feel the heat fading away from my elbow back to our palms.

"I've never felt that before," I said, remembering that I was unconscious the last time our powers were magnified by our touch.

"It wasn't that strong last time." He smiled wide. "I've *never* been able to do that. It's gotten stronger."

I glanced back at the canopy where the injured waited, still recovering from their frenzy. "Good. Stay close. I'm going to need all the extra healing power I can get."

––––

"I'M SORRY," A MOTHER APOLOGIZED AS I TREATED the burns on her daughter's face. "I don't know what came over everyone. We just...we're scared."

"It's okay," I said as I dabbed blood on the young girl's cheek. She squirmed in discomfort at first, but calmed as the skin re-grew. Chloe followed close by with water and rags to clean up after me. She stayed quiet, and I could tell she had seen a little more than she could handle.

"You all right?" I asked as we made our way to a man who had been stabbed multiple times.

"I'm just glad you're okay," she answered quietly. "I didn't know where you were during the fight, and then just now..."

I pulled her close into my left side so I wouldn't get my blood on her. "I'm fine," I said. Though I knew once this was over, I probably wouldn't be. I kissed her forehead, and she smiled at me. "I love you, Chloebug."

I healed as many as I could, but even with William amplifying my ability, I could only do so much.

"I think I know where we can go," someone said from behind me as I washed my wrist in the creek. As soon as I recognized Kara's voice, I jumped up and wrapped my arms around her. She was guarded, still holding on to that hardened version of herself, and she tensed up as I hugged her.

"You're alive," I said with relief.

"So?"

"So, I'm glad you're okay."

Her lips were stubborn. They resisted the smile, and curled up only slightly at the edges.

"We need a new camp."

"We do," I agreed, wondering where we would put all of these people.

"I was thinking. My family's been hiding out. So far so good. We could stay there, too."

CHAPTER FIFTEEN

—

KARA SHOWED ALEX THE PLACE IN HER MIND, AND
he had us there in seconds. Alex, Kara, William, and I
stood looking out into the distance at the central plains of
North America. Behind us was a small cabin settled into a
hill, surrounded by trees and tall grass that reminded me
of *Little House on the Prairie.*

"It's a little exposed," I said.

"But it's in the middle of nowhere. They'd never find
us," Kara said with a grin.

I could tell she was getting excited to see her family.

"Well, let's just go say hi first. We'll talk about the
location later." I was eager for her. It had been years since
she'd seen them in person, though I wasn't sure how many.

The four of us approached her family's home with
anticipation.

"Is your sister pretty?" Alex joked. "You might have
to set us up."

"She might be," Kara laughed. "I haven't seen her since I was seventy."

Then, her pace slowed, and the smile fell from her face.

"What?" I asked, reaching for my dart gun.

"Something's wrong." She looked at me, her eyes wide and worried. "I can't hear them." She shook her head and tried to concentrate as we waited. Without another word she took off toward the house at a full sprint.

"Kara," I yelled after her. If something was wrong, we needed to be careful. Still, I ran after her and the guys followed.

I watched from a distance as she ripped open the door and fell to her knees, her sobs carrying through the air like howling winds. The sounds she made were involuntary and unnatural. They cut through me, worsening the ache in my chest. When I reached her, I wrapped my arms around her shoulders, but she threw me off.

"No. It's okay. They're going to be okay," she screamed. She stood and stumbled toward their bodies, which remained where they had fallen after they'd been shot to death. Blood stains covered their clothes, their skin, the floor. It hadn't been long. We were only hours too late. If not for the blood, they could be sleeping.

She cried over her mother as I tried to comfort her, but she pushed me away again. I sat on the wood floor next to her, and when the guys ran in, they had no words. None of us did. I was too sick with anger to think about anything but destroying Christoph.

I looked at William. "Alex is right. We have to kill Christoph."

He nodded.

"We need to get her out of here," Alex said, watching Kara. It was strange to see his face sink with sadness. I had never seen him feel anything but anger.

"No," she shouted. "Just leave me here and get out."

William didn't listen. Instead, he walked toward her, reaching for her shoulders, and pulled her into his arms. "I'm sorry," he whispered, clutching her body tightly to his. She wept into his shirt, clinging to him, needing him like I'd never seen her need anyone. "I'm sorry."

"We should bury them," Alex said after a while, his eyes still sad. "You don't have to help if it's too much."

I shook my head. "I'll help."

We found two shovels behind the cabin and dug three holes. I ached everywhere and wanted to give up, but I wouldn't let myself. I forced my muscles to lift piles of dirt from the earth until the holes were big enough. Then we carried Kara's family out back to the graves and waited for her to be ready.

She knelt down beside each of her family members, placing blades of long grass under their folded hands and coins over their eyes. As she moved from one to the next, fixing their hair and adjusting their clothing, she set crowns of braided reeds atop their heads. After each adornment she whispered something in Latin under her breath and kissed their cheeks. A final goodbye.

"I'm sorry it couldn't be more," she said when we lowered them into the ground.

It was hard to see her so distraught. To me she'd always been unbreakable.

None of us spoke as we let her take that final moment with them.

"*Réquiem ætérnam dona eis, Dómine,*" William said, breaking the silence. I looked at him, surprised. His head was bowed in prayer, and his eyes were closed. "*Et lux perpétua lúceat eis. Requiéscite in pace.*"

We buried them in silence. Only after I poured the last shovelful over Kara's sister did I say anything.

"We have to find out how he's getting to us." I was beaten and tired, my clothes filthy with ash, but my mind wouldn't quit. "If we don't, we might as well start digging our own graves."

"You need to sleep first, Ellie," William answered, still holding Kara close. "You can't save the world in a night."

"Sleep?" I said, staring at the three mounds of dirt that rose out of the ground. As if that was even possible. Kara's face was red and her eyes swollen. "I'll sleep when he's dead."

———

WHEN WE GOT BACK, THE BODIES OF OUR PEOPLE HAD been buried as well, but a nervous tension kept everyone quiet and unsure. They were waiting for me to give them a reason for this, for answers. I didn't have them. Those who weren't injured gathered and whispered in groups under the tents, their expectant eyes following me as I walked among them.

I squeezed William's hand before I stepped forward to face the crowd.

"Remember what you're fighting for," he said with a nod.

I started to pick at my fingers, but stopped immediately. I needed to be strong.

I cleared my throat. "We lost some great people today. Friends and family. War has consequences, but we can't let the deaths of those we love be in vain." I glanced at William. I believed in what his father said about Luke. We had to stand up for the virtue of those who'd died for this cause. "The best way to keep them alive is to fight for what they stood for. What we all stand for. Freedom. The future isn't going to be easy, but it will be worth the fight."

"What now?" a man yelled from the crowd. He held his motherless daughter in his arms, and I scanned the numbers of devastated faces around him. Some sat on the ground still injured. Some looked off with empty expressions. The rest were desperate, and unsettled voices began to chatter.

"Are we safe?" someone shouted, quieting the rest.

Their questions threw me off, but I needed to be the leader they expected me to be. "We can't stay here," I answered. "They know where we are. It's only a matter of time before they come back." I turned to Mac, communicating my plan, and he nodded in agreement. "We don't know how they're finding us." Nervous voices started back up again, but I spoke over them with confidence and they silenced. "Alex will be moving us ten at a time to a new location. We'll do the best we can to set up security. If there is a next time, we'll be prepared for it."

———

"HOW DO YOU THINK THEY FOUND US?" I ASKED MAC as he collected maps that were saved from the flames.

Kara and William stood next to me, hoping he knew more than we did.

"No idea," he answered, "but it was Christoph's attack. He stripped my ability, took away the safe haven. Not sure it'll do much good this time, but..."

He was distracted, paying attention to more than just us. Always alert and ready for more.

"Let me heal that," I said, noticing the sleeve around his forearm was wet with blood.

He opened his shotgun, checking the rounds, and began rolling up the cuff of his flannel.

"Your ability is back, though?" I asked.

"Yeah. I suppose he doesn't see it as much of a threat. Not if he knows where we are."

"How could he know?" William asked as I treated the gash on Mac's arm.

None of us had an answer.

"I'll be checking the minds of those who come with

us," Kara added. "I think I would know if there was a mole, but it's worth a try to dig a little deeper."

"As soon as we get there we'll go over an evacuation plan," Mac said, flexing his fingers as the wound healed. "And we'll need to have lookouts during the night. We'll get volunteers, but you three and Alex should start us out."

"I'll go first," Kara said. "I won't be able to sleep anyway."

That night we slept on the floor of the Lenaia caves. It was too obvious a place to hide, so our theory was they would never look there. At least we hoped. Kara hadn't found a spy, but it was still hard to sleep. None of us truly felt safe. Instead, I lay awake and worried. On top of everything, nobody had been able to verify that our friends had left on their recon mission. I hoped that was where they were and that they were okay.

My lids lifted in frustration as my mind ignored their attempt to shut out the world. Above me, lights that looked like twinkling stars cast a gentle blue light throughout the dark cave. I wasn't sure whose ability it was, but it was beautiful. I sat up from under the covers and looked out over the sleeping bodies huddled together for safety's sake. The only person awake was Kara sitting against the stone wall.

I slipped out from under William's arm, and made my way over to her. She didn't look up.

How are you?

We sat for a while in silence before she decided to

answer.

If I had just brought them to the camp, maybe I could have protected them.

It's not your fault, Kara.

I thought they'd be safer on their own. You're the target. I thought if they were far enough away…

I knew she didn't want my sympathy, but it was in my nature to at least try and comfort someone when they needed it. *Maybe they would have been safe with us.* I remembered the fire, the bodies lying out along the ground. *Maybe not, though.*

Maybe not.

Can I tell you something? I hadn't told anyone about the dream I had before the fire, not even Anna. *I saw it before it happened.*

What do you mean?

The fire. I had a dream about Christoph, about him burning everything around me.

She looked at me, her eyebrows creasing with confusion. *I can't see it,* she said.

Just like you couldn't see it when I saw Christoph at training. I looked down at my belly, still flat and unchanged. *Do you think?* I didn't feel pregnant. Wouldn't I know if I was?

I guess it's possible. Her eyes drifted toward William, and I wished for a moment that I could hear what she was thinking for a change.

She smiled. *I'm thinking you're lucky.* Her gaze lingered

on him as she pushed black flyaway curls behind her ears. I pretended not to notice. *You should tell him.*

The air seemed harder to breathe at the thought.

It'll worry him. You know how he gets. He's protective. Besides, I'm not even sure it's true.

Maybe you should be protected.

I shook my head. *I can't just disappear. If I tell William, things will be different. There's no guarantee I'm pregnant anyway.*

I think you'll find out eventually. I mean, if you are, your belly's not going to be getting any smaller.

I glared at her. *Thanks.*

My reaction made her laugh. She tried to hold in the sound, but that only made me start laughing. Both of us gripped our mouths as we suffered through a silent laugh attack. By the time it was over, we were sucking in deep breaths and smiling. The mind has strange ways of dealing with grief. I sat with her in silence for a while longer, both of us holding on to the moment, before I returned to William for a few brief hours of sleep.

The next morning sadness hung in the air. We'd lost so many in the fight. But despite the battle, no one had left. Instead the group was focused, finally realizing none of this was for fun. This was war.

We spent the next few weeks building up camp. The caves were cold and unwelcoming at first, but with so many helping hands, it began to feel like home. Alex took small groups out to gather supplies. The guys hung lanterns on poles in a circle around new tents at night. During the day, Mr. Williamson mimicked sunlight, so that the entire cave was alight. The women built fires and set up tables for cooking. A girl named Christine grew trees from the bare ground to give the place the feel of Lenaia. Her mother had been responsible for last year's forest, but had died in the attack. Sofia's friend was able to draw water from the ground, and built a streaming waterfall a ways away from the camp for bathing, and a smaller pool closer to the tents for drinking.

My focus was on the enemy. We sent recon scouts to Beverly Hills to verify Christoph's location, but the house was abandoned. Others sought out places his workers were known to meet, hoping to discover how they'd found us. So far no one had returned. Those of us who stayed were developing security protocols and escape plans in case of another attack. I couldn't fail these people a second time. I carried the guilt for every person killed, as if their lives were mine to redeem.

"You need a break," William said from behind me as I poured over lists of bloodlines and locations with a flashlight.

"No, I'm fine," I answered without looking up.

His shoes crunched the dirt as he moved closer. He set his lantern on the table and put his warm hands on my shoulders.

"You'd rather stare at that paper than sleep with your fiancé? I think you're starting to lose it," he teased.

Maybe I *was* starting to lose it.

He brushed my hair aside and pressed his soft lips against the delicate skin on my neck. "Come on."

I followed him to the tent, though my mind was still dwelling on our next move. Like most nights it was hard to sleep, but at some point I must have dozed off. I woke abruptly, disoriented. Something was wrong. My vision wasn't clear, but I heard voices behind me. William. Kara. I opened my tent, needing to get to them. I needed help.

"Ellie?" William said, but his voice was muffled by something.

I couldn't respond. Everything was starting to pull away from me, stretching, disappearing, and the world around me changed. What I saw in front of me wasn't camp. At first I thought I was in a military facility. I cowered in the back behind lines of soldiers, my heart racing. Rows of people stood at attention, but they were not in military clothes, and some were too young or too old to be soldiers.

The warehouse was lined with people from wall to wall. I heard something, maybe footsteps coming from ahead, but those around me were still as statues. I chose to get closer. I wanted to see their faces and figure out why they were so still. As I walked past the first row, trying to understand, I made eye contact with a short blonde wo-man. The intensity in her gaze made me jump, but she didn't flinch. Instead she acted as if she didn't see me and continued to look around desperately. They all did, thousands of worried eyes silently pleading for help. Something was keeping them from moving. I recognized that look, and suddenly I felt my stomach rise up into my throat. I had only known one person to restrain people like that—Ryder.

I shook my head in disbelief. He couldn't be alive. William had killed him. As I turned to walk down another row, my question was answered. There, in front of a child's frightened stare. It wasn't Ryder. It had to be his son. He was younger, but with the same block jaw and body frame. His hair was a lighter brown that wasn't streaked with shades of gray, but he wore the same hard expression. At first I stood still, expecting him to come at me seeking revenge, but he didn't so much as turn his head. He couldn't see me. None of them could.

Though my body still fought the idea, I inched closer. I had to make out what he was doing. A young girl was with him, and tears slid down her dark cheeks as she wheeled a machine behind her. Tubes of red blood connected her to it, but as I stepped forward, things seemed to dissipate.

Everything evaporated around me, and I found myself on my knees with William at my side.

"Are you all right?" he asked, helping me to my feet.

I looked up, brushing the dirt off of my hands. "I'm fine."

"You fell pretty hard," he said, looking at Kara.

"Just tired," I answered, not knowing how to explain.

"Do you need some water?" Kara asked. I could see from the look she gave me. She knew what I was thinking. *Another vision?* Her voice sounded unspoken in my head.

"Sure," I said, and I nodded answering her other question. *I think so.*

She handed me a water bottle. *What did you see?*

I pressed it to my lips and drank long and slow as I summed up what I saw in quick silent sentences.

"Any word from Sam and the others?" I asked, trying to sway the focus of William's worry. We hadn't heard anything from them. Not in weeks.

"Not back yet," William answered, but he was too concerned to be distracted. "Maybe you should sit down."

He took my hand and led me to a chair next to Mac.

"Look who decided to show up," Mac said.

In front of us was a brown foldout table with maps spread across the top of it. Red circles signified groups of Descendants who had broken away from the communities, and asterisks pinpointed those with beneficial abilities.

I looked over the maps, considering our next move. Before I could get a word out, Alex was in front of me.

"Rachel's hurt. I need you," he said as he disappeared.

"What?" I asked aloud. I looked at William for answers, but he shrugged.

"Clear the table," Kara yelled. "She's been shot." She swept the maps to the ground, and within seconds Alex was there with all of them. Sam and Nics stood behind Paul who carried Rachel in his arms. She hung limp, covered in blood and unconscious.

I'd never seen Nics cry, but tears were running down her cheeks. "Can you help her?" she pleaded.

Paul set Rachel on the table, his face white with shock. He didn't speak. He couldn't seem to look away from her face.

At first there was no doubt in my mind that I could help her, but as I pulled up her shirt I realized there were bullets lodged in her chest. "We need to get the bullets out before I heal her, right?"

"I don't know," William answered. "I'll go try and find someone."

After he took off toward the supply team, Sam put a heavy hand on my shoulder. "We don't have time for that."

I nodded, hoping it wasn't too late. I snapped the buttons on my bracelet while terrified eyes watched in silence, and let the blood drip into her mouth. Maybe if I healed her from the inside, the bullets would make their way out on their own. The fingers of my left hand rested on her neck, searching for a pulse. There wasn't one, and my heart began to ache. *Please,* I thought. *Work.*

Her face stayed locked in a peaceful sleep, her body jerking as Paul pulled at her shirt, begging her to wake up. Nics's tears brought on my own as I watched the skin heal around the bullets. I fed her blood until I was light-headed and weak, but she didn't revive.

When I pulled my wrist away, Paul screamed at me. "Why isn't it working?"

I didn't dare say the words, but I thought them. *She's dead.* "I don't know," I said instead.

"Here," William yelled, as he ran toward us. "I brought Mr. Gransky. He can..." When he saw us all sitting in silence, he lost his words.

Paul's eyes were ringed with red as he looked up. "It was my fault."

CHAPTER SIXTEEN

—

I WAITED FOR PAUL TO EXPLAIN WHAT HAPPENED, but he didn't. He stayed silent too long, and I noticed that everyone around me was frozen like time had stopped. There was no sound, no movement except for the person walking up behind me.

"Helen," I said, surprised. The last time I'd seen her was in her classroom. "How did you..." My head felt so light from blood loss I could hardly finish the sentence.

"One of your recruiters found us, told us you could provide refuge." Beside her were two boys. The one that came to her hips had blond hair and a missing front tooth. The other was taller, with darker hair. She squeezed his shoulders and pulled him in next to her. "My husband was taken by The Council." She looked at my dripping wrist. "Are you all right? Do you need my blood?"

I shook my head. "No, I'll be okay." The older boy kept his head down. I didn't know what to say. There was nothing I *could* say that would make his father come back. "Well, you're safe now."

Helen's eyes drifted to Rachel, who could be sleeping and frozen like the rest of them. "Are we?"

Maybe she was right. After the attack, I couldn't promise her that. "It's Rachel," I said instead, but she already knew who it was. Rachel had been her student. "I couldn't help her. She's...we lost her." Saying the words aloud made my throat tighten. I bit my lips, trying not to cry.

"Practicing Abilities Defense is much different than living it. I did my best to teach all of you..."

Tears slid down my cheeks, but I tried to ignore them. "You taught us well."

"Apparently not," she said. She moved around me to look over Rachel, not bothering to hide the death from her boys. They followed her, staring at Rachel's blonde hair spilling over the table's edge. "How'd she die?"

My whole body felt damp with sweat, and my head spun as I stepped toward them. I reached for something to steady me, but her smallest son caught my hand. I smiled at him. "She was shot," I answered. My chest ached with guilt. "I didn't know how to get the bullets out. I healed over them."

Helen brushed the back of her hand over Rachel's cheek. "Is there someone who can help us with that?"

I wiped away tears, defeated. "It's too late."

"If we get the bullets out, my son Aaron can bring her back, and you can heal her wounds."

My heart skipped with hope. "He can do that?"

"I'm descendant of Clotho." The older boy stepped forward to speak for himself. "I inherited my father's bloodline." He looked at me for the first time. "I can revive the dead within the first hour, before the spirit transcends." His voice was young, but I could see he was trying to be brave, to take on the role of his father.

"Transcends where?" I asked.

"Wherever it goes. Heaven, the other side. I don't know. Wherever my father is." His eyes found the ground again.

"We don't know he's dead, son," Helen said, but I could tell he didn't believe her.

"I'm not sure how long it's been." As I rushed to Rachel's side, my vision faded to black for a few seconds.

"There's time," Aaron said.

I looked at Helen. "We need Mr. Gransky."

She flicked her wrist, and Mr. Gransky blinked. He was disoriented at first, but he must have been familiar with Ms. Stanzic's ability to freeze time. "Nice to see you, Helen," he greeted her.

"You too, Rick," she said with a smile. "We need you to remove the bullets from her chest before we revive her."

I watched him, unsure if he'd be able to do it. I remembered the interdepartmental mail, office furniture, and janitorial objects passing in the air above students as they walked to class. I was pretty sure he'd never been asked to remove bullets from a girl's body before, but he didn't hesitate.

He sighed at the sight of her. "Of course."

Maybe he *had* done this before.

He moved toward her, stepping around the still figures of people stuck where they stood. I watched Rachel's
unmoving body as he stared at her, concentrating.

"Wait," I said. Things were starting to blur together,
and I was afraid I didn't have enough blood to heal her, at
least while conscious. "I need more time. I just...I'm a little
light-headed."

"We don't have time," Helen said. "Not enough to
wait for you."

"But time is stopped."

Her son shook his head. "It doesn't work like that for
the dead."

"Okay," I answered, working up the strength I needed.

Helen put a hand to her son's shoulder, holding him
back while she considered something. Then she waved her
wrist. William's eyes fell on me first. "What's going on?"
he asked, realizing not everyone was moving.

"Elyse needs your blood," Helen answered.

"Sure," he said. "But why are we stopping time?"

"Privacy," she replied calmly. "We're going to try and
revive Rachel."

He nodded, moving quickly to grab the knife inside
Kara's boot.

I'd never had to drink blood before. I watched while
Anna did, when I healed her, and when I healed others

after the fire, but each time it repulsed me. I couldn't imagine doing it myself. I pressed my lips together. "Really, I think I'll be okay, just let me—"

"Elyse," William interrupted, looking me over. "You need it." Maybe he was right. I felt dizzy and could see the remnants of the loss on my blood-covered hands.

He slid the blade across his wrist without flinching.

"What are you doing?" The words came out high-pitched. "That's too much. You'll—" He pushed the cut to my lips to quiet my protest.

"You'll heal it in a second," he said, grabbing my hand. I nodded and pinched my eyes tightly together, like if I didn't see it happening it wouldn't be so bad. My heart pumped harder against my ribs, and I felt the warmth pulse between our palms like energy, heightening my power. I tried to block out the taste by not breathing through my nose, but that only lasted so long. I inhaled and my taste buds registered the flavor of William's blood, surprisingly sweet. Refreshing, like water after a long run. Not what I expected.

My eyes opened as I was rejuvenated, but when I finished, the sight of William's cut arm made me regret needing him. My weakness meant his pain.

"Thank you," I whispered as I rushed to heal his wrist with the blood left in my bracelet.

He brought our clasped hands to his lips and kissed my knuckles. "It's what I'm here for."

Mr. Gransky had already started to remove the bullets.

I watched in horror as they re-emerged from her healed flesh and fell onto the table. Each one left a trail of crimson across her powder white skin.

"All right, Elyse," Helen instructed.

I twisted the bracelet and created fresh wounds to stimulate the flow of blood. Drops slipped into the bullet holes, and her skin mended.

"Be ready to give her more," Helen instructed. "Your turn, Aaron."

I stepped away, and Aaron held his hand to Rachel's chest. I waited for her to gasp or jolt with life, but nothing happened. It was taking too long.

"Is it too late?" I asked when Aaron removed his hand. I wasn't sure I wanted to hear the answer. I couldn't handle anything that wasn't good news.

"Give her time," he said, though he seemed uncertain. He was young, no more than sixty-five. I wasn't sure I believed him.

There was no jolt, no gasp, no shimmering image of a soul floating back to her. Her eyes simply lifted as if she were in a deep sleep and was having trouble waking up.

I pressed my wrist to her lips. She seemed confused at first but took the blood willingly and smiled at me with her eyes.

Helen set time in motion again, and Nics's sobbing picked up where it left off. Everyone still stared at Rachel, but for the first time the rest of them saw her open eyes. She was very much alive.

"Rachel," Paul breathed. "How...you're...are you..." His hands cupped her face, and he kissed her over and over, though her lips were still stained with blood.

"I'm okay," she said, half a question, half amazed. She felt her chest with her hand and smiled wider.

Paul ran his fingers through his short dark hair, shaking his head in disbelief. He turned to look at me. "Thank you."

"Oh, it was..." He flew into me so fast I nearly fell to the ground. "Aaron." I laughed as he hugged me tight enough I couldn't breathe.

"Did you tell them?" Rachel said to Paul, and I wondered if she had any idea what had just happened.

He let me go and shook his head, still too shocked at the sight of her to speak.

"We found Descendants of Mnemosyne," she said.

I looked at William, not sure what she meant.

He tapped his temple. "Mind-wipers."

CHAPTER SEVENTEEN

—

"SO WHAT'S THE BIG DEAL ABOUT MIND-WIPERS?" I asked at lunch. Everyone seemed to have pulled themselves together by then, as best they could at least. Paul still hovered over Rachel, like he could lose her at any moment.

"Christoph has been trying to find them for years," Kara answered as she took a seat across from me and put her plate on the table. "There were rumors that we killed them all. *We* as in the bad guys..." Her guilty eyes searched those around her for judgment. She raised her hands defensively. "...which I'm not anymore."

I leaned forward. "*Did* you kill them?"

She didn't answer at first. Instead she gave me a look, clearly tired of being thought of as ruthless. "No. Actually, we were always told to bring them in alive."

"Well, Christoph's found them, or at least he thinks he has," Rachel said. She was back to her normal self, like she hadn't died earlier today. I still couldn't believe she was sitting here talking to us. "He's planning something."

"Why does he want them so badly?" I asked, before taking a bite of my sandwich.

"It's a powerful ability," William answered. "Think about it. If he can erase things from someone's memory, he's got power over them, over you, over us, over humans."

"Exactly," Kara said.

So I wasn't the only one Christoph was after. I wondered how deep his plot went, how long he had been waiting and planning for this war. There was no way I was anywhere as prepared as he must be. Still, what could I do about it? I could only think of one thing.

"We have to find them first," I said.

Everyone stayed silent. Sam glanced at Nics, and for once I saw agreement in her eyes.

"What?" I continued.

Rachel laughed. "If it was that easy, I wouldn't have almost died."

Sam raised his eyebrows. "Um...You *did* die."

"Jeez, Sam," Nics said, shoving his shoulder. "Be a little more sensitive."

"What exactly happened? How did you get shot?" I asked Rachel.

"Adrianna," she answered. "I was..."

"We were outside The Institute," Nics continued for her. "We think they're using it as a meeting place these days. It's been cleared out. No school. No Headquarters."

"It's chaos out there. Descendants are leaving communities. They aren't safe anymore," Rachel explained in a high voice. "People being accused of treason are disappearing."

Nics nodded. "Anyway, The Institute was our best shot at getting a lead. I had to keep us hidden because Christoph's men were everywhere. It was really a great plan..."

"We heard two of them talking about mind-wipers, so we followed," Paul spoke up. "My idea." He shook his head. "Rachel decided to fly ahead. Nics had her covered, but...Adrianna. She just came out of nowhere."

"I fell from pretty high up when she took away our abilities, and I actually landed on my feet," Rachel said with a sense of pride. "I just landed in front of two guys with guns."

"I got her out," Paul said, "and we called Alex."

Nics nudged Alex in the arm with her elbow. "Thanks, by the way. If you hadn't shown up..."

"Just doing my job." He'd been so quiet I'd hardly noticed he was there. I wondered what he was plotting. I knew it was something. He wasn't the shy type.

"Well, we can't do anything about it now," William said, trying to get everyone's mind off of what happened. "They'll be expecting us."

I focused on Alex whose gaze lingered on something in the distance.

William turned to me. "We'll have to wait for another opportunity."

We rounded everyone up for target practice after lunch. Since the attack, we'd moved on to weapons training. Guns mostly, but now that Helen was here, she wanted to focus on the use of abilities and weapons simultaneously. The idea made me nervous, but after what happened to Rachel, I realized it might actually be necessary.

I loved target practice. It was one of the few times we got to spend outside the caves. Nics provided a shield in addition to the safe haven, but even if we didn't have either of those, we'd still be hidden under a tangled canopy of bare branches. Alex transported us to a forest for the day's session. The trees made for good targets, and none of us felt as vulnerable as we did on open land. Cardboard cutouts were scattered throughout the shooting range, pressed against tree trunks at different distances, and a table littered with various types of hand guns was set up to the side.

William walked ahead to speak with Mac about today's session, so when I felt a hand on my arm, I flinched. I turned my head just in time to see Alex's face before we disappeared. We were gone in seconds, reappearing in a separate part of the forest.

"Look," he said immediately. "If you think it's too dangerous, that's fine, but I'm going. On my own if I have to." His eyes sharpened ready to take on a challenge.

"What are you talking about?"

He looked away irritated. "The mind-wipers."

"I knew it," I said quietly. "You were planning something. You know William's right. The Council will see you coming if you go back there. They'll be waiting for you." Deep down I was glad William had made the decision for us not to go, even if it wasn't the right one. I didn't know if I was ready to face what was out there. Not yet.

"You can use whatever excuse you want, but we have a lead here. You can't just sit on it." The words came out like fire. "Because you're scared."

"I'm not scared. I'm being smart," I argued, but inside I knew that was a lie.

"That's what you call it?"

Without giving me a chance to answer he grabbed my wrist, and we were back before anyone realized we were gone. Helen turned to face the front of the group of fifteen, and William headed back in my direction.

"This is real training. This isn't for fun," she said.

"Sure it is," Mac laughed under his breath.

Helen looked at him a little taken aback. "Excuse me?"

William took my hand as he joined the group, his face tensed with concern.

"It's all a game if there's nothing at stake," Mac answered.

She raised her eyebrows. "Do you have a better idea?"

"First of all, we need moving targets." He stepped out in front of us standing almost a foot taller than Helen. "Nothing you'll be shooting at ever stays still."

From the minute he said moving targets I knew where

this was going.

"Mac," I said, trying to discount the idea.

"I'm sorry, Elyse. People have died. War ain't no picnic."

"I'm in," Sam said before he knew what he was signing up for.

"We'll be starting off in groups of three," Mac yelled. "One will be the shooter, one will be the protector, and one will be the target."

William gave me a look like he'd seen this coming.

"No way." Nics laughed. "I'm not doing that."

"Look," Mac said, pulling a Glock from the weapons table. "Anyone who's going to learn how to shoot someone should know what it feels like to get shot." He shrugged like it was a simple fact. "If you don't want to be on this recon team, go ahead and leave."

Everyone looked at each other, waiting for someone to move. No one did.

"Good," Mac said with a nod.

Sam's face was suddenly wary of what he'd volunteered for. "Is he serious?"

"Well, I already know what it feels like to get shot," Rachel huffed with resentment.

"Yeah," Paul said, worried for her. "Can she just sit out?"

"No excuses," Mac bellowed, making eye contact with every one of us. "You can always leave."

"Let's just say, on the off chance, one of us gets killed,"

William said sarcastically. "That might be a little bit of a problem, don't you think?"

"Nope. We've got I-bring-people-back-to-life boy right here." He nodded toward Aaron. "And Elyse knows how to heal. Suck it up. You'll be fine. Besides, it's the protector's job to make sure that doesn't happen."

"So we're going to shoot at each other?" Sam asked like maybe it was all a joke.

Mac loaded the Glock in his hand with a click. "Yep."

William shook his head, but I couldn't argue. As ridiculous and crazy as it sounded, Mac was right. We needed to train under pressure, to feel the fear of getting shot while trying to aim a gun or take out a mark. I felt guilty for thinking that. Maybe I had lost some of my humanity to the fight.

"Any volunteers?"

No one moved.

"I'll go," I said before anyone else. "I'll be the target."

"Elyse," William said without thinking.

"It's fine." I stepped forward. "Someone's got to go first." My toes flexed and curled inside my shoes, my feigned confidence masking the fact that I was nervous.

"Good," Mac said, pleased by my offer. "Nics, you're the shooter. Ian here will be the protector." He slapped a gruff hand against the back of the youngest boy in our group.

"I'm not doing it," Nics said with attitude. "No way."

"All right. You're out."

"Nics, it's fine. I'm a healer. I know pain. I can take it," I said, hoping she believed the words coming out of my mouth. "Besides, maybe I'll shoot you before you shoot me." I adjusted my dart gun on my thigh, moving it higher.

She eyed the Glock Mac held out in front of her and looked back at William before taking it. "We'll see," she said, trying to joke about it, but she was nervous, too. I could tell.

The crease deepened between my eyes as I realized this was really going to happen.

Ian and I walked out about twenty paces from where Nics stood. He was maybe fourteen years old in human terms with frizzy curls and freckles. I tried to tell myself it didn't matter. With Descendants, it was all about the power of your ability that determined a person's strength. I didn't know what Ian's was, but I hoped it would protect me long enough to shoot the first dart.

"Ian, step back a ways. Protect her from a distance," Mac yelled. I moved my bracelet back and forth nervously, readying myself to draw blood from my left wrist.

The minute Mac said go, everything changed. My vision went black, and all I could do was listen. I heard Nics steady her footing. I heard the watching crowd inhale and exhale in staggered patterns. I heard Nics swallow, grip the gun tighter. Then I realized I shouldn't be able to hear those things. Nics stripped me of my sense of sight, but Ian must have been amplifying my hearing. I could make out everything. The bullet released from the chamber, cracking the air like shattered glass, and I jumped. It was so loud it hurt, but I could hear it flying toward me, a buzz that broke through the atmosphere. I heard William suck in a breath, heard him curse quietly to himself as he watched. I stepped to the side quickly, and the bullet whizzed by my left ear hitting a nearby tree.

Adrenalin kicked in. I steadied my feet, listening to the direction of the breeze as it pushed the old dry leaves around like nature's wind chime. I heard the crunch of nervous feet, the click, the bullet. I knew exactly where it was going, heard it so clearly that I could reach out and catch it. I ducked as it flew over my head. The group whispered. They were impressed. So was I.

Nics shot three more bullets, and I dodged them all. I heard the last one hit the dirt with a dull thud, burying itself into the earth. It was too easy. I could've probably taken her out just by the sound of her shuffling feet, but I was having fun. I smiled. I felt invincible.

Then things changed. I could see again. Nics must have realized the blackness wasn't fazing me. I caught sight of William, a proud grin gracing his face as he looked back. He was a distraction. That's what she wanted. I was too slow moving out of the way of the next bullet, and it grazed my arm. I winced and fell to my knees. I looked back at Nics expecting to see remorse, but she only raised an eyebrow and shot again. The bullet passed so close to my ear, I felt the air move. My heart kicked into gear, pumping harder. The bark behind me broke and splintered into pieces. I reached for my holster and grabbed a dart, but by the time I had it between my fingers I realized something was wrong. The world was pulling away from me. This had happened before. Everything distant, blurred. I heard nothing. I needed the sound. It was my only protection. I shook my head and brought my hands to my ears, trying to make them hear. Too late. Nics smiled and aimed one last time.

"Nics," I yelled, trying to get her to stop, but the bullet sank into my shoulder, tearing my flesh. I felt the pain everywhere and cried out. The last thing I saw was William rushing toward me before they all disappeared.

This time when my surroundings began to transform, I was aware that what I was experiencing was a vision. Adrianna stared at me, only I wasn't staring back at her. I was somewhere outside my body, watching the two of us have a conversation. I couldn't hear what we were saying, but I didn't seem to be in danger.

We were in an office. I didn't think it was hers. She sat against the front of the desk, not behind it. There were Latin textbooks on the shelves to her left, and light filtered through the windows on the right. The moment didn't last long, only a few seconds, and the next time I blinked I thought someone turned out the lights. Then all I saw was a face. Small, young, skin the color of milk chocolate, and wide weepy eyes. It was her face. The one Christoph was looking for, the girl at the warehouse. The mind-wiper.

Everything around me pulled away again, disappearing,

leaving me in blackness.

When I came to, William's face was hovering above me.

"Ellie," he said, his eyes searching mine. He brushed my hair back and grazed my cheek with his thumb. "Are you okay?"

I grabbed his hand, confused as he pulled me up to sitting. His palm was bloody and my shoulder tender. People were huddled around, staring at me.

"What happened?"

He laughed. "Well, Miss I-want-to-play-the-target, you got shot. Big surprise, I know."

I shook my head. I'd completely forgotten about target practice. "I'm fine. I think..." I looked around at their curious faces. Prying eyes, listening ears. "I need to talk to you."

"All right, next three," Mac yelled to the crowd.

William lifted me to my feet as the group around us began to mill about wondering who was next.

"Sorry," Nics said as I rubbed my shoulder. "I got a little carried away."

"No, you did good. You got me," I said with a half-smile.

"Yeah," she shrugged, smiling back. "Got you good."

William led us to the back of the group while another three were selected.

"Something happened before you got shot," he said. "What was it?"

"I don't know. I just…" I knew I should tell him about the vision, but that would mean telling him about my theory, about the baby. I couldn't, not until I was sure there actually was a baby. I didn't want to think about it. There was no baby. I wouldn't believe it. "We just…have to get to the mind-wipers," I said, unwilling to be more specific.

He laughed uncomfortably. "Now? You just got shot, Elyse."

"Yeah, well—"

"It's too dangerous," William responded without thinking.

"Things are going to be dangerous, William," I said. "We can't hide forever."

His eyes narrowed with suspicion. "What happened? Why'd you change your mind?"

The visions replayed in my head. The warehouse, the girl, Adrianna. Alex was right. I had to make a move.

"It doesn't matter," I answered. "What matters is that we have a lead. We can't just sit on this information and do nothing."

"No." He crossed his arms, resisting the idea. "You could get hurt or—"

"William," I interrupted. "It's not your choice."

He rubbed the back of his neck nervously.

"You always tell your dad I'm the one who calls the shots, right?"

He looked away and nodded. "I'm sorry I get like this.

I can't help it." He sighed, giving in. His hands reached for mine, and he pulled our laced fingers to his lips. "All right," he said. "How are we supposed to find them? There's probably a reason everyone thinks they don't exist. Anyone who gets close probably gets their mind wiped."

"I'm not sure, but we should make a plan over dinner. Maybe Kara has some ideas."

A gunshot made me jump. "Elyse!" Helen shouted. "We need you."

CHAPTER EIGHTEEN

—

THE REST OF TRAINING WAS A LIGHTHEADED BLUR. I'D lost a lot of blood healing gunshot wounds, and I couldn't concentrate on anything but the vision. Whatever these visions were, they meant something.

We stayed in the woods until nightfall. Until our muscles ached. Until our hands were blistered. Until I had no more blood to give.

Back in the caves the smell of food wafted around the camp. Normally I wouldn't be looking forward to the grilled chicken and beans we'd been having every night. Making food for a large group was more complicated than it used to be, and I missed Cearno's cooking. Our nightly meal was bland, and dry, but tonight my mouth watered at the smell of it. I was starving.

"So are we going to talk about the plan?" Alex asked from his seat beside me. I knew he only sat there because he wanted something.

I'd called a meeting. Over dinner was the best way to be subtle about it.

"What plan?" Dr. Nickel asked.

"We have new information," I answered. "Christoph is after mind-wipers. It's important we find them first."

Dr. Nickel, Mac, and Anna sat across from me, like a panel of judges I felt I had to get approval from.

"How?" Anna asked.

"We need to find Adrianna," I said. "She helped us once. I think she's the key."

Anna shook her head. "You can't go back to that house, Elyse."

"The last place she was seen was at The Institute," Rachel added from a few seats down, and she was right. Adrianna would be there. In an office. I'd seen it.

"You sure you want to risk it?" Mac asked, stabbing a piece of chicken with his fork. "Didn't go over so well getting that information in the first place."

William raised his eyebrows. "He has a point."

I looked out at the groups of people gathered at tables talking cheerfully over dinner. All of them were here to see me take down The Council. They expected things of me. "We're going to try."

"All right." Dr. Nickel nodded. "Tell us what you want us to do."

"I'd like to start at The Institute. I'll need Alex for transportation and Kara, but no one else needs to come." I waited for William to protest, but he didn't. He avoided my eyes and didn't say a word. "Mac, you should stay to look after those here, and Dr. Nickel, it's best you lay low. I just need a few minutes with Adrianna. I don't want her to feel like we're launching an attack."

"When do we leave?" Kara asked.

"I want to go tomorrow tonight. We'll be well rested by then."

William looked up. I knew he didn't like this plan, so his words surprised me. "You'll need Nics for cover, and my ability would be useful as well."

I opened my mouth to shut him down, but stopped myself. His ability *would* be useful, and if I expected him to let go of his protective nature around me, then I owed him the same.

———

IT WAS DARK WHEN ALEX LANDED US SOME DISTANCE away from The Institute, but the city lights made the night glow. The plan was to approach on foot from a few blocks away. We didn't know what to expect inside the building. Cool night air chilled my lungs as the five of us walked without speaking. The sound of the once familiar city seemed newly foreign. It was louder than I remembered, the noise of so many people and cars creating a busy chaos. I fed off the energy.

I watched the building as we got closer. To anyone else it was nothing special, but I saw beneath its cosmopolitan camouflage. It was dangerous, unstable. It stared down at me with a thousand eyes, night windows that could be hiding anything behind their shadowed panes.

I expected to feel nervous, doubtful even. Instead I felt alive, like my life finally had purpose. Tonight I'd prove that I could make a difference, or at least bring justice to the lives that were lost. Blood pulsed so fast in my chest it almost tickled, and for once it wasn't fear that quickened my heart. It was the rush.

Wait. Kara's voice was hesitant. We all stopped. Cars passed by without notice as Nics hid us beneath her shield, and Kara stood there in silence for a moment, eyes closed.

What is it? I asked, the thrill of the mission still egging me on.

They're watching from the windows. Lookouts. Though the words were in my head, they were hurried and tense.

"Should we go back?" William asked.

"No," I answered. "We have to try. They shouldn't be able to see us."

Kara shook her head. They know we're here.

Nics's dark brow pulled together, and adrenaline made my blood pump faster. How? I asked. This wasn't how it was supposed to go.

They're waiting to see what we do. Keep walking. Slowly. I turned to lead the group, keeping my eyes forward as Kara spoke. It's Claudia, she said. She's of Selene. Nics can't manipulate the Moonlight. *Not for her at least. She has power over it.*

So we're not hidden?

My eyes darted back and forth across the building hoping to catch sight of something suspicious.

Not to her, she answered.

The building grew taller as we neared it, rising up like a giant, frightening and monstrous. I'd been overly confident, foolish, for thinking we'd get in without a fight. *Help me out here, Kara,* I said. *What's she thinking? What's our best move?*

I waited for an answer as I kept on, but I didn't get one. Instead, I turned around to find Kara stopped behind us, staring up into the night sky like nothing else mattered.

"What is she—"

"Don't look," William whispered. He shot a hand out to cover my curious eyes as they lifted upward. "It's the moon."

We lost Nics next. Her gaze became fixated on the glowing orb above her, as if she were hypnotized by its light. Before I could react, Kara's body jerked as a soundless bullet sank into her arm. Then another to her thigh, and her knee buckled beneath her.

"Kara," Alex yelled, and he was there to catch her as she fell. Her eyes stayed locked on the moon. No scream. No reaction.

I panicked. I couldn't move. Things were falling apart. If it wasn't for William's hand in mine, I would have been next. He pulled me toward Alex, and grabbed Nics by the arm. "Get us inside," William said to him, and seconds later I was blinded by the white world of the upper air.

I was grateful for the nothingness, the absence of oxygen, the silence. It meant we were safe. No one could touch us. But the moment was brief, and when my eyes could see again, they found the barrel of a gun in a dimly lit hallway.

"Don't move," the woman said, but even if I wanted to I couldn't. Almost instantly I felt sick. Her ability, whatever it was, was crippling me by the second. Someone collapsed to the floor behind me, and William fell to his knees at my side. It didn't take long before I recognized the feeling. Hunger. Thirst. To the point of pain. I felt the burning need throughout my body. I had no strength, no will, no life left in me. She was starving us. I hit the ground before I realized I was falling. Too weak to stand.

"Stop," William pleaded, hardly able to get the word out. "Give me the gun."

I watched from the floor, hoping William had the strength to get a hold of her. All he needed was a moment of power. Just a moment.

She didn't move. With her hand settled on the radio on her waist, she stared back, indecisive.

"Please," he whispered.

Her lips moved gradually into a smile. It had been enough. With every breath I felt the relief come as the harsh feeling of starvation dissipated. William held his gaze strong, until we'd all risen to our feet.

"The gun," he said, holding out his open hand. She handed it to him willingly. It was large. Not a handgun. William pointed it at her, and she looked wounded, but didn't retaliate. "Is there anyone in there?" He gestured to a closed door to the left of the hallway.

"No," she said, unable to look away from him.

"Open it," he commanded.

Only then did I begin to hear Kara's moans as she breathed through clenched teeth.

"What happened?" Nics asked, helping Kara into the safety of the dark office. "I don't remember any of it."

"Yeah, you weren't much help either," Alex scoffed.

Both William and I ignored the question as she laid Kara out on the floor. "Sit there. Don't talk or move," William told the woman. He looked back at me. "What do you need?"

"Just something to soak up the blood, so I can heal the wounds."

William slid his shirt over his head.

"Here." He handed it to me and found the small tear in Kara's jeans where the bullet had passed through, his fingers ripping it wider.

"Ready?" he asked her.

She nodded, and I pressed the black cloth against her wounded leg. She covered her mouth and clenched her jaw to keep from screaming as I dug for the bullet. It was messy. Too deep. I couldn't get it.

Kara let out a breath, and her head fell back against the floor.

"Just let me try again," I said as I examined the wound. "I can do it." I'd practiced this over and over again in training, but never under this much pressure. My heart was beating fast. I hadn't realized how much I'd come to care about Kara. I felt her pain as if it were my own. Every second she writhed and moaned made my stomach ache with regret. *I'm sorry. I'm so sorry, Kara.* I dug deeper as she cried out, unable to hold back.

"Elyse," William interrupted. "Maybe you could give her something. Just enough…"

I looked at him confused at first, but he glanced at my left wrist with reason. Maybe I could knock her out long enough to remove the bullets.

"I don't know. What if I—"

"Do it," Alex demanded. His eyes never faltered from her face, and something in them was desperate.

Just a drop. She nodded, and I moved closer to her, pressing the buttons on my bracelet. She opened her mouth, and I let the blood hit her tongue. As soon as she was out I felt thankful I could give her such quick relief.

I moved back to her leg, trying to find the hard metal in her fleshy thigh. I couldn't see through the blood, so I focused on Nics's feet. She moved nervously, shifting her weight back and forth, rocking her body without realizing it. She couldn't look away from the woman against the wall.

"You want me to try?" William asked.

"I got it." I found the bullet with my fingers, carefully pinching them around the slippery surface, and threw it to the floor. I unlatched the bracelet and placed it on my other arm, pressing the buttons without hesitating. The blood ran over the open flesh sealing the wound with fresh skin.

"One more," I whispered, moving on to her arm. I'd just gotten the bullet out when Nics stopped me.

"Elyse," she said.

"Hang on."

"Someone's coming."

The room went quiet. As I lifted my eyes, I recognized something. The books. The desk. This was the room where I'd spoken to Adrianna in my vision. The excitement I'd felt before found its way back into my chest.

"Maybe it's her," I whispered.

Footsteps. Murmurs. William held a finger to his lips, his brow cinched as he tried to make out words through the walls. He reached for my hand and nodded at Nics to make contact with Alex.

"Wait." I stopped him. "What if it's her?"

William looked at me. "What if it's *not*?"

Our eyes stayed connected for what seemed like minutes. Only when the door knob began to twist did we look away from each other. I squeezed William's hand as we waited. Then something hit me. This wasn't how it was in my vision. Things were different. I was alone. No blood on my hands, no darkness outside the windows. This wasn't it. I was wrong.

"Go," I shouted as the door began to open. "Go now, Alex!"

The last image burned into my eyes and followed me even as we were surrounded by white. Christoph's face glaring back at me, hungry for his prize. If we'd taken a second longer we'd be trapped, unable to use Alex as an escape. I'd been so stupid.

I waited for the caves to appear, for the air to fill my lungs, but it didn't come. The emptiness pressed in on me, the nothingness stole my breath, trapped me in a timeless prison. Air. I needed air. I felt my unseen body thrash with panic. Were we stuck?

Alex! I had no voice in this void. No body I could see. No control. Alex!

My heart hammered. My chest fought for life. This was it.

I felt the ground before I saw it, hitting hard from high up. My teeth sank into my lip as my mouth hit the dirt, and I tasted blood on my tongue. My white surroundings had released me, but my pupils let in too much light. Everything was pulsing and blurry from lack of oxygen. I heard the rest of them fall beside me with gasps and groans. I wasn't the only one stuck in the nothing for too long.

"William," I said, squinting as my eyes adjusted.

"You're okay. We're okay." I crashed into his chest.

"Did you see him?" I asked, wiping the blood and dirt from my lips. "I was wrong. I'm sorry. It wasn't how I saw it. Things were different. If I—"

"What things were different?" he asked. I could see him now, and his soft eyes settled my trembling hands.

When I didn't speak he held me closer. "We got out. That's all that matters."

As I looked around I recognized the crevice Kara had summoned me to at Lenaia so many months ago. At least we were home.

"What the hell was that, Alex?" Kara complained, suddenly conscious. She sat on the ground nearby clutching her still wounded arm in her hand.

"He took my ability away mid-travel," Alex answered, his face unable to let go of the shock. "I thought it was over. We were dead." He disappeared and reappeared in seconds. "I don't know why, but he must have given it back."

"We were already gone. He wants us alive," William said.

"Alive?" Alex asked, pacing in the small space. "Why?" The idea seemed ridiculous to him, but he didn't know what we knew.

"It's none of your business," I snapped. I moved toward Kara, trying to busy myself with healing her wound. I didn't want to get into this right now.

"Okay." He crossed his arms over his chest. "Now I *really* want to know. Why would he want any of us alive, Elyse?"

"It doesn't matter. We're out," Kara answered. She closed her eyes as the healing blood sealed her wound. "Thank you."

"It's really great that you're all so happy we're breathing," Alex's voice raised with each word. "But does anybody else realize that we came back with nothing? It was all a waste."

"At least we tried," I said, sitting down next to Kara in the dirt. I hated him for being right.

"Well, I'm sorry," Nics said, hands on her hips and scowling. She'd been so quiet, I'd forgotten she was there. "It was my fault. Take somebody else to protect you next time."

"Nics!" I called after her, but she squeezed through the crevice opening without looking back.

Alex's eyes moved back and forth between William and me. "You two know something."

"Yeah, well, it's private," William answered for me.

"Nothing's private anymore. This is ridiculous." He turned to me. "I should never have listened to you when you said go." He kicked the wall in front of him causing pieces of rock to fall to the ground. "He was right there. I could have killed him."

"Then why didn't you?" I challenged him.

"I don't know," he yelled, but his eyes gave him away. They drifted toward Kara, as she rubbed her freshly healed arm. There was something more in the way he looked at her. Then, as though he had called out her name, she glanced up, speaking something to him silently. "It's just... killing him is the only way to get my father back."

I stared at him in shock. "He has your father?"

"Yes and no." He shook his head, uncomfortable

opening up. "Christoph claims he has my sister." His lips pulled down in disgust. "So my father does what he says. In exchange for her life."

"But *you* left," I said, not understanding.

"His arrangement was with him. Not with me. I stayed for my father, until I realized he was never going to give her back." His voice was quiet, but all of us were silent as he spoke. He'd never said a word about anyone in his life until now. "My dad, he still has hope, but...why would Christoph give her up? Not when he has a messenger in his back pocket." He took a deep breath and looked around, like he just realized he was speaking aloud and not to himself.

"We all have our reasons for wanting him dead," William said, grabbing Alex's attention. "And he will be. Trust me." I wondered what his reason was. His brother's death, his need for our baby, the war, me?

"How can I trust you," Alex laughed, "if you won't even tell me why he wants us alive?"

"Not *you*," I answered. "Us." I glanced at William. "He wants the next generation oracle."

Alex was quiet for a while, digesting the idea. "So he wants both?" he asked, a little surprised by my honesty. "Mind-wipers and the oracle?" He brushed a hand through his dark hair. "And you're sure talking to Adrianna will lead us to the mind-wipers?"

"Positive," I answered. "I'm going to need you to take me back."

"Are you serious?" Kara asked.

"Well, I'm not going to give up," I said, defending my choice.

"How can you be positive, Elyse?" William asked, kneeling down in front of me. "You don't have any way of knowing what she'll say. I'm trying to be supportive but...I can't let you go back there. I shouldn't have let you go in the first place."

"*Let* me?" I said, my voice lifting.

"You know what I mean." William rested a hand on my knee.

"He's right, Elyse. It's too dangerous," Alex added.

I looked up at them. "Since when are you two calling the shots around here? If I want to go back, I'm going back—"

"Wait," Kara said, stopping me from ranting. She was quiet for a minute, thinking or maybe speaking to one of the others in her mind. "Actually, Alex has a pretty good idea."

"So you're pilfering my thoughts now?" Alex smirked at her.

"Yeah, well, say something next time," she said, embarrassed she had been in his mind. "What if Alex goes out on his own looking for Adrianna? It's easier for him to get in and out of places unseen if he's alone. When he finds her, he'll come get you, Elyse, and take you to her."

"I'm okay with that," William said.

"Are you sure, Alex?" I asked. "You'll have no protection. If Christoph catches you—"

"I'll be fine."

Tell him it has to be that room. She'll be there, I said silently to Kara. *I saw it.*

"All right," I agreed. "Thank you."

With all the commotion going on at camp, hardly anyone noticed as we approached. Groups of people were gathered around to watch as Sam and Paul prepared to race.

"What's going on?" I asked Rachel.

"You're back!" She squeezed me tightly and smiled at the others. "Did it go okay? Nics won't talk to me."

"Yeah. Fine," I lied. "What is everyone doing?"

"Oh. Paul and Sam decided we should start our own Olympics. In honor of our soon-to-be changing world. Olympics with abilities would be a lot more fun, don't you think?"

"Yeah," I said, feigning excitement. I wished I could take part in the fun, but I was weighed down by fatigue. I wanted nothing but sleep.

When the two of them took off, the crowd cheered, and I watched for a moment as Paul stuttered and zigzagged drunkenly in the air. Those around me laughed, but my eyes searched for Anna. I needed her, and just as I thought those words, I found her staring back at me as if she'd been looking for me, too.

"I'll be back," I said to William. He nodded, but I could feel him watching me as I walked away. My secrets were building tension between us, and he was starting to notice.

"I was so worried," Anna said, pulling me into a hug. "What happened? Is everyone all right? Did you get what you needed?"

"Come on," I said, grabbing her hand. "I need to talk to you."

I followed the edge of the rock wall until the cheers were background noise.

"What's wrong? Are you okay?" she asked.

"No," I said sitting on the dirt. "Something's happening to me."

She sat down beside me. "What do you mean?"

"I think I'm pregnant, Anna." As soon as I said the words I began picking my cuticles, nervous that uttering it aloud would make it true.

Her eyes brightened. "That's great! Oh my gosh. You were acting like it was something bad."

"It *is*," I insisted. "I can't have a baby. Not now. Not here in this cave. Not when I'm supposed to lead a war."

"Are you sure you're pregnant?"

"No, but if I'm not, then I'm going crazy. I keep seeing these visions, and I don't know if they're real, but they feel real. I feel like I have to listen to them, but what if I'm wrong and...tonight just...I thought I knew what I was doing."

I covered my face with my hands, trying to hide from everything.

"What visions?" she asked pulling my hands away.

"Of Christoph and the future. At least I think it's the future...I don't know." I stared off into the distance. "Things...an oracle should see."

"Well, I know you're not crazy. Maybe these visions are supposed to happen. Maybe you're supposed to listen to them. Try not to over-think everything. You do that, you know? You over-analyze. I mean, isn't there some prophecy that says you'll succeed in all this?"

I bit the inside of my cheek. "Yes."

"So trust your gut, and if you're pregnant, be happy about it. Don't waste these precious moments on worrying that it's not the right time or place."

"I'm just..." I rested my head against the stone wall behind me. "I'm just scared."

"You should be scared. It's the scariest thing in the world to become a mother. Your life will never be the same, but it's all worth it."

"It's not just that." My voice raised a little as I admitted what was really bothering me. "We're at war, Anna, and the thing Christoph wants the most is *my* baby." My eyes welled with tears, and I looked up trying to hold them back.

She leaned toward me and pressed her cheek to mine as we hugged. "We'll never let that happen."

I nodded, hoping it was true. We weren't able to save everyone from the fire. What if my child's life slipped through my hands, just like the others?

She pulled away and shoved my shoulder playfully. "I can't believe you didn't tell me it was even a possibility that you were pregnant. What happened to best friends for life, huh? Girlfriends always kiss and tell."

I laughed, dabbing away the tears with my knuckles. "I'm so glad you're here." Her lids squinted around her deep brown eyes as she smiled. It was nice to see her healthy, back to the Anna I remembered. "I think being around all these Descendants is rubbing off on you. You look younger."

"Yeah, right," she scoffed. "So tell me what happened tonight. I was going crazy waiting for you."

I shook my head. "It was a complete disaster."

Anna and I stayed away until voices began to quiet in the distance.

"Thanks," I whispered to her before ducking into the tent I shared with William. I slipped beneath his arm quietly in the dark, and though there was still tension between us that I couldn't deny, it felt good to have him hold me.

His lips pressed against the back of my neck. "I'm sorry," he said quietly. "For saying I wouldn't *let* you go back."

I turned to face him, the fronts of our bodies pressing together, and we kissed. The touch of his mouth was gentle against mine, but I still winced.

"Your lip."

"It's okay," I said. "It's not that bad."

He reached for his bag anyway and pulled out a flashlight and a small pocketknife. I watched as he ran the blade across the same thumb he always used to heal me. "Here." He slid his finger over the cut, making sure it closed up with focused eyes. When he was finished I tested the new skin with my tongue.

The silence tempted me to talk, but I stayed quiet.

"I'm trying not to be controlling and protective," he said. "I really am."

"I don't think it's working," I teased, but maybe he had a right to be protective. I wasn't sure I trusted myself these days.

"I just don't want to lose you."

The way he looked at me as his hand found my face. I'd forgotten that look. I'd been looking past it, taking it for granted.

"I don't want to lose you either."

We kissed slowly at first, remembering how sweet these moments could be, the moments where it was just us and the world falling down around us didn't matter. I inhaled with surprise as he pulled me on top of him, heat building between our bodies. He lifted my shirt up over my head and kissed my bare shoulders.

"I love you, Ellie," he whispered, his breath tickling my neck.

"I love you, too."

CHAPTER NINETEEN

—

AS IF ADMITTING MY FEAR TO ANNA HAD MADE IT a reality, every morning for the past week I was hit with the same relentless nausea that woke me out of a deep sleep. I was covered in night sweats and had to move fast to my secret spot to keep from waking anyone. Most were still sleeping in tents around me, but dim light had begun to spread across the rock walls. Mr. Williamson was awake, and the supply team would be up soon to prepare for the day's missions. Backpacks were already set out on tables waiting to be filled with weapons and food as I passed.

I tried to swallow the sick feeling down, but the bitter taste of rising stomach acid made me gag. My fingers tightened around my water bottle, and I nodded at the two night guards standing watch near the edge of camp. They nodded back, assuming I had somewhere important to be. In truth, I just needed to be alone, where no one would hear me vomit. Tears came as I wretched. I knew what it meant. It was proof that it was real, and I couldn't deny it anymore. I was pregnant.

When it was over, I moved to a different spot and slouched against the cave wall wiping the tears from my cheeks. I rinsed my mouth out and drank big gulps of water trying to wash the taste away. How was I supposed to have a baby now? The fearful thoughts returned the tears. I felt guilty for not wanting her, even though there was already love building between us in a way I couldn't explain. I *did* want her, just not now. Not here. I looked around at the dimly lit cave, our home, with floors of red dirt. This was no place for a newborn. How was I supposed to fight with a baby to care for? How would I lead? A different kind of nausea formed in my stomach as I considered the fact that I might never make up for the lives Christoph had taken.

"Hey," William said from a distance.

I jumped with surprise and wiped my tears discretely, hoping he couldn't see my swollen eyes in the faded light. "Hey."

"You okay?"

He didn't need to see my eyes to know something was wrong.

"Yeah," I said. He sat next to me, and I put my head on his shoulder.

His body slouched beneath my cheek as he sighed. "I know you're not."

"I'm fine. Just a lot on my mind."

He nodded. "You don't have to carry everything on your shoulders. I can carry some of the burden, you know."

"I'm stubborn that way."

"One of these days you're going to have to start telling me things."

I bit my lips. Did he know? "I tell you things."

He stared at me, waiting for something more, but I stayed silent.

The sound of voices growing louder in the distance caught my attention, and I looked away. "I brought something for you," he said, giving up on the subject. He pulled two new toothbrushes and a small tube of toothpaste from his back pocket.

I smiled at his perfect timing. "Thanks."

He poured the water for me as I brushed my teeth and cleaned my face. I tied my hair back in a ponytail, and washed the dirt off of my arms.

"I like this look," he said.

I laughed because I knew I was a mess. "I'm pretty sure grimy camper isn't fashionable these days."

"It's kind of cute." His warm hand found my face, and he pressed his full lips to mine. The feel of his kiss never got old. As my mouth pushed against his, my heart beat with excitement. He reached for my waist, pulling me closer. I wanted to be closer, but when his fingers grazed the bare skin of my stomach, I thought of the baby and pulled back.

"So, what's the game plan for today?" I asked, breaking

away from the moment.

I left him standing alone, his eyebrows sinking in confusion as I walked away. "What's wrong, Ellie?"

"Nothing," I said too cheerfully. "We just need to get back. See if there's any news about Adrianna. That's all."

He nodded and pressed his lips together, unconvinced.

"I knew this would happen." His voice wasn't harsh, but sad.

"What?" I asked, walking back to him.

"That I would lose you to this war."

I grabbed his hands. "You haven't lost me."

"You're far away lately." He tightened his fingers around mine. "I don't know where you've been, but..."

"I've been here," I said growing defensive. "I just..."

He shook his head, and my chest felt nervous. I had to tell him. I wanted to tell him, but things couldn't change.

"You have to let me be who I'm supposed to be. I have to be strong. I have to lead. I can't be weak like I've been."

"And I'm supposed to help you be strong, but you're forcing me out."

"Well, I'm sorry," I said, tears fighting against my lashes. "I'm pregnant." There. It was done. The words were out, and there was no going back.

His face was still for a moment, like he couldn't process what I'd said. Time seemed to stretch on forever as I waited for his reaction. My ears blocked out the sound of the distant voices. My eyes stared into his, expecting fear, panic, or anger, but his lips slowly revealed a smile and a breathy laugh escaped. "I thought...you said..."

"I was wrong," I answered with a gentle voice, still trying to accept the truth. "Some things seem to come true no matter what I do or say."

He moved closer, slipping his fingers into my hair and pressing his lips to my forehead. "I'm glad you were wrong. I was hoping you were."

Our eyes met, and he kissed me. His lips folded into mine with love, soft and familiar. I wrapped my arms around his neck, and he pulled me closer. I always felt safest when he held me. For that moment all the uncertainty of the future faded to the background.

His hands lowered to my stomach, still flat enough to keep our secret. "So you're sure?"

"Aside from the vomiting, either I'm going crazy or there's an oracle inside me."

"What do you mean?"

"I've been seeing things," I answered, moving to sit down against the rock wall. "Visions." If he was going to know about the baby, I had to tell him everything.

He sat next to me and rested his forearms on the tops of his bent knees. "What kind of visions? Dreams?"

"They're not dreams." I remembered the way the world pulled away each time, the loss of control as my consciousness was swept away. I hated the feeling. "I saw Christoph light the forest around my parents' house on fire. I've seen warehouses of people that I know Christoph is planning to use for something, and I think I know how to stop him. One of the visions is of me talking with Adrianna. That's why I've been so insistent on finding her. If I can get to her, I know she'll help us."

He stared at the dirt with high eyebrows before he looked at me. "And you say you tell me things."

I shrugged, trying to casually play off the secret I'd kept from him. "I just did, didn't I?"

"Okay so you *eventually* tell me things." He laughed, but I could hear the frustration behind it. "*If* I beg."

"Ninety years of keeping secrets has made me a little... secretive."

He laced his fingers through mine. "Just a *little*. You know, only about babies, visions, things like that."

I stared back at him with tight lips, embarrassed that I'd kept so much from him, but he only smiled at me.

"I didn't think you'd take it this well."

"I'm not taking it well. I'm livid. Can't you tell?" He narrowed his eyes at me, faking a glare. "Okay, I know I should be, but I couldn't be mad if I wanted to." His smile widened. "You're pregnant. I'm too happy to be mad."

"I'm glad *you're* happy," I said, shaking my head. "I'm...nervous."

"Don't be. It'll be fine. It's meant to be, Ellie." He turned to face me and brought our laced fingers to his lips for a kiss. "I've been waiting for this for a long time."

My heart relaxed, finally releasing the secret I'd been holding in, and I let myself enjoy his happiness.

"Marry me," he said, tilting my chin up so I would look

at him.

"I already told you I would," I laughed.

He leaned in and kissed me with smiling lips.

"Today," he said, our foreheads still pressed together.

I pulled away surprised. "Here?"

He shrugged. "Yeah. Why not? Everyone is with us."

I let myself get carried away by the fantasy for just a moment but shook my head instead. "We can't."

"I thought we weren't going to let Christoph control us."

"He's not. It's not that. I'm supposed to be a leader. We just can't stop our efforts to have a wedding."

"It's one day," he said, not seeing my point. "Besides, some of us could use a break."

I shook my head. "We have to stay focused."

Throughout breakfast William's face seemed brighter as he spoke. Everything was said with a smile, and though I was still unsure about how he would react in the future, I enjoyed seeing him happy.

After we ate, Anna dragged me off to join the women at the bathing pool. I was anxious to get updates from Alex about Adrianna, but I hadn't seen him around, and if anyone needed a bath it was me. We left our shoes at the entrance of the pool so no men would enter and stripped down naked before diving into the cool water. I washed and combed my hair, trying not to be shy as I bathed. No one else was. They splashed and screamed, chasing each other through the water.

"Why are you so smiley this morning," I asked as Anna dipped her head back in the water. She'd been looking at me differently.

"What?" she asked, obviously hiding something. "I can't smile?"

I rolled my eyes at her and grabbed the soap from the ledge. "I've known you too long. Come on. Spit it out."

She avoided my eyes, but couldn't hold back her grin. "The girls are having fun," she said, trying to distract me. I watched for a moment as Chloe dove through the waterfall, and someone else covered the surface with blooming white roses.

"Is it Mac?" I asked, not letting it go.

"Maybe." She shrugged, squeezing the water out of her black and silver hair. "He's cute, huh?" It was funny to hear her talk about a crush, like we were back in junior high again.

I laughed. "*Cute* isn't exactly the word I'd use."

"You know what I mean." Her smile still lingered as I passed her the soap.

"That's not it, then?"

"Oh come on, Ellie. You're the queen of secrets, and I can't have one?"

"No. Look at you. You're dying to spill it. Just tell me already." I dunked my head to rinse as I waited for her to answer.

She looked behind us toward the shoes at nothing. "All right. Fine. Let's get out. I'm sure it's been long enough."

I wrapped a towel around my body and followed her, searching for whatever it was she'd been looking for. When we reached our clothes there was a white box sitting next to mine.

"Open it," she urged.

I looked at her under low lashes and untied the blue ribbon. Inside, on top of the white tissue paper, was a note.

All is fair in love and war.

Marry me.

His words made me smile. I shook my head, folding the note up and digging into the tissue paper. "I told him I would," I mumbled, but Anna only watched with anticipation. Beneath the wrapping was a white silk dress. I lifted it out of the box by its straps and my mouth opened a little at its beauty. It was a halter with a billowing skirt, much like Marilyn Monroe's famous wind-swept dress from *The Seven Year Itch.*

"It's gorgeous," Anna said, her voice low and dramatic. "Now, come on. You have to put it on. They're waiting."

"Now?" My eyes widened in surprise.

"Yeah. Put on your clothes. You can change into the dress in the crevice." She had me by the hand, rushing me through the camp before I had time to protest.

"Can you believe this is happening?" Anna asked, once we were alone.

"No." I shook my head, heart pumping faster and harder in a way it never had. "We were supposed to wait. Who's out there? Does everyone know?"

"Ellie, relax," she said, shoving the dress into my hands. "It's all hush hush, okay? William made it pretty clear you didn't want to have any fun with this."

"That's not true," I said, sounding defensive. "I like to have fun. It's just a bad time. What about the camp? What if something happens? We need to be alert at all times…"

"Elyse," she said, taking hold of my shoulders. "Can you for once just allow yourself to have a moment? The world isn't going to fall apart in an hour."

"It might."

She sighed through her nose. "You really are a master of excuses, you know." We looked at each other, and she smiled at me in a motherly way. "How long have you wanted this? A lifetime? You've sacrificed so much for so long, and you finally have what you've always wanted, and you're letting this war take it all away from you. Life doesn't happen when it's convenient, Ellie. It happens when it happens. Just let yourself enjoy it."

I bit my lip, reluctant to see her point, but what was I going to do? Leave him at the altar? "Okay," I said. "You're right. I can't let this war consume me." That's what William was afraid of, and I was starting to see his point.

"I always knew you would fall in love," Anna said, as I stepped into the dress.

I rolled my eyes at her. She had not.

"You wanted it too badly for it to not happen."

I tried to hold back my smile, because it was true. I'd never wanted anything so badly, and as nervous as I was about it happening here and now, at least it was secret. I promised I would let myself have this moment. It might be the last good memory I'd have.

"Oh, here," Anna said, handing me the pearl ring on her index finger. "Something borrowed."

I slipped it on and ran my fingers across my necklace, my something old. In the box there had been a set of pearls that once belonged to William's grandmother. "Thanks." I smiled at her. "It matches."

"You look beautiful," Anna said, tying my wet hair back with the blue ribbon from the box. She pressed her lips to my cheek. "Nobody deserves this more than you."

When I was ready, I followed Anna along the cave wall away from camp, kicking up rust-colored dust around my white shoes. I stopped as the oasis came into view. Like the trees around our campsite, it was a paradise sprung from nothingness.

The aisle was lined with cherry trees that showered light pink petals onto the ground. Beneath the petals lay a path of mossy green grass sprinkled with wildflowers, and at the end of the walkway was something even more spectacular.

An altar of trees shot up in a semi-circle so entangled they created a canopy of leaves. Light from somewhere I couldn't see shone through the branches the way it does when the sun breaks through the clouds, like heaven. I'd never seen anything so beautiful.

When my eyes met William's, he smiled and lifted his

eyebrows at me, pleased with his scheme. I shook my head at him, but couldn't keep from smiling back. Next to him was Mac, and to his right William's parents and sister. On my side there was only one person, Chloe. She clasped her hands together in excitement, and Anna tugged at my arm.

As I started forward, something tapped the sole of my shoe, and I looked back. With every step I took, green shoots emerged from the earth, each one blooming into a white tulip. I looked at William in amazement, but he seemed to be watching nothing but me, as if I was what amazed him.

"Who gives this woman to be married?" Mac asked as I reached them. He tried his best to sound formal, but his voice was too rough for such delicate words. It made me smile to hear him.

"I do," Anna said. She and Mac made eyes at each other like they were next in line.

"You really want to marry this kid?" he asked.

I laughed with the group and nodded. "I do."

I took William's hands in mine, the heat between our palms familiar and reassuring. His green eyes held me the way they always had. His full lips, defined jaw, his smile, all perfect, but none of it was the reason I felt in love with him. It was the way he looked at me, like I was the only thing he needed. I couldn't stop smiling. My cheeks hurt.

———

WORD HAD GOTTEN OUT BEFORE THE CEREMONY

was over, and by the time our small group made it back to camp, an entire reception had formed in The Cavern. The natural pillars, formed over the ages by stalactites and stalagmites, were decorated with vines of jasmine, filling the place with their scent. Floating stars lit the dark cave ceiling, and a lighter version of Lenaia's traditional drum beats and flutes played, reminding me of the last time I'd danced in these caves. A buffet of meats and Greek delicacies lined one edge of the dance floor with tables set off to the right.

"What is this?" I asked William. I had expected to announce the news and that our friends would be excited, but this?

He shook his head as we stared down on to The Cavern floor. "It wasn't me." His face was just as shocked as mine.

Anna stepped up beside me. "I may have told some people." The corners of her eyes creased as she smiled, hoping I wouldn't be mad.

"Anna," I said, my voice spiking with irritation.

"Oh, lighten up. What's the harm in having a little fun?"

"Fun." I laughed. "Sure. We're only at war. Why not?"

Anna looked at me more seriously. "Exactly, and I don't expect it's going to get any easier. So have fun now, while you still can."

I sighed. There wasn't much I could do about it anyway. "I knew this was a bad idea."

"It might be for the best," Mrs. Nickel chimed in. "In times like these, people need a little distraction."

Maybe she was right. Maybe all anyone really wanted was an excuse to dance and drink moonshine.

Without warning Rachel popped into form next to us. "Come dance with us, married lady!" she pleaded.

I resisted, but Anna was still giving me that look.

"Please," Rachel persisted.

"Okay," I agreed, knowing I had no choice in the matter. "Okay."

William followed us and took my hands once we'd joined the crowd.

"So, Mrs. Nickel." He spun me under his arm. "Ready to have fun?"

I shrugged. "Yeah, I guess," I teased, but I couldn't keep a straight face. My hard shell was cracking. He pulled me close and I smiled wide.

"Shocking," he laughed.

Despite my hesitancy about all of it, I couldn't deny how happy I felt. Marrying William was the best moment of my life, and no matter how many awful things loomed in my future, tonight, that happiness was untouchable.

Suddenly Alex was next to us. "We need to leave," he said. "She's there. Adrianna."

CHAPTER TWENTY

—

ALEX'S WORDS CAUGHT ME SO OFF GUARD IT TOOK me a minute to really understand what he was saying.

"What?" I asked. "Now?"

"We might not have another chance before it's too late," he said, his voice insistent.

William's gaze dropped to my stomach as people continued to dance around us. I could feel the conflict building within him.

"I'm..." I hesitated, not knowing what to expect from him.

"I'll go alone then," Alex snapped, turning away.

"Wait," I said, catching his arm. He looked back at me and so did William. "If my visions are true, William..."

"I know but—" He stopped himself and rubbed the back of his neck with his hand. "What is your gut telling you? Will you be safe?" I could see the tension in his face as he waited for my answer.

I nodded, feeling guilty. As much as I wanted to deny it, I'd been waiting for this moment for weeks. Everything in me knew it was now or never. "It's telling me to go." I took his hand. "I'll be fine. I will." I waited for him to look at me. "Trust me."

"Okay," he said, still unsure. I knew it took everything in him to let me leave.

Before I had a chance to say goodbye, Alex pulled me away from him, and we were gone.

When I opened my eyes we were in the crevice. "You need to change," he said, walking out of sight. "Call me when you're ready."

I slipped out of my dress as quickly as I could, regretting my choice, but knowing it was the right one. I pulled on my army green pants, black shirt and boots, strapping my dart gun to my thigh. This was what I'd been wearing in the vision. It had to work.

"Alaximandrios," I said when I was finished.

I only saw a glimpse of him before we were swept away by the white. We appeared in the same hallway we had before, the one where I learned what it felt like to starve to death. This time it was empty. Daylight shone through the tinted windows exposing us to whatever threat might be lurking around the corner, but all was silent.

"Don't stay here. Just listen for my call, okay?" I said to Alex.

He didn't move. Instead his eyes challenged me.

"Alex, go," I demanded, and he disappeared.

I stared at the blue door for a moment, trying to relax my shoulders. I had to seem confident. I took a deep breath and turned the knob.

"I'm just here to talk," I said as I entered.

She didn't look surprised to see me. Instead her arms were crossed, as though she'd been waiting. She leaned back against the front side of the desk, just as I'd seen it.

"I have to tell you," she said, sweeping her brown curls behind her shoulder. "You're either very brave or very stupid for coming here."

"Probably a little of both," I answered.

"You should be careful using that messenger. He was on our side once, you know."

I glanced around the room feeling the tension between us.

"He's not anymore."

"You realize Christoph has one, too, and his is faster, more precise. I press one button and he'd have Christoph here before you could blink. So much for your revolution."

"I need your help," I said, hoping she wasn't as hard-hearted as she pretended to be. My child's life was in her hands. I needed her to be on my side.

"And what makes you so sure I'll help you, Elyse?" A smile pulled at her lips that could be every bit as dangerous as it was curious. I couldn't trust her, but she was the only one who had the answers I needed.

"You helped us escape." I said. "I don't think you're as bad as you make yourself out to be."

"Maybe, maybe not," she answered.

"We need to know where the mind-wipers are. We can't let Christoph get to them."

She laughed. "So you really do have faith in the human race?" I didn't know exactly what she meant, but I answered.

"Yes, I do."

"You're naïve." She shook her head. "Do you think generations before us haven't tried integration?" My throat felt dry as I swallowed, realizing she knew more about our plan than she should. "It doesn't work, and the consequences cost even more lives than keeping us a secret."

"I don't think that's true."

"It's history."

"Is it? Or has Christoph manipulated you like he has everyone else? Into thinking he's the only one who knows what's best for our race." I stood taller. "He's wrong. You're wrong."

"Don't test me, Elyse."

"You're better than him...I just..." I could see her expression hardening. Apparently their relationship was a delicate subject. "Will you help us or not?"

"Even if I wanted to, I couldn't," she answered. "Christoph has who he wants. You're too late."

That wasn't the answer I needed. This had to work. I'd seen it. "I don't believe you."

She walked toward me, and I tried to resist the urge to back away. Her presence was threatening. I didn't know what would happen if she got too close. She wheeled around behind me, but I kept my gaze forward, though I felt her hand settle onto the top of my shoulder.

"You realize," she whispered, "if I really thought you could even come close to us, I wouldn't have set you free. I'm sorry, Elyse. I just don't think you have it in you."

I didn't know if it was the tone in her voice or the feeling of her breath on my neck that reminded me she wasn't a friend, but I knew I needed to get out while I still could. William was right. There was a fine line between bravery and foolishness. I was a fool for coming here.

I turned to face her. "You're wrong."

As I walked past her, toward the door, I clenched my jaw willing her to let me leave. How could I have put my-self and my child in such danger for nothing?

"Elyse," Adrianna said, stopping me with my hand on the doorknob. I waited, knowing at any moment she could choose to betray me. I turned to look at her. "This time there will be no going back." Her expression softened, and for a moment I thought I saw sympathy.

I didn't fully relax until Alex had me back in the caves. Back to William.

"Thank you," I said as we appeared in the crevice, but he was gone before he heard me.

William sat alone as he waited. He looked out of place in his tux, his elegant apparel clashing against the rustic backdrop of earth and stone. His heavy eyes lit up when he saw me, letting go of their worry.

"I shouldn't have gone," I said as I approached.

"I'm just glad you're back," he answered, wrapping his arms around me. "You're alive."

I buried my face into his shoulder. "I shouldn't be."

He held me closer. "I've learned that I have to trust you—"

"Don't trust me," I interrupted. "I'm crazy. I don't know what I was thinking."

He pulled back and looked at me. "Trust me, don't trust me. What, are you pregnant or something?"

I smiled at his attempt to make me feel better, but it was the fact that I was pregnant that made me so mad at myself for what I'd done.

"It was all for nothing, William," I said with remorse. "I was wrong. I'm surprised she didn't kill me on the spot or hand me over to Christoph."

"Well at least you were right about that," he said, pulling me closer. "We'll find the mind-wipers some other way."

"I was just so sure. I saw her face in a vision. We found her."

"Her?"

I rested my head against his shoulder, still baffled. "There's a girl. A mind-wiper. She's the one he needs."

"If you saw her, then we'll find her."

I shook my head. "It's too late. She said Christoph already had who he wanted. He has her. Who knows where?"

At first he didn't say anything. Then he kissed my

forehead. "It'll be fine," he whispered, but I knew he didn't believe it. "If it's okay with you, from now on I'm just going to let you be mad at me instead of letting you go."

My body shook as I laughed into his chest. "Fine," I said.

"We should get back. I'm sure everyone is asking where we are."

"What should we tell them?" I asked.

"We're newlyweds," he answered with a grin. "We'll just tell them to use their imaginations."

I was still a little shaky when we rejoined the party, but William kept close, with a warm firm grip on my hand.

"Where the heck have you been?" Chloe asked, finally ripping me away from him. "Why'd you change out of your dress?" She had a whine to her voice that made me think she had either been sneaking sips of moonshine or Sam had done her a favor.

"It was uncomfortable," I said. "This is more me."

"Come dance with me," she slurred as she pulled me into a crowd of smiling, happy people. Her black hair was damp with sweat, and she tossed it over her shoulder.

"I like Peter," she blurted out, but the music was too loud.

"Who?"

"Peter," she yelled, pointing to a young boy dancing with a toddler. I didn't recognize him, but I was happy. I wanted her to be accepted, to be a part of this.

I smiled and twirled her under my arm. "He's cute," I

said. "Where's your mom?"

Her eyes gave them away, and I followed her gaze to Anna and Mac dancing so closely nobody could pull them apart. Her head snapped back with laughter, and he swung her delicate body back and forth with ease. I watched them for a second, loving Mac for giving her something she'd lost.

"I'll be right back, okay?" Chloe said before she bounded off toward her crush. I knew she wouldn't be, so I left the dance floor and found my friends lounging against a stone pillar in the distance.

"And so the queen finally decides to grace us with her presence," Sam bellowed as I walked toward them.

I bowed and curtsied. "Hello, minions," I said with feigned arrogance.

"So how did it go with Adrianna?" Nics asked.

I immediately glared at Alex. "You told them?"

"Oops," he said with a shrug.

I shook my head, annoyed with him, and sat across from Nics. "It didn't go well."

"Um, I'd say it did," Rachel huffed. "You're still *alive.* What were you thinking going by yourself?"

Paul kept quiet, but I could feel his disapproving eyes on me after what had happened with his girlfriend.

"You're right. It was stupid," I said. "I don't want to talk about it." I glared at her half joking, half serious.

Rachel smiled at me. "Only because it's your wedding day." Her voice spiked with girly excitement. "Where's your husband anyway?"

"*Husband.*" I twisted the gold band of braided olive leaves around my ring finger. "I'm going to have to get used to that. It sounds funny." I looked around, scanning the crowd, but he was nowhere. "I don't know where he is."

"Probably hiding," Alex said. "It's game over now. No more making girls fall in love with him. He's stuck with you. One woman...for the next 400 years...forever."

"Shut up," Rachel scoffed, giving him the look of death. "Besides, they were always stuck with each other. They're meant to be."

As my eyes continued to search through the chaos, I finally found him and Kara off to the side of the dance floor. She looked sad, but he smiled at her and tousled a hand through her hair. She shoved him back playfully, but her face still showed the hurt she felt. He hugged her, letting her bury her face into his chest.

"I don't think she's taking it well," Rachel whispered to me.

Everyone stayed up far later than normal. Mac was distracted and failed to announce "lights out" until half of the camp was already passed out in their tents. Even after the music stopped, voices and laughter carried through The Cavern.

That night William and I claimed the bathing pool.

"I had Christine mimic what we had at Lenaia," he said, proud of his surprise.

Willow branches draped over the edges of the pool,

and the surface was covered with petals that rained on us from a massive cherry tree in the center of the water.

I smiled wide, anxious to dip my toes in. "It's amazing."

William slipped his shirt over his head. "You want to get in?"

I nodded and did the same, stripping down to my underwear. As I unbuttoned my pants, something fell from the pocket. A note. It had been folded over and over into the smallest square it could make. My fingers pulled open each tightly bent crease until it bloomed into a full page.

"Come on," William yelled from the water.

"I'll be right there," I said glancing at the signature along the bottom of the letter. It was a message from the oracle.

My Dearest Elyse,

You've done well. I know you don't understand my choices. They have been difficult to make. One day you will realize that there was always a purpose behind my actions, and though at times the price of those actions was high, they were necessary. It was I who betrayed your location at your parents'. Far more lives would have been lost in a different battle had I not led them to you that day.

Understand that it is in your child's nature to protect you. The visions she shares will be meant to guide you. To help you know the future that should be, not only the future that will be. You need to believe in what you see, to believe in her. My choice to betray you and William to Christoph is what gave you a daughter, and make no mistake you will need her to win this war. Trust her. She's the only gift I have to give you. Let her show you where to go from here.

Christoph has made a mistake. He has indeed captured descendants of Mnemosyne, but he has the wrong pair. You still have time to find the girl, but you must act now. Kara has seen the house. She's been there, but the memory has been taken from her. Have Alex look into her mind, and he'll know where to go.

As for me, my time is coming to a close, and though Christoph has my body in captivity, he will never have control of my mind. Be strong for the both of us, Elyse. Challenging times are ahead. The legacy of the oracle is in your hands. She will not lead you astray.

- Florence

I clutched the letter in my hand, my heart beating out of my chest. It hadn't been a waste. I smiled at Adrianna's two-tongued ways. She'd planned to help me all along.

CHAPTER TWENTY-ONE

—

"WHERE DID YOU GET THIS?" WILLIAM ASKED THE NEXT morning.

"Adrianna must have slipped it into my pocket when I was there," I answered, pulling my shirt over my head.

"This is something, Ellie," he said, raising his eyebrows. "I mean, we could really stop him from doing whatever it is he's up to."

"I know." I smiled, ready to go share the news. "Are you going to get ready or what?"

He lay there in our tangled blankets, his sculpted chest exposed.

"Does it have to be over?" he asked, pulling me back down. His hand rested on my stomach, and he looked at it with warm eyes. "Not very big."

"Not yet. I'm hoping she'll stay that way for a while."

"She? You mean *he*, right?" he teased.

"She," I clarified.

"All right, *she* must be happy," he continued, his warm palm sending heat across my belly. "You didn't get sick this morning."

The word sick was enough to make my mouth taste sour. "Uh-oh."

"What?"

I scrambled for the zipper on the tent door and opened it just in time.

———

"WELL HELLO, MARRIED LADY," RACHEL TEASED AS I sat down next to her at breakfast.

I laughed. "Hi." She lifted a backpack to her lap that was full to the brim with supplies and stuffed some bread rolls in the side pocket. "Where are you going?"

"Another recon mission," Sam said sitting beside me. "We think the Hunters have information, but Dr. Nickel is taking us this time. Me, Nics, Rachel, and Paul."

"Are you ready for that?" I asked Rachel.

"Not really," she said without looking at me, "but being ready doesn't make much of a difference." She shrugged. "It's what we're here to do."

I pulled the letter out of my pocket. "I guess you're right."

Once the rest of my inner circle had joined us, including Dr. Nickel and Mac, I read it aloud. When I looked up they all stared back at me.

"I think that settles it," Dr. Nickel said. "We'll postpone our recon mission and team up with you—"

"Not a good idea," Mac interrupted. "Small groups have been working. You won't know what to expect there. It could be a trap. Large groups are harder to manage." He tipped his head at me. "It's up to you, Elyse, but my advice is to take no more than three."

The letter had decided two of them for me already. "All right. I definitely need Kara and Alex," I said, thinking aloud.

William stared at me intently, willing me to see his point of view after what happened last night. I was carrying his child.

"Sorry," he spoke up. "I'm not letting you go without me again. You can be mad if you want, but I'm coming."

"All right," I agreed. "We leave tonight."

Dr. Nickel left with our friends on their recon mission not long after that. If anyone had information on what Christoph was planning it would be the Hunters. I didn't disagree with their plan, but it still had me worried for them. It was hard to see things as a leader when my friends were the ones risking their lives for this war. Hunters weren't merciful.

"You okay?" William asked.

"Huh?" I was still lost in thought, my mind on our friends. He nodded to the gun in my hand as I flicked the safety on and off for the tenth time. "Oh. Yeah," I answered, handing him the weapon. "Give this one to Alex."

In front of me, atop our planning table, was an array

of weapons glinting under the lantern light. Knives, guns, and a mound of freshly carved darts I'd been making to keep myself busy until nightfall. We'd get the best coverage at night, but the waiting was torture.

"Let's go then," Kara answered my thought. "It should be dark enough." She stood and tucked a bigger knife into her boot.

"I still need to see where we're going," Alex said, leaning on the back two legs of his chair.

Kara pretended not to hear him at first and busied herself with her already tied bootlaces.

"You might not find anything," she said without looking up. For some reason she was resisting this part. "I guess you can try..."

Alex let the chair fall back on all four legs and jumped to his feet. When he placed his palms gently against either side of her forehead, I could tell his closeness made her tense. Something had changed since the last time he'd looked into her mind. Their eyes connected for a moment before Kara closed her lids and let him in. Maybe they felt more for each other than either was letting on. The two of them stood still and quiet as William and I waited.

"Get out," Kara said suddenly, shoving Alex in the chest. He stumbled backward. "Those thoughts are private."

He stared at her, guilty and defensive. "Like you're not in my head all the time. You know how I feel."

Her lips tightened, and she shook her head at a loss for words.

"I have a right to know if you feel the same," he continued.

"No you don't," she yelled back at him. "Not if I don't want you to."

William and I stayed quiet, but I couldn't keep from watching them. From the look in their eyes, they were either going to make out or kill each other.

Kara pressed her fingers to her forehead, like the conversation was giving her a headache. "Let's just focus on the mission, okay?"

"Look, I'm sorry," Alex said, trying to recover. He reached out his hand, but she caught it before he could touch her, twisting his arm until he was on his knees.

"You're a real jerk, you know that, Alex?"

He didn't struggle or try to disappear. Instead he looked up at her, grimacing a bit as she put pressure on his shoulder. "So are you. Maybe that's why you like me."

She let go and turned back to me and William. "Can we leave?" she asked with an edge to her voice.

William dared a glance at Alex. "Any chance you found out where we're supposed to be going during all that?"

"Yes," he answered, still on his knees.

When Alex transported us, it was to a place somewhere outside, and the glow of the moon was the only thing that helped me make out our surroundings. The silver light glinted in William's eyes as we made our way up a dirt path surrounded by pine trees and boulders. Kara and Alex were close behind, both of them silent, or perhaps taking part in a silent conversation. I walked faster than normal, the muscles in my legs burning as the path led us uphill. I was anxious to feel right about my choices. Some part of me believed that after we foiled Christoph's plans I'd feel better about the fire, maybe I'd be able to let it go.

When we got closer to the house, Alex disappeared. "The place is empty," he said after appearing in front of me. He shrugged. "You're sure she's here?"

"Yeah, she's probably just hiding," I said. "Do you hear her, Kara?"

She shook her head. "We need to get closer."

The four of us walked up the winding path toward the porch light that blinked like the North Star in the distance.

"I don't hear anything," Kara said, and my heart sank into my stomach. I didn't want to believe that Christoph had her.

"I still want to check. Maybe there's something there. A clue."

As we got closer the place looked more like a shack than a house. It was nothing more than an old one-room cottage made of gray, weathered wood and broken windows. From where I stood, it looked abandoned.

I soaked a dart and loaded it just in case Christoph's men were close, but I'd already lost hope. I knew they were gone, *she* was gone. William sped up and went through the front door before the rest of us. I didn't think anything of it. All I could think about was Christoph and the girl, about how I'd failed.

"Wait! Stop." I heard William yell from inside the house, but something was wrong with his voice. The words were a struggle. I ran, my heart picking up with each quick step that propelled me forward.

I reached the door before Kara, and though Alex was already there, he just stood, staring at the girl with two open slits down her wrists. For a moment I was relieved. I could heal her cuts, that didn't matter. William had found the girl. Her familiar face stayed locked in his trance, immobile with false love for him, but my smile faded when I caught sight of William who had fallen to his knees.

"What is it?" I asked, scrambling to the floor where he sat. His hands clutched a large knife that protruded from his chest. As soon as I saw it, I started to shake.

"I love you," he said, like it was over. His eyes closed, and he lost his hold on her.

I knew we were here to save the girl, but when his body fell to the floor, I immediately shot a dart into her neck, and she fell too.

"Help me," I screamed to Kara and Alex, who were still frozen in shock.

They turned him over, and I readjusted my bracelet, stabbing two fresh wounds into my right wrist.

Kara's hands were covering her mouth, and all Alex could do was stare as I waited for the blood to come.

"I didn't hear her," Kara said over and over under her

hands.

"Take it out," I said to Alex.

He pulled the knife from William's chest, and blood began to flow faster from the wound. It spread onto the wood floor, soaking into my pants, but I refused to think about it. I couldn't. If I did, I'd come undone.

"He'll be okay," Kara repeated to herself, but she was rocking nervously.

I tried to ignore the doubts in my head, the voice that told me he was already dead. Instead I forced myself to breathe, to move, to heal him.

I lifted his shirt, and my throat tightened at the sight of the open wound over his heart. *Please keep beating*, I thought as my blood dripped into the opening. I'd rip out my own heart and give it to him if I could, but all I could do was grip my forearm and force more blood out. *Take it all, just live.*

I got a lot of it into his body before the skin healed, but he still didn't wake up.

"It's not working," Kara yelled at me.

"It *is* working," I yelled back, too determined to cry. I pressed my wrist to his lips. "Wake up, William."

As if acting on my command he coughed and sat up taking in deep breaths. Blood dripped from his chin, and all of us went silent. I felt the tension lift from the room, as if we'd all started to breathe again. My heart beat with relief, and a laugh escaped my lips. I was too overcome for words. Only then did runaway tears drip down my cheeks.

We all watched as William wiped the red from his lips and face. He looked down at his blood-stained shirt. "What happened?" he asked, confused.

I took his face in my hands and kissed him like I hadn't seen him in months, but something wasn't right. His lips didn't kiss me back. They stayed still and tense.

"What's wrong?" I asked, as his eyebrows lowered.

Kara touched my shoulder. "Elyse..."

"Who are you?" William asked, his stare vacant and unfamiliar.

CHAPTER TWENTY-TWO

—

I LOOKED UP AT KARA AND BACK AT HIM. "WILLIAM,"
I said, forcing him to see me, to know me. "It's *me*. Elyse."

Kara shook her head and sank to the floor next to the
door. Alex followed her.

I felt the panic rise up in me again. "Hey," I said,
taking William's hand, hoping it was just a daze. "You're
all right." I kissed his knuckles, waiting, but he stared past
me at the girl on the floor. She looked dead with my dart
sticking up from her neck.

He turned to me and pulled his hand back, running
his fingers through his hair like he was nervous. "What...
What's going on here?" He moved away and stood, wiping
his bloody hands on his pants. "Did you *kill* her?"

"No," I said defensively, standing with him. "William,
don't worry. You're okay."

"He's not," Kara whispered, but I couldn't look at her.
I didn't want it to be true.

"Great," Alex said with indifference. "He can't remember her?"

"He can't remember anything," Kara answered.

"William," I said desperately. I walked toward him, but he backed away, like he was afraid of me. "You don't remember me?"

He looked me up and down, and I could see him thinking, but when his gaze met mine he only shook his head. "No."

I nodded, trying to ignore the sick feeling in my stomach. "It's okay. When she wakes up," I said, looking at the young girl on the floor. "We'll fix it. Okay? Okay."

I walked over to the girl and gently removed the dart from her neck then pressed our wrists together, healing us both. Her eyes were still closed, and her hand fell limp as I laid it on the ground. I could feel William watching me. Did he remember we had abilities? He didn't say anything. Instead he sat against the wall taking in his surroundings.

The tension in the room made me anxious. It felt wrong. Awkward. I didn't like it.

"Can we be alone for a minute?" I asked Kara and Alex.

"Sure," Kara answered. The way she looked at William, I wished I knew what she was thinking.

"Don't have to ask me twice," Alex said. He grabbed Kara by the arm, and the two of them disappeared.

"Are you okay?" I asked, sitting next to him. I could feel him tense up. He didn't feel comfortable so close.

He shrugged. "I guess." His fingers played with the hole in his shirt. He looked down at it, and his hair fell into his face. I wanted to reach out and push it away. I wanted him to look at me. I wanted him to remember. "Why don't I remember what happened to me?"

"The girl," I answered, pulling my knees in. "She can make people forget."

He nodded. "That still doesn't explain the blood."

"She stabbed you, I guess." I bit my thumb nail and looked down at my belly. "I didn't see it happen."

"And then you healed me? Like you healed her?"

"Yes."

We sat for a while. The room was quiet, but there was unsettled air around us. It wasn't a comfortable silence. I looked at him, and he glanced at me, then away again.

"I guess when she wakes up..."

"Yeah," I said.

I wasn't sure how much time passed, but I had nothing to say so I picked the grooves between the wood planks of the floor. The porch light and the moon illuminated the room with a grayish yellow glow, and as I looked around for the first time, I could see evidence of The Council's attack.

The two windows next to the front door were shattered and pieces of glass were scattered inside. A few chairs at the kitchen table to my right were on their sides, and the couch that sat against the left wall was disheveled. I wanted to sweep up the glass and put it all back together, to undo what they'd done to this poor girl, but I couldn't bring myself to move away from William. Being next to him, no matter how uncomfortable he seemed, was the only place I wanted to be.

The girl gasped when she woke and scrambled to her feet as she caught sight of us.

"It's okay," I said, trying to calm her before she dug up another weapon.

William and I stayed still as we stared into her wide fearful eyes. "Who are you?" she asked, her chest rising and falling quickly with panic.

"We're friends," William said, slowly getting to his feet. His words surprised me, but I nodded in agreement and stood with him.

Her eyes moved back and forth between us, and I raised my hands to show her I wasn't going to hurt her. It seemed to have no effect. Descendants could hurt with their minds. Some of us needed no weapons.

"Are you okay?" I asked. It was the only thing I could think to say that might convince her we were not there to hurt her. My eyes moved to her wrist and she followed my gaze.

She looked confused.

"I healed you," I said. "You can trust us."

Her shoulders relaxed, but in the moonlight, I could see the glisten of tears on her cheeks.

"What's your name?" I asked.

"Hannah." She was in her fifties from what I could

tell, with spiral curls that stopped at her chin.

"I'm Elyse," I said. "This is William."

She shuffleed her feet, still unsure. "They took my family."

"Who?" I knew the answer, but I needed details.

"A man with black hair and a scar on his lip." She traced her finger from the corner of her mouth to her chin, but I didn't recognize the description.

"How long ago?"

"Two days."

"We need to go," I said to William like he was himself. He didn't look at me the same way, but he nodded. I watched the girl as she stared at William's bloody shirt. I could see questions swimming behind her eyes. "They'll be back for you soon. If you come with us, we can keep you safe, but I need you to give him back his memories before we leave."

Suddenly she was afraid again.

My throat pinched with worry. "You can do that can't you?"

"My brother," she said, her voice staggering. "Or my father...only their blood can give the memories back."

"He has them both?" I asked, my stomach tightening. She nodded. "Yes."

I was sick. I couldn't stand anymore. I headed for the couch and my knees buckled just in time for me to collapse on the deflated cushions.

"I'm sorry," she said, stepping toward me. "I thought

you were with them. I thought you…I didn't know."

"It's all right," William told her. He didn't know any better. It wasn't all right.

He sat next to me and put his hand on my shoulder, but his touch was unnatural, forced. The familiar warmth didn't comfort me. It made me cry.

Kara stepped through the door. "Let's go home, Elyse."

There was no home. Not anymore. William was my home, and he was gone.

Alex took us back in an instant, but being back in the caves didn't make me feel any better. I was too numb to cry, to be angry, to care. My brain simply decided to shut off my emotions. It's own survival technique. Thankfully the camp was asleep when we returned.

"She can sleep in my tent," Kara said when we arrived, and as the two of them turned to leave, Alex was already gone.

"We normally sleep in the same tent," I said quietly to William. "Is that okay?"

"Sure," he answered, looking around.

Inside the small space I rearranged the bedding, moving his sleeping bag to the opposite side.

"How did we know each other?" William asked as he watched me tear apart our bed.

"I'm your wife," I answered trying not to let my emotions back in.

"My *wife*," he said, staring down at his wedding ring. "Okay." He cleared his throat. "Well, it's…nice to meet you."

I stared at the back of his head as he slept, unable to find comfort with my eyes closed. It was a restless night, the kind that had me gasping with fear as I woke from my dreams, only to find the nightmare was real. Tears came at their own will, whether I was asleep or awake. I put my hands on my belly for comfort. She was my secret again. Why didn't she show me this? I tried to believe there was a reason, and my mind ran until sleep found me again.

In the morning, I watched from a distance as William's mother and sister were confronted with the news. Sofia's face tightened with concern as she saw the same unfamiliar look he had with me. I sat in a corner alone, picking at my breakfast, too ashamed to address them. I was no leader.

"How are you?" Kara asked, though she already knew the answer. She sat down next to me, but my eyes stayed on William. "You look like hell."

"Thanks," I said, faking a smile. "That really helps."

She laughed. "I'm sorry." She brushed her black curls behind her ears, and we sat in silence for a moment. "You think it's your fault, but it's not," she finally said. "It's mine. I didn't hear her."

"Why not?" I asked.

"I think because she took away my memory of her. It's like my ability doesn't recognize she exists."

"Why do you get to remember everything else?"

"Usually she doesn't take away every memory. She just uses a drop to erase the last day or so," Kara answered.

"That knife just had too much of her blood on it. She feels really horrible. She was just so angry about her family. She assumed we were there to take her, too."

I nodded. What was there to say really?

"It'll be fine, you know," Kara said.

"Yeah," I answered. It felt wrong to say I didn't believe her. My issues with William paled in comparison with what had happened to her family.

I could tell she'd heard my thoughts by the way she looked at me, but she didn't say anything about it. "Once Dr. Nickel is back, he'll mimic that ability and make him remember," she said instead.

I picked at the skin around my thumbs leaving my food untouched. The idea made me feel better. I hadn't thought of that. "What if he can't?"

"He can."

"We don't know how long they'll be gone, and we can't contact them. It could be months." I dug my spoon around in my oatmeal. "What if he doesn't come back?"

"You're overreacting," she said, taking a bite of hers. "Maybe this is a good thing."

"Yeah," I scoffed. "For you. He's fair game again. Maybe he'll fall in love with you this time."

She rolled her eyes. "I'd punch you if you weren't pregnant."

I couldn't help it. I knew I was acting childish, and maybe it was the pregnancy, but something in me knew she was hoping to win him over.

Seriously? she said without speaking.

"Do you *always* have to be inside my head?"

"Okay," she said. "I *do* love William. I always have. But it's different, and he'd never be with me anyway. I would never try and take him from you."

I looked up, dropping my spoon against the bowl. "Why not?"

"Because he doesn't love me back." She sighed. "Trust me. I've been inside that head a thousand times."

"It doesn't really matter anymore what was in his head. That was before. It's all gone now."

"I don't think his love is the kind of thing that just goes away."

CHAPTER TWENTY-THREE

—

THE PERSON NEXT TO ME WAS NOT WILLIAM. HE wasn't my husband. Kara thought she could jog his memory, but I didn't want to bank on false hope. I told myself it wouldn't work. It was just us three, and we used the crevice for privacy. The one I had used to change into my wedding dress not so long ago.

"All right," Kara said. "Hold hands."

I tucked my hair behind my ears, stalling.

Is this necessary? I asked as I caught sight of William watching me.

No, she said with a laugh, *but it's fun. Just go with it.*

William held out his hands, and a sideways smile pulled into his cheek. It was the first time since last night that I'd seen a glimpse of the person I knew.

"It's worth a shot," he said with a shrug.

I slid my fingers between his, still afraid to be hopeful. It felt good to touch, though. The warmth was still there.

At least that couldn't be erased.

"Do you feel that?" he asked.

I nodded timidly. How could he not know what it meant? He'd always known.

"It means you have the hots for me," I joked, trying not to scare him. It was what he had told me when I first asked, when I was the one who didn't know anything. I knew he didn't remember that night on the beach, but it still made me smile.

He tilted his head. "Might be true."

"Maybe you don't need me here," Kara said, caught between the tension.

"No," I said. "We do. I do."

"All right. When you're in," she said to William, "just try and remember Elyse, using my mind. I'll guide you to a memory of the two of you."

She placed her palms against our foreheads, and we were drawn in by her ability. I could feel William there, hear his searching thoughts, amazed by what was happening. Chaotic images of Kara's life, along with flickering memories of William and I, reeled behind my closed eyes. It was overwhelming and made me dizzy.

Focus, I thought.

On what? I heard William ask.

I was too surprised he heard me to respond, but before I needed to, everything stopped. I was watching William kiss me on the couch in my old apartment. This was my memory. His fingers ran through my hair, and his lips pressed against mine. They moved to my cheek, my neck, my ear. I missed his kiss. I'd taken it for granted.

I tried to ignore the ache in my chest as I relived the night with William, but there was another emotion glaring from somewhere that I couldn't suppress. In the memory, I rested my head on his chest. I kissed lightly beneath his jaw, so in love in that moment. The nagging emotion was persistent, though somewhat distant, like it had been buried but wouldn't die. It throbbed from the corner of Kara's mind, and when I found it, it crushed me.

It was more than jealousy. It was longing, emptiness, and infinite loneliness. It was a love for William that went deeper than I could ever have guessed. I hated her for it, without wanting to.

William's hand loosened around mine. His mind pulled away, and I knew he'd sensed it too, every bit as powerful as I did.

"I don't think this is working," he said, his jaw clenching nervously.

Kara wouldn't look at me. "I'm sorry," she said, but I had no response for her. All I could do was stand and walk away.

I kept to myself the next few days, finding quiet places far away from camp. I didn't want to talk to anyone. I felt restless and trapped in my own head, like I had all the space in the world to run but nowhere to go. I wasn't sure how long it had been since the night I'd gotten pregnant. My stomach was still flat, but I knew she was in there, and

I let her comfort me.

"You're going to have to come join us eventually," Anna said, trying to coax me back to normal.

"Why?"

"Well, first, you're going to go crazy sitting here all day doing nothing. I know you. Second, people are starting to worry, including me."

"I just…"

"No excuses. Come on."

The first week was painful. Anna refused to let me seclude myself, so I spent the days studying maps at the planning table with Mac.

"Still no word from my father?" William asked, approaching us. The question was for Mac, but my eyes drifted toward him as they had over the past few days.

He stood three feet away, but the distance between us might as well have been infinite. He was no longer mine. It made me ache with the hollow feeling of heartbreak, like my whole body might crack into pieces and float away. I couldn't focus.

"Sorry, kid," Mac answered.

That evening I caught myself watching him again as he helped load newly delivered food supplies into the cooking area. I imagined the hard body I knew lay beneath his shirt as the toned muscles in his arms flexed. He caught me, and I looked away too quickly. I wasn't used to being estranged. I wanted an excuse to touch him somehow, to walk by and graze his side by accident, just to feel him again or hear him speak. My eyes didn't obey, they found him when he wasn't looking and lingered on the soft skin of his neck. I wanted to press my lips against it, hide my face in that warm secret place that existed when he held me. Instead I snuck off to be alone in the crevice.

I wasn't there long before footsteps approached.

"You want company?" William asked, peeking his head in.

I didn't, but it was him. I was desperate to get him back. "Sure."

He sat down beside me on the dirt floor. "I don't really remember anyone, so it's sort of...depressing."

"Tell me about it," I said. The broken shards of my splintered heart dug a little deeper.

He smiled. "I'm sorry it didn't work before. That Kara wasn't able to jog my memory. We can try again if you want."

"It's okay," I said, shaking my head. I risked a sideways glance. "It was probably more confusing than helpful."

"Not really," he said. "Just because I can't remember you doesn't mean there isn't something between us."

"What do you mean?" My words were stammered and soft. I could hear the embarrassment in them, making my cheeks burn and my ears flush.

My eyes stayed focused on his perfect hands as they toyed with his bootlaces, unable to look directly at him. He exhaled a laugh and smiled to himself.

"There's something about you that's...I think something pulls me to you." He bit his cheek, trying to hide his bright smile, but it didn't work. "That sounds stupid."

"It's not," I said. I took his hand, no matter how strange it felt that he didn't recognize my touch. The warmth beat between our palms, and his eyebrows lifted in curiosity. "You asked me what this meant. It means we're meant to be together."

He pulled his hand away, nervous and unsure. "Even if I can't remember?"

"Yes," I said, forcing myself to believe it.

I waited for him to say something, taking in all the details I could from the corner of my eye, but he didn't.

"You don't have to stay here with me," I said, trying to break away from the image of his mouth.

"No. I want to. I keep hoping if I'm around you..." He looked at me like if our eyes connected he might remember. "Maybe it will come back."

I stared at him, my heart racing with hope as his face moved closer to mine. His lips taunted me. His green eyes drew me in. When he reached for my cheek, I didn't care that he didn't know how it felt to kiss me. *I* remembered. I needed it.

"Is it okay if I..." I didn't let him finish. Our lips touched softly, as if he was afraid I'd pull away. I wouldn't. I might never get another chance. I pressed my mouth into his, and he kissed back. It wasn't the same kiss, but it was familiar enough to take away the hurt. At first, we kissed through the tears as they rolled down my cheeks, but after a moment, he brushed them with his thumbs.

"I didn't mean to make you cry."

I laughed. "I always cry." I left out the part that I was pregnant, not wanting to scare him away. "Did it help?"

"Well, it didn't make my memories come back, but I sort of want to kiss you again."

I wiped my face with my sleeves and smiled. "It was worth a try," I said, hoping to keep from looking sad.

He lifted my chin with his hand. "Can I? Kiss you again?"

Our lips met, this time more confidently than before, like he'd discovered something new and wonderful in my kiss.

"You know," he said, still close. "It might be fun to fall in love all over again."

I smiled and slid back to lean against the rock wall, shyer than I was used to being around him. "What makes you think you'll fall in love with me and not Kara?"

"Yeah, because I just kiss random people I don't feel anything for. At least I don't think so." He looked at me, a little concerned. "I don't do that, do I?"

"No." I couldn't hold back a laugh, and for a moment, I almost forgot anything was different at all. "What exactly do you remember? Do you have any memories left at all?"

He shook his head. "I mean, clearly I remember how to talk and walk. I remember how the world works, that there are Descendants and humans. I remember being places, but I don't remember who was there with me or why I was there, what happened, or where *there* even is. It's like everything's gone but the basics. Relationships, emotions, purpose...there's nothing."

"That must be hard," I said. I was glad he was opening up to me. I could feel a connection growing between us, even if it wasn't the same.

"Something in me must remember you, though." For a second, he looked at me like he used to.

That night I relived one of my visions as a dream. It was the same dream I'd been having for a week now. I walked down the rows of people until I found Ryder's son, only this time Hannah wasn't there. It was someone different. I didn't recognize him, but tears slipped down his young cheeks just as they did Hannah's. He pressed his fingertips to the foreheads of each person, their eyes darting back and forth in fear only to settle when he finished. Saving Hannah hadn't changed anything.

The Ryder lookalike turned and walked my way. As he got closer I imagined his father's yellow teeth and foul breath, the look in his eyes that had haunted me since his death. My heart started to quicken even though he stared past me. When he was only inches away my eyes snapped open, and I was drenched in a cold sweat.

"You okay?" William whispered across from me. He was on his side, watching me as the mini stars glowed above us through the mesh of our tent.

I nodded. He was lying more than an arm's length away. I couldn't reach out and touch him even if I wanted to.

"Come here," he said, opening his sleeping bag. I wondered briefly if he was just being kind or if he really wanted to be closer. It didn't matter though. I slipped out of my bag and slid myself in next to him. His smell was familiar, like cool, crisp limes.

"Thank you," was all I could say as he folded himself around me.

"Bad dream?"

"Yeah," I answered. It was the easiest response.

He rested his arm cautiously over mine and pressed his body against my back. At first he was tense, but even he couldn't deny how natural and good it felt to be close. He rested his head on the pillow and relaxed into me. The rhythmic rise and fall of his chest was exactly what I needed to help me close my eyes again, so I could face the horrors that found me in my sleep.

—

"PEOPLE ARE STARTING TO TALK," KARA SAID AS I took my seat next to her at breakfast.

"About what?" I asked.

"Well first, that you're completely non-functional these days. Second, that we need to make a move. You talk about human integration and freedom, but we're still hiding in a cave. Our people are still being controlled and abused, and we aren't any closer to winning anything against Christoph."

"Says who?" I retaliated. "Do they realize he was going

to use Hannah to enslave people or whatever it is he's planning on doing with them?"

"No," Alex answered. "Nobody realizes that. You haven't told anyone anything."

"It just happened."

"A week ago, Elyse." Kara eyed William who sat down beside her. "They want to be involved. They want to see some progress. They're afraid and need to know their leader has a plan."

I sighed. "What am I supposed to do? I can't just send people out into the world to expose our race. They'd all get killed or captured as soon as Christoph found out. The transition has to be gradual. We have to take out Christoph first."

"So maybe we need to focus on finding Christoph. He has Hannah's family, and we need to help her get them back," William added.

We all looked at him.

"I think that's a good plan," Alex said.

"Yeah? What are we going to do?" I asked. "Walk right up to him and shoot him in the head?"

"Something like that," he answered.

Kara shook her head. "That's suicide."

"We've done it before," Alex scoffed. "We were right there. We could have killed—"

"If it's too risky," William interrupted. "You shouldn't do it."

Our restless group, Christoph's plan, William's memory,

my pregnancy, too many burdens weighed me down.

"Tell everyone I'll update them at dinner."

———

THAT NIGHT WHILE EVERYONE WAS SLEEPING, I SET out to be alone, to think. It had only been a few minutes when I heard footsteps behind me.

"Sorry," William said, finding me at the bathing pool. "I didn't see your shoes."

They were sitting next to me, so I held them up. "It's okay. I'll leave."

"No, don't," he said, slipping his sandals off and sitting down beside me. "I was actually looking for you. Can't sleep?"

"Never can these days," I answered.

I kicked my bare feet around in the lukewarm water and made ripples with my toes. "Feels good," he said as he dipped his in, too.

"It's a little cold."

I was the only one who remembered that cold night on the beach, but he smiled anyway and shook his head. "Wimp."

I glared at him playfully and reached down for a handful of water. Without thinking I batted it into his face. His mouth fell open in shock, but all I could do was laugh. He clenched his teeth to keep his lips from curling into a smile, and the next thing I knew I was under water breathing out bubbles of air.

I resurfaced with a half-angry face. "You pushed me in!"

"Yeah," he said. "You started it."

I grabbed the leg of his jeans and pulled. He tried to hold on to something, but there was only brittle dirt. His eyes pinched shut, and I dragged him into the water, using my whole bodyweight to shove his head under.

"You're secretly trying to kill me, aren't you?" he asked as he popped up some distance away, water dripping from his lips.

"Wimp," I mocked with a smile.

He raised his eyebrows and disappeared beneath the surface, the waterfall's ripples making him invisible. My eyes narrowed, searching.

I felt his fingers against my waist before I saw him. I liked the feeling, but I liked the game more so I shot away with a laugh and swam toward the falls. His hands grasped at my feet as they kicked, and I flailed trying to pull myself through the sloshing swells. Something caught my pants, which were heavy and loose. I didn't care. I wriggled free from them, and the cool water slipped over my bare legs. I moved easily without the weight of the fabric, and swam away, breathing hard from the fight.

Behind the waterfall it was quiet. I turned and waited for him to come through the veil of rain, excited and nervous.

When he did, he approached slowly, lifting my sopping pants into the air. "Um...pantsless woman. You forgot these." His voice echoed slightly in the space.

I shrugged. I didn't know what had gotten into me. "Gotta do laundry somehow."

I swam toward the cave wall and sat on a ledge exposing my white thighs. I smiled at him as he floated toward me, but my eyes were more serious. Did he still want me like before? Maybe a part of me just had to know. Maybe I just wanted *him* like I used to, like I always had.

When he reached me, he pulled himself onto the ledge, and I didn't have to ask to be kissed. He knew. Our wet lips melded together like I remembered. His soft and careful as they moved. Mine eager. I reached for his shirt, wet and clinging to his chest. I expected him to stop me, but he didn't. I breathed out, satisfied and happy as the falling water splashed tiny droplets onto our faces.

"This is okay with you?" he asked, unsure of where we'd been together.

Our eyes connected like they hadn't in a while, and I nodded. "Technically, you are still my husband."

He smiled and peeled my wet shirt from my body. I wanted nothing more in that moment.

———

I FELL ASLEEP AS SOON AS MY EYES CLOSED THAT night, like a kid who had played too hard. My hair was wet, my body damp. William held me differently, tighter, closer. It was the first night I didn't have visions or nightmares, my first night of peace since he'd been taken from me.

CHAPTER TWENTY-FOUR

—

THE SOUND OF MY TENT DOOR UNZIPPING WOKE ME up.

"There's something you need to see," Alex said shaking my leg. "Get up." The look on his face made me nervous. It was grave, like something tragic had happened.

William and I dressed quickly and in silence, but the quiet between us meant something different now. We had a secret. He smiled at me as he handed me my boots.

Outside, Mac and Alex waited at the planning table. There was no time to reminisce about my wonderful night with William.

"What is it?" I asked.

Alex nodded for William and I to make contact before he transported us.

When Mac didn't reach out, I looked at him. "What about you?"

"I'm gonna stay back. I heard about it. No need to see

the details," he said. Moments later we were bathed in white.

We reappeared in an apartment. It was dark, and the only sound was the television. Kara was already sitting on the couch, staring at it. The windows were shaded and the blue light of the TV reflected off of her face. She looked at me, and I followed her gaze back to the screen. Where the Statue of Liberty once stood, smoke billowed like some evil force escaping from the rubble.

"Was anyone hurt?" William asked.

I couldn't speak. My stomach turned to knots, and I felt like there was nothing beneath my feet to hold me up. I tightened my grip on William's hand.

"We don't know," Kara answered. "They aren't telling us anything."

"What happened?" I managed.

"They're calling it a terrorist attack," Alex said as he sat next to Kara and flipped the channel. Each one reported on the same story, and I was sure the entire world was watching, waiting for answers.

"What does this mean?" I asked. "War?"

"It's been war," Kara said.

A blonde woman prattled on in front of the camera, but I couldn't look away from the image behind her. I didn't hear a word she was saying. All I could think about was Christoph.

"Do you think it was him?" I asked.

"We know it was," Kara answered.

"This is what he did before, right?" I combed my hair back in disbelief. "He'll just keep killing innocent humans until…"

You surrender yourself? Kara finished for me. *Yeah. Probably.*

"It's more than him just killing humans," Alex added, looking at me from his spot on the couch.

"What do you mean?"

"It wasn't a Descendant who attacked. It was a human," he answered.

"Something bigger is going on here, Elyse." Kara stood and walked around to face me. "The Hunters have been collecting humans," she said. "He's doing something with them, and whatever it is has to do with this attack. I'm sure of it."

The warehouse in my vision. What was he doing to them?

"How do you know all this?" William asked.

Rachel's voice came from behind us. "I told them." She was sitting against the wall in the back of the room.

"Rachel," I beamed, but her face didn't brighten as I expected. "Where is—"

"We were ambushed on our recon mission to get information from the Hunters. There were too many." Her eyes were empty as they looked away. There was no hope in them.

"Hunters have the others, Elyse," Kara continued for her.

"And my father?" William asked.

Rachel nodded as she lifted herself off the floor and came to join us by the TV.

"How?" It was hard to believe anyone could touch Dr. Nickel.

"They're well trained," Kara answered. "It's what they do. They use a sedative to debilitate most of their victims. That's how they're keeping them down I'm sure."

"Do you know what they want?" I asked Rachel.

"They let me go to deliver a message," she told me, but she couldn't look into my eyes. "You for them. They're going to kill them if you don't cooperate." Her lips quivered as she spoke. "Tonight."

My heart sank, and all I could feel was fear. Christoph knew how to play me. All he had to do was threaten those close to me. Love, something I'd tried my whole life to avoid, was my greatest weakness.

The room was silent. "All right," I said. "Just tell me where they are. Mac won't approve, so keep quiet about it—"

"Wait," Kara said. "Let's think about this. You can't just turn yourself over to them."

"What other option do I have?"

What about the baby? Kara insisted.

I didn't have an answer for her, but I couldn't just leave all my friends with the Hunters to be murdered. *I don't know,* I admitted, *but I'll be safe. They won't harm me as long as I'm pregnant. How long until she's born?*

I had no idea how long Descendant babies were in the womb.

Our growth rate is faster before we're born. Ten months from now, give or take, Kara answered, but her eyes were anxious.

"All right," Alex interrupted. "What's going on? No secret conversations."

"Look," Kara said. "I know a lot of Hunters. Maybe I can sway them to see things our way. Not all of them are happy with Christoph."

Alex crossed his arms, and I could tell he didn't like the idea. "You do realize they've all been told to kill you on sight, right?"

"Do you think they will? Kill you?" I asked.

She thought about it and shook her head. "No."

I wasn't sure I believed her.

"Can I talk to you?" William asked, touching my arm. "Alone." He turned to walk down the hall of the unfamiliar house without waiting for my answer, and I followed him.

"I don't think you should do it," he confessed, sitting on the bed as I closed the door behind me.

"I have to," I said, swallowing down the nausea. I stared at the carpet in defeat. "What choice do I have?"

"I don't know," he answered, standing and stepping closer to me, "but everything in me is telling me not to let you go."

He reached for my face, and his fingers grazed the back of my neck. I could feel the look in his eyes becoming more and more familiar.

I had to pull away from that vulnerable place. If I was going to be strong, I couldn't let him in.

"This is supposed to happen," I explained, remembering Beverly Hills. "I keep getting stuck in the same situations. Maybe he's supposed to have me. Maybe it's all for a reason. I can't just let them die…"

"Elyse," William said, forcing me to look at him, but he couldn't find the words. Instead his lips touched mine, and tears spilled over my cheeks. Our kiss, wet with tears, was salty and desperate. "I'm coming with you."

His green eyes yielding so much power made my chest feel empty. They didn't know the loss that I knew. Even so, I had to be thankful for that. The old William would never have let me leave him.

I pressed my face into his warm neck, pinching my eyes tightly shut, trying to keep this moment. I would need it later. "Thank you."

———

WHEN MY FEET FELT THE GROUND I SAW IT, THE only building for miles along the dusty highway. Harley Davidsons were parked in a jumbled mess out front, their menacing faces grimacing with black and chrome. The name of the bar, Tartarus, was illuminated in old red neon that flickered on and off in the midday sun. No one knew we were there yet. We could go back. My throat felt dry, and I tried to swallow.

"Has Mac called?" I asked Alex.

"Not yet, but he'll realize it's been too long soon."

I stared ahead at the building, knowing he'd disapprove of this. "If he does, don't answer."

"You want me to go first?" Kara asked.

"No," I answered immediately. "We go together."

I glanced at William. I should never have let him come. I could tell he wanted to say something, try to convince me this wasn't the right choice, but he stayed quiet with stubborn disapproval in his eyes. "Be careful, okay?" He squeezed my hand, his silent way of pleading with me.

"We'll be fine. Alex will be with us, so we can get out at any time."

I started for the door and heard the clatter of men before I walked in. The air was dank and the light dim. The smell of leather and sweat lingered. As I took my first steps into the bar, everything went silent. Big-bodied men sat on stools in front of a wall of liquor at the back of the room. They surrounded pool tables and dartboards that hung over the windows. Thirty sets of eyes zeroed in on me, each face harder than the next. Their thick hands reached for weapons, but I couldn't move.

I cleared my throat. "I'm Elyse."

The sound of a pistol sliding a bullet into place clicked behind my head. I froze. "We know who you are."

"We want to talk to Luther," Kara said from beside me. The gun didn't make her tense. She looked up at the

Hunter without flinching with fear as I would have.

The men laughed, but I heard the gun's lever click back into place, and I released the breath I'd been holding.

"You've got a lot of nerve showin' up here, Kara." His hard face looked angry behind his long greasy black hair. His dry, thick knuckles clenched into fists.

Just leave, I told her.

She shook her head subtly. *I know him. He's softer than he looks.*

"They want to see Luther," the man announced to his fellow Hunters. He cocked his head to the left, staring from Kara, to William and Alex, then back to me. "Sure." He shrugged. "It's been nice knowin' ya."

William's eyes scanned the men who taunted us with smirks as the four of us moved deeper into the bar. We followed the Hunter to the back, the light growing dimmer, until we reached a dark hallway with a door.

I looked behind me, still feeling threatened by the Hunters we'd left behind, but I only saw William's face. "Where's Alex?" I hissed, irritated that he hadn't followed the plan.

"I don't know," William answered under his breath. "He was right here and then he just disappeared."

I clenched my jaw in anger. I didn't like not having an escape. If things went wrong, we were on our own.

When we entered, there was a man sitting behind a worn wooden desk. He seemed gentler than the rest, but his low guttural chuckle made my heart beat in my stomach.

His long gray ponytail hung at the base of his neck, and the white of his goatee reminded me of someone wise and kind. I was sure my impression was wrong. I felt William next to me, like a shield, tense and ready.

The Hunters have made calls to the Council, Elyse, Kara warned. *We don't have a lot of time. They've called Antec, and he'll bring others.*

"So this here's it? A three man army come to take out the Hunters?" Luther nodded to the black haired man to shut the door. "Gonna have to do better."

"We're not here to fight. We're here to talk," I said.

"Hunters are better at killin' than talkin'," he laughed. "But since ya made it so easy, go ahead."

"I know this isn't what you want," Kara said, getting to the point. "Why do you kill for him? It isn't right."

"What I want and what's right ain't always the same thing," he answered. "Killin' for him saves more lives than you're willin' to admit."

They were quiet for a moment, staring at each other, speaking secretly while we waited.

"I'm just doin' my job," he said aloud.

"Your job is to defend our people," Kara disagreed.

"I am," he sneered. "Even if it means taking out Descendant rebels who want to bring on war." He nodded to the man in the corner. "I'm sure Christoph wants her alive. Make sure she stays conscious."

He looked away as the greasy man headed toward me, but there was no missing the guilt he felt with his head hung low.

"So this is what you are now, cousin?" Mac said, appearing in front of us with Alex.

"Mac," Luther grumbled. "Here to give me grief over this, too?"

I glared at Alex and shook my head at him for not listening to me, but he only rolled his eyes and looked away.

"There was a time Hunters stood for something," Mac answered. "Something good."

"We do what we have to. What we were born to."

Mac took a defiant step forward. "You were born to protect. Have you forgotten your bloodlines?"

"Protection means different things to different people."

"You're descendant of heroes, of Hercules. You should be fighting for what's right. Keeping our people safe, not killing senselessly and following blindly. That's weak. You're slaves."

I could see shame in Luther's eyes, even as his face stayed stern and unyielding. "If we had a choice, maybe it'd be different."

"You do have a choice," I spoke up. "We all do. Christoph thinks he can control us, but what does he have without you?"

"He has The Council. He has followers. He ain't afraid to kill those who oppose him, including us."

"You think he doesn't want to kill us? Kill me?" Kara added. "You're supposed to be the heroes, Luther. Stand up. Be brave—"

"Something's wrong," Alex interrupted with force. "I was getting calls, and they just stopped." We all stood there watching him. "I can't..." His eyes lifted in fear.

"Christoph," Mac said.

"What do we do?" Alex asked, lost without his ability.

"Antec's here," Kara said in a rush, trying to concentrate on distant thoughts. "He's here for you, Elyse. You've got to go."

"Go where?" I asked, feeling just as stuck as everyone else.

Mac nodded toward the side wall. "The window."

Before we could move, the door flew open, and for the first time I stood face to face with Antec. Black hair hung like a horse's mane around his face, and a scar cut through his bottom lip. His bold eyes locked onto me.

"Feel like making this easy?" His voice was slick, and his face twitched with anticipation.

"Don't take another step," Mac threatened as he drew his gun, but Antec's lips only stretched into a half smile around his scar.

It won't work, Kara warned us. *He has a descendant of Loxo with him.* Sure enough, the Hunter standing watch at the door was gone, and in his place was a tall thin man with blond hair and a twisted grin.

What does that mean?

He can divert the paths of things. Change their direction.

Antec took his first step forward with confidence, daring Mac to shoot him. When the gun went off, I dropped into a squat, taking cover against the side of Luther's desk. The bullet ricocheted away from Antec, and Kara cried out as it grazed her arm.

Don't let him touch you with his hands, Kara said in my mind.

Every part of me wanted to dive at him, tackle him to the ground and drive a dart into his neck, but I couldn't bring myself to act. Some other instinct kicked in that told me to hide, run, protect my child. I fumbled with my bag of darts trying to find the largest one I could. My blood wouldn't work on a Council member, so I gripped the wooden spike in my hand. If he came at me, I wanted to be ready.

The sound of breaking glass, gunshots, and men's deep battle cries erupted outside of the little room where we'd been cornered. If we didn't get out soon, more would be coming. When Antec took his next step, Mac lunged at him, then Kara, but he was faster than they thought. All I could do was sit and watch as the two of them tried to bring him down without success. He dodged every blow taunting them with his hands as if he was enjoying the fight and could end it at any time. His fingertips brushed Kara's arm as he ducked under her punch. Within seconds Kara and Mac were gone, carried away to Antec's Underworld like they'd never been here at all.

I couldn't keep myself from screaming as they disappeared. Before I knew it, I was on my feet. "I'll go with you. Just let them go."

"No," William yelled as he grabbed a bat from against the wall. "Get her out of here, Alex."

Antec walked slowly toward him, and there was nothing I could do as William took a challenging stance in front of me.

"What are you doing?" I screamed at him, but Alex had me by the waist, pulling me toward the window. "Let me go."

I struggled enough to get free, but Alex darted out in front of me, too careless without his ability. In seconds, Antec lurched forward and his hand found Alex's arm. Another friend, gone.

Luther grabbed me by the wrist, pried the dart from my hand, and yanked me back. It didn't matter how strong he was. I still struggled. My eyes were focused on William. Each time he swung the bat he missed, all while my voice was going hoarse from yelling, begging to be set free.

As the bat made contact with the side of Antec's face, I went quiet. He spit blood onto the floor and looked at William ready for revenge.

Luther pulled me toward the window, and my eyes met William's one last time before glass was crashing around me. "Run!" I pleaded, but I was the distraction that caused him to let down his guard. A hand clamped down on his shoulder, and he was gone like the others.

I landed on Luther's thick body as we hit the ground

below us. I tried to scramble to my feet, but he was strong enough to break bones. It was no use. He threw me over his shoulder and carried me flailing to his bike.

He sat me in front of him and wrapped his left arm around my waist, locking me in my place. I struggled, but it was pointless. He had me, and I collapsed in defeat. I felt dead. My chest was heavy, and everything inside me hurt. The roar of the motor drowned out the riot, which had spilled out into the front, and as we drove away I didn't try to look back.

CHAPTER TWENTY-FIVE

WE DROVE SO FAR MY BODY ACHED FROM SITTING. The wind burned my face and made me numb, but none of it mattered. My lifeless eyes took in our surroundings with indifference. I assumed we were in the Sierras. The mountain roads were lined with pine trees, and there was snow on the ground, although it was old and melting under the sun that beat down on us. Passing cars were few and far between. Their license plates read *California*. Signs for campsites flashed by us as we drove. I didn't know where he was taking me. I didn't care.

Luther turned off onto a dirt road marked by a brown wooden sign—Pine Knot Campground. Nobody was there, not even a park ranger. It was too cold for camping. As soon as we stopped, I tried to push and shove my way off of the bike. "Let me go," I screamed.

"Sure," he said, letting me slide off the side. "If you try and run, I'll shoot you."

I stared at him, so much hate and anger seething through me I couldn't take it. "I could have saved them," I said quietly.

He lifted his leg over the back of the bike and stood tall next to me. "No." He shook his head, tossing a large pack to the ground. "You couldn't have."

I watched as he unloaded weapons from the leather satchels that hung on the sides of the bike. Guns. Bullets. Knives.

"Are you going to kill me?"

His laugh was a deep rumble. "You think I'd o' brought you this far to kill ya?"

"Maybe."

"If I wanted ya dead, you'd be dead."

"So why are we here?"

He unzipped the pack and pulled out a tent, blankets, and food.

"Safety," he answered. "Had to get ya outta there. They'll be searchin' for ya in all directions from that place."

I looked at him, unsure of what to make of this change of heart. I grabbed a pole and started copying him, sliding it through the sleeve of the tent. He watched me as my fingers inched along the fabric.

"None of us never meant it to be like it is," he said.

"You had a choice," I answered, trying not to look at him.

"True." He lowered his blood-shot blue eyes. "Never was any savin' me, though. My soul's been black too long, but maybe helpin' you will undo some o' the bad I did."

"Helping me?"

"Helpin' you go where ya need to go. Do what ya need to do."

"There's nothing I *can* do." My voice spiked with frustration, and I let go of the tent. Why was I trusting him anyway? "Your men or Christoph, someone's going to kill my friends tonight." My chest started to tighten at the thought.

"That'd be Christoph," Luther said, "but he ain't keen on killin' his kind. It's not likely he'll go ahead when he knows he won't get nuthin' for it."

His words were reassuring, but I didn't know if I could believe him.

I picked up my end of the pole and fit it into the metal fastener. "Why would you help me? You were about to turn me over to him a few hours ago."

"Eh, Kara was right. Always is. Just been livin' by somebody else's rules for too long," he said. "Seein' as you're alive, though, there's still hope o' changin' that."

I shook my head. "I tried believing that. I'm just not sure it's true."

He looked at me across the canvas dome. "Well, here's to hopin'."

When the sun went down, the heat went with it. Luther built a fire, but even that couldn't keep me warm. The shame, the cold, the emptiness all made me shake and tense until I felt sick. Who knew if I'd ever see William again? I blew hot air into my hands as Luther cooked beans over the flames like we were in the old west.

"Want a blanket?" he asked.

"Okay."

He wrapped it around me with the same heavy hands that had killed so many. It was hard to accept kindness from those hands, but I did.

"Imagine Christoph's fixin' to rip apart the world. You have a plan?"

"No," I answered, disgusted with myself, my lack of leadership. Even if I did, I probably wouldn't tell him. I still wasn't sure how much I could trust Luther.

"He's doin' somethin' with those humans. Poor souls."

I rubbed the skin around my fingernails. I hadn't even thought of the humans. All I could think about was William, Kara, Mac, Alex, and the others. If I had any plan it would be to save them, but I didn't. I had no idea where to go or what to do to get them back.

I wrapped the blanket tighter around me. "I don't even know where to start."

"Well, what's yer heart tellin' ya?"

Wisps of gray hair had fallen from his low ponytail, and the light of the fire made him look like a native medicine man or some sort of warrior spirit.

"It's telling me to save my husband. To do whatever it takes to get him back."

"If you had the strength and the will, how would ya do it?"

"I don't know," I said louder than was necessary. Our eyes met across the fire. "Even if I could find Antec, I couldn't kill him, and the only other way I can think to get them back is to get to Lilia. Get her away from The Council so all their abilities are stripped. If Antec lost his ability William and the rest would be set free. But I don't know where Lilia is or how to get to her. I've got nothing to go on."

He nodded his head and stirred the beans. So much for not telling him anything.

"What about yer head?" he asked.

"What?"

"What is yer head tellin' ya? Lotsa times it's different than yer heart."

At first I didn't have an answer. My head was confused. I tried to think outside of myself. If I weren't me, what would be best for my people?

"Try and find the rest of my team with Dr. Nickel and continue the fight against Christoph."

"And yer gut?"

I knew immediately what my gut was telling me. The warehouse vision had been lingering in my mind unfinished, unresolved. Everything in me said to go there. It was like a beacon drawing me in, but that would mean giving up on my friends, on William.

"I can't...I mean, how do I know what's right? What if I make the wrong decisions?"

He poked the fire with a stick, sending sparks into the

air, like fireflies dancing in the night.

"Just make a choice and trust it's right. Follow it 'til the end and maybe it'll put ya exactly where ya need to be."

Knots formed in my chest at the thought. Choosing meant losing someone or failing one way or the other. "I can't do that. I can't risk everything for a maybe."

"There ain't no wrong way. There's only the way ya choose. It'll happen the way it's suppose to. Even if it's not what you expect. Even if it turns out bad, there's always a reason."

"It's different for me," I confessed. "I see things, the future. I should know which way to go, what to do."

"I'm not talkin' about oracles and visions." My brow pulled together in surprise. I didn't realize he knew so much about who I was. "I'm talkin' about there's something bigger guidin' us where we're suppose to go."

My eyes lifted. "You mean God?"

"Somethin' like that."

His face glowed orange from behind the flames.

"Do you really think you were meant to kill all the people you have? That killing innocent humans was for a reason?"

He spooned the warm beans back into the cut open can, stuck a spoon in, and handed it to me. "I'm not sayin' I done right. I know I haven't, but the things I done put me here, made me the perfect man to help ya do what ya need to do."

I held the warm meal between my palms. "You act like

you know what that is. Even if my head is telling me to find Dr. Nickel or my gut is telling me to get to the humans your men have been collecting. I have no idea where any of them are..."

"I do," he said, "and lucky for you, I think it's the same place."

I didn't sleep well that night. Partly from the cold, but mostly because I was afraid to make a choice that felt wrong, even though I knew it was right. William and the others were gone, forced to sleep in the prison of the Underworld. I had no way of knowing what that was like. There was probably a reason it was known in myths as a place for dead souls. I couldn't imagine anyone had come back. The thought made my heart twist until I thought I'd be sick. How could I leave them?

I woke up with Luther's blanket draped over me. Though it felt like I hadn't slept at all, I knew I had. I'd dreamt of the warehouse again. It was the first thing I thought about when I woke up. Only it wasn't my thought, it was hers. She was pointing me in the right direction. I remembered the oracle's words, Listen to her. I rested my hands on my warm belly. It had been growing. Just enough that I could tell.

When I peeked my head outside the tent, I saw Luther. There was a fire, and roasting on the end of two long sticks were some sort of skinned animals. Rabbits maybe.

"Hungry?" he asked, pulling one back from the flames.

"Yeah."

I sat on a log and reached my hands toward the heat. It was still cold enough to see my breath. He ripped the leg off one of the cooked animals and handed it to me. I took it without hesitating and bit into the warm meat.

"Been collectin' wood this mornin'. Yer gonna need more darts than what ya got."

I nodded as I chewed, letting him know I'd made the decision to follow him. Maybe it was never a choice. It seemed like the only thing I could do.

"Thanks," I said, eying the small pile of twigs, each one straight and smooth to make for easy carving. "How'd you know I could make the darts?"

"I know Mac taught ya right," he answered. "I taught him." He grabbed the other stick off of the fire and reached into his back pocket. "Here." He handed me a fold-up blade. "Better get goin'."

As I carved, he talked.

"There'll be a lot of 'em. Best to go slow. Take out one at a time and hide the bodies. The longer ya stay invisible the better."

"I can't do this alone," I said to him. "There are others who can help. Maybe if we—"

"Where ya were before, the ones there, none of it's o' use to ya. Best assume the place has been found. Christoph has ways a gettin' information from people. We're on our own."

The ache I'd been carrying around in my chest sank

into my stomach. Anna, Chloe, Helen, Rachel, Edith, Sofia, so many were left unprotected.

"We need to go—"

"No. Too risky."

I was starting to wonder if Luther wasn't just using me to right the wrongs of his past.

I opened the knife with weak fearful fingers and took a deep breath, hoping he was wrong. Luther stayed quiet for a while, watching me as I slid the blade across the wood.

"It's better this way," he said. "They'll be expectin' more than just you, watchin' for numbers. Alone is yer best chance to slip in unnoticed."

I nodded and continued carving.

"Hunters'll need double the blood at least. Don't be afraid to kill 'em. Better them than you. If it's them in yer shoes they'd kill without thought. Ya need to be the same."

"You want me to kill your men?"

He nodded. "If it comes to that. Like I said. Sometimes doin' what ya want and doin' what's right ain't always the same thing."

I thought of Kara, of putting on that hard mask and becoming the person I needed to be. Forgetting the person I was. Forgetting the hopelessness. Forgetting my weaknesses. I had to be a killer.

"The place has a couple levels, rooms for experiments and such—"

"Experiments?" I looked up from the blade.

He nodded, watching me, as if waiting for me to crack or give up because it was all too much. But I couldn't.

"Been goin' on for years that way. Not sure what he's lookin' for."

"When do we leave?" I asked.

He shrugged. "Whenever yer ready."

"Tonight," I said, carving a little faster.

CHAPTER TWENTY-SIX

—

THE IDEA OF TAKING ACTION MADE MY HEART CHUG. I wanted to leave sooner, before I changed my mind. I rode on the back of the bike this time. It was easier, and we could ride at higher speeds without Luther having to restrain me. I wrapped my arms tightly around his thick body as we drove, clinging to a man who could have easily decided to kill me. Maybe that was still his plan, but I had to trust him. He was my only option.

Jets of cold air rushed past us making my ears numb, and my hair whipped around in an angry fury, like wildfire. I buried my face into his back, hiding my eyes, pulling myself out of a reality I didn't want to confront. My breath kept my nose warm and parts of my cheeks from feeling the biting air. When I looked up, I couldn't see anything but the blackness that surrounded me. Even the moon was hiding tonight. The bike's engine tore through the quiet, filling my ears with enough noise to keep my mind still.

When he exited the freeway I bit at my dry lips until I tasted the salty tang of blood. I lifted my head from his jacket, surprised to see buildings. They seemed out of place along the country roads. Smart, I thought, not secluded enough to be suspicious, but far enough out that screams wouldn't be heard. He passed them all and drove into the rising hills that sat behind the industrial garden.

"What are we doing?" I asked when he shut the bike off in the middle of nowhere.

"We'll need to go in through the back. They'll be watching the roads. Prob'ly be watchin' the hills too, but it's our best shot."

We hiked through trees and brush with no paths. Up hills, clawing at dirt and roots. Then I saw it, the building from my vision. It shined a dull gray under the stars. It looked deserted, but I knew better. The sight of it made my blood hot.

We stayed low, hands and knees against the ground.

"I count ten," he said. "How 'bout you?"

"Ten?" I asked. "I see six."

"Look harder. Not just the obvious places. Them are decoys."

I scanned the hillside to our left and right. There was a man on either side. Snipers. I saw another body flash quickly around the backside of the building. "Okay, nine."

"Right below us," he whispered.

Sure enough, down the sloping hill, a small girl in black hid crouched against the dark earth.

"Can you get her from here?"

I looked at him, still shocked that this was actually happening. "Yeah," I said with a nod. I pulled a medium sized dart out of my satchel, but Luther stopped me.

"You'll be needin' a hollow."

It seemed harder to breathe all of a sudden. "You want me to kill her?"

"That's the idea. It's her or you."

I pulled out the thick hollow dart and filled it with my blood. Something felt wrong about killing someone I wasn't defending myself against, like it was murder, but I'd seen things that had readied me for this. I'd had to heal the wounded, grieve the dead. I'd lost those closest to me. I'd lost William. I was here to end this, and if that meant killing those who were in my way, so be it.

I took off toward her, willing myself to muster the courage I needed. All I could hear was my breath as I crept up behind the girl. Her raven hair fell over her back and glistened with a blue sheen under the moon. She lay silently on her belly in the dry grass, and I didn't wait to find out what her ability was. I didn't think. I didn't question. I just shot.

The hollow buried itself into her right shoulder, and she arched her back, flinching from the pain. I froze as I watched, keeping low and quiet until she was still. I'd killed Christoph's people before, when they attacked us at my parents', but I never felt guilt like this. This time it was *my* choice to kill her, and there was a price to pay for that.

"It's done," I said, over the soft crunch of my footsteps as I returned.

"Good." Luther's eyes drifted to my shaking fingers, and I clenched my fist to make it stop. "I'll take out the man to the left, you get the one on the right. Meet back here. Can you do that?"

I nodded. "Yeah." I needed to be stronger, to force that softer side of me out.

I crept with careful feet, stepping quietly over pine needles and dirt. *Breathe*, I told myself. In and out. The rhythm kept me at a steady pace, kept my heart from racing ahead of me. I went around to come up from behind the man. He wasn't a Hunter. Nothing about him seemed overly-threatening, aside from the gun tucked under his arm. When I saw him, I lost focus and a twig snapped beneath my boot. He lifted his head from the scope, and my shoulders tensed. I made myself fit behind a tree before he looked back. I waited. I didn't hear anything.

When I peered around the trunk, he was gone. My stomach sank. I couldn't think. Where was he? *Focus*, I thought with clenched teeth. My eyes were sharp, my ears open. I punched the buttons on my bracelet and soaked another dart. A hollow. I would aim to kill. It was him or me.

He wasn't as quiet as I was. I heard him to my left, saw him prowling. Hunting me. I slid around the trunk so I was hidden. Loaded the dart. *Breathe.* I stepped. Toe, heel.

Toe, heel. Backward and to the left so I always had eyes on him. His back was to me. I pressed the gun to my lips. Wind check. Adjustment. Aim. I punched the air with my breath, and the dart hit him in the back of the neck. He reached for it, but fell. Dead. Eight more. Seven if Luther had killed his man.

As I crept back through the trees, I thought of what Luther said. *Maybe it'll put you right where you need to be.* Maybe Lilia was here, or Adrianna. Maybe this was the way I got them all back, even if it meant saving the humans and the others, but being captured myself. Maybe that would get me close enough to the ones who had the answers. It was a slim chance, but I had no other plan to get to William, and if I couldn't get William back, I wanted to be dead anyway. I tried to push that thought from my head. Tried to pretend I didn't think it, not with a baby on the way. I was supposed to love her. I did love her, didn't I? Somewhere in me, I knew I did. But right now I couldn't feel it, and I was afraid it wouldn't be enough when she was here.

Back at the meeting spot, Luther was nowhere to be seen. I stayed guarded. Loaded a dart. Looked around carefully for any sign of a threat.

I felt a gun to my back, a hand to my mouth, and I stiffened.

"Yer dead," but the voice belonged to Luther. I swung around with a scowl.

"Keep them eyes and ears open," he said as he tucked

the gun into his pants. "You got to be smart 'round here."

I nodded as he walked past me and crouched down to get another look at the building.

"Did ya kill 'im?"

"Yes."

He nodded, but his eyes stayed locked ahead of him. "The two on the right is next. You get the one closest to us an' I'll do the one combin' the outside."

Again, I crept up from behind. I got close enough that I knew I'd make the shot. My target, a short muscular woman, paced back and forth. She was spinning a knife in the air over her open palm as she walked from one end of the building to the other. My eyes were the only part of me that moved. They followed her as I planned the shot. How far in front of her I'd have to aim, the slope of the hill I was on, what part of the body to target. I'd aim for her back. She'd be out before she had time to turn and throw her knife.

I filled the hollow, loaded the gun, and inhaled, waiting for the man watching the opposite side of the building to be out of sight. The dart flew through the air soundlessly and hit her in the left shoulder. I moved right, slinking low and hiding amidst the sagebrush. After she fell, I knew I had to get her body out of there. My heart raced as I ran toward her on impulse. I pulled her by her hands, straining every muscle I had to drag her into the brush. I knew I shouldn't, but I looked down into her still open eyes. Dull brown, dead, gone. My shoulders started to shake, and my throat ached with regret. But a man walked around the corner, and I didn't have time to fall apart.

I recognized him as he leaned against the warehouse wall. I thought he was dead, but apparently William hadn't killed him that day. He was smoking a cigarette, looking bored, but I knew it was a ruse. He threw fire, and the burning ember was all the spark he needed to burn me like he had before.

Even on this cold night I was sweating. I wiped my damp forehead with my palm. This guy should be easy. I had a reason to kill him, but the sight of him had me flustered. The memory of my scorched back was still fresh. I was shaky and couldn't hold the dart gun steady. If I missed, it would give me away.

He pushed away from the building and gave me his back. The perfect shot, but I couldn't do it. Fear held me in my place. *Be someone else*, I thought. *Be Kara.* I didn't know what made me act, but I crept toward him, leaving the woman in the bushes. My steps were silent, and I didn't stop until I was close enough to touch him. I gripped a blood-soaked hammer dart and stabbed it into his back, through the heart. My hands still shook, but I had made the kill. My stomach lurched as he fell forward to his knees, but when he looked back into my eyes as he died, I remembered how many people he'd murdered. Innocent Descendants and who knows how many humans. I wasn't sorry.

"Nice one," Luther said from behind me. He grabbed

the man by the arm and pulled us both into a dark corner, shadowed by an adjoining wall of the building.

"They're gonna start noticing' things ain't right. We gotta make our move."

I nodded in agreement, even though everything in me knew we'd get caught. There were too many of them. If we went in, there wouldn't be any getting out.

"I'm gonna go in the main entrance. I'll take out as many as I can, cause a diversion." As he talked he went through the pockets of the dead man, pulling out a set of keys. "You sneak in here." He nodded to the door behind me on my right.

He handed me the keys and started to turn away, as if I'd see him in a few minutes. I knew I wouldn't. This was it.

"Wait," I said, catching his arm. "How am I supposed to get the humans out without you?"

"Prob'ly won't save most, but at least you'll save some."

"What if you get caught? They'll let you go, right? You're one of them."

His eyes looked out at nothing in the distance. "Don't worry 'bout me."

"Thank you," I said when he looked back.

He nodded and disappeared into the tall brush without a word.

The shakes came in waves, making the keys jingle as I fumbled with them. I had to find the right one. With each wrong key I felt a sense of urgency. What if I couldn't find it? What if I couldn't get in? Then the lock turned, and I slipped behind the door, praying I wouldn't be seen. When I closed it behind me, I clicked the lock and pressed my back against the cool surface. My chest worked hard, pumping up and down rapidly. Once I saw what was in front of me, I couldn't move.

Blood. It was everywhere. Not in a messy scene-of-a-crime kind of way, but neatly organized in large vials as tall as the ceiling. The white walls glowed pink, bathing the room with it. Tubes were connected to bodies outstretched on sterile silver tables, rows and rows of them. I covered my mouth with my hand, and walked down the line of unconscious people being milked. Their blood was being siphoned and collected. For what, I didn't know.

Slowly I began to recognize some of them, descendants who'd been with us but never returned from missions. Guilt throbbed in my chest. As I walked down the line of tables, I stumbled over my feet at the sight of a familiar face—Dr. Nickel. I made myself move closer, ignoring the sick feeling in my stomach and the knot in my throat. A few tables away there were other faces amongst the bodies—Sam, Paul, and Nics. A sound escaped my lips, but I stopped it before it became a sob.

I stood still and listened. The room was quiet, so I stepped closer to my friends. Nics and Sam were next to each other, their bare legs and arms sticking out of hospital gowns. My feet were heavy as I walked across the white tile floor. All I could do was stare.

The sound of screams snapped me out of it. Voices and clatter echoed from somewhere distant. The diversion. As I reached forward to rip the first tube from Nics's arm, my surroundings blurred and stretched. *Not now,* I thought, trying to resist it, but the room pulled away from me. No matter how deeply I breathed, how wide I kept my eyes, I couldn't stop it. I was carried off to some other place.

In the vision I stared back at Christoph. I couldn't make out what was behind him or around us. The moment was brief, a dark empty blur.

"I'm here to surrender," I said, and at those words everything shifted.

First blackness that seemed to stretch on forever, solitude, loneliness, fear. Then I stared into new eyes, familiar, loving eyes. William's eyes.

I woke up on the cold tile, dripping with sweat. How long had it been? A few seconds? A minute? An hour?

Nothing had changed. Their bodies lay unmoving on the tables, but it was quiet. Luther, the fighting and clatter, gone.

I scrambled to my feet, frantically ripping the tubes from their bodies as fast as I could. I shifted my bracelet to the right wrist and punched the buttons. I opened Nics's mouth first, letting the drops flow over her tongue, then moved from one to the other doing the same.

I waited. Every second I expected someone to burst through the door and shoot me, leaving the four of them to be bled dry, but all was still.

Nics was the first to move. Her head turned to look at Sam, but she didn't sit up.

"Nics, it's me," I whispered. I held my finger to my lips. "It's okay."

She blinked her eyes and swallowed, and I knew I didn't have much time before the others woke up. Until the vision, I assumed I'd leave with them. That Dr. Nickel would mimic Alex's ability and take us home. But I had other plans now.

I removed my dart gun, my bracelet, and my satchel of darts. "Here," I said as I handed them to her. "I'm not going with you."

"What?" her voice was hardly audible. She was still dazed.

I squeezed her hand and eyed the door on the other side of the room. I was hoping it would lead me to the humans. "Don't try and follow me. Just leave."

Through the door there was more blood, more bodies, but these weren't the neat kind. I'd found the warehouse, the humans, but all of them were dead. My boots tracked blood across the floor as I searched for movement. A rising chest, a blinking eye, but they were all lifeless.

Not a single soul had survived. I thought of the clatter. The screaming I had heard. I was too late. What was it he'd said? "Prob'ly won't save most, but at least you'll save some." Had he tried to save them without me?

The industrial hanging fluorescents flickered dim, ghostly light that reflected up from the floor. I could hear my heart in my ears, the breath move in and out of my lungs, my footsteps as I made my way across the room.

My stomach felt hollow, and just as I thought I couldn't take anymore of it, I found a familiar face. Luther. I knelt down beside him, taking his hard hand in mine. "I'm sorry," I whispered, closing his eyelids with my fingertips.

With the hopelessness dragging me down, there was only one thing left to do—give up. It felt wrong, but if my vision was right, giving up would lead me to William. He was all I cared about now.

"I'm here, Christoph," my voice echoed against the tall factory ceiling. "You win."

The cement floor made the place cold, and I rubbed my arms as the chilled air bit my skin. I listened in the emptiness, waiting for him to show. I knew he would.

I felt the air change, and sensed he was behind me. I could feel him, like a sixth sense that tells you when someone's eyes are on you.

"Hello, Elyse," he said.

It didn't startle me as I was sure he intended. I only turned to face him. Another man stood at his side, a messenger, but my eyes never veered from Christoph's. Being so close to him made my hands shake. Whether out of fear or anger wasn't clear, but I tried to keep them still. *Be strong.*

"Here to make a trade?" he laughed.

"No. I'm here to surrender."

His eyes narrowed with suspicion. "I don't believe

you."

"Innocent humans shouldn't have to pay the price for our conflicts."

"I tend to disagree. After all, they're the *reason* for our conflicts."

My nails bit into my palms as I looked around at the loss of life, the brutal end these people had to face. "Why did you kill all of them? Obviously Luther didn't set them free. Why slaughter them?" My chest ached. I'd failed.

His empty eyes moved to a body splayed beside him, and he nudged a boy's arm with his foot. "They were... defective." His voice was indifferent, as if he'd simply bought the wrong brand of human. "Don't worry, though. They would have been eliminated regardless of Luther's attempt. No need to carry the guilt."

I didn't see it that way. I should have saved them.

"If it's me you want. You can have me." I swallowed down the knot in my throat. "Just don't kill anymore. Please. All I want is peace."

"Peace always comes at a price, Elyse."

CHAPTER TWENTY-SEVEN

—

AT MY LOWEST POINT, ALL I HAD WERE THE ORACLE'S words to keep me from breaking. *Listen to her.* I'd given up everything based on that advice, and put all of my hope into the idea that she was right. But as I lay in the dark alone, in a basement prison with no windows or light, what hope was there?

In the beginning I was strong. I memorized the room with my hands. There were stairs leading up to the ground floor, but the door was locked with no keyhole to pick. A thin lumpy mattress lay against the back wall, along with an empty plastic bucket with no handles. To the right I found an air vent in the floor. I tried prying it loose, but even if it had worked, the grate was no bigger than a shoebox with holes that fit my fingers just barely. At first I was confident that I'd plot my way out, but no matter how many times I circled the room, nothing worked, and soon the darkness closed in on me.

Solitude is a special kind of torture. It uses your thoughts against you, until your own mind is the one thing you're most afraid of. After more time passed than I could keep track of, I drifted in and out of madness, reliving my regrets over and over until I was trapped inside myself.

One thing pulled me out of it—her.

If my belly hadn't grown with the weeks, I would have nearly forgotten about her. Since I'd been here, the baby had gone quiet. She didn't share her visions anymore. The demon in my mind wondered if she was even alive.

I was crouched against the stone wall the first time I felt her move inside of me. It woke me from my thoughts and stopped my trembling. I straightened up, waiting for it to come again. It was a very subtle sensation, like the flutter of butterfly wings, but I had nothing else to concentrate on. It was that feeling that saved me from myself. After that I knew I needed to stay sane and steady. Whenever darkness threatened to take me over, I forced it out. She was my only reason for not giving up. I had to be strong—for her.

"Hello," I whispered to her. I lay on the lumpy mattress, staring at a ceiling I couldn't see. My voice sounded strange in the empty room, but it was worth a try. "How are you in there?"

I lifted my shirt to place my hands on my bare belly and was met with a gentle flutter from inside that made me smile. I'd never talked to her directly. A pang of guilt tightened in my chest. This was the first time I had truly acknowledged her. I was in denial before, like if I didn't think about her or talk about her I could put off having her long enough for me to be ready.

"I'm sorry, baby girl," I said softly. "I never thought I'd be a mom." My throat burned. "I don't know how. I don't know what to do."

I pulled my shirt down, the fabric tight around my slightly rounded stomach. At least I wasn't alone.

"We'll get out of here," I told her. "I promise."

I never saw who swapped out my waste bucket and brought me food. Whoever it was never entered through the door. He was a ghost. My whole life I'd taken everyday things for granted, things like toilets and light, even comfort. Each night it got harder, until I felt like I might go crazy.

"Let me out of here!" I screamed after what seemed like the thousandth day of eating alone in the dark. I threw my fists against the locked door until they were sore and swollen. It was a last resort. I had given up after waiting in vain for the next vision, my answer, my way out. It never came.

I slid with my back to the wall and cried into my knees. Why had I been so naïve? I would never get out of here.

Then, as though my silence was the key, a sliver of light stretched across the floor.

"What did you expect?" Christoph said from the doorway.

I stood when I caught sight of him, my eyes squinting

away from the brightness. My heart knocked against my ribs. I couldn't speak. In my mind, I was strong. I would find a way to get information from him. But my gut didn't agree. It clenched in the pit of my stomach.

"I hardly think these conditions are worthy of such a fit, but I suppose you could use a shower." His eyes were oddly gentle. It had to be a trick. He gestured for me to step through the open door.

I watched him with suspicion, thinking he might reach out and grab me as I stepped cautiously into the hallway. I waited for the trap, but there was nothing. "If you try and escape. I *will* kill William and your friends."

My eyes shifted, and I glared at him but said nothing.

"The washroom is down the hall to your left."

The walls were lined with maple wood panels. Artwork decorated the space in what seemed to be someone's vacation home. A cabin. There was a window at the end of the hall, but it was pitch black outside, no lights, nothing. As I moved toward it I fought the urge to press my face to the glass. Could I break it? Christoph lifted his eyebrows at me, as if wanting me to test him.

I glanced back at the window, but turned into the bathroom as expected, locking myself inside. My shoulders slumped, and I leaned against the door once I was alone. I didn't see any options with Christoph watching so closely.

I saw myself in the mirror for the first time in months. I was a mess. Ratty hair, dirt-stained clothes and face, like a homeless child. My muscles were weak from inactivity, but my eyes were determined. I hardly recognized my face. The girl who stared back looked strong and unbreakable despite her frailty. Inside I was lost. I lifted my shirt to expose my belly. It was much bigger than I'd imagined now that I could see it in the light. I was grateful she was in there, protected and safe. No one could get to her.

I showered until the hot water was gone, trying to wash away the guilt and hurt, but all of it was stuck inside. It couldn't be rinsed away.

I thought of the window, of getting us out like I promised. I needed to keep that promise.

On the counter there was a new set of clothes. They weren't there before, and I cringed at the thought of someone being in here with me naked and vulnerable. Was I always being watched?

The sound of raised voices and bickering made me turn my head. I stopped moving and got quiet so I could hear them. The words were mumbled, but there was a woman. I pulled the jeans on quickly and whipped the black t-shirt over my head. I needed to know who the woman was.

The voices stopped when I opened the door, but as I reached the end of the hall, I saw Adrianna standing next to him. Her face was tight with anger, and she wouldn't look at me.

"You know, I really want to hate you," Christoph said. He was sitting at a table in the middle of the kitchen. The windows were black behind him.

"Go ahead," I said, crossing my arms in defiance. "I hate *you*." My words were strong, masking the fear he instilled in me.

He looked away with indifference. "You've put quite a damper on my plans."

"Good," I sneered. Although, I didn't know what he meant. I'd failed. I hadn't saved any of the humans.

"I've worked for years on that formula," he continued, "and the only thing I needed was the mind-wiper. It's the human memories that are the weakness. If I was working with a blank slate, I'd have complete control. They wouldn't know any better. The memories influence their decisions. They feel guilt, and they sabotage the missions."

"Why are you telling me this?"

"You know where she is, don't you?"

Adrianna was watching me, and I tried to hide the wave of relief I felt. He hadn't found our camp. Anna, Chloe, and the others were safe.

"Even if I did, why would I tell you?"

"See," he said, "how can I hate someone who doesn't know any better? You may think you know our world, that you are fighting for a moral cause, but you're naïve. You haven't been around as long as I have. You don't know what humans are capable of."

"I know what *you're* capable of. Just because you've had bad experiences with humans doesn't mean they are all that way."

His eyes opened wider. "And just because your best

friend is human doesn't mean the collective masses won't try and destroy you."

"You don't know that's how it will go."

"That's how it has *always* gone."

"I know more than you think. I know why you are the way you are, about your mother and father, about Nettie."

The name threw him off, and I could tell he wasn't expecting me to know that.

He tapped his fingers on the table. "Kara." His lips tried to form a smile.

"It doesn't justify your actions," I said, making my point.

"I disagree."

"Of course you do. Because I'm not the one blinded, you are. You're blinded by hate. It doesn't have to be like this."

"And what do you suggest? That we bow down, let them slaughter us willingly? That our race become test subjects, experiments for them to exploit?"

"That's what you're doing. You're no better."

He pulled a chair out from the table and pushed it in front of him. "Please sit." He gestured. I stepped forward, sensing him opening up. Maybe I could get to him, convince him he was wrong.

"Sometimes you have to make hard choices," he said once I'd taken the seat. "If it's us or them, would you rather it be them? Would you have them kill us all? Because I assure you, they will try."

"Not if we present ourselves as equals instead of gods."

He shook his head. "They'll never be our equals. You'll learn that soon."

I felt someone behind me before I saw the change in Christoph's face. Something was holding me, and I couldn't turn around to see who it was. "Thank you, Philip," he said, before his gaze shifted back to me, cold and distant. "Sometimes certain things are necessary. To get the upper hand."

I breathed in sharply as my body stiffened in a way that filled me with terror, in a way I never imagined I'd feel again. Though I was frozen still, my body trembled from the inside. My heart kicked at my chest like it was trying to bring me back to life. Everything in me feared what was coming. When Ryder's son stepped into my line of sight, I seized up.

"Nice to see you, Stephan," Christoph greeted him before continuing. "You see," he said to me. "I'm not so naïve to think I'll be able to stop a prophecy. I know what's coming. You've made sure of that, but humans cannot win. Mark my words, there will be war between the races." He shrugged, a smug smile stretching across his face. "A war I never wanted."

He did want it. I could see the lie in his eyes. Suddenly it was all clear to me. It was *exactly* what he wanted. It was the perfect excuse to retaliate against humans, a real reason to kill them. It was his final solution, war, and I had handed it to him on a silver platter.

I thought back to the last world war I had been around for. I'd only been in my twenties. The memories were vague, but I remembered the aftermath. When news of the Holocaust had sunk in, when anti-Japanese sentiment still hung in the air. He hated humans that way. He wanted them eliminated.

"Your people have already started coming out into the open, Elyse. They weren't sure what to do without you. Tragic."

Another man stepped in front of me. I recognized him somehow, his dark gray hair and light skin. His eyes were wide and intense. They were trying to tell me something, but I didn't know what. We held each other's gaze for a moment, and I knew what was coming would be bad. I just didn't know how bad.

"It really is fortunate that you're here," Christoph continued. "The oracle isn't of any use to me dead." Breath caught in my throat, the only part of me that could physically react. The oracle...dead. He spoke of it so casually I felt sick. A new sense of dread opened up in me like a black hole, stealing any shred of hope left. "Her blood really wasn't working anyway." His right cheek wrinkled as he smiled. "Then it occurred to me, I might have something far better to work with."

The gray haired man lowered to his knees, his eyes never leaving mine. He lifted up my shirt just enough to expose my stomach. My chest hurt, as his gentle fingers roll up the fabric. Please, no, I pleaded from within my head. His eyes fell to the floor before he stood.

"This is a bad idea, Christoph," Adrianna said from behind him. She was tense. So was I, trapped in my body, unable to run, scream, or fight. The air was thin, ready to shatter.

Christoph didn't look back at her. He only shook his head, before pulling out the needle. "It must be done."

It was too big and too long to be meant for me. They wanted something from her, from my baby girl. My body thrashed inside. *I won't let you touch her!* Every muscle in me was desperately trying to move. I went crazy within, flailing, screaming, panic-stricken mad as Christoph walked toward me.

Stephan's evil grin fueled my rage. As Christoph placed a hand on my belly, I cried out inside my head, piercing and desperate. Tears blurred my vision, and my heart felt ready to burst. I willed my muscles to work, pulling strength from places I didn't know existed. I had to break free.

Then, somehow my knee swung forward, overcoming Stephan's hold and smacking Christoph in the face. He yelled with frustration and stared at me with wild eyes as his nose began to bleed.

"Hold her," he growled. Stephan's strong hands gripped my legs, pinning my still immovable body to the chair.

Quiet moans slipped past my teeth. Even Stephan couldn't hold them back. I breathed like I was on fire. As the needle penetrated my skin, I didn't feel the pain. I didn't watch what was happening. I told her she'd be fine.

It's okay, baby girl. It's okay.

Stephan had no hold on her. She flipped and turned. My heart burned like someone had mashed it into bits with a hot poker. *Tell me what to do, baby girl. Help me.*

The needle was all the way in, and I was powerless. My mind went numb. My body gave up.

"All right," Christoph said with a chipper tone to his voice. "Not so bad." He looked at the syringe with satisfaction. I wanted to kill him. "You can take her back now, Philip."

My muscles stayed locked in place as Philip slid his arms under my body and carried me into my prison. The moment I was free from Stephan's hold I collapsed in agony on the basement floor. I clutched my belly in my arms, letting all of my angry cries spill out of me. I was sick with hate. I wanted him dead.

I felt a hand on my back, and I batted it away with force. "Get away from me," I wailed, the garbled words lost to hysterics. I breathed in gulps of air as I cried and buried my face into the musty mattress.

That night, darkness was my friend. It helped me hide from myself, from everything. I never wanted to come out.

After that, I felt grateful for the days spent in the lonely silence of the basement. I got used to the quiet, the solitude. It comforted me.

On the days they came for more, those were the times I broke into pieces.

CHAPTER TWENTY-EIGHT

—

I'D RIPPED NINETEEN TINY HOLES INTO THE MATTRESS when the basement door opened again, one for every day since the needles had started. Or at least what I was guessing were days. I knew what they wanted. The aching tightened in my throat, and angry tears welled up in my eyes when Stephan stepped down the stairs. Not again.

"Get away from me," I said through clenched teeth, clinging to the darkest places of the room. The shadows only hid me for so long. Fighting back wasn't an option. Not with Stephan locking up my bones and muscles until I was no more than a statue, trapped inside myself.

In the kitchen I was forced to relive my worst nightmare. The same people, the same chair, the same needle. I closed my eyes, my only defense, the only part of me that could move. *It's okay, baby girl,* I repeated over and over, like the words would brace me for what was to come.

"I don't suppose you've heard," Christoph said as he

knelt down in front of me with the syringe. "It's getting quite chaotic out there in the real world." My frantic eyes opened and watched as he lifted my shirt exposing my prenant stomach. My chest heaved in and out with anxiety I couldn't control. "If our people don't start behaving themselves, the humans are going to retaliate, and what a pity that would be. Don't you agree? No doubt we'd have to eradicate that kind of an enemy." He pressed the needle in slowly, and I winced though my body remained still. I watched my stomach move as she twisted inside me. "And what better way to fight an enemy than with their own kind? My mutated human army against the human race. It's brilliant, really. All we'll have to do is sit back and watch as they destroy themselves. They won't even know the difference. They'll be like clones fighting in our place."

I gagged involuntarily as he pulled out the needle. I could feel the bile rising, burning my throat. Tears wet my lips, but I couldn't lick them clean. All I could do in my frozen state was stare at the man that was breaking me. Try to kill him with my eyes.

"There we go," he said with a smile, examining the fluid he'd extracted. "The last batch killed the poor man I used it on, but we'll make some adjustments." He placed the cap on the needle and tucked it in his jacket pocket. "I'll be sure to let you know how it goes."

It wasn't until I emerged from my devastation that I began replaying it all in my head. What had he said? It was important, but in that moment, nothing was more important than my child and what was being taken from me.

One thing stood out. The words *mutated human army*, then something about the world in chaos, humans fighting humans. Whatever the details, what he'd said meant one thing—it was all falling apart. He was winning. I punched the wall in anger, and my hand burned as blood rushed to it.

Which Descendants were revealing themselves to the human world? My people? Or was it his? Did I do this? Was he instigating this chaos or letting the pieces I'd set up for him fall perfectly into place?

I covered my face with my hands and sighed into my palms. None of it mattered as long as I was in here. There was nothing I could do about any of it. Where was this prophecy savior now, because clearly I was never the one. How could I be? Not trapped in here while our world was crumbling. Maybe there never was a prophecy. Or maybe this was it. Would the humans be the last part of the equation, the final thrust that destroyed The Council?

I lay on the mattress, curled around my belly, and tried to bring my thoughts back to here and now. To my baby. To surviving. To holding myself together long enough to make it through this.

Over the next few weeks, my baby girl was all I had, helping me through the moments I felt like giving up. I never realized how much I'd grown to love her, never expected how fiercely attached I'd become.

"We're going to get through this. Right, baby girl?" I

whispered to her. I felt a nudge from inside and smiled. One thing that lived like fire inside me was the need to free her. Nothing could stifle that flame. Not Christoph, or needles, or the world coming to an end. None of it was more important than my daughter. I lived for her.

———

ANY NOISE THAT BROKE THE SILENCE ALWAYS GOT my attention, but it was never anything like this. A voice drew me to the right side of the room, a quiet hum that carried through the wall. A woman. My ears strained as I listened for the place it was coming from, and I found the grate in the corner. I wanted to lie on the floor and press my ear to the opening, but my belly had gotten too big for that, so I lowered into a squat instead.

"Hello?" I whispered the word into the vent, and the singing stopped almost immediately. I let my knees fall to the ground and waited for an answer. There wasn't one. "Hello," I said again, louder, but there was only silence. I waited, wondering if I should just let the woman be, but I couldn't. What if she could help me?

"Who are you?" I asked, keeping my voice low. If Christoph found out, I was sure he would move us away from each other. The humming picked back up, sweet and comforting, a lullaby to nurture a lonely soul. "I know you can hear me." I sighed, irritated that I was being ignored.

"Ssh," she answered.

I opened my mouth to reply. I couldn't stay quiet

now, but the sound of a scuffle kept me from speaking, then the clank of metal on metal, though no one spoke.

There was another voice, a low mumble. "...the greater good," were the only words I made out, before the latch of a door.

"Elyse?"

My fingers curled through the holes in the grate.

"Yes," I whispered. "Who are you?"

"Lilia."

I felt lightheaded with a mix of hope and frustration. "How long have you been here?"

"Today."

"Why? Will they take you away? Are you..." Was it too much to hope she'd want to help me?

"I don't know," she answered. "It's Christoph and Adrianna's turn to keep me."

Without her near at least two members of The Council, none of them had any power. She was their key, but she was also mine. If I could get her away from them, Antec's ability wouldn't work and my friends would be free. I stood and paced along the wall like a wild animal trying to think its way out of a cage. In the end I was back at the grate on my knees.

"I can't get out of here."

"No. You can't," she answered matter-of-factly.

"Can you help me?"

"No. I'm in chains." She stayed quiet for a moment. "If you're here, there's no helping any of us."

"Christoph lets me out sometimes." I didn't mention the needles. I didn't like to think about it. "Is there any way to escape? If I can get outside the house—"

"No."

The single word sank like a weight around my heart, taking the fleeting moment of hope with it.

I didn't try talking with her any more that night, but I listened to her song. The clang of a plate on cement told me my dinner was there, but I didn't feel like eating. I huddled in the corner of the cold room, welcoming the darkness. If there was no hope, why bother?

I spent days just a wall away from her, hoping that any moment I'd think of a way to escape and take her with me. I dreamt of releasing them, of finding William, but after a while even the sound of her song couldn't bring me to open my eyes.

"Do you believe in fate?" Her voice echoed up from the floor.

I lifted my head from my knees. "I used to," I answered in a whisper. "Not anymore."

"The oracle told me you would save me. Back when I thought I knew what was right. I didn't believe her. Then, I didn't need to be saved."

"She told me a lot of things."

"Were they true?"

"Not always."

I rested the back of my head against the wall and disappeared again inside myself. This was my fate now.

I didn't know how long I was out. Maybe it was only a few seconds, maybe hours, but when I heard her scream my whole body jerked. That kind of scream meant fear or pain. I could still hear it when it was over. I swallowed saliva down my sandpaper throat. Was I next?

The latch on my door clicked, and I stood. Light spread across the room like an open fan. I was close to giving up, but I would not die tonight.

I waited. Still nothing came.

The door stayed open, inviting escape. I couldn't resist. It had been weeks since I'd been allowed outside of my prison. I crept toward the stairs, protecting my belly with my arms.

The hallway outside was dark. I hesitated before I stepped beyond the threshold. Out of the corner of my eye I saw a shadow to my left. I gasped with surprise and darted to the right, slipping through the first open door I saw. As I closed it behind me, I realized it wasn't a door but a part of the wall, a secret entrance to a secret room.

When I turned around, I knew exactly where I was. A single window shed gray light onto the floor, and Lilia's slim body hung in chains from the stone wall. Above her, her hands were suspended in shackles. Her knees hovered, not quite reaching the floor. She was slumped forward, causing her sleek blonde hair to hang over her face.

"Lilia," I said, rushing to her side. I brushed her hair away, lifting her head. "Lilia, come on." When I pulled my hands back, my fingertips were wet with blood. It was bright, like the only splash of color in a black and white world. The back of her head had been bashed against the wall, and if I didn't stop the bleeding soon, she might not survive.

I needed her to live. Separating her from Christoph and Adrianna was my only chance at saving William, my only chance at saving any of them. If she died, Council abilities would shift to their heirs. I'd never get William back. *The oracle told me you would save me.* I couldn't ignore those words. This was meant to happen.

My eyes scanned the floor for something sharp. A loose nail sat at her feet, and I dug the point into my wrist.

I pressed a hand to her forehead and lifted the other to her mouth, hoping to heal the wound from the inside out. I waited for her eyes to open, for her to groan and come to, but she hung limp, lifeless. "Come on!" I urged. Maybe I was too late. Then it hit me. My ability wasn't working on her. It wouldn't work on her. Abilities didn't work on Council members.

I stepped back, grabbing my bleeding wrist.

"Keep going," said a voice behind me.

I jumped and whipped around ready to fight for survival. "Philip?"

"I said, keep going before it's too late," he snapped.

I shook my head. "I can't. It won't work on her—"

There was a look in his eyes. It frightened me. "I really don't want to have to force you, but I will."

I pressed my arm to her lips once again, tilting her

head back so the blood dripped down her throat. Philip watched me. I didn't know why he was so adamant that I save her. Soon I felt the familiar heaviness begin to weigh me down with the more blood I sacrificed. The baby kicked nervously in my belly, sensing the stress. I started to worry. I wouldn't put her at risk for this. It was useless anyway. I pulled my arm away to demand he let me stop, and Lilia inhaled like she was coming up for air. The chains jangled as she tried to stand.

"It worked," I said under my breath.

She heard me. "Elyse?"

"I'm here." I reached out to her. She took my hand, and our eyes connected for a moment before she saw him.

"No," she whispered. "Don't hurt me." The way she withdrew into the wall, I knew he was the one who did this.

His fingers curled around my arm. I looked back to yank it away, but suddenly found myself trapped in white, breathless space. I realized who he was as I felt the familiar emptiness press in around me.

"Wait," I said, when I could breathe again. I had to stop him before he bashed my head in next. "I know Alex." I couldn't see, but I recognized the dank smell of my prison.

"Yes," he answered. "He's my son."

I stood still in the blackness expecting him to do something, but both of us waited in silence.

"Was it you?" I asked, once I realized he wasn't going to attack me. "Why would you ask me to heal her if you meant to kill her?"

"It worked, didn't it?" His voice was low and empty like he had given up on emotion. "You healed her. A Council member. It worked, even though it shouldn't have."

I nodded, still confused by it. "How did you know it would work?"

"I didn't."

"What if she had died?" My voice spiked.

"It was a risk I was willing to take," he answered. "I needed to see the extent of your ability. Ensure it was strong enough."

He switched on a small flashlight illuminating his face. It hung like he'd been hurting for longer than he could take. I knew that look. I knew what it felt like to lose the ones I loved.

"Alex and your daughter," I said, seeing a way out. "You could free them." My words became hurried, desperate. "If you took Lilia away from here, you could have your family back. If you—"

"You don't think I've thought of that?" he interrupted. "And then what? Run? I know what Christoph is capable of. It's a death sentence. I don't want my family to live that way. To die that way..." His voice trailed off.

"It's worth it," I continued carefully. "I'm the last healer. I'm supposed to bring The Council down. If you could get Lilia out, and if I could come—"

"I plan to," he said, and suddenly a fire was ignited in

me again. He took my wrist in his hand. "But I need you to do something first." *Anything,* I thought as he slid a pocketknife across his palm and placed it on my wound. I hadn't even noticed the pain until it was healed. "Take this." He handed me the light. Then in a matter of seconds he was gone and back again. "Here's some water and a towel for the blood. You can keep the light, so you can see in this place."

"Thanks." His eyes flashed up at me, glinting in the dark. They were sad. Desperate. So was I. "What do you want me to do?" I asked, though it didn't matter what his answer was. I would do anything if it meant he'd help me.

"I want you to kill Christoph."

I laughed a little. "What?"

"It's the only way to be free."

It was impossible. He had too many people's abilities at his fingertips. Though the idea was tempting, I wasn't in any position to kill him. "Why don't you do it?"

"We tried." His feet shuffled against the cement floor. "I watched a colleague shoot the man six times in the chest, and he didn't even stagger. He's gotten too powerful, developed new abilities somehow."

The experiments. I remembered the blood dripping from his nose when I first faced him. He'd been experimenting on himself.

"He has my children," Philip continued. "I want him dead."

Philip's eager voice fueled my own need to free them,

but as much as I wanted the same thing, it was more complicated than that. "As soon as he's killed, Council powers will pass on to the heirs. Distancing Lilia won't save your family or anyone else."

"I'll make sure to get her out beforehand. They'll be set free, and Christoph will be all yours."

My hand tightened around the flashlight. If the timing was wrong, it could all backfire. But this was my only chance. Maybe I could help him. "What do you need me to do?"

"Christoph will be back for you, for more fluid from the child." His words were rushed with excitement and nerves. "Before he comes, I'll be here to draw blood from your left. I'm sure he'll have you restrained, so I'll have to kill Stephan. It'll be a good distraction, and it will set you free. Then all you have to do is inject him with the blood."

I shook my head. "My blood loses effect the longer it's outside my body. If it takes too long, it won't kill him."

"Then you'll have to find a way to give him more."

He disappeared before I could agree, but I nodded anyway. This could work.

CHAPTER TWENTY-NINE

—

I WAITED DAYS FOR ALEX'S FATHER TO SHOW. EVERY night since I healed Lilia I had the same vision—me with the syringe full of baby fluid in my hand. I didn't like what it meant. I had to let them take it from me, from her, but she was finally trying to tell me something. I needed to make sure to get that fluid.

Philip arrived just as I was starting to believe he would never come.

"Are you ready?"

I scrambled to my feet, startled by his sudden appearance. "Yes," I said, flipping my flashlight on so I could see him. I could feel his urgency, everything that was at stake. "But you need to let them take the fluid from me before killing Stephan."

His eyes squinted away from my light. "Why?"

"Agree or we have no deal."

His brow wrinkled, but he nodded. "All right. I'll wait."

I extended my arm and handed him the light. "Okay," I said. "Take it." He held the small light between his teeth as he examined the crook of my elbow. I looked away as he stuck my arm. It wasn't the pain or the blood that bothered me; it was the needle.

"They'll set out a chair for you like they normally do." He clutched the syringe of blood in his hand. "This will be taped underneath it when you're ready, on the left side. There'll be a knife on the right if you need it."

"Okay," I said. It was all I could manage.

"I'll see you soon."

Soon felt like hours. I had no way to tell time in my prison, no more light to click on and off nervously. I paced back and forth in the dark, my mind playing tricks on me. It focused on every sound as I waited, every creak or tick that might mean it was time.

When the door to the basement opened, my feet stumbled backward, and I cowered against the wall. No matter how necessary this was, I couldn't bring myself to step forward. It would be too suspicious if I were anything other than unwilling anyway, so I let myself feel the fear. I egged on my nervous heart. I closed my eyes and looked away.

A rough hand grabbed hold of my wrist and yanked me forward. I let the tears come and fall down my cheeks, scowling at the floor as I was dragged toward the door.

"I see you've accepted there's no use resisting," Christoph spoke as Stephan thrust me in front of him.

I glanced at the chair in the middle of the room, then spit into his face. He stared at me with disgust, wiping his cheek with a clean white handkerchief. I stared into his dead eyes hoping it was the last time I'd ever have to.

"Get on with it," Christoph snapped at Stephan.

I searched the room for any sign of Philip. He was nowhere, and my heart began to slam. Stephan pulled me by the arm, forcing me to sit in the chair. I grabbed the sides of the wooden frame, curling my fingers underneath before I felt my body lock up. They were there just within reach, the syringe and the knife.

Christoph glared at me with tight frowning lips before he took the needle out. I closed my eyes not wanting to watch, but listened to his words, hoping for an update on what was happening outside these walls. "I suppose you'll enjoy knowing that things aren't going quite as planned with this," he said, and I could hear the aggravation in his voice. "Another dead." I felt his hand on my right arm, and my eyes snapped open. This time he drew blood from my vein, not from my belly. Though in that moment I felt nothing but relief, my mind was quick to remind me. I needed that fluid. I watched as the blood swirled into the tube, waiting for his next move.

He was so close I could see his imperfections, the wrinkles and dark circles that made his face look sunken like he was a corpse. "This should help," he continued. "We are very close." His eyebrows lifted as though I was supposed to share in the excitement. "The last woman saw her death after the injection. She knew it was coming before it happened. We're getting there."

I waited, hoping for another needle as he capped the syringe and placed it in his coat. When he removed a larger one from the same pocket, my lids closed. Somewhere in me I was feeling relief, but I still shook inside, dreading what was next.

"I'm sorry to put you through this," Christoph said, his voice soft and genuine. If I hadn't known any better, I might have believed him, but apologies didn't make up for the wrongs he'd done.

I forced my eyes open, willing myself to face this fear so that he had to look at me while my child squirmed inside. Tears streaked my cheeks. My body shivered with distress. Still, nothing in his eyes said he was sorry. He stared into me while he took what he wanted, what wasn't his. When it was time, I'd take it back.

As he pulled out the needle, I exhaled with relief and tightened my fingers around the knife under my chair. In that moment I realized I was regaining mobility. I tried not to move.

"Stephan," Christoph said as he rose to his feet.

Now, I thought. I grasped the syringe of my blood and plunged it into Christoph's thigh. It wasn't the perfect place, but it was unexpected.

He screamed with fury, his eyes narrow and enraged. I ducked out of the way of his angry hands, but he didn't need to touch me to hurt me. He kicked the chair to the ground as I fell to my knees in agony.

"What is this?" he demanded, but I couldn't manage a response. Every nerve seared with sharp unrelenting pain. My bones felt like they were splitting and splintering inside my body. I went into shock. I couldn't stand or fall or breathe or cry. He glared into me, breaking me with his stare as he used a Descendant power that wasn't his own. Then he staggered, blinking, trying to catch himself on the table. In that moment of relief, just as I thought I might die from it all, I sank to the floor, and so did he. With my head against the kitchen tile, I heard the sound of him collapsing, but couldn't move my head. My body shook with painful tremors.

I knew the blood I'd injected wouldn't be enough to kill him, but I couldn't bring myself to move. The aching lingered even after he'd fallen.

Though I was still, my baby girl moved inside me, as though she were encouraging me to finish what I'd started. I wouldn't have another chance. I tilted my head so I could see across the floor. His lids were closed. Out, but not dead. With all my will I dug my fingers into the grooves of the tile and dragged my heavy body toward him. Our faces were inches apart. I reached for the chair, grasping at the knife with my fingertips until I had it in my hand.

I slid the blade across my left wrist, hardly noticing the feel of the cut. It was so dull in comparison to what I'd just endured. When I looked back at him, his eyes were open, watching me. His cold stare locked me in my place, and I waited for the pain to come again, but it didn't.

"Don't be a fool," he whispered, too weak to retaliate. Scarlet dripped from his nose. "You'll never win."

I looked down at my wrist, puddling and dripping with blood. *Do it,* I told myself, but I hesitated. What about Lilia? Was she far enough away?

"Kill him, Elyse, please," Philip's voice came from behind me. I turned my head, dropped my guard. I felt the knife leave my hand and watched it fly into Philip's chest. Something had compelled me to do it. Some urge that didn't belong to me. Christoph's eyes gave him away.

"No," I cried, as Philip grasped the blade and fell to his knees. *What did I do?*

"Kill him," Philip pleaded.

Christoph smiled up at me, weak but defiant. I forced my wrist to his lips, holding him down as best I could despite my still-aching bones.

He choked and sputtered on the blood, but I didn't let up until well after he'd stopped moving. I pried the syringe from his hand and rushed to Philip's side.

"I'm sorry," I whispered, pressing the knife to my right wrist, but he stopped me. "Just let me—" He lifted his shirt revealing a deep gash that cut into his abdomen. His chest fought for breath.

"Got him with a sedative and left him in the Sahara," Philip sputtered, wincing and coughing up blood. "Wasn't quite fast enough though." Our eyes met, knowing it was too deep to be healed in the moment. "We need to get to

Lilia. Others will be coming."

He wrapped his bloody palm around my left wrist, sealing up the cut without meaning to. My body tensed, still feeling jolts of the pain, as the white washed everything away.

I fell hard onto the ground but found soft dirt under my hands and knees.

An open valley stretched out in front of us covered in tall grass and shrubs. Trees were scattered across the land providing shade for hawks and field animals. A distant ranch was the only sign of civilization, and a single highway not too far off ran straight across the land. The sky was clear, a brilliant blue. I smiled. We were free.

"Where are we?" I asked, making my way to Philip. He was lying feet away from me. "Philip?" I touched his face, eyes closed. I was too late. I stayed sitting next to him, holding his hand in mine.

"We need to go," Lilia said, touching my shoulder. Her eyes flickered toward the ranch. "Away from here."

"Why?" I asked, getting the sense we still weren't safe.

"The ranch," she answered. "He wasn't able to get us far." She looked back at it nervously. "That's where we were."

I stood, trying to figure out what we could do, where we could run. "Okay," I said, still flustered by the thought of a dead Christoph a little more than a mile away. There was nothing around, only the road. And what about Philip? I looked back at him. "We can't just leave him."

"We have to," she answered quietly.

I dropped to my knees next to him, folding his hands across his chest. I straightened his legs, his clothes, and brushed his dark gray hair back. "Thank you," I whispered as I kissed his cheek. "We'll find Alex." I took a breath before I uttered his full name. "Alaximandrios."

I waited.

"Alaximandrios," I said again, more forcefully. When he didn't show, I began to panic. What if it didn't work?

Lilia shook her head at me. "We don't have time to wait."

We headed for the road. It was the only place we could go. We walked along the abandoned pavement until I could see the only car on the highway coming from a long way off. I pressed my hand to my back and jutted my belly out. Lilia stood next to me, tired, scared and weak.

My face was already desperate, and my clothes and hands a bloody mess. I didn't have to act. I truly needed this person to stop. As the truck approached I waved my right arm in the air, pleading for help. It worked. I tucked the syringe and the knife in my back pocket before it rolled to a stop.

"What y'all doin'?" said a lone woman from the window of a pickup truck. She combed her walnut-colored hair behind her ear with a look of concern. "Hitchhiking 'round here's not too safe for us ladies."

"We know, it's just—"

"No need to explain," she interrupted. "You're a mess.

Hop in."

"Thank you for stopping," I said as I scooted my awkward body over the bench seat. Lilia stayed quiet.

"It's no problem." As soon as she started driving, I breathed with relief. The distant ranch grew smaller and smaller behind us. Ahead, the sun sank below the horizon, setting the sky alight with orange fire like the end of the world, dangerous and beautiful. "So where y'all headed?"

"Anywhere," I said at first. Then I realized, I didn't know where to go from here.

"I'm Trisha," I offered, just in case. I wasn't willing to trust anyone at this point. "This is Janet."

The woman nodded. "Name's Jeanie," she said. "Nice to meet you."

"This might sound like a strange question," I continued, "but where exactly are we?" I looked around at the vacant land. There was nothing for miles.

"Good ol' state o' Texas," she answered without hesitating. "Home sweet home."

West, I thought. I checked for signs. We were headed the right way. I just hoped we wouldn't have to drive all the way back to California.

"How far do you think you'll be able to take us?" I asked.

She switched on the radio, and her words were lost a little to the sound of a country guitar. "Well, given the fact ya'll are runnin', as far as you like I guess."

I looked at her. "I never said we were running."

Her eyes drifted to my blood stained wrist. "Aren't you though?"

Something about her tone gave her away. A secret. Her lips pulled at the edges, like she knew I was on to her.

"Listen, we don't—"

I started choking on my words. I couldn't get them out. Something was wrong. I tried to take a breath, but there was no air. Before I could react, the woman plunged a needle into Lilia's neck, and her eyes closed.

"I believe you killed my cousin," the woman said, remaining calm, almost pleased to see me struggle. I was suffocating. I needed air.

I leaned over Lilia and tugged at the door handle. I tried to roll down the window, unlock the door. Nothing worked. We were stuck.

"Don't bother," the woman said, and her needle found me next.

With my last ounce of breath I uttered one last word. "Alaximandrios."

CHAPTER THIRTY

—

I FELT AIR IN MY LUNGS. I DRANK IT IN, GRATEFUL, BUT didn't dare open my eyes. My head rested against Lilia's side, her body rising and falling beneath me. My arm draped over my hip, and I felt something hard beneath my palm. The knife in my pocket. I'd have to be quick if I were to get to it.

I kept still as I opened my right eye enough to peer through my lashes, trying to get a sense of my surroundings. We were in the same truck, still driving. I couldn't make out the woman, but I could feel her presence next to me. Without hesitating, I ripped the knife from my jeans, flipped it open and sat up with the blade drawn, ready to attack.

"Holy—" Alex blurted out before he disappeared from the driver's seat. My eyes widened in surprise.

"Shoot!" I yelled, grabbing the wheel as the truck drifted off the road.

Gravel popped against the tires, and Lilia woke to my screaming. We fishtailed, and the car jerked back onto the pavement. Then Alex was there again, like he'd never left.

I shoved his shoulder. "Why'd you do that? We almost crashed."

"*Me*? You had a knife." His eyebrows pulled together as I caught my breath.

We stared at each other for a moment before we laughed.

"What about the woman? Did you kill her?"

He shrugged. "No, but I left her in the middle of the road." Both of us looked out at the desert landscape ahead of us. "The walk might kill her."

I let my body relax into the seat. "I never thought I'd say this, but I'm happy to see you." I laughed again. It had been so long since I'd had a reason to. "Thanks."

"Same here." He nodded. "Turns out the Underworld isn't all that great." His eyes drifted to my belly, which had grown quite a bit since he'd last seen me. "You're huge by the way."

"I hadn't noticed," I said, rolling my eyes.

He gripped the steering wheel tighter, becoming more serious. "So, how long have I been...out? A little longer than a few days, I'm guessing."

"You don't know?" I asked.

He glanced at Lilia, who continued to stare out the window in silence. "No." He shook his head. "The last thing I remember was Antec. I got this vacuum feeling when he touched me. After that is was like living in a conscious coma. Just blackness...nothing. Next thing I know I wake up in my parents' old house." He looked over at Lilia again. "I think I should be thanking you," he said. I nudged her thigh so she'd know he was talking to her, and she smiled a shy quiet smile.

"Have you seen the others? Are they free?" I asked.

"I've been getting calls," he answered, "but I didn't want to answer until you woke up. I don't know what things are like out there. I don't know how long it's been or what's going on. Is it safe?"

"It's been months." I looked down at my stomach again. "And I don't know if it's safe," I answered honestly. "I've been with Christoph."

"You *what?*"

"He's had me held captive, but he's dead. I killed him."

I saw the relief on Alex's face as I said it, like he could finally let go of the anger he'd been battling for so long. "Good." He nodded. I chose not to mention his father. Not yet at least.

"Where should we go?" he asked.

"Have you heard from..."

I didn't need to finish. He shook his head with regret. "It's my fault. I forgot to tell him my call name after the memory loss. I'm sorry."

"It's fine. We'll...figure something out. Take us to camp."

I touched my fingers to Lilia's hand and reached out for Alex's shoulder. The white upper air was pure and cold and clean. It pressed in on me and stole my breath, but it was more than just an escape; it was my way home.

We landed easily on the stone floor of the Lenaia caves. The place was deserted, but for some ten or twenty that milled about. When we appeared, those around us stopped and went quiet.

"Elyse!" Rachel's voice echoed loudly against the cave walls. A stream of rainbowed light tore through the air until her full form was wrapped around me in a hug. "Look at you! You're..."

"Pregnant," I finished for her. "Yeah. Have you heard from William?"

She shook her head, sad for me, as the others walked up with smiling faces.

Sofia and Edith were at Dr. Nickel's side, Anna and Chloe cried happy tears, and Nics, Sam, Rachel, and Paul nearly tackled me to the ground.

"Don't tackle a pregnant lady," I laughed, though my eyes were on Lilia.

She stayed back, unsure of how she'd be received amongst the group, but I watched as Dr. Nickel drew her in for a hug. He whispered something in her ear, words I couldn't hear, but I was sure it was a thank you. Without her, none of us would have ever been set free.

Within seconds Alex appeared with Kara and Mac. I'd never seen him smile so wide.

After months of separation, everyone was there. All but one. Even after all the hugs, all the happiness and laughter, I didn't feel whole without William.

"I need to get out of here," I whispered to Alex as Kara and Mac stole the show.

"What? We just got here," he said.

"I need to go to the lake," I pleaded. It was the only place I hoped he could be. "Please."

He stared at Kara from a distance and sighed, frustrated at my timing. "Fine."

Before we left I grabbed Rachel's hand, "I'll be right back," I said, under the noise of the reunion.

Her brow pulled together, but she nodded.

———

WE LANDED NEAR THE WATER, THE CLAY DIRT uneven under my feet. My eyes darted around, but my heart sank. "I just want to stay for a while," I said.

"Sure," Alex answered, leaving me to myself.

I walked the muddy shore, making my way to the tree I'd leaned against when William had healed my burns so many months ago.

I'd find him, I told myself. No matter what I had to do.

After everything I'd been through, my soul knew what it wanted, and it was willing to sacrifice anything to get it. My world. My pride. My life. Something in me sought without reason. It pulled me through the unseen, toward the only thing that mattered.

Then I saw him sitting against our tree, looking away from me. The wind blew his golden hair forward, his strong forearms rested against his knees. I needed nothing else. My heart stretched, reached, like flowers toward the sun. Like the moon on dark nights. Like hope in the deepest, emptiest places.

"William," I called out. His head turned, and our eyes met.

I walked toward him, then ran, my face twisting into that awful scowl everyone makes before they cry. I was not beautiful in that moment, but somehow I knew he saw beauty in me. He stood when I reached him, amazement in his eyes, like I wasn't real. His hand touched my face. I never appreciated it before, the simple touch of his hand to my cheek. Now it was everything.

"How are you here?" I asked. His aching eyes moved over my face, like he was trying to memorize every part of me. "Do you...remember?"

He shook his head. "Nothing but this. Frenchman's Lake. I don't know why. We were fighting Antec, then...I just showed up here."

I closed my eyes, and my heart slowed. "It's where we said we would meet if we ever lost each other."

He remembered. Even if it was only the lake. It was something. Nothing in his eyes told me he had forgotten me.

His gaze fell to my stomach. "I had no idea. Is it..."

"Ours." I smiled, pressing his palm to my belly. He touched my face with the other, his thumb grazing my cheek. I welcomed his kiss like warm skin on cold nights, and we clung to each other. Afraid to pull our lips apart, afraid to ever let go.

CHILDREN OF THE GODS
DESCENDANTS LIST

COUNCIL

Adrianna

Bloodline: Hera

Ability control for female Descendants

Antec

Bloodline: Hades

The ability to confine Descendants to the "Underworld"

*The Underworld is a void of nothingness where Descendants are trapped in a semi-conscious limbo.

Christoph

Bloodline: Zeus

Ability control for male Descendants

Dimitri

Bloodline: Demeter

The ability to age or grow living things

Dr. Nickel

Bloodline: Ares

The ability to mimic Descendant powers

Lilia

Bloodline: Hestia

Ability control for Council Members

*Must be in the presence of two Council members for Council abilities to work

ELYSE & FRIENDS

Alex

Bloodline: Aether

Messenger—The ability to move from place to place using teleportation

Call Name: Alaximandrios

Elyse

Bloodline: Asclepius

The ability to heal or poison with her blood

Kara

Bloodline: Prometheus

The ability to access to the mind

Mac

Bloodline: Soteria

The ability to create safe havens

Nics

Bloodline: Nix

The ability to manipulate light and create darkness or invisibility

Paul

Bloodline: Hermes

Messenger—Flight

Rachel

Bloodline: Iris

Messenger—Flight (changes form)

Sam

Bloodline: Dionysus

The ability to change liquid to wine

William

Bloodline: Aphrodite

The ability to persuade by infatuation

OTHER DESCENDANTS

Aaron

Bloodline: Clotho

The ability to revive the dead before the spirit transcends

Amber

Bloodline: Aletheia

The ability to decipher the truth of someone's words

Cearno

Bloodline: Comus

The ability to make food or drink with extraordinary flavor

Christine

Bloodline: Hegemone

The ability to conjure plants and trees from the earth

Claudia

Bloodline: Selene

The ability to control the moonlight and hypnotize those who stare into it

Edith

Bloodline: Ares

Council Heir – Can mimic Descendant powers once her ability is manifested

Florence

Bloodline: Delphic Oracle – Pythia

The ability to see the future

Hannah

Bloodline: Mnemosyne

The ability to erase memories with her blood

Helen (Ms. Stanzic)

Bloodline: Chronos

The ability to stop time

Ian

Bloodline: Homados

The ability to amplify or impair hearing

Iosif

Bloodline: Metis

The ability of intuition

Luther

Bloodline: Hercules

Lead Hunter

Mr. Gransky

Bloodline: Hecate

The ability to move objects with telekinesis

Mr. Williamson

Bloodline: Helios

The ability to mimic daylight/sunlight

Officer Gomez

Bloodline: Pasithea

The ability to make others feel relaxed

Philip

Bloodline: Aether

Messenger—The ability to move from place to place using teleportation

Call Name: Philotheos

Richard Adler (Elyse's Father)

Bloodline: Hephaestus

The ability to manipulate metals, woods, and stone

Riley

Bloodline: Kratos

The ability of great bodily strength

Ryder

Bloodline: Sophrosyne

The ability to restrain the body and Descendant abilities

Sarah Adler (Elyse's Mother)

Bloodline: Asclepius

The ability to heal or poison with her blood

Sofia (Mrs. Nickel)

Bloodline: Aphrodite

The ability to persuade by infatuation

Stephan

Bloodline: Sophrosyne

The ability to restrain the body and Descendant abilities

Unnamed

Bloodline: Tethys

The ability to draw water from the ground

Unnamed

Bloodline: Astraeus

The ability to create the illusion of stars

Unnamed

Bloodline: Penthus

The ability to induce extreme sadness

Unnamed

Bloodline: Anchiale

The ability to conjure fire

Unnamed

Bloodline: Limos

The ability to cause extreme hunger or starvation

Unnamed

Bloodline: Loxo

The ability to manipulate an object's trajectory

Unnamed

Bloodline: Hecaterus

The ability to control objects using the hands

Victor

Bloodline: Lelantos

The ability to control the air

REDEMPTION

CHILDREN OF THE GODS
BOOK 3

JESSICA THERRIEN

FROM THE TINY ACORN...
GROWS THE MIGHTY OAK

PROLOGUE

—

OUR SECRET WAS OUT. AS I LAY AWAKE BESIDE William the night after my escape, it was the first time I allowed that thought to sink in. Of the hundreds of Descendants who sought refuge in these caves months earlier, only my friends and family had waited for me to return. The rest were out there, and the world was watching.

A part of me felt relief. It was out of my hands. Those who'd trusted and followed me were free, and in a different way, so was I. No more prophecy weighing me down. Still, as the twinkling lights that lit the cave at night dimmed and withdrew into darkness, I couldn't find peace enough to sleep.

After all I'd been through, the fighting, the death, the seclusion, I'd survived. We'd won. But I still felt like I'd lost the one thing I'd always counted on—William. I stared through the pitch black to where he slept next to me, warm and real. He was alive. He was mine. For that I was grateful, but my heart felt empty. He didn't remember.

He'd always told me he'd lose me to this war. I never imagined I'd be the one to lose him.

The moment I killed Christoph, the Council shifted generations. Dr. Nickel's power fell to his daughter, Edith. Now she was the one who could mimic the ability of any Descendant she came into contact with. The cave's stars belonged to her tonight. At first I was hopeful she could give her brother his memories back, but at her young age, she hadn't been in contact with many abilities, mind-wipers included.

A piece of me had been convinced I'd get William back, the man I married, the man who loved me before I knew him. Now our love was one-sided.

I stared at him through the darkness. He used to know me intimately. Knew my fears. My secrets. Now all of our wordless moments were lost. I wondered if he'd ever get any of it back, the tangled legs and warm skin of so many nights together.

WE MOVED OUT OF THE CAVES THE NEXT DAY. WITH so few of us left, there was no reason to stay. Dr. Nickel arranged for a house in a small town called Sattley nestled deep in the Sierras. It was private and surrounded by pine trees that reminded me of home. As the weeks passed, it inherited a nickname: The Compound. It was large enough to house all fourteen of us. The Nickels, Mac and Anna, and William and I had our own rooms on the top floor, while Nics, Sam, Paul, and Rachel shared rooms on the bottom floor across from Edith, Chloe, Kara and Alex.

In the mornings the kitchen warmed with the smell of breakfast, and at night the cool evening air carried the fresh smell of freedom through the open windows.

Things were too normal. Too calm. It had me on edge.

"Yes!" Sam jumped to his feet in the middle of the living room. "Did you see that?" He slapped William on the shoulder as he passed, forgetting his best friend wasn't who he used to be. They shared an awkward moment before William continued on into the kitchen.

"Okay, so you beat me." I struggled over my pregnant stomach to pick up my cat's eye shooter from the floor and moved to the leather sofa. "I'm terrible at Marbles." I smiled, pretending I wasn't dwelling on what was happening in the real world.

William stepped in front of me with a bowl of stew.

"Is that for me?" My mouth watered at the smell of garlic and beef broth.

"No. It's for the baby," he teased. He sat next to me and put the bowl on the coffee table. "*This* is for you." He lifted a napkin off a plate like a magician revealing his trick. Voila—two chocolate chip cookies. "Mrs. Nick—" He stopped himself. "Mom just baked them."

Mrs. Nickel smiled at me as she closed the oven door. She'd been extra doting since she'd found out her first grandchild was on the way.

"I see how it is," Sam complained. "The pregnant girl gets all the good stuff. I wish I could get pregnant." He winked at me.

"Ha!" Nics laughed. "I'd pay to see that."

I rubbed my gigantic watermelon-sized stomach. "Believe me. If I could trade places with you, I would. You want to carry this belly around for a while?"

Sam chewed on his lower lip. "Yeah, not really."

"There's plenty more," Mrs. Nickel said, placing a plate on the coffee table. "Save some for Paul and Rachel." The two of them were gone more often than not these days, taking advantage of their freedom to fly wherever they liked.

Sam grabbed a cookie and took a bite. "Okay, who's next?" he asked, turning his fingers into guns and shooting them at Nics.

"Only if you want to get crushed," she said from her seat on the floor.

Chloe scooted closer to the yarn circle taped to the oatmeal-colored carpet. "I'll go."

I opened my mouth to egg her on, but stopped as I heard laughter down the hall that wasn't there before.

"At least take this with you." William reached for the bowl of stew as I pushed myself off the couch.

The door at the end of the hall closed with force, but

I didn't care. I needed to know how things were out there. I turned the knob and stepped into the room.

Alex pulled his lips from Kara's as soon as he saw me. The two of them straightened up and tried not to smile.

"You could knock," Kara said, giving me a look.

"You can hear my thoughts." I glanced away. "You knew I was coming."

She turned back to Alex, who brushed a thick black curl away from her apple cheeks, and shrugged. "I was... distracted."

"So what happened?" I asked.

"What do you think happened? Same thing every time, Elyse," Alex answered. His hair, a shade darker than Kara's, made his eyes seem too blue. "Why don't you just watch the news?"

"They won't let me," I said, my voice raised with irritation.

"It's on all the time," William said from behind me. "We needed a break." He raised his eyebrows. "*She* needed a break."

Alex nodded, his constant smirk pulling into his cheek. He reached into his back pocket and pulled out a rolled up magazine. "Those crazy humans can't get enough." He threw it at me, and I caught it against my chest. "The paparazzi do get a little annoying." He kicked his shoes off and stretched out on his bed, hands behind his head like he was sunbathing in bliss.

I unrolled the magazine and shook my head. A smug

picture of Alex posing on top of the Golden Gate Bridge took up most of the cover, and around the edges were other Descendants flaunting their skills. In the four months since Christoph's death, there were those who'd made names for themselves. They had fans, appeared on talk shows. They'd become celebrities overnight, and Alex was one of them.

I threw the glossy roll of pages back at him. "This isn't a game, Alex. It's too soon for this."

"Come on, Elyse. We finally have freedom. What did you expect?" Kara said, loosening the laces on her army boots. "Besides," Alex's cocky tone seeped into her voice, "they love us."

"I'm just saying that we should be preparing for their reaction, not posing for pictures."

"What if this is their reaction?" Alex jumped in.

I crossed my arms. "I know you don't honestly believe that."

"No, we don't," Kara added, "but we're going to enjoy it while it lasts. You should too."

I turned to leave, too frustrated to continue the conversation. They were being reckless, and they knew it. Or maybe I was just being pregnant. Either way I needed to get out of this house.

I stopped before I went through the door, my fingers lingering on the wooden frame. "Did you find anything?" I asked without looking back.

Soon after my escape we'd returned and buried Alex's

father, but that still hadn't given him closure. He claimed these adventures were just for fun, but I knew he was searching for her. His sister.

"No," he answered.

I let my fingers fall and heard William shut the door behind me.

Nobody looked up from the marble game as I passed through the living room and walked out the front door. They were used to my fits of paranoia by now. I headed for the shed. I knew Mac would be there. At least he was on my side.

I pushed the door open with force. "Alex is on the cover of Starz posing on top of the Golden Gate Bridge."

Mac grunted with disapproval. "I'd say they're gonna get themselves killed, but I might end up doing the job." He turned back to the twelve-inch TV above the mini fridge, accidentally knocking a can of nails to the ground. He was a giant in this shed. So was I. Both of us stared at the pointed metal pieces and silently agreed to leave them.

I hoisted my awkward body onto the stool beside him.

"You forgot your food," William said appearing in the open doorway.

"Thanks." I took the bowl and stared down at my belly. "There's a lot in my stomach already. I'm not sure this is going to fit."

I took a bite and he laughed. "So you *do* still have your sense of humor." He stepped inside the shed. "Don't worry. I won't tell anyone."

"Yeah, we wouldn't want anyone to think the pregnant lady was acting normal, right? Then they might actually take me seriously."

"Imagine that," Mac mocked, his eyes still glued to the local news. I watched with him as a cocky Alex-type grew webs between his fingers for a crowd.

"It's not me. It's them," I said through another bite. "Right?" I raised my eyebrows as I waited for an answer.

William squinted like he was trying to see through me. "This isn't some pregnancy trap type question is it?"

I laughed. "Yes, it is. And the correct answer is, *Right, Ellie. You're absolutely right.*"

He pulled up the empty stool so he could sit next to me. "Do you really want to know what my memory-less head thinks?"

I licked the salt from my lips and answered with a sigh. "Yes."

"Okay." He swiveled a little on the stool. "I think you're stuck in the past. The war is over, Ellie. You killed Christoph, broke up the Council, and Descendants and humans are living together in peace. There's nothing else for you to do."

I stirred my stew in vicious circles as I tried to keep myself from bubbling over. "I see what you're saying. It's just...what if something happens? What if the world gets scared? What if this gets out of hand?"

He nodded at the bowl, and I took another bite. "First of all, that's not your problem anymore." For the briefest moment I saw the old William shine through, the one who wanted to keep all of this war away from me. "And second of all, yeah, it probably will get out of hand. But until it does we just need to live our lives."

Elyse's Story Continues...

OPPRESSION (BOOK #1)
UPRISING (BOOK #2)
REDEMPTION (BOOK #3)

—

THE CHILDREN OF THE GODS SERIES

The Descendants have waited long enough
for freedom...

ABOUT THE AUTHOR

JESSICA THERRIEN spent her youth in the small town of Chilcoot, California, high up in the Sierra Nevada Mountains. In this town of nearly 100 residents, with no street lights or grocery stores, there was little to do but find ways to be creative. Her mother, the local English teacher, inspired her to do all things artistic, and ultimately instilled in her a love for language.

Her Children of the Gods trilogy has been translated and sold through major publishers around the world, such as Editions AdA (Canada), EditionsMilan (France), Dunwich Edizioni (Italy), and SharpPoint Press (China).

Aside from her Children of the Gods series, Jessica is also the author of Carry Me Home, The Mercenary's Daughter, and a kid's picture book called, The Loneliest Whale.

Jessica currently lives in Southern California with her husband and their three children.

You can visit her online at

WWW.JESSICATHERRIENBOOKS.COM

ALSO BY JESSICA THERRIEN

THE MERCENARY'S DAUGHTER

"A hugely entertaining novel. It pulls you in and doesn't let you go."
—**TOM O'CONNOR**, SCREENWRITER *of*
THE HITMAN'S BODYGUARD and IRONBARK

"One of the coolest and downright fun books I've read in a while."
—**TOMMY WIRKOLA**, WRITER/DIRECTOR *of*
HANSEL & GRETEL: WITCH HUNTERS and DEAD SNOW

"Completely compelling. The pages might rip from turning them so fast."
—**NEIL TOLKIN**, SCREENWRITER *of* LICENSE TO DRIVE
and THE EMPEROR'S CLUB

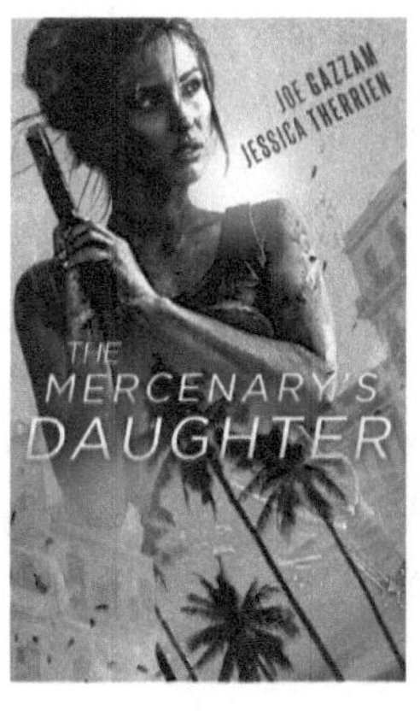

When Special Ops recruit, Tara Kafee is dishonorably discharged, there's only one place to go—Home.

But there's more waiting for her there than she's ready for.

It's been four years since she's been back and ten since her mother walked out on the family never to be heard of again. She's determined to rekindle things with her father and keep him close. That is, until he goes missing.

Soon after stumbling upon a safe room full of weapons, fake passports, and a mission's dossier marking a target in Cuba, she reluctantly accepts the help of her angsty teenage brother. He's the only one she can trust, so together, the two set out for Havana.

Tara is determined to get her father back, whatever it takes, but things are never easy when you're the mercenary's daughter.

CARRY ME HOME is a work of fiction inspired by the true story of a teenage girl's involvement in several Mexican gangs in San Jose and Los Angeles. The members of her crew call her, Guera, Spanish for "white girl" and it doesn't take long for her to get lost in their world of guns and drugs.

* * *

Lucy and Ruth are country girls from a broken home. When they move to the city with their mother, leaving behind their family ranch and dead-beat father, Lucy unravels.

They run to their grandparents' place, a trailer park mobile home in the barrio of San Jose. Lucy's barrio friends have changed since her last visit. They've joined a gang called VC. They teach her to fight, to shank, to beat a person unconscious and play with guns. When things get too heavy, and lives are at stake, the three girls head for LA, seeking a better life.

But trouble always follows Lucy. She befriends the wrong people, members of another gang, and every bad choice she makes drags the family into her dangerous world.

Told from three points of view, the story follows Lucy down the rabbit hole, along with her mother and sister as they sacrifice dreams and happiness, friendships and futures. Love is waiting for all of them in LA, but pursuing a life without Lucy could mean losing her forever.